Changeling Press, LLC
ChangelingPress.com

Merlin's Legacy Vol. 1

Angela Knight

D1737346

# Merlin's Legacy Vol. 1
## Angela Knight

All rights reserved.
Copyright ©2019 Angela Knight

ISBN: 9781080781942

Publisher:
Changeling Press LLC
315 N. Centre St.
Martinsburg, WV 25404
ChangelingPress.com

Printed in the U.S.A.

Editor: Margaret Riley
Cover Artist: Angela Knight

The individual stories in this anthology have been previously released in E-Book format.

# Table of Contents

Master of Seduction (Merlin's Legacy 1)...............4

   Chapter One ........................................................5

   Chapter Two.......................................................25

   Chapter Three ...................................................38

   Chapter Four .....................................................53

   Chapter Five ......................................................69

   Chapter Six .......................................................86

   Chapter Seven .................................................104

Master of Valor (Merlin's Legacy 2) .................122

   Preface .............................................................123

   Chapter One .....................................................130

   Chapter Two.....................................................145

   Chapter Three ..................................................162

   Chapter Four .....................................................180

   Chapter Five ......................................................195

   Chapter Six .......................................................214

   Chapter Seven .................................................232

   Chapter Eight ...................................................252

   Chapter Nine....................................................264

   Chapter Ten......................................................282

Master of Fate (Merlin's Legacy 3)....................293

   Chapter One .....................................................294

   Chapter Two.....................................................309

   Chapter Three ..................................................326

   Chapter Four .....................................................341

   Chapter Five ......................................................358

   Chapter Six .......................................................377

   Chapter Seven .................................................393

   Chapter Eight ...................................................409

   Dedication........................................................428

Angela Knight.......................................................430

Changeling Press E-Books....................................431

# Master of Seduction (Merlin's Legacy 1)

## Angela Knight

All her life, Sheriff's Deputy Rachel Kent has dreamed of becoming one of the immortal Magekind witches who protect humanity from itself. But first she must prove herself to the handsome vampire whose job it is to decide whether she'll become a danger to those she's supposed to save.

Nathaniel Allard is a Court Seducer who has been sent to trigger Rachel's witchy transformation by making love to her three times. The problem is, gaining such incredible powers may drive Rachel insane and force Nathaniel to kill her. Otherwise she may kill him -- and anyone else who gets in her way.

Nate vows he'll only agree to complete Rachel's transformation if she proves she can be trusted with the powers she'll gain. But as he tests her -- and makes love to her with every test she passes -- mutual lust becomes something more. Will love be enough to save Rachel's sanity?

# Chapter One

Deputy Rachel Kent ran flat out, though her ribs ached with every stride, every breath. The bullet had left a bruise on her chest the size of a silver dollar.

Still better than being dead.

The sun had dipped below the horizon, but it wasn't entirely dark yet as she pounded down the two-lane rural road. Shadows gathered in the thick woods on either side of the blacktop, and the sky overhead purpled as the last of the sunlight bled away.

Sweat slicked Rachel's skin, gluing the T-shirt to her heaving ribs and rolling down her legs as her feet hit the pavement. Normally she liked to do her running at dawn this time of year, before the July sun made South Carolina's humidity even more miserable. That wasn't an option tonight. She needed to exhaust herself. Otherwise she'd lie awake for hours, looking for a way she could have avoided killing Don Gordon.

So far, Rachel hadn't thought of one. Not if she hadn't wanted to watch him murder his wife and daughters. Yet every time she closed her eyes, she heard Emily's heartbroken scream, "Daddy, daddy, daddy!"

*Daddy tried to blow your brains out, sweetheart.*

The moment flashed through her head yet again: Don turning his gun on his wife as Eileen huddled against the wall, trying to shield their kids. Rachel had been too far from him or his victims to reach either, so she'd stepped between them. It was the first time she'd fired her Glock in the line of duty. The two guns boomed almost simultaneously.

The impact of Don's bullet hitting her Kevlar vest felt like a baseball bat to the sternum. She'd fallen to one knee, fighting to breathe.

When she looked up, Don lay on his back a few feet away, staring up at the ceiling as the life drained from his eyes. The neat hole in the center of his chest barely had time to bleed before his heart stopped.

*Daddy, daddy, daddy!*

It wasn't killing Don that bothered her. He was an abusive asshat she'd taken to jail three times in six months. Two of those times, his wife had ended up in the ER. His death had greatly improved his family's collective life expectancy.

No, what bothered Rachel was giving four-year-old Emily a memory that would haunt her for life.

*Cut it out. You're wallowing.*

Unfortunately, trying to repress her growing obsession only strengthened it. Rachel knew she had to get her mind on something else. Even the ache of her chest made a useful distraction. Which was why she was pushing so hard when bruised ribs made a three-mile run borderline stupid.

Rachel took a left into the apartment complex that had been home for the past three years. Four long buildings stood on either side of the street, sheathed in cream vinyl siding and surrounded by neat green hedges.

Breathing hard, she slowed to a walk as she turned into her unit's parking lot. And stopped to mutter a curse. Two boxy trucks stood in front of the building, each topped by a satellite dish.

News vans. Great. Just great.

*I am not in the mood for this.* And not exactly camera ready either, given the sweat that glued her shorts and T-shirt to her skin. Bending over, Rachel braced her hands against her knees and fought to get her breathing under control. Her ponytail flopped against her cheek, damp from the run.

She'd be tempted to walk away, but she knew both crews would still be staking out her building when she returned. Besides, Gee would disown her. *Kents don't run from anything, kid.*

When she thought she could speak without gasping, Rachel straightened and rolled her shoulders back. Ignoring her aching ribs, she headed for the red awning that shaded the building's door.

The news crews stood in a little cluster, chatting in the bored way of people on a stakeout. Catching sight of her, the videographers pivoted to aim their cameras in her direction as the reporters went on point like bird dogs.

Until they got a good look. Judging by their disappointed expressions, she wasn't who they were expecting. Probably didn't recognize her from her Sheriff's Office photo. *Yeah, let's see you look spit-and-polish after a run in this heat.*

But just as she was hoping she could sneak past, the female reporter brightened and stepped into Rachel's path. She looked like an ex-Miss South Carolina -- blonde, toothy, and the proud owner of two miles of leg. "Deputy Kent? Debbie Rice, WTAY News. People are saying you're a hero since Amy Gordon's video went viral. What can you tell us about that night?" With a toothpaste-ad smile, she tilted her mic toward Rachel.

*Why in the hell did Amy have to live-stream the whole thing on Facebook?* But Rachel knew why. The kid had thought whipping out her phone would keep Don from beating her mother -- again.

Nope.

"I did what the taxpayers pay me to do. Excuse me, I need a shower." She pushed past, amused as Rice recoiled from her sweaty, smelly self with a murmur of disgust.

Debbie's big African-American rival wasn't so easily put off. He shouldered in and stuck his mic in her face. "Darren Mayfield, WACN. Eileen Gordon said you deliberately stepped between them and her husband's gun. Weren't you afraid he'd kill you?"

"I was wearing Kevlar. They weren't."

"Which wouldn't have saved you if he'd shot you in the head."

"No." She dodged around him and edged a few steps closer to the door.

Debbie flashed those teeth and hip-checked Mayfield out of the way. "Would you be willing to grant an interview?"

"You'll need to take that up with the department's Public Information Officer." She fished in her shorts pocket for her keys.

"It was obviously a justified shooting. Does it bother you they put you on leave anyway?"

"Nope. It's departmental policy." The brass didn't really question her actions, but they did think any cop involved in even a justified shooting needed a few sessions with a shrink before going back to work. Given her nightmares, it was probably a good idea. Not that she'd share that little tidbit with this flock of vultures.

"Deputy…"

Having sidled to the door while they were distracted, she quickly unlocked it, stepped in, and closed it in their collective faces. Leaning against the door, she breathed out in sheer relief.

Someone knocked. "Deputy! Deputy Kent, do you…"

Ignoring them, Rachel headed up the two flights of stairs to unlock her apartment door, slip inside…

And damn near jumped out of her skin.

"There you are! I was getting ready to send out a search party." Grinning, the woman sprang up from the rust sectional couch. Tall and model-slim, she wore skinny taupe trousers with a pair of black stilettos. A sleeveless black blouse bared lean arms and an inch of flat belly. Honey blond curls tumbled around her shoulders, artfully streaked with paler gold, and her blue-gray eyes gleamed clever in a heart-shaped face.

She sure as hell didn't look like anybody's great-great-great-great grandmother.

"Hello, Gee." Despite her exhaustion, Rachel's smile was genuine. Like the rest of the Kent clan, she adored her witchy ancestor.

Ignoring her drying sweat, Oriana Kent swooped in for a hug that smelled of exotic flowers and the ozone tang of lightning. "You really made me proud, kiddo. That jerk would have killed his whole family if not for you."

"Thanks." Spotting something dark looming from the corner of one eye, Rachel turned.

The man leaned a muscular shoulder against the gas fireplace's tiny mantle, one dark brow lifted in sardonic amusement. He towered over them both, broad shouldered in a black knit shirt that bared powerful biceps and corded forearms. Black jeans, faded in all the right places, drew the eye to muscular legs. His sable hair was barely long enough to curl, and a goatee framed his erotic mouth, lending a little scruff to the striking contours of his angular face. *Somewhere a GQ cover is missing its model*, Rachel thought.

Then she saw his eyes, and her amusement vanished like a popped soap bubble. Those blue irises were dark and cold as a polar sea, assessing and predatory.

Which is when it hit her he wasn't Gee's boy toy. *Oh God, he's a Magus.*

An agent of the Magekind.

A vampire.

When Rachel's eyes widened in awe, a half smile crooked one corner of his goatee in cynical amusement. "Don't you think you'd better introduce us, Oriana?"

Gee shot him a *Mind your manners* glare Rachel recognized from childhood. "Rachel, this is Nathan Allard. He's a Magekind Court Seducer." Despite her obvious irritation with him, a radiant smile spread over her face. "The Majae's Counsel has approved your Gifting!"

Rachel's jaw dropped as her eyes darted back to the big man. "Oh. Wow." *Eloquent, Kent. Way to sound like an idiot.* She tried to come up with something more intelligent, but the best she could do was a hoarse, "Thank you. Excuse me, I'm a little... stunned." Mechanically, she held out a hand. "Nice to meet you, Mr. Allard."

Nathan's hand enveloped hers with long, strong fingers and a warm palm, rough with calluses. "Call me Nathan." His remarkable eyes took on a glint of humor, turning the Arctic to sunlit blue. "Court Seducers aren't big on formality."

Rachel blinked up at him, feeling a little dizzy, as if she'd stepped into the middle of a dream. *God, I'm supposed to make love to him*? "I... can see that." She swallowed and tried for sophistication. "I'm open to informality." *That sounded a lot less lame in my head.*

Oriana eyed her, her expression darkening with maternal worry. "Are you all right? You look like hell."

"It's been a rough couple of days, Gee." She forced a smile. "Look, I need to get a shower. I probably smell like a goat."

The Maja lifted a graceful hand, a precursor to one of those sweeping gestures she used to cast spells. "I can fix that."

Rachel took an instinctive step back. "Thanks, but I need a minute. I'm a little off balance."

"But…"

"Let Rachel take her shower." The vampire gave her a long, perceptive stare. "You don't feel as clean from magic."

"Thanks. Give me fifteen minutes." *Get your shit together, Kent.*

"Of course, dear. And after that, Nathan and I will take you to dinner in Avalon."

Rachel's brows shot up. When she'd been a kid, she and her sister and cousins used to beg to visit the magical capital. Gee had always turned them down. *"Sorry, kids, if I tried to lead a mortal tour group through town, Morgana Le Fay would turn us all into frogs."*

*This is real.* Rachel's gaze slid to the vampire. *He's going to Gift me. And he'll have to sleep with me to do it.* If it went well, she'd become an immortal witch with fantastic abilities.

If it went badly…

"Sounds great," she rasped, and started down the short hallway into the bedroom.

"Wear something loose enough to exercise in." Nathan said, his voice a dark, seductive rumble. "I'm going to put you through your paces."

"Sure." Rachel shut the door, wondering whether she should be more terrified or turned on.

\* \* \*

Nathan Allard waited until the shower started running. "I told you we should give her another week to settle down. The first time you have to kill messes with your head."

"She can handle it," Oriana said, all stubborn confidence.

"We'll see." He prowled around the room, examining the furniture and knickknacks. You could learn a lot about someone from the things they surrounded themselves with, knowledge he found invaluable in establishing a rapport with his Latents. Otherwise being a Court Seducer could feel like whoring, regardless of the higher goals it served.

Rachel's apartment was small, no surprise given the salary of a sheriff's deputy in Tayunita County, SC. It was also as neat as a monk's cell, its walls painted eggshell white, with the kind of thin beige carpeting common to apartment complexes. Besides the sectional, the furniture consisted of a square coffee table and a long bookcase, both built of black laminate that suggested she'd bought them at Target.

Nathan's attention fell on the painting that hung over the sectional. A woman's arm thrust from the surface of a lake at nightfall, a sword raining magical sparks over her graceful hand as she held it aloft. A few feet away, a bearded man in plate armor crouched in the water wearing an expression of awe.

King Arthur receiving Excalibur from Nimue.

Like most Arthurian legend, the story was complete bullshit. Rachel obviously knew that, yet she'd bought the painting anyway. *Kid must have a romantic streak.*

He wandered over to the bookcase. Double rows of dog-eared paperbacks filled the shelves, wedged into place with trophies from martial arts tournaments and shooting contests. Evidently the girl had a competitive streak to go with the taste for romance -- and a hell of a lot of practical training. Oriana had been serious about making sure her descendants could handle themselves in a fight.

"By the way," the witch said tartly, "Would you please quit looking at her as if she's someone you may have to execute?"

"She is." Though God knew he had no desire to do so. Rachel was lovely, with big honey brown eyes under arched chestnut brows, a long narrow nose, and a certain cool strength to her oval, high-cheekboned face. She'd pulled her dark, curling hair into a messy tail that swung like a restless cat's when she moved. Even in a sweaty blue T-shirt and shorts, her long-legged body and full breasts made his dick sit up and take notice.

"Merlin's Gift is not going to drive Rachel insane," the witch snapped. "She's too disciplined and intelligent."

"That's not your call. It's mine. If I see any indication she isn't suitable, I'm pulling the plug."

Oriana's gray eyes went glacial with warning. "The Majae's Council agreed with me that she's an excellent candidate."

"Yeah, well, the Council doesn't have to deal with the fallout if this goes sideways. Rachel's going to damn well prove herself before I so much as kiss her."

"I don't deny we've made mistakes, but she's not one of them."

"It's not a mistake when somebody dies. It's a fuck up." Christine had been a fuckup -- and not just the Council's. The ultimate responsibility was his, because he hadn't recognized the problem in time to keep his dick out of her.

"Gifting Rachel is not a fuck up," Oriana told him impatiently. "Look, Nate, I'm the last one who wants to lose that child." She rose from the sectional, radiating enough magical menace to lift the hair on the back of his neck. "But if I find out that you refused to Gift her without good reason, you're going to regret it."

He gave her glare for glare. "You do what you have to do. And so will I."

\* \* \*

Rachel poured a handful of shampoo into her palm and started washing her hair under the warm, pounding stream of the shower. Her stomach felt tight with a combination of excitement and anxiety. *They chose me. I'm going to get Merlin's Gift. I'm going to become a Maja.*

She could barely believe it.

To most people, Merlin, King Arthur, and the Knights of the Round Table were nothing but misty legends from the fifth century. The ancient stories got most of the details wrong, but they all had a kernel of truth. For example, the real Merlin hadn't been an elderly Druid magician.

He'd been an alien.

His people, the Fae, were a race of star-faring magic users who'd discovered the galaxy's intelligent species tended to wipe themselves out through war or ecological disaster. Hoping to prevent more mass extinctions, the Fae chose guardians from among each species they encountered, training and empowering them to help their worlds survive.

When Merlin came to Earth in 450 AD, King Arthur, his knights and their ladies were among those he considered for the job of guardians. Those who passed Merlin's battery of tests were permitted to drink a potion from his enchanted Grail.

The potion transformed them into Magekind, with the men becoming Magi -- vampires -- and the women, Majae, or witches.

Mission accomplished, Merlin went on to the next world, leaving Arthur and his people to fight for the survival of humanity.

Because the potion altered their genetics, the Magekind passed Merlin's Gift down to their descendants, the Latents. Unfortunately, suddenly gaining magical abilities could drive susceptible people insane. To give the agents a chance to vet candidates, the Gift had to be triggered by a member of the Magekind. If the spell was never triggered, Latents lived and died as ordinary mortals.

Very, very few made the cut.

*And now I'm one of them*, Rachel thought, feeling dazed.

Just like Oriana, who'd been one of Sir Percival's many bastards. The immortal Knights of the Round Table evidently did not practice birth control.

Gee had been a Maja for the better part of three hundred years now. A century ago, she'd gone on the Mageverse version of maternity leave, taking twenty-two years off to raise three children on Mortal Earth. You didn't rear mortal kids among the immortals of Avalon, since it wasn't good for their mental health.

In the decades that followed, Oriana had urged her descendants to seek lives of service even if they were never chosen for the Gift. As a result, members of the Kent family had fought in every American war of the twentieth and twenty-first centuries. They'd also been police officers, firefighters, doctors and nurses, even government agents.

Still, the ultimate Kent goal was to become Magekind. Most of the clan had never been considered, despite their dedication and hard work. Rachel had no idea why the Majae's Council had picked her.

*I need to tell Mom. She'll be over the moon.*

And probably scared out of her mind, because if Rachel failed this test, she could end up insane.

Worse, she'd have the power to make every lethal impulse reality. The thought of it made her feel a little sick.

*Daddy, daddy, daddy...*

*That's not helping. And I'm running out of time.* Dragging her mind out of the dark spiral that was becoming habit, Rachel stepped out of the shower and toweled off. She hurried to the tiny mirror over the sink, dug out her makeup kit, and went to work on her face. One eye on the clock, she blow-dried her hair, made strategic use of a curling iron, then headed for her tiny bedroom closet.

She hadn't felt this damn nervous staring down the barrel of Don's gun.

Nathan had told her to wear something she could work out in. *Wonder what kind of workout he has in mind? And does he take requests?*

*Aaaand I'm running out of time.*

Rachel pulled on a snug red cotton tank over a pair of black leggings, then slid her feet into black flats. Contemplating her reflection, she sighed. *Well, at least I don't look desperate to impress.*

Of course, she *was* desperate to impress, but that was beside the point.

Firmly squelching her nerves, she walked into the living room to find Oriana fidgeting on the sectional. In contrast to her earlier joy, Gee looked wired, even a little pissed.

The court seducer was on his feet in front of the bookcase, a paperback in one big hand. Glimpsing the cover and finding it all too familiar, Rachel felt her cheeks flame. *Vampire Trinity*.

Great. Juuuust great. He'd discovered her collection of erotic romances. Lately, those books had been as close as she came to getting laid.

Without looking up from the book, the vampire said, "You're three minutes late."

Rachel bit back a flustered excuse. She'd known she was taking too much time on her makeup. "You're right, of course. My apologies."

"Don't be an ass, Nathan," Oriana said, as she rose to her feet.

At that he looked up, his gaze narrow, a muscle flexing in the corner of his jaw. Ignoring him, Gee made one of those theatrical gestures of hers. The scent of ozone filled the air like smoke.

A glowing point appeared in midair, expanding rapidly into a wavering doorway that looked like something out of a science fiction movie. Which is basically what it was: a dimensional gate to the magical city of Avalon. Rachel had seen Gee conjure gates any number of times over the years, but she'd never used one herself.

"Come on, kiddo," Oriana said, gesturing at the opening. "We've got a lot to discuss."

"Okay." Rachel squared her shoulders and stepped through the gate. As she passed through, an indescribable sensation rolled over her skin, making every hair on her body rise.

The feel of Oriana's magic.

She found herself in a long, arched room floored with Italian marble in shades of umber, gold and cream. Chandeliers dangled from the ceiling between thick wooden beams, shedding gold light and glints of rainbow reflections from long crystal pendants.

Stained glass windows lined the plaster walls. Glowing in brilliant colors from the house's exterior spotlights, each depicted a different scene from Arthurian legend. Beautifully upholstered chairs and couches stood in conversational groupings, their oak frames intricately carved and gleaming. "Oh," Rachel breathed, staring around the sitting room in awe. "This is gorgeous!"

"Thanks." Oriana strolled through the gate, Nathan following her like a dark shadow. "It's not as grand as some, but it's not exactly a single-wide either."

"That's putting it mildly." Rachel moved to study a figurine of a woman in armor standing on a side table. It appeared to be solid gold. "This looks like something from an art museum."

"Oriana is a magpie," Nathan observed dryly. "If it's shiny, she swoops down on it and carries it off to her nest."

"Better than living in an armory like that pile of yours," Oriana told him.

These two knew each other. Knew each other well. *And why does that thought make me feel a little jealous?* Rachel wondered. *And am I jealous of his friendship with her -- or hers with him?*

"Come along, dear." Gee headed for a doorway at the other end of the room. "I was cooking all afternoon. I want to celebrate."

"You cook?" Rachel followed her down a corridor lined with paintings. One of them looked suspiciously like a Michelangelo. "I figured you just conjured."

"Oriana is considered one of the best cooks among the Magekind."

Rachel dared a mischievous smile at him. "How would you know? Vampires don't eat."

He grinned with such charm, she blinked. "I've heard rumors."

Rachel expected the dining room to look like something out of Beauty and the Beast, but it turned out to be more intimate than that, designed for eight rather than eighty. Even so, the table fairly groaned under the weight of a feast of Thanksgiving proportions. Among the dishes were several of her favorites, all steaming gently.

"It looks delicious, Gee." But probably wasted. She doubted she'd be able to eat a bite with her stomach coiled in its current nervous knot.

Moving with the automatic courtesy of another age, Nathan moved to pull out the chair at the head of the table for Oriana. Rachel waited for him to seat her, too, knowing Gee's attitudes about gentlemen and ladies. Hand-to-hand combat wasn't the only thing the witch had taught her.

But when he stepped up behind Rachel, a ripple of pure sensual awareness rolled down her spine. There was something about all that alpha male presence that made her feel keyed up and juiced.

Rachel sat, then watched him stride to the place opposite hers, his big body moving with a fluid, athletic ease. As Oriana began pointing out the dishes, Nathan picked up the elegant bottle that sat by his elbow, plucked out the cork without the use of a bottle opener, and poured something dark red into a cut crystal glass. It didn't look like wine. "What's that?"

He gave her a dark smile. "You wouldn't like it. It's a very nice Chateau Oriana."

When Rachel frowned in confusion, Gee explained dryly, "My blood. I bottle it magically for vampire guests."

Okaaay. Though she supposed it made sense. Oriana had told her Majae needed to donate their blood as badly as Magi needed to drink it. Otherwise their blood pressure would shoot too high, and they could suffer strokes, even fatal aneurisms. Apparently Merlin had designed the two Magekind sexes to be interdependent.

As Nathan took another sip, Rachel's gaze fell to his big, scarred hands. Interesting, those scars. They must date back to his life before he became a vampire; any injuries suffered afterwards would have long since healed.

His gaze flicked up, apparently noticing her interest in the pale lines. "I was a professional duelist when I was mortal, back during the Renaissance. Even with gloves, the hands take a beating."

"That was a job?"

He shook his head. "Don't they educate kids at all anymore?"

Stung, Rachel worked to hide her irritation. "Actually, I did well in history."

Oriana looked up from filling her plate with thin slices of rare beef. "Nate, if you don't quit being an ass, you're going to find yourself with really long ears."

"And deprive Rachel of my tongue?" He arched a sardonic eyebrow.

"He's not usually like this," Oriana told her, eyeing him with disfavor. "I don't know what his problem is, but if he doesn't solve it, he's going to find himself looking like a cast member from *A Midsummer Night's Dream*."

"That was a play," he explained to Rachel, his tone elaborately helpful.

"Now that you mention it," Rachel said through her teeth, "there is a certain resemblance between him and Nick Bottom."

"Ah, she does read." His lips curled up. "Something other than *Vampire Trinity*."

Rachel stiffened as her temper went up in flames. Enough's enough. "Look, I may have to fuck you, but that doesn't give you the right to abuse me."

There went that dark brow again. "Given your taste in reading material, I'd think you'd like that."

She studied him in baffled fury. "Are you trying to goad me?"

"And I seem to be succeeding, not that it's taking much effort." He sat back in his chair, hooking a muscled arm over the back of it. "For future reference, Majae need better self-control. You don't want to kill someone because you lost your temper."

"I've been a cop for three years. I've dealt with more than my share of drunks, idiots, and assholes, all of whom thought I was fair game simply because I'm both a cop and a woman. My self-control is fine."

"Three whole years. My. That many?"

Which was when Rachel remembered he was four hundred years old. She clamped her teeth shut, realizing he was right -- she had lost control. She usually maintained a tighter grip over herself.

"Keep it up, Nate, and you'll be braying to go along with the ears," Oriana told him, thoroughly irritated.

The vampire ignored her. "Let's get one thing straight." He rose to his feet and leaned across the table until his face was inches from Rachel's. His eyes snapped blue flame. "I don't *have* to fuck you. I'm not going to give you the Gift until I'm convinced you can use the power wisely. And at the moment, I'm not impressed."

"That's. Enough." Oriana snapped. "You are not the only Court Seducer in Avalon. If you consider the job so distasteful, I'll find someone else."

"You didn't give me this assignment, Oriana. Arthur did. And he's the only one who can take me off it. I accepted it, and I'm going to use my best judgment whether you like it or not."

Oriana hesitated, as if recalibrating her argument. "Nate, we need her. The Council's conclusion was that she'll make an excellent agent. She can be trusted."

"That's not the question. The question is, can she survive the Gift?" He turned to Rachel, who sat frozen, wondering exactly when the conversation had gone to hell. "Look, I don't doubt you're a good kid. You've got guts. You proved that when you stepped between Gordon's bullet and his daughters. But it doesn't matter how good you are if the Gift burns out your sanity. If it does, it'll be my job to put you down like a rabid dog. Are you sure the risk is worth it?"

Rachel stared up at him. "I..." She broke off. The fact was, he had a point.

"Yeah, think about it. You need to think about it hard. Because even if the Gift doesn't go bad on you, that's not going to be the end of it. You're going to end up fighting and killing. You're going to end up watching everyone you love die. Not only your mother and father, but your sister and your nieces and your nephews."

"I... don't have any nieces and nephews."

"You will. And if you have kids, you'll watch them die, too, if they're not chosen to get the Gift. I lost

four of mine to old age, three others to smallpox, two
to cholera and one to murder. Why do you think
Oriana's so determined to secure immortality for one
of her children's descendants? Because all her kids
died and you're all that's left of them. That's a wound
that never heals."

"Yes, I'll admit that's a factor." Oriana leaned
toward her, voice low and intense. "But it's also true
that you're needed. Morgana Le Fay and Gwen both
have had visions, and they agree there's something
nasty on the way. Something every bit as bad as
Warlock or the Dark Ones, or any of the other bastards
we fought in the last decade." There was something so
coldly desperate in Gee's normally warm gaze, Rachel
felt a chill. "That's why we're recruiting. Magekind
agents are going to die, and the world trembles on the
edge of chaos. You can make a difference in this fight."

"Maybe," Nathan said softly. "Or maybe you'll
end up cannon fodder. Maybe you'll end up insane,
and I'll have to put you down. Make damn sure you
want to risk both possibilities before you say yes."

Rachel's first impulse was to drop her eyes from
his hard gaze, but she knew that would be a mistake. If
she showed him any vulnerability at all, he'd keep
pounding it. So instead she let her attention dip to his
mouth.

*Damn, his lips are downright erotic.* Abruptly she
realized she was almost painfully aware of him: his
height, his broad shoulders, those big, scarred hands.
What would it be like to make love to him?

No, not make love. He was a Court Seducer.
Screwing women into the Gift was what he did. *This
will never lead anywhere or mean anything to him. It's only
a fuck.* Rachel raised her chin. "If I wanted to live
forever, I wouldn't have stepped in front of a bullet

two days ago." She turned to Oriana. "I've never wanted to be anything but Magekind. Not for the power, not for the immortality -- to make a difference. Lately it feels like this entire damn planet is balanced on a knife blade over hell. If I can help stave off the fall, that's a chance worth taking."

Nathan sat back in his chair with a grunt of disgust. "Jesu, you did a good job brainwashing this kid."

Oriana snorted. "You know, the asshole act would be more convincing if you hadn't spent the past four centuries trying to save the world."

He shrugged. "Yeah, well, it needed saving."

# Chapter Two

Somehow they got through the rest of the meal without things getting any more heated. Rachel felt all too aware of Nathan's brooding gaze as he worked his way through the bottle of Oriana's blood. There was something about that dark stare that made her skin feel too tight.

Especially her nipples. She sneaked a downward glance to check whether they were as hard as they felt... *Oh. Yeah. Crap.* But he was so damned male. Those Arctic eyes made her acutely aware of her mouth, her breasts, her... everything.

*Well, at least it's been an hour since I've even thought about that damned shooting.* She sipped from her glass of wine. *Maybe I'll even be able to sleep.* Though she'd have to do it in the morning...

"Are you done?" Nathan asked at last. "It's getting late."

Rachel looked down at her empty plate, where one hand fiddled restlessly with her fork. She put the utensil down. "Yes."

"Good. We've got only a few hours until sunrise, and I'd like to get started."

*On what?* Rachel suspected her eyes were little bit too wide.

Nathan turned to Oriana. "Did you get those circlets finished?"

Gee nodded and rose. "Of course. I'll go get them." She hurried out.

"What circlets?" Rachel asked cautiously, not sure she liked the sound of that.

"They're magical devices we use in training. I had her program them with a couple of new scenarios."

"What, like a video game?"

"Video games are primitive compared to these. They simulate situations we've encountered in the field. I asked Oriana to create an illusion that you have magical abilities. Watching what you do with those powers will give me a chance to evaluate your judgment."

Rachel nodded. "Oh yeah, I did something similar at the Academy during training." Called 'shoot-don't shoot' scenarios, the equipment projected video of training situations on a long screen. She'd had to determine whether to shoot a laser pistol at images depicting either bad guys or innocent bystanders. If you chose wrong, you got shot -- or "killed" some poor sucker who'd only pulled out a cell phone.

Rachel had done well in those tests, but she knew that might mean precisely zip when it came to whatever Nathan had in mind.

"I suspect you'll find the Avalon version a little more challenging. We fought some pretty weird crap a decade or so ago. Demons, giant bears, an enormous snake the length of a bus." He grimaced as if in a particularly nasty memory.

Rachel stared at him. "I thought you guys fought people like Nazis and assorted witch-burning assholes."

"We did, for most of our history, but we went through a very bad stretch in the mid-2000s. A demonic alien escaped from a prison Merlin locked him in centuries ago. He caused all sorts of chaos even after we killed him, thanks to his assorted nasty followers. It took a long time to clean up that mess, and we're still dealing with the fallout."

"Oriana didn't mention any of that."

"She damn well better not have. That crap was 'I'd tell you but I'd have to kill you' stuff." He shook his head. "If you think being Magekind means you'll always be ridiculously overpowered compared to the normal humans you fight, think again. And it's important to remember that even when we do fight normal humans, they've got us outnumbered millions to one."

Rachel opened her mouth to question him further, but then Oriana walked back in. She handed Nathan a flat wooden box. "As requested. One headset for her, one for you, both loaded with those scenarios you wanted. But be advised -- they also record, and I will be double checking the results." Judging by her glower, she'd better agree with any conclusions he drew.

Gee gave Rachel a look that was considerably warmer. "If you need me, don't hesitate to call. When you decide to head home for the day, I'll be happy to open a gate back to your apartment."

A new thought occurred to Rachel. "How? This is the Mageverse. I'm pretty sure Verizon doesn't have a cell tower in Avalon." She bit her lip. "Damn, I hope nobody from the Sheriff's Office called while I was here."

Oriana held out a hand. "Give me your cell, and I'll enchant it."

She obeyed. Gee took it and closed her eyes. The ozone tang of magic stung Rachel's nose, though she didn't actually see anything. A moment later, the witch handed the phone back. "Don't worry, you didn't miss any calls from the department."

"That's good to hear."

Nathan stood. "If that's all…"

He headed out. Rachel got up to follow him, but Gee grabbed her forearm. "If you need me, I'm here."

"You always have been."

Nathan stopped at the door to shoot them an impatient look. "If you ladies don't mind, we have a lot to get done before dawn."

"Bye, Gee." She hurried after his broad, black-clad back as he strode through the house.

They emerged through an intricately carved door onto stone steps that led down to a cobblestone drive. Rachel glanced up at the night sky -- and stared, her jaw dropping. Alien constellations spilled overhead in a river of light brighter than any stars she'd ever seen back home. The sky was dominated by a swirl of iridescent light she knew must be a nearby nebula. A quarter moon hung in the cloudless sky, spilling pearlescent light over the clusters of trees and elaborate flowerbeds that filled the lawn.

*I'm really not on Earth anymore.*

This was the Mageverse -- a parallel dimension where magic was a law of physics, making this universe's Earth a much different place than the one where she'd been born.

"Are you coming?" Nathan demanded, turning to look at her from halfway down the drive.

"Oh. Yeah." As she hurried in his wake, she stared around in dazzled awe. Buildings from a hundred different times, countries and architectural styles stood together: French chateaus like Oriana's, honest-to-Arthur castles, Federalist and Georgian architecture, plantation houses, Italianate mansions. The street was cobblestone, and huge marble fountains stood here and there, surrounded by topiary and filling the night with the gentle splash and murmur of falling water.

"Oh wow," she said softly.

Nathan chuckled. For once, there was no mockery in his voice. "Witch ego in action."

"What?"

He gestured at one particularly impressive Gilded Age manse. "Everything you see was created by witches, either separately or acting in groups. But the idea is basically to show off. The bigger the building, the older and more powerful the Maja -- at least most of the time. The really old Majae consider this kind of thing a little vulgar, because they don't have to prove anything to anybody. After all, if you've been Magekind for 1500 years, everybody knows you're a heavy hitter."

Even more awed, she eyed the Gothic stone spires and massive walls. "So... I'll be able to conjure something like that?"

The humor fell from his eyes. "Assuming you survive the Gift -- and I give it to you."

He was starting to piss her off. "Look, I'll survive. This is what I trained for from the time I was a child. Oriana did not go easy on us. Yes, I do understand what the price of being a Maja may be. Gee never sugarcoated anything."

His sensual mouth flattened. "Then why are you the first Kent in two generations to be offered the Gift? It's not because we didn't need the personnel. It's because the Majae's Council concluded the others would have gone mad. Oriana submitted name after name for consideration, but they were all turned down."

She stared at him. "You mean my mother... ? My aunt... ?"

"Weren't approved. The fact is, the majority of Latents wouldn't be able to survive the Gift -- and there are a hell of a lot of people carrying that spell in their DNA after fifteen hundred years of us running around siring kids. Only a fraction of one percent are chosen, and some of them still go insane despite everything we can do to weed them out. And we don't know why."

"Can't the Majae do anything to save them? I mean, as powerful as they are..."

Nathan didn't answer for a long moment. Finally, he sighed. "A few years ago, Morgana created a magical collar designed to contain a new Maja's power. The idea was to let each candidate gain her abilities gradually, with the hope she'd be able to control it better. It should've worked. That collar was even able to contain Morgana's power -- and she's the most powerful Maja we've got. But the very first Latent they tried it out on blew out the collar. Merlin's Gift was simply too powerful for it. The girl went into a paranoid rage, and Bonnhome had to kill her."

"Damn," she murmured, chilled. "Why would Merlin cast a spell that does that to people?"

"He didn't design it that way. It seems to be a side effect of the Mageverse hitting some human brains." He studied her as they walked. "I want to give you every chance to survive. These tests will give both of us a chance to think about this, to make absolutely sure it's what you want to do."

"But it *is* what I want to do."

"And every single Latent I have ever Gifted -- including the ones I had to kill -- said the exact same thing. I'm sick of killing girls I just made love to. Especially considering I'm the one who turned them into magical IEDs."

*Daddy, daddy, daddy...*

"I appreciate the concern. But I'm not going to give up. And I *will* survive my transition."

Nathan's face went stony. Turning away, he lengthened his stride. Rachel didn't have to break into a run to keep up, but it was close.

A few blocks away, he turned down a walkway that led to an impressive Greek Revival home with tall arched windows and wrought iron balconies. It wasn't that large compared to most of the houses they'd passed, but it wasn't exactly tiny either.

"If Majae use magic to build their houses, where did you get yours?" Vampires couldn't work spells beyond healing or turning into a wolf. For anything more, they needed a witch.

He shrugged. "I rescued a Maja after she was captured by a team of Geiroff's psychotic followers. She built the house for me to show her gratitude."

"So where do the other vampires live?"

"Depends. The Majae built an apartment complex for the rookies. Sometimes a Maja you partner with frequently will build you something. It's a big favor -- it takes a lot of magic, and it wipes the witch out for days."

"So the houses are permanent? Because it would really suck if the place disappeared around you while you were on the second floor."

He laughed. "Yeah, they're pretty sturdy. Though I'll admit, if the witch who created them dies, they do go away. Luckily, Majae don't generally die that often." He grimaced. "Not unless something nasty and magical is doing the killing. We don't get that a lot, thank Merlin."

The house was as impressive inside as out, with tile floors, stained glass windows, and massive furniture, all leather and dark wood. The house wasn't quite as packed with art and antiques as Oriana's, but it was obvious why Gee had called it an armory. Exquisite swords, spears, axes, shields, dueling pistols, and assorted other weapons hung on the walls. A suit of plate armor, elaborately engraved, stood gleaming in the house's foyer. As Rachel followed him over elegant black-and-white marble tiles, she found herself imagining how she'd decorate her own place.

Assuming she survived the transition.

Better not even think about that. It was never a good idea to dwell on all the things that might go wrong before you went into a dangerous situation. That could become a self-fulfilling prophecy.

Nathan led the way into a long, narrow space with an arched ceiling she first assumed was a ballroom. But what really riveted her attention were the pair of murals that ran the length of opposing walls. The paintings depicted Renaissance duelists facing off against each other armed with rapiers, all deadly grace and lethal intent. One of them bore a distinct resemblance to Nathan.

While she paused to admire one of the murals, he walked to a huge armoire that stood against the room's back wall. Swinging its double doors open, he revealed an impressive collection of swords, axes, daggers, and quarterstaffs. Nathan put the box Oriana had given him into a drawer, then paused to contemplate the blade collection.

He really did have the most incredible back -- broad shouldered, narrowing to a tight waist and a deliciously muscled ass under those black jeans. When he started to turn, she jerked her eyes guiltily away. A hint of a smile curved his seductive mouth, and she knew he'd caught her staring. "Keep your mind on business and off my dick. It's by no means a sure thing you're going to get it." He tossed a sword at her.

Startled, Rachel almost missed the catch. Her cheeks heating ferociously, she studied the weapon. Though it had the heft and metallic gleam of steel, when she touched the blade, it gave beneath her fingers. "What's this made of?"

"It's spelled for use during practice, giving it the same weight and balance as a real blade. You'd have to work to hurt someone with it, and even if you did, I could call a healer." He sauntered to the middle of the room and gave her a taunting finger wave. "Let's see what you've got."

"I thought we were going to use Gee's circlets."

"Not this first time. She said she trained you in swordplay. I want to see whether the lessons took."

*In other words, I'm about to get my ass kicked.* Rachel had no illusions. Not only was Nathan a vampire, he was six or seven inches taller than she was, he'd been a professional swordsman during the Renaissance, and he had four hundred years of combat experience.

Still, it wouldn't be the first time she'd had her butt handed to her, and, one way or another, it wouldn't be the last. Her mind flicked feverishly through every bit of combat advice Gee had given her. *Do the unexpected, especially when you're badly outmatched.* And it didn't get much more outmatched than fencing a vampire duelist.

Standard procedure in any sword fight was to circle and test your opponent, looking for weaknesses before you committed yourself to an attack. To do anything else was a good way to end up diced into sushi.

Taking a deep breath, Rachel moved to face him, lifted her sword, and settled into guard.

Nathan brought his weapon up and settled into position, balanced and graceful as a dancer. "*En garde.*"

She exploded toward him with a roar, as loud and startling as she could make it, swinging her sword in a furious arc that would have decapitated him if the sword had been real. His blade thumped rather than rang against hers in a parry that knocked hers off line, then slashed downward to slap against her extended thigh. It stung like a bitch. Her bruised sternum howled.

"Slow." He shot forward, his blade licking out.

Rachel immediately leapt back, snapping a cut toward his ribs that he parried in a blur of speed. This time his retaliatory smack landed across her forearm. She gritted back a cry of pain.

She'd always loved swordplay. Gee had counted her as the best of her generation; she'd even bested her male Kent cousins. Though shorter than most men -- which meant her reach was also shorter -- Rachel was fast, and her endurance was greater because she didn't have as much mass to move around. She knew how to take a beating too, since her cousins never pulled their shots.

But in all the matches she'd fought -- even against Gee -- she'd never had her ass handed to her with such a cold lack of mercy.

As she circled with Nathan, parrying his lightning attacks, her ribs took on a grinding ache. To make matters worse, that three-mile run earlier meant she didn't have as much in the tank. Her attacks and parries slowed with each bruising impact.

But damn it, she was going to land a strike if it killed her. Rachel charged, teeth clenched. He parried her swing so hard her arm seemed to reverberate. The flat of his blade slapped across her chest just beneath her breasts, right over the center of the bruise.

Her knees gave, dumping her flat on her back, unable to even breathe.

Nathan looked down on her, frowning in irritation. "I know I didn't hurt you that bad. Get up."

The snap of command in his voice jolted Rachel into motion, but when she tried to sit up, pain slashed across her ribs like a whip. She fell back, curling around herself and fighting to breathe.

"Oh, shit. What's wrong?" He fell to one knee beside her. Before she could stop him, he grabbed the hem of her red T-shirt and snatched it up.

* * *

"What the fuck?" Nathan stared at the deep purple bruise that bloomed across her sternum. Gently, carefully, he tugged the tee off over her head, despite her hiss of pain, and studied her lean, athletic torso. A lacy white bra cupped delightfully full breasts he'd normally be a lot more interested in -- if not for that God-awful bruise.

It was shaped like a teardrop and about two inches across. He knew damn well he hadn't given it to her: it was too old, deep purple, going green around the edges. "What the hell?"

"I got shot the day before yesterday." There was a distinct wheeze in her voice. "Hit me in the vest."

Belatedly, he remembered a line in the news report Oriana had shown him about Rachel's shooting incident. Damn it, he wished he'd remembered that little detail before he'd dragged her in here and beat the hell out of her.

As he studied the bruise, measuring its location against his knowledge of human anatomy, a chill stole over him. "He'd have killed you if you hadn't been wearing that vest."

She shrugged. "Maybe. Hard to tell."

And what if the bastard had shot her in the head? The thought made Nathan feel a little sick. Anger rolled over him, replacing the shock. "Why in the fuck didn't you mention this before we started? Don't you have any sense?"

Now she looked annoyed. "It's just a bruise. Gee says you don't let injuries stop you in combat."

"This wasn't combat, you little twit. This was a practice session." Nathan reached out to delicately probe the contusion. He didn't think her sternum was broken, though it was hard to tell without X-rays. "And in any case, you don't go into combat injured if there's time to see a healer. You'll end up getting yourself hurt worse, and someone will have to risk his life to save your ass. Which wouldn't have been necessary if you'd been healed ahead of time."

She spoke through her teeth. "I'll keep that in mind if it happens again."

"You'd better. You do realize that little display of feminine machismo was self-defeating? I'd thought Oriana exaggerated how good you are, since your speed and range of motion sucked. Hell, you could barely breathe."

Now he found himself impressed by her willingness to go after him so hard despite the pain. He'd fought with more serious injuries, of course, but still, bruised ribs were hell when it came to a sword fight. They impaired breathing and ached viciously whenever you tried to attack or parry.

She hadn't let it stop her -- until he'd hit her right across that bruise. No wonder she'd fallen on her ass. "Idiot." This time the curse wasn't aimed at her. He'd worked with enough gung-ho little twits to know you couldn't trust them to take care of themselves. The kid had no sense of self-preservation whatsoever.

Nathan was no longer sure it was even possible to discourage her. But he had to try. He really didn't want her blood on his hands.

# Chapter Three

Nathan rose and returned to the armoire to open the cabinet where he kept the first aid supplies. Rummaging through the assortment of bottles, jars and powders, he found the one he was looking for, plucked it out, and returned to her. She hadn't tried to sit up -- probably an indication of how lousy she felt.

"Take off your bra."

A mulish expression crossed her lovely face, and she opened her mouth.

"Considering we're supposed to sleep together, don't you think modesty is a little out of place? Take off that bra."

Rachel frowned at him, but arched her spine and tried to reach around under her back to unfasten it. When she winced in pain, he realized there was no way she could do it without hurting herself more.

"Never mind." He caught hold of the band between the bra's cups and tore the fabric carefully, trying not to put any more strain on her bruised sternum. The twinge of pain that crossed her face revealed he hadn't quite succeeded. Rather than try to maneuver the straps off, he snapped them one by one, then tossed the bra aside.

And froze. Under normal circumstances, he suspected it would be a very nice view. Her breasts were full and round on her leanly muscled chest, topped by pink nipples that crinkled in involuntary reaction as he stared at her.

Unfortunately, he was feeling too guilty to appreciate the view. Reaching out, he delicately traced the contours of the bruise again. "What the hell were you thinking? You could have broken ribs. You had no business fencing like this."

Rachel glowered up at him as her cheeks flushed a becoming pink. "Give me credit for some sense. I got a chest X-ray after the shooting. Nothing was even cracked. It's only a bruise."

Nathan grunted, and twisted off the jar's lid. The ointment it contained was cool and white, and his fingers tingled from the magic as he scooped it out.

"What's that?" she asked as he started spreading it over the blue-black lump. She sucked in a breath in surprise as the magic went to work, brown eyes widening.

"Magical salve, specifically designed for bruises. Anything more complicated than that needs a healer." He traced a finger through the red line left by his sword stroke.

"I thought you vampire types turned into wolves whenever you needed to heal." Her tone was cool, but her throat worked as she swallowed, her gaze following the movement of his fingers as he sought out each mark his blade had inflicted. On her arms, with their smooth skin over long female muscle, along one shoulder... His hands began to slow, savoring the textures of her body.

"Shifting to wolf burns a lot of magic, and I don't like to do it to heal relatively trivial injuries." His voice sounded a little hoarse, and he swallowed and cleared his throat.

His gaze landed on her breasts again. The ugly purple bruise was beginning to fade as the magic did its work. Without its guilty distraction, he grew even more aware of the lovely, pale curves with their tight peaks. *What do they taste like?*

This was a very bad idea. The whole point of this little exercise had been to build distance between them, not to erode his self-control even more. Self-control that was more than a little rickety to begin with, given that intoxicating Latent scent he smelled every time he drew a breath in her presence.

His fangs began to ache.

*Give her the damn jar and get out*, his common sense told him. Trouble was, he'd spent the fight watching her -- and found himself reluctantly impressed by her grace and guts, by her refusal to back down, by her sheer willpower.

His stubborn hands reached for the waistband of her leggings even as his common sense whispered *Don't do it*.

The whisper was way too faint.

\* \* \*

Rachel swallowed as those big scarred hands tugged the leggings downward. "What are you doing?"

He froze, staring at the triangle of red panty he'd revealed. His throat worked as he swallowed. At least she wasn't the only one feeling the effects of this. Whatever the hell *this* was. "Checking your legs for bruises."

"Yeah? Because it looks like you're taking my clothes off." Which would've sounded a lot more cynical without the rough note in her voice.

"Even a vampire can't see through fabric." He looked up at her, and she drew in a hard breath at the dark blaze in his eyes. "Unless you don't want me to."

The heat in his eyes made her heart start pounding in long, furious lunges. What did she want? She had no idea. But her nipples were drawn tight, and she could feel her sex going slick. He blinked, and his nostrils flared.

And Rachel remembered Gee had told her vampires had a sense of smell as acute as a bloodhound's. *Oh God, he's smelling how turned on I am.*

Her attention slid helplessly downward.

A bulge swelled below his belt, thick enough to choke an anaconda. She didn't quite manage to suppress her gasp.

Nathan's lips curled in a half smile in the black frame of his goatee. He kept pulling the leggings down. The red panties didn't go with them.

Quite.

He got the leggings down to her knees, then stopped. Deliberately, he took her flats off and placed them neatly to one side. When he turned away, she shot a quick look between her thighs. There was a dark patch on her red silk panties, silent testimony to her arousal. She almost reached down to cover herself, but arrested the gesture. *We're supposed to sleep together, damn it. I'm not going to act like a virgin debutante from a Victorian romance.*

So she made herself lie there as he scooped out more of the magical salve. Again, he traced the line of a long sword stroke that cut the length of her thigh. Again, the cream felt cool going on, only to heat a moment later as the magic went to work, building rapidly into a sting that reminded her of alcohol on an open cut.

Nathan stopped to study her legs, searching for more bruises. Spotting one, he hesitated a long moment. Following the direction of his eyes, she saw why. The long red mark stopped barely an inch below the crotch of her panties.

He dug out more of the cream and slowly spread it along the welt. Again, ice soothed the ache, followed by the sting of healing, until it was all she could do not to writhe with growing need.

Nathan sat back on his heels, his hot eyes scanning her body. This time, he wasn't looking for bruises. Raw possessiveness glittered in those blue eyes.

She cleared her throat. "There's a bruise on your arm."

His gaze met hers. For a moment she felt she was tumbling in free-fall. "Yes." His voice sounded deeper, rougher than it had a moment before.

Rachel sat up and took the jar from his hand. Nothing hurt. "That salve's good stuff." She scooped out some of the cream, and traced her fingertips over the hard contours of his biceps. At her touch, the thick muscle twitched.

Acutely aware of the sway of her bare breasts, she reached for the hem of his shirt and pulled it off over his head. And froze, much as he had.

Nathan looked as if some classical sculptor had carved him out of marble, all smooth, hard curves and ridges. His wasn't the heavy build of a weightlifter, for whom muscle was an end in itself. Nor did he have the gangly appearance of a marathon runner. Instead, his body struck the perfect balance between the two like an Olympic swimmer, with enough bulk for strength, but not enough to slow him down.

Scars marred that perfect body here and there, thin lines that reminded her of his duelist career. Old sword wounds, probably inflicted with a rapier.

A long red line slashed over his belly that looked like an abrasion from her practice sword. Rachel scooped up more of the cream and leaned forward to trace it over the injury. Muscle moved under her fingers as though he drew in a breath.

She looked up automatically to find Nathan staring down at her, his eyes intense and hot.

Broad hands slid into the hair at her neck, pulling her head back. His mouth covered hers, lips soft in the frame of his beard. The kiss started out slow, almost gentle, more request than claiming.

Until she groaned.

Nathan growled. It was a rough, animal, very male sound, fierce with hunger. He opened his mouth wider, increasing the pressure until he fed at her lips in deep, eating kisses.

Ravenous.

Excitement burned through her like a flame licking along a fuse, heat building toward an explosion.

A big hand came up and cupped her breast, palm rough with calluses and scars. The faint abrasion made her heating lust leap higher. Rachel dragged her mouth away from his, sucking a breath. "I thought you didn't want to do this. Didn't want to give me the Gift."

He stared into her eyes from inches away. His gaze was so feral with lust, it was like staring into the eyes of a tiger. "Once won't do it."

"Three will."

His lips lifted in a quick flashing grin. "Which gives me one more time before I have to make up my mind."

"Asshole."

"Get used to it." This time when his mouth crushed down on hers, she felt the prick of his fangs. One hand tightened on her breast, thumb raking over her nipple, each rough brush sending an intoxicating rush of flame through her, until it felt as if her veins began to glow. He gripped her hair in a big fist.

Something about the stinging hold heated her blood even more.

He surged against her, bearing her backward, his hand cradling her skull, preventing it from knocking into the floor as his weight hit her. Instinctively, she wrapped her legs around his hips, and her arms around his powerful torso as thick brawn worked under her hands. Her short nails dug into his skin. The feel of that velvet flesh indenting under the pressure was wildly arousing. She growled herself, a little rumble in the base of her throat, a little animal, a lot hungry.

He growled back. And bit her lower lip, not quite hard enough to draw blood with those fangs, but the threat was there. And God, it aroused her.

She dug her nails and tightened her thighs. Felt the bulk of his cock through the rough fabric of his jeans. Rachel moaned at the thick promise of it. The raw, erotic tease.

She wanted more.

He pulled away a fraction, arctic eyes wide, the pupils huge and eating the light. He began to kiss his way along the length of her jaw, tongue swirling, tasting her. She threw back her head, gasping, tightening the grip of her thighs so she could grind her silk-clad pussy against his cock.

Wet. She was so wet, and he was so hard. And he was going to fuck her. God, she wanted it, whether or not it was the first step to getting the Gift. Rachel really didn't give a damn about the Gift just now.

She wanted Nathan.

He tasted his way along her jaw to her ear, paused to swirl his tongue around her lobe, press the delicate flesh between his front teeth. Careful not to break the skin.

His lips found her pulse and paused. She gasped, feeling the heat of his mouth against the throbbing beat of it. *He's going to bite me. He's going to feed. And it's going to hurt.* Yet there was a wicked arousal in that thought, a perverse need to feel the sting and penetration of his teeth. To listen to the sound of him swallowing her blood.

Claiming her.

Rachel had never wanted anybody to claim her. Hell, yesterday the thought would have outraged her. But now she froze against him, breath held, waiting for the sink and sting of his fangs. Waiting for the liquid sound of his swallows.

Instead he jerked his head away from her throat, met her gaze, his narrow and wild. His lips curled into something halfway between a smile and a snarl. "Not yet."

When she hissed in frustration, he laughed. Went back to kissing and licking his way down her throat. He pulled tighter on her hair, drawing her spine into an arch. Rachel tried to fight his hold, but his vampire strength overwhelmed her easily.

She was helpless.

*God, that's exciting.* She ground against his erection, nails digging deeper into his skin.

"Keep that up, and you'll draw blood."

"Good," she gritted. "You deserve it."

He laughed, deep and rough, a tiger's purr. "Maybe I do, at that." He lowered his head until his mouth hovered over her nipple. His eyes flashed up at hers. "The question is, what do *you* deserve?" The tip of one fang flashed white over the thrusting peak, an implied threat that made her breath catch.

Something wild and hot spun through Rachel, making her crave that dark, erotic pain. She'd never considered herself a masochist, but something about Nathan's stare seemed to draw out an answering wildness. Made her crave things she'd never known, never even dreamed of wanting.

Made her want to leap into the dark after him.

* * *

Nathan stared up at her as hot lust fisted his balls until the roots of his fangs ached. He shouldn't be doing this -- it was a bad idea -- but he didn't give a shit. He'd wanted Rachel since she'd stalked into her apartment covered in sweat, her eyes dark with pain and black memory.

He should have known it was going to end up like this, regardless of what his common sense told him.

He had to have her. Now.

Nathan closed his mouth over her breast, sucked hard, and was rewarded by the sting of her nails drawing blood. He loved that he'd driven her so wild, loved the grind of her panty-clad pussy against his dick.

He reached down, wrapped his fist in that ridiculous scrap of red silk. Twisted. Jerked. The panties tore like spider silk in his hand.

But he was still wearing his jeans. And he needed them the hell off. He levered himself off her, jolted to his feet, jerked off his ankle boots. Sent them banging against the nearest wall while he went for his snap and his zipper and began dragging the jeans off.

Rachel propped up on her elbows and watched him, a long chestnut curl falling into glittering brown eyes, color riding high in her cheeks. He could smell her arousal with every breath he took. Nathan jerked his pants off, and almost fell on his ass in his haste. He sent them sailing after the boots.

That he bent down, scooped her into his arms, and headed out of the room and down the hall.

She looped her arms around his neck. "Where are we going?"

"Bedroom. I'm damned if I'm going to fuck you on the floor."

Rachel gave him a gamine smile. "Well, as long as you've got a plan."

He returned the smile with one deliberately evil. "Oh, I have a plan, all right."

She laughed, the sound throaty and a little wicked. His cock bucked at the erotic promise in her voice. Damned if he could remember the last time he'd been this turned on.

Never mind that he practically fucked for a living. Deep in his mind, a voice said, *This is different.*

*No, it's not,* insisted his sense of self-preservation.

He ignored both and carried her up the stairs. It was the kind of maneuver he used frequently with his Latents, romantic and dominant at once.

This time, it wasn't part of his act. There was something about having her in his arms that felt different. As if he were claiming her rather than simply seducing her.

Nathan looked down into her face, and saw a flicker of vulnerability and unease in her gaze. But beneath that emotion was a glitter of erotic excitement.

She wanted him.

He couldn't think of the last time he'd wanted a woman this badly.

Nathan carried Rachel down the hall to his bedroom, enjoying her awed murmur as she looked around at the huge brass bed and the stained glass window that took up one whole wall. He strode to the bed and lowered her to the enchanted mink throw that lay across it. She purred in approval at the press of the pelt's silken texture against her bare skin. Then she frowned slightly.

"And before you ask, no, it didn't come from real animals," Nathan told her, having previously encountered Millennial objections to skinning the small and fuzzy. "You can lie back and enjoy it with a clear conscience."

She grinned wickedly up at him. "Okay, you talked me into it."

He straightened, admiring the carnal contrast between her lush, pale body and the dark fur. As he watched, she scooted toward the middle of the bed, lovely breasts bouncing. Her eyes were hot with anticipation.

Before Rachel could scoot any further, he grabbed her ankles and lifted them so he could drape her thighs over his shoulders. He practically dove for her pussy, enjoying her sharp indrawn breath as his mouth covered her. He thrust his tongue deep, eyes slipped closed at the salty pleasure of her taste, tinged with that hint of magical spice that meant Latent.

Distilled sex. God, he loved that taste. He released his grip on one thigh to spread her vaginal lips and stab his tongue deep.

\* \* \*

Rachel gasped, both hands fisting the fur at the burning pleasure of his long licks, the elegant swirling patterns over clit and between lips. God, he was good at that. She rolled her head back against the pelt as delight leapt with every tiny flick and nibble.

She felt as if he were winding her up like the key of an old-fashioned toy, some inner spring compressing tighter and tighter. Squeezing her eyes shut, she panted. Craving his teeth.

The thought of his bite sent another shiver of sheer lust through her, a driving hunger for that thick, flushed cock.

His arms tightened around her thighs, and she dug her bare heels harder against his muscled back. Pulling him closer, increasing the pressure of his tongue against her pussy and clit.

But it wasn't enough. She wanted him, and she wanted him *now*. "God, Nathan, fuck me!"

His only response was a dark, rumbling chuckle against slick folds.

The vibration was maddening. Rachel writhed against him, deliberately grinding, until she began to feel the hot tensing that signaled the beginning of an orgasm. She gasped, reflexively reaching out, meaning to grab his short hair in one hand.

A male hand closed around her wrist before she could get a grip, pushed it down to the fur, and pinned it there. Nathan's tongue licked and swirled, urging the maddening sensations even higher. She writhed, unable to stop herself. Close, so close…

"Nathan…" She gasped it, desperate, begging.

The hand around her leg released it, reached up her body, and found her nipple. He began to squeeze and milk and twist it, every stroke sending another stab of delight through her. Built her lust even more.

"Nathan!" Need made the word so high-pitched, it was almost a whine. "Fuck me, you sadistic son of a bitch!"

He lifted his head and shot her a glittering stare. "That is not the way you talk to me." The naked menace in his voice somehow aroused her even more.

*Vampire Trinity* notwithstanding, she'd had no idea she was this kinky.

Abruptly he released her wrists to land astride her like a cat pouncing on a catnip mouse. She didn't quite suppress her yelp.

Nathan loomed over her his eyes glittering, broad shoulders blocking the light as he sat back on his heels and took his thick cock in hand. "Do you want this?"

Her laughter sounded a little wild. "You're kidding, right?"

His palm slapped against her bare thigh in a smack she should've kicked him for. "I asked a question."

"Yes! But if you ever spank me again, you'll wind up with donkey ears if I have to get Gee to give them to you."

Nathan's mouth curled into a dark smile framed in beard. "I'm terrified," he drawled. And lowered himself over her, guiding the thick shaft into her wet, snug heat.

The feel of it was so raw, so intense as he worked in deep… Gasping, Rachel stared up at him, wild-eyed, as he braced himself over her on thickly muscled arms.

Licking her lips, she spread her legs wider for him.

Nathan began to thrust. Slow, deep, grinding in and out, angling his hips to make sure his pelvis made contact with her clit. Winding her building pleasure tighter and tighter until it seemed to press against the back of her eyes. She hooked her calves over his ass and ground up at him, wrapping both arms around his torso. Muscle worked and rolled under her hands with every long stroke.

Nathan sank to his elbows, so the length of his strong body touched hers. Wrapping his arms around her, he pulled her body into an arch. He kissed her, one of those deep, suckling kisses he did so well. With a groan of arousal, she kissed him back, tongues circling and swirling.

The hard muscle of his abdomen flexed against her softer belly, shuttling his cock in and out, teasing her with its length and thickness. Each stroke felt exquisite, and she lost herself in him, in his taste and heat and hardness.

A crazed kind of hunger built in Rachel, more intense than anything she'd ever felt with any other man. She tightened her grip and met the drive of his hips with hers, taking him as deep as she could get, trying to fill that maddening emptiness, that breathless craving.

Still riding her, he drew away from her mouth, found the underside of her jaw. Groaning, knowing what he intended, she tilted her head back. Giving him access to her banging pulse.

His mouth touched her skin there, tongue laving the spot tenderly. One hand angled her head. She sucked in a breath, impossibly aroused -- an arousal that only grew as he bit down in a hot, sweet sting. A thought flitted through her mind -- *I thought it would hurt more* -- and then he began to drink, taking her as he fucked her harder. Each long plunge made the bed shift under her as his big body rolled against hers.

On and on he thrust, still drinking, as the pleasure wound tighter and tighter until she groaned and shook with it, clawing for the orgasm barely out of her reach.

He stiffened with a snarl, shoving deep. Coming. And as he shot within her, her orgasm struck like a snake, a savage burn more ferocious than any climax she'd ever had. "Nathan!" She screamed it, helpless, as raw sensation blasted through her.

He released her throat and lifted his head. "Look at me!"

Her eyes flew wide as she gasped through the blazing orgasm. He stared down at her, his gaze fierce, pupils blown with lust, his handsome face drawn in a rictus of ecstasy and triumph. A bead of something crimson shown on his lip.

She had no idea why that made the whole thing even hotter.

Finally, he collapsed on the bed beside her, then reached out and pulled her over on to him, cradling her in his arms. Listening to the furious thump of his heart, Rachel felt herself truly relax for the first time since the shooting.

She'd slept barely a handful of hours in the past seventy-two. And yet five minutes later, she fell asleep in the vampire's arms.

# Chapter Four

Nathan lay staring up at the stained glass skylight, bright even at night in the illumination of the house's exterior spotlights. Otherwise he'd never be able to enjoy it, thanks to the magical Day Sleep that would knock him cold the minute the sun rose. The colored glass served a practical purpose; without it, the sun's light would inflict serious burns he wouldn't even feel until he woke at sunset.

Being a vampire might give you fantastic strength and speed, but it came at a price. A liquid diet and never seeing the sun were major line items on that bill.

The fact that he found Latents like Rachel incredibly tempting was yet another price to be paid.

He looked down at her, feeling her warm breath puff across his bare skin. Her lashes looked ridiculously long as they lay on her cheeks. She was asleep.

*What the hell am I doing*? He'd fully intended to keep his distance tonight. And yet here he was.

Nathan frowned, intensely conscious of the feel of her, her body soft against his in so many tempting places, strong in so many others. She looked so innocent in sleep, as untouched as a maiden from a medieval ballad.

Which made a startling contrast to the cold determination on her face when they'd fenced. She was a warrior, no matter how sweet she looked in sleep. She also made love like a courtesan, as wild with arousal as he'd been himself.

His self-control was usually better than this. If he weren't damn careful, he'd end up Gifting her before he knew what hit him.

And then he might have to kill her.

The thought of Rachel going mad made him feel sick at what he'd have to do then. Killing Christine had been bad enough.

Dr. Christine Phillips had been a pediatric oncologist who'd devoted her life to saving children from childhood cancer. She'd told him once how the patients she lost ate at her.

Christine had believed becoming a Maja would give her the opportunity to heal those she couldn't save through merely human medicine. He'd warned her it wouldn't be that simple -- she'd have to give up practicing medicine among the mortals. She'd almost turned the Gift down then, but the thought of being able to do something about the terrorism and injustice of the world seduced her into going for it anyway.

She should have been fine. The witches of the Majae's Council had predicted she'd survive her transformation with her sanity intact.

They'd been wrong.

He'd come within her that third time, felt the blast of raw power that was the Gift activating within her cells. In those first moments, he'd thought she would be okay. She'd looked around the room with such wonder, entranced by the magical forces all Majae could see when they transformed the first time. Springing from the bed laughing like a child, she'd conjured one ball of sparking magic, then another. Then another.

He realized something was wrong when the first of those spheres changed from sunlight gold to bloody red.

Christine turned her head and looked at him. As he watched in helpless horror, madness flooded her gaze like the red staining her magic. She whirled and flung all three balls at him like a Major League pitcher, one right after another. He dove off the bed barely a heartbeat before the first blast blew a hole in the stained glass window.

As Nathan rolled aside, he'd snatched his sword from under the bed, where he always left it when he Gifted a witch. Christine dove at him, shrieking in rage and madness...

And he'd run her through.

For a heartbeat, she stared at him in bewildered accusation. Then she'd fallen, the life draining from her beautiful blue eyes.

Nathan hadn't loved her. That was by design -- he never spent enough time with the Latents he Gifted to fall in love.

*But none of those girls was Rachel*, whispered a soft voice in his mind.

*Oh, shit. Oh no, I am not doing that. No way in hell.*

A little spurt of unaccustomed fear drove him to lift Rachel off his chest and settle her on the bed's furry coverlet. He needed some distance. Badly.

Nathan eased off the other side and padded naked down the hall to descend the stairs. Moving in long strides, he headed for the living room and its well-stocked bar. He stepped behind the gleaming length of dark walnut, reached up into the shelves that held his liquor collection, and pulled down a shot glass and a bottle of Glenlivet. He poured himself three fingers and downed the fiery liquor in one swallow.

Galahad would be outraged at his sacrilegious treatment of the Scotch.

He poured another glass and did it again.

As the liquor seared the lining of his throat, Nathan tried to reason with his instincts. He was not, damn it, falling for Rachel Kent. The very idea was ridiculous, especially considering how little time he'd known her. Yeah, she was pretty enough, but so were the other women he'd slept with in his career as a court seducer. Yes, she was bright and courageous, but both characteristics were pretty much a prerequisite for any Gift candidate.

*I'm feeling guilty and vulnerable because of Christine. It doesn't mean anything.*

Nathan threw himself down on the long black leather couch, scooped up the remote, and turned on the wall-length screen that hung across the room. By all rights, the thing shouldn't work in the Mageverse, but witches had a way of sidestepping the laws of physics. Pretty much every cable and online service known to man was available in Avalon.

Brooding, he started surfing the program menu, trying to find something he actually wanted to watch. He'd settled on one of the 24-hour news channels when his vampire hearing picked up a soft moan of pain coming from upstairs.

Nathan tossed the remote aside and hurried out of the room to take the stairs two at a time. Striding to the master bedroom door, he swung it open and headed for the bed. "Rachel?"

Gloriously naked in the colorful light shining through the stained glass windows, she twisted restlessly against the fur, moaning in distress. The moans grew into a ragged, pleading sound, strangled with pain and terror.

Nathan's first instinct was to shake her awake, but he knew that was the worst thing you could do to someone in the grip of a nightmare. Instead he called sharply, "Rachel? Rachel, you're dreaming. Wake up."

Her entire body seemed to spasm, and her eyes flew wide. She looked around, her expression panicky, as if she had no idea where she was or what was going on.

"Rachel, you're at my house. Everything's fine."

Her head snapped around and she stared up at him as he stood by the bed, wild-eyed and confused. "Nathan?" Her voice shook.

Then the confusion faded, replaced by embarrassment. She groaned, rubbing both hands over her face. "Damn it."

Nathan squashed the impulse to take her in his arms. He was on the verge of losing all pretense of objectivity as it was. Neither one of them could afford that. She needed him to make her think -- really think -- about whether she wanted to risk the Gift. This wasn't something she should do simply because Oriana had brainwashed her to believe it was her duty. He was all for duty, but the thought of looking into those beautiful eyes and seeing madness…

No. He had to get a handle on the situation. Had to maintain some emotional distance so they both could stay on an even keel.

If she chose to risk the Gift, fine. It was her life. She needed to make that decision without being swamped by emotion that might lead her into self-destruction. He had a responsibility to provide that distance, not tempt her into suicide by treating her like a lover.

And if some part of him hated the idea, that was too fucking bad.

\* \* \*

"Bad dream?"

"Yeah." Rachel rubbed her hands across her face again, trying to rid herself of the last sticky psychic cobwebs of the nightmare. *Daddy, daddy, daddy…*

In tonight's variation, she'd been unable to move when the killer turned his gun on his wife and children. She wanted to step between them, shield them as she had in real life, but her body hadn't obeyed. She'd stood frozen and helpless while Don killed them one by one -- and then turned the gun on Rachel.

"I dreamed about the shooting. Again."

"You'll find you do that a lot in the aftermath of combat," Nathan told her. His voice was cool, sounding nothing like the man who'd made such passionate love to her. When she shot him a startled glance, his eyes were as distant as his voice.

The hell?

He made a show of looking down at the old-fashioned wristwatch he wore. "Sun'll be coming up in about half an hour. I don't have long until the Day Sleep. You may want to head to Oriana's, have her open a dimensional gate for you if you need to go back home. Be back here tonight at sunset and we'll continue the testing."

A spark of anger shot through Rachel as she remembered an old southern saying about rude hosts trying to get rid of inconvenient guests. "'Here's your hat,'" she muttered. "'What's your hurry?'"

"I'm not your boyfriend, Rachel. You're my assignment."

Her jaw dropped. She wanted to tell him exactly what he could do with his assignment, but she had the humiliating suspicion she'd be unable to hide the hurt under her rage. "Yeah, you made that more than clear."

Furious, Rachel stalked toward the door, only to break step when she realized she was stark naked.

"Your clothes are still in the dojo."

Without acknowledging what he'd said, she headed naked down the steps, blinking her stinging eyes. Damned if she was going to cry for the son of a bitch.

Her leggings, tank, and shoes lay on the floor of the practice room. He'd reduced her bra and panties to scraps. *Looks like I'm going commando*, she thought, and got dressed anyway.

Still seething, Rachel let herself out, resisting the urge to slam the door. It was only when she hit the cobblestone street outside that she realized she didn't remember how to get back to Oriana's.

Fuck it. She turned right and stalked off.

Which was, of course, the wrong way. She realized her mistake more than a mile later, turned around, and went in the other direction.

*Asshole.*

\* \* \*

Rachel poured out her outrage while Oriana cooked breakfast for the pair of them. They were eating before she ran out of steam. "I can't help but notice…" She stabbed her fork into her eggs. "That you haven't said anything."

Gee took a bite of her bacon, chewed and swallowed. At last she said, "I don't blame you for being pissed, but I think he was trying to do you a favor."

"Are you saying you don't think I should get the Gift either?"

"Don't be ridiculous. You'll make an excellent Maja. I'm simply concerned you may be getting a little too involved with him. Nathan's right. He's not your boyfriend, and he's never going to be."

"I know that. I'm not an idiot."

Oriana gave her a long, cool look. "Do you?" When Rachel opened her mouth to retort, Gee held up a hand, silencing her. "Look, it's natural for Latents and Magekind to feel an intense mutual attraction. Merlin's spell reacts to the magic in any member of the Magekind, especially someone of the opposite sex who could trigger the Gift. And Court Seducers are naturally seductive people to begin with. That's why they're chosen for the job."

"Yeah, Nathan just oozes charm."

"Actually he does, at least when it suits him. He's always loved women -- has a positive talent for making whomever he's with feel like the center of the universe."

"He must really hate my guts then, because he doesn't make me feel that way."

"Oh, really?"

Rachel started to answer, then remembered the moment when she'd lain in his arms. "Okay, maybe once."

Gee sighed. "Look, being a Court Seducer can be difficult. Ninety-nine percent of the time you're sleeping with someone you don't know, so you're supposed to make it easier for the Latents by romancing them. Seducers aren't supposed to lie, but they are told to make their partners feel this isn't just soulless sex. The best Court Seducers make their Latents fall a little bit in love without actually breaking their hearts."

Rachel toyed with her fork. "Tricky balance to strike."

"Exactly." Oriana leaned closer and caught her in an intense gaze. "Now imagine that out of every thousand Latents you seduce, one of them goes insane and tries to kill you. And if you don't stop her, God knows how many people she's going to kill."

"Yeah. He's told me all about that. More than once."

"But think about how it must really feel. Here's a woman you were making love to not five minutes before, and now you've got to kill her -- if you can. Vampires may be much stronger than we are, but our magic gives us a tremendous advantage. In any fight between a mad Maja and a Magus, the vampire could easily lose. And if he dies, she'll be turned loose on an unsuspecting Avalon. Yes, eventually somebody's going to kill her, but others could get ambushed and murdered. All because the seducer screwed up."

Rachel winced. As a cop, she was all too familiar with the public cost of lethal mistakes. Hell, even when you did the right thing, there was a price to be paid. And you might not be the only one to pay it. *Daddy, daddy, daddy…*

"My point is, no matter how he makes you feel, he doesn't share your emotions. He can't afford to. And you can't afford to let three fucks mean more to you than they should. You're going to get hurt."

Pride stinging, Rachel glowered. "Look, I'm not some dippy little Victorian virgin. I've had lovers."

Oriana snorted. "None of whom were anything like Nathan Allard. There's nothing wrong with enjoying your time with him, but you need to keep in mind it doesn't mean anything. It can't. Have fun making love to him, by all means, but don't let him get to you. Don't let him piss you off when he tests you. And for God sake, guard your heart even when he makes you come so hard you see stars. Otherwise you're going to regret it."

"Yeah," Rachel said. "I see your point."

*I don't like it, but I see it.*

* * *

Oriana opened a gate back to Rachel's apartment, promising to return her to the Mageverse at sunset.

Rachel took a shower and fell into bed, hoping to catch up on the sleep she'd missed since the shooting. She tossed and turned before finally drifting off.

Her alarm went off at two, and she staggered out of bed to get ready for her appointment with the therapist. She supposed she could go ahead and quit her job, but she didn't want to trigger rumors that there was anything unjustified in the Gordon shooting. Besides, it was possible she might decide not to become a Maja after all. She doubted it, but the possibility existed.

So she spent fifty minutes at the therapist's office rehashing the shooting -- again -- and explaining she felt fully justified and would do it again if she had to.

She wasn't sure the therapist believed her.

Next Rachel swung by her parents' house to tell her mother what was going on. She'd briefly considered waiting until it was all over so her folks wouldn't worry, but what if she didn't survive her transformation? She didn't want them blindsided like that.

Barbara Kent worked the second shift at Tayunita County Regional Hospital, but it was her day off, making this a good opportunity for a visit.

Though she'd become a nurse when her Magekind ambitions failed to materialize, Barbara was still tall and athletic even in her fifties. She was so thrilled when Rachel told her the news, it was obvious it never even occurred to her that her daughter might not survive the Gift. Rachel decided not to bring that possibility to her attention.

When she left the family's brick colonial, her mother was already making plans for the party they'd throw to celebrate Rachel's becoming Magekind.

Buoyed by Barbara's confidence, she called her Highway Patrol trooper father to give him the news. Richard might not be a Latent, or even a Kent by blood, but he knew the family secret and had embraced its traditions. He'd even taken his wife's name, a move that had raised some eyebrows in his very conservative family. He'd been willing to do it anyway to make his wife happy.

He'd even submitted to the secrecy spell Oriana cast on family members to ensure none of them talked about the Magekind. The measure was *de rigueur* for any mortal who knew the secret; Avalon was more paranoid about security than the NSA.

Richard also knew what it took to become a Maja, and he wasn't sure he liked the idea. Nor did he approve of Court Seducers, particularly when it came to his daughter.

"So how's this vampire treating you?" Dad demanded, sounding every inch the big, intimidating cop he was.

"Oh, Nathan's a perfect gentleman," she told him without missing a beat. She didn't lie to her father often, but there were some things he didn't need to know.

"He'd better be, or I'll kick his ass." Dad would give it his best shot, too, never mind that a vampire was several times stronger than any human.

By the time Rachel hung up, she was smiling.

A call to her firefighter sister was the next order of business. Teresa wanted to know if the vampire was cute. She admitted he was, and resisted the temptation to add that he was also an asshat. Anything Teresa knew, her parents would find out. Her little sister couldn't have kept a secret in a bank vault. She loved to talk, and she was compulsively honest. If not for Gee's Top-Secret spell, she probably would've outed them all on Facebook by now.

Duty done, she headed home and fell into bed for another desperately needed nap. She dreamed about the shooting only once, but it was still bad enough to make her claw her way to wakefulness.

By the time Oriana finally arrived at sunset, Rachel was glad for the distraction.

Gee treated her to dinner before she set off for her appointment with Nathan and another glorious night of banging her head against the wall.

Though she was tempted to do it with the vampire's stubborn skull instead...

\* \* \*

Rachel strolled in wearing a black tank top and another pair of skintight leggings that made Nathan's vampire appetites rumble approval. She'd tied her hair back in a curly ponytail that swung between her shoulder blades, and her brown eyes were narrow and wary.

*Good*, he told himself. If she wanted to keep her distance, all the better. His disappointed libido would have to get over it.

Once again they headed into the dojo, but this time he gave her one of Oriana's simulation circlets. She studied the engraved silver circlet dubiously, but she put it on anyway.

He did the same, feeling the familiar buzz of magic along his skin as the spell activated.

Suddenly they stood in an alley between two brick buildings. The ground trembled beneath their feet.

It had good reason.

A creature fifteen feet tall raced down the alley toward them on two powerful legs, thick tail lashing behind it as it ran. It was covered in emerald green feathers, its gaping muzzle revealing teeth like daggers. A blue gemstone shown above its bright orange eyes.

Rachel recoiled, staring at the dinosaur in shock as it thundered closer. "What the hell is that -- a Tyrannosaurus Rex?"

"The team that fought it called it Super Chicken." He didn't blame her for looking horrified. He was glad he hadn't had to fight the thing himself. Facing it in the simulation was bad enough. "But technically I think it was a raptor."

"Real raptors were the size of German shepherds!"

"Super Chicken wasn't a real raptor. A werewolf wizard created it from another werewolf."

"Oh, come on! Werewolves don't use magic any more than vampires do." Apparently Oriana had briefed her descendants about Merlin's assorted creations.

"Warlock did." And they'd had a hell of a time killing him, too.

The monster thudded to a stop, tail whipping, and roared, breathing the stench of blood and meat over them.

"Back off, KFC!" Rachel snapped up at it, before turning to glare at Nathan. "No. Forget it. I was willing to play along with the sword fight yesterday, but this is ridiculous."

The raptor started to dive at them, jaws open wide as if to eat them both. With a huff of disgust, she snatched the circlet off of her head. And promptly vanished from the simulation.

Nathan did the same before the creature had a chance to take a bite out of him. Both the dojo and Rachel reappeared. He glowered at her. "I told you I was going to test you. Are you giving up on becoming a Maja?"

"No, I'm refusing to go along with this bullshit."

"Majae don't get to turn their backs on a mission because it's dangerous."

"And exactly how many times have Majae had to fight magical raptors in the past fifteen hundred years?"

"Once," he snapped back. "But they *did* have to fight it."

"And how many of them were brand new Majae who'd never fought anything at all with magic -- ever? I have had zero training in the use of my power because I don't have power to use. You can't tell me Morgana Le Fay would send a rookie Maja against a monster like that with no backup."

"Look, all you have to do is picture what you want to do -- create a fireball or whatever -- and the spell will create an illusion of that attack to let you experience what it would be like. The point is to see how you would use magic if you had it."

"The *point* is to scare me off. Look, I get that you don't want to have to kill another insane Maja. I don't blame you. I'm not real thrilled about the possibility I might have to shoot somebody again. But giving me Merlin's Gift is your job. The Majae's counsel cleared me to get the Gift. Do your job or quit."

"This *is* my job," he ground back. "I make the final decision about whether you can survive the transition. So take the test or go home. Those are your options."

"May I remind you, you're not the only male court seducer in Avalon? I can also go to Dominic Bonnhome."

At the thought of Bonnhome taking Rachel to bed, a stab of vicious jealousy knifed through him. "He's on a mission."

"Fine. Half the people in this town have dicks. I'm sure Gee can talk one of them into doing it."

And they'd probably be more than happy to oblige, too. "Not if I appeal to it to Arthur. As I told Oriana last night, he's the only one who can rescind this assignment. If I judge you're not safe to receive the Gift, he'll back me up."

Her delicate jaw jutted. "Are you honestly saying you think I'm too weak to survive?" When he hesitated, she demanded, "Is that what you think?"

He couldn't quite bring himself to lie. "I don't know. I do know your life hangs on this decision. Yes, Dominic would happily bang you into the Gift, but if you lost it, he'd also cut your throat without a second thought."

"Would *you* have a second thought?"

"Yes, damn it, I would. I'd never fucking get over it. Is that what you want to hear?"

Rachel looked startled for a moment before she frowned. "Even if I pass your tests, is there any guarantee I'll survive the transition?"

"No," he said reluctantly.

"Then what's the point? And what gives you the right to take this chance from me if you don't know?"

Nathan started to retort, then closed his mouth. Yes, if he gave her the Gift and she failed, he'd be cheating her out of her normal lifespan. But if he refused to Gift her when she could have passed, he'd be depriving her of centuries.

He didn't have that right.

And yet the thought of looking into those big chocolate eyes and killing her was unbearable. He'd survived Christine's death. He really wasn't sure he'd survive Rachel's.

*It's time for me to quit this job and go back to being a straight field agent.* Nobody would be surprised. Court Seducers had a notoriously high burn out rate.

The question was, what was he going to do about Rachel? He'd accepted this assignment. Nathan didn't back out on missions. Never had. Never would.

"Well?" she demanded.

"I'll make you a deal. Take these two simulations and I'll give you the Gift -- as long as I don't find reason to believe you won't make it."

She studied him in suspicion. "Again, why bother?"

"It'll give us both a chance to think. Make sure we're making the right decision."

The suspicion intensified. "So after I fight Super Chicken, you'll make love to me? And then the third time after I do the next simulation?" When he nodded, she thought of a loophole. "What if it takes more than three?" It usually didn't, but it wasn't impossible.

"Then we'll make love until you get the Gift."

She stared at him, eyes narrowed in thought. Finally she nodded slowly. "You've got a deal." She gave him a tight smile. "And I will hold you to it."

Then she put the circlet on. With an irritated grunt, Nathan did the same.

# Chapter Five

*I,* Rachel thought, staring up at the gaping jaws of the magical raptor, *Am out of my mind. Why did I let him talk me into this?*

*You know perfectly well why,* retorted a disgusted mental voice. *You've got a thing for him, and you want his approval.*

*Idiot.* She'd be lucky if she didn't get herself eaten. Never mind that this was an illusion -- it felt real.

It wasn't merely the gleam of moonlight on Super Chicken's feathers, or the thing's ear-shattering roars. It was the heavy reptilian scent of the creature, the reek of blood and meat on its hot breath and clinging to its gory claws. The whole effect made her hindbrain gibber like something out of an old *Monty Python* movie: *Run away! Run, run away!*

One thing was for damned sure. She didn't want to find out what the simulation would feel like if Super Chicken ate her.

A huge clawed foot slashed at her head, and she threw herself aside. Her enchanted plate armor rattled as she hit the pavement rolling. She had to admit, she liked the armor. Unlike her bullet resistant vest, it weighed little more than her tank top and leggings. Which might be because a tank and leggings were what she was really wearing…

A deep male voice roared a battle cry, and Nathan leaped at the dinosaur, swinging an enormous claymore in a glowing arc. The magical blade was four feet long, with another foot of hilt so it could be swung two-handed. It was a good choice; nobody in their right mind would want to get any closer to the giant reptile than they absolutely had to.

As Nathan hacked at its muzzle, the creature jerked its head up. The gemstone over its eyes flared blue, and the blade rebounded off the blue hemisphere of the raptor's magical shield in a shower of sparks. The dinosaur shrieked and darted its head at Nathan, toothy jaws open wide. He dodged as it snapped, teeth biting empty air. Whirling the blade as if it weighed no more than a chopstick, he darted in, slamming the weapon again and again against the raptor's shield.

What had Nathan said about using magic in the simulation? "Look, all you have to do is picture what you want to do -- create a fireball or whatever -- and the spell will create an illusion of that attack to let you experience what it would be like. The point is to see how you would use magic if you had it."

"Okay, what the hell." She pictured a fireball appearing over her hand in the kind of spell she'd been watching Oriana perform for years.

*Woosh*! The ball of flaming sparks burst into being, its heat warming her palm. *Wow, it worked*! She hurled it at the raptor.

The ball of fire splattered against Super Chicken's shield, raining sparks. And doing absolutely no damage whatsoever.

*Crap.*

How the hell had the original Magekind team defeated the thing? Rachel conjured another fireball and hurled it after the first. It, too, splashed off the shield.

Damn it. Taking a deep breath, she circled the monster, darting in, then dancing back, flinging blasts at the monster the whole time.

The attack served its purpose. Super Chicken quit chasing Nathan to turn its beady orange glare on her again.

*Yeah, that's a real improvement. Think, damn it,* she told herself, summoning another fireball. *The original team beat it somehow. What the hell did they do?*

"Come on, KFC!" Rachel bounced on her toes in a mocking little dance as she conjured a fireball in either hand. "I've got your eleven herbs and spices ready!"

The raptor lunged toward her, swinging tail narrowly missing Nathan's head. The vampire whirled aside like a bullfighter, his cold blue eyes locked on the creature, looking for an opening. The raptor twisted its long neck around, jaws gaped wide, and darted its huge head at him. With a shout, Nate leaped back a heartbeat before those jaws snapped shut.

Rachel strangled a scream, summoned a fireball, and hurled it at the raptor, missing its fanged muzzle by a fraction of an inch. *At least I got closer that time.*

Her eyes widened as realization struck.

The two other times she'd thrown a fireball at it, Super Chicken's shield had blocked her blasts three feet away. This time she'd missed by inches, as if the shield hadn't been up. *Of course not.* KFC was trying to bite Nathan. It couldn't bite through its own shield. That's it. That's the key!

Her mind worked furiously as she saw what she had to do. But fuck, if she miscalculated…

Tough. She had to do something. Sooner or later, they'd start slowing down -- and it was all they could do to stay ahead of the monster now. She had to take a chance.

"Here, chicky chicky chicky!" she caroled, and flung a trio of fireballs at him one after another. It hissed in displeasure. "I've got a bucket with your name on it!"

The huge creature hesitated, glaring toward her. Nathan swung his sword at it, and it wheeled to snap at him. He backpedaled, whirling his sword in arcs that sent sparks raining off Super Chicken's shields. "Quit smarting off at the monster and keep your mind on the job!"

*Damn it, Nate, work with me*! Gritting her teeth with frustration, Rachel darted forward, readying her spell as she ran. She'd only have a fraction of a second...

But she wasn't used to running in plate armor. The inner edge of her right thigh plate caught against her left, tangling her legs. She fell, tucking and rolling as years of martial arts training came to the rescue.

"Rachel!"

Heart pounding, she flipped onto her back -- to find herself staring up into the raptor's throat through a forest of teeth as its head shot toward her face. With a shout, she conjured a spear just as she'd planned, then rammed it between those open jaws, into the creature's soft palate.

It threw its head up with a squeal of agony. Before it could rear away from her, Nathan raced up, leaped onto the raptor's back, and began chopping furiously into its neck with his claymore. Blood flew. She barely rolled clear as the raptor collapsed to the ground, the vampire hacking at it like a berserk lumberjack.

Before she could conjure a sword of her own, alley and dinosaur disappeared.

* * *

Rachel blinked. She stood nose to nose with Nathan, as she'd been when she put on the circlet. Startled, she stepped back a pace. She would have felt a little shamefaced at the reaction, but he looked as off-balance as she did.

For a moment, they stared at each other, both breathing hard. "Did we actually do any of that? I mean, were we running around the dojo fighting an imaginary lizard? And if so, how did we avoid slamming into walls?"

Nathan hesitated. "I don't think so. As I understand it, the spell suppresses your voluntary muscles the same way your body doesn't act out dreams."

Rachel staggered over to the nearest wall, leaned against it, and slid down to sit on the floor. "Then why do I feel like I went ten rounds with a giant prehistoric chicken?"

Nathan walked over and sank down to sit at her side. "Because it was one hell of a simulation."

They spent the next few minutes trying to breathe. Finally, he turned his head to look at her. "So, was falling on your face all part of your cunning plan, or are you just clumsy?"

"Some of both."

"Yeah, that's what I thought. You do realize if you'd tried that shit in real life, you'd have gotten yourself killed. And maybe me with you."

"Only if it didn't work."

When her heartbeat finally slowed, she asked, "So did I pass?"

Nathan turned his head to give her a smile that sent a bolt of wicked heat through her. "Yeah, you passed. Quick thinking with the spell."

She studied him, a little suspicious. "Does that mean I get my prize?"

He gave her a slow, dark smile. "Oh, yes."

Rachel hesitated. She wasn't sure she was ready to make the transition from fighting for her life -- illusion or not -- to kinky vampire sex. Her gaze dropped to his incredibly erotic mouth, to its firm curves, to the plump lower lip. *On the other hand…*

"Need a little encouragement?"

"Maybe."

"Well, I *am* a Court Seducer…" That bearded smile of his took on a pirate's wicked tilt. He leaned in and cupped her jaw in one large, calloused hand, black pupils dilating, darkening the arctic blue. Her breath caught as she stared back, and her slowing heartbeat began to speed again. Taking his time as if thoroughly enjoying the anticipation, he lowered his head and took her mouth.

It was a long kiss, his lips warm and silken against hers. His tongue traced the seam of hers, until, with a moan of surrender, she opened to let him slide inside. Wet, delicious, he thrust in and out in a swirling, seductive tease, until desire kindled low in her belly, growing hotter when he growled against her mouth. He angled his head, eyes closed as he tasted her, slow and hot and passionate. His thumb brushed back and forth over her cheekbone in tiny caresses that seemed to promise her body more.

Nathan gave it to her a heartbeat later when his free hand found her breast. His fingers tightened, seeking the peak of her nipple, teasing it until arousal became outright lust. She gasped against his working mouth. *God, he really is good at this.*

Bracing herself against his chest, Rachel felt hard muscle roll under her palms. She dragged up a leg, threw it over his hips. Rachel sat up, deliberately grinding against the erection she could feel growing behind his zipper. He opened his mouth, inviting her tongue inside. With another soft moan, she thrust in deep. Moaned deeper when she felt the smooth edge of a lengthening fang.

He slid that warm hand into the hair at her nape, cupping her head in long, possessive fingers. She drew back until she could meet his burning gaze. "I think I want to shower. I'm feeling…" Her lips curled into a smile that felt almost as wicked as his. "Sweaty."

His own teeth flashed as he smiled back, slow and dark. "Can't have that." He lifted her off his lap like a kitten, and she scrambled to her feet as he rose, graceful as a panther.

For a moment they stood there looking deep into each other's eyes. His glittered vividly blue with lust as he took her hand and led her from the dojo.

* * *

By the time they walked into the master bedroom, Nathan's cock felt hard enough to hit a fastball. His gaze fastened on the long line of her neck as she stepped in front of him, at the pulse throbbing under the skin. His attention slid down her lithe back to the lush curves of her ass in those skin-tight leggings, his fangs aching almost as much as his dick.

His mind flashed back to her fall, when the raptor pounced on her with open jaws. Though he'd known it was a simulation, in that instant it felt utterly real.

It wasn't the first time Nathan had seen a female partner endangered in combat. Hell, twice in the past four hundred years, Majae had died in battle beside him despite everything he'd done to save them. Yet he'd never felt such icy terror for any of them. Desperation, yes. Fury, yes. Their deaths had left such deep scars, he sometimes still woke from nightmares of guilt and grief. But not such deeply intimate *panic*, as if

Rachel meant far more to him than any Latent ever had. Ever should.

Then there'd been the look on her face as she'd stared up into all those teeth. Fear had contorted her features for a split second, only to vanish as the spear popped into her hand. She'd driven it between the raptor's open jaws with a fluid surge of power and courage.

Nathan had endured some truly horrific things over four centuries, but he wasn't sure he could have dared those fanged jaws without flinching. And yet she'd only been a cop for three years.

*Damn. Just damn.*

Ahead of him, Rachel stopped in the doorway of the bathroom, drawing in a startled breath. Jolted back to the present, Nathan smiled, knowing exactly what she was reacting to.

Like his bedroom, his bathroom was designed for seduction. A huge Jacuzzi bath took up one side of the room, while the other was dominated by an enormous glassed-in shower. Both were more than big enough for two -- or three.

"Want a bath?" he purred, enjoying the thought of Rachel neck-deep in bubbles.

She looked back at him, big brown eyes taking on a sexy twinkle. "Not this time. Baths tend to wash away certain… lubricants."

"That would be inconvenient." Because as hard as his cock was, she needed all the lubrication she could get.

She eyed the glass enclosure. "I think a nice pounding shower might be more the ticket."

"I'm definitely in the mood for some kind of pounding."

She laughed, the sound throaty. "You're a bad, bad man."

"Lady, you have no idea. Yet." He caught the hem of her black tank top and pulled it off over her head. She made a purring sound of approval as he unsnapped her bra, baring the smooth, curving line of her back.

They undressed each other slowly, hands stroking, leaning close now and then to kiss a shoulder or nibble some sensitive spot. When he slid a hand to the cluster of curls between her long legs, he found her deliciously wet, tight around his thrusting fingers.

Then her cool little hand encircled his hot cock, and he almost swallowed his tongue. She stroked him slowly, her dark eyes locked on his face, a smile curving her seductive lips. Her free hand cupped his balls, squeezing gently even as she milked the length of his cock with the other. Shuddering, he let his head fall back.

With a wicked little laugh, she tugged gently on his shaft, leading him to the shower by his cock. Arousal coiled deep in his belly, heating his balls and drawing them tight.

She released him and turned away with a taunting little twitch of her bare ass, slid the shower door open, and reached inside to turn on the spray. His hands curled into fists of need as she took her time adjusting the temperature to her satisfaction.

Nathan was seriously considering grabbing her when she moved into the enclosure and reached for the bottle of body wash in its wall niche. He followed, his cock leading the way.

Rachel's eyes dropped to the thick, aching shaft. A grin of pure lascivious anticipation spread over her face as she squeezed body wash into her palm. The air filled with the scent of vanilla, intensifying as she put the bottle down and lathered her hands. As he stared hungrily down at her, he glimpsed a flash of dark brown irises as she watched him through her thick lashes.

The little minx knew exactly what she was doing to him. And she liked it.

But then, so did he.

She reached for him with those soapy hands, stroking them over his pectorals, tracing the rolling ridges of his abdominal muscles and ribs.

Breath caught, he watched her, feeling hypnotized by her sensual absorption. As Court Seducer, he was normally the one who did the seducing. His Latent partners were more likely to lie back and let him do whatever he wanted to.

But she was more ambitious than that. And she wasn't simply teasing him, either. Fascination filled her lovely gaze as she stroked him, traced each muscle and hollow with her fingertips in ticklish, tempting brushes.

She seemed captivated by his chest hair, which he'd refused to shave despite the demands of Millennial fashion. There was something intensely erotic in the sensation of those gentle fingers touching him, spilling long rolling streamers of foam. Spray from the shower pattered warmly on his shoulders and back as he stood there, submitting to whatever she wanted to do.

Enjoying it all. Needing it all.

And every time she touched him, he grew harder, the ache in his balls building until they felt as heavy as lead.

Rachel fell to her knees on the tile and slid closer to stroke the length of his shaft with her soapy hands, washing him, caressing his full testicles, then rinsing off the soap. And driving him slowly insane. Forcing him to fight the need to reach down, snatch her off the ground, and shove his cock deep.

Leaning forward, Rachel opened her mouth. Nathan stiffened in anticipation. Slowly, so slowly, she took him into her mouth an inch at a time, lips engulfing his cock in a maddening possession.

The sight of her, kneeling there at his feet -- looking submissive when he knew damned well she was anything but... He shuddered, fisting his hands against the need to snatch her off the floor and jam his way into that tight, creamy pussy.

Her lips tightened around his cock, began to suck so hard her cheeks hollowed. The blazing eroticism of the sensation made his head fall back in a low, rough groan of frustrated lust. She sucked harder, drawing deeper, letting him feel the wet, snug grip of her mouth. The pleasure blinded him with its primal intensity.

Unable to help himself, he began to roll his hips, savoring each velvety slide. Every sweet entry and retreat scalded his nerves with a pleasure so intense it was almost pain.

He wondered how much longer he could take it.

* * *

Rachel closed her eyes as she concentrated on the hot weight of him in her mouth. His shaft was so damn long and thick she couldn't take it all, but the effort to do it anyway was impossibly arousing.

She angled her head, working him another fraction deeper, remembering the way he'd looked swinging that claymore as he tried to behead the raptor. All that incredible muscled strength and speed, that vampire grace. The raw essence of masculinity.

She drew off his shaft until her lips encircled the fat corona of his cock, savoring the heated sensation of his velvet skin in her mouth. Before she could sink deep again, he seized her shoulders. "Let go!"

She obeyed, and he jerked her off her knees and into his arms. Her wet body slapped against his as he pulled her into a biting kiss that let her feel the tips of his fangs. He swirled his tongue between her lips, and she opened wide for him, groaning in yearning.

He'd pulled her off balance, forcing her to stand on tiptoes in his arms. Every ridge and hollow of him branded itself on her senses. So very hot and male. He pulled back, his hands clamping into the flesh of her ass, lifting her right off her feet. Raising her high, he looped an arm around her waist and used his free hand to aim his cock. She hissed in shocked excitement as he impaled her on his thick length.

"Oh God!" she gasped at the stark delight of his cock stuffing its way so very deep. Calloused hands gripped her thighs, and he began to drive. Deep, burrowing thrusts ground the big shaft in and out.

They were eye to eye in this position. His vivid irises were thin rings around black pupils, his fangs bared and fierce. She clung to one brawny shoulder, gripping the back of his neck with her free hand to brace herself as he dug in, fucking her hard, until the air filled with the slap of wet bodies.

Helpless, hypnotized, she stared into his face, dewed with water droplets from the shower, hair lying in glossy curls over his forehead, his black goatee dripping.

Each sawing thrust drove her another inch closer to the climax she could feel maddeningly close. Almost. Almost…

"Rachel, Merlin's Cup, Rachel..." he hissed between his teeth, his handsome face set. "You drive me insane!"

"Nathan!" she gasped back, eloquence utterly beyond her, aware of nothing but the sensation of that powerful cock shuttling in and out. He worked her body as if she were a rag-doll. The climax built deep in her belly, a hot spring coiling tighter and tighter and tighter... and...

A fountain of fire blazed up her spine, jerking and twisting her body in his hard arms as she howled. Helpless. Utterly overwhelmed.

He roared, head thrown back, fangs glinting white. *Coming. Coming...*

As she writhed under him, he lowered his head, eyes glittering, and buried those fangs into her throat. She screamed in shocked arousal. He drank her blood while his body emptied itself in her.

And the spell that was Merlin's Gift awoke deep in her DNA.

It seemed each tiny hair on her body rose, and she smelled ozone, sharp and metallic. A heartbeat later, every one of those hairs burst into flame as a wave of heat seared her skin. Rachel screamed in shock at the sensation -- not pain, but so overwhelming it rattled her brain in her skull like a pea in a tin cup.

Light exploded all around her, sparks flaring among the shower's falling water. *The Gift!* The thought lashed her consciousness with a combination of joy and stark terror. *It's the Gift! No, it's too soon, this is only the second time...* But the light grew brighter and brighter...

Until it all went black.

* * *

One minute, Nathan was coming like a fire hose as he drank from Rachel's slim throat. The next, it felt as if the head of his dick seemed to detonate in a rolling magical explosion that made him see stars. It felt like the first pulses of the Gift.

He pulled his fangs from her throat as sparks showered around him. *No, it's too soon! Unless some other vampire -- I'll kill the son of a bitch!*

Another blazing vibration shook him, burning up his cock, deepening his fear. *Not yet, I'm not ready to give her up...*

Then the convulsion of magic sputtered and bled away, leaving him shaken. *Damn, that was close.* As the fireworks faded from his vision, he found himself staring into her huge brown eyes, wide and startled -- before they rolled back in her head. The grip of her long legs around his hips suddenly relaxed, and she went limp so fast he almost dropped her.

"Rachel!" Tightening his hold on her ass with one hand, he snapped the other up to brace her back. She sagged boneless in his arms, out cold. "Fuck!"

His heart pounding, he slid his shaft carefully out of her, then leaned her against his chest as he freed one hand to turn off the water. "Rachel? Rachel, what's wrong?"

But she made no answer, her head lolling, eyes closed. Concentrating on his vampire senses, Nathan heard the beat of her heart, still strong and steady. Cursing under his breath, he slid the shower door open, shifted his grip to cradle her, and strode into the bedroom.

He laid her carefully down on the bed, ignoring the way they both streamed water on the silk sheets. "Rachel?" Patting her cheek, he tried to rein in his growing panic.

He'd spent too many years in combat to freak out like this. She'd simply fainted. It was probably a little precursor to the Gift, something he'd seen before. Yet still, fear gave his mouth a brassy taste. "Rachel!"

To his relief, her long lashes fluttered, opened. She blinked at him, more than a little dazed. "Nathan?" Her voice cracked on the second syllable. "What was..." Her eyes widened in abrupt panic. "The Gift!" Jolting against him, she tried to sit up.

"Shhh," he soothed her, stroking her wet hair back from her face. "You haven't transitioned yet." He tried out a seductive smile, despite his own lingering alarm. "We get to make love one more time, remember?"

The reminder didn't seem to soothe her, judging from the way her eyes darted around as if looking for something that wasn't there. Nathan felt a chill of alarm, reminded of the times he'd seen new Majae staring at magical energies vampires couldn't perceive.

Some of those witches had gone crazy.

He shut that thought down hard; she didn't need to read it on his face right now. "Everything's fine. Latents get these little precursor jolts from the Gift during the second session. Some people even have visions. It's no big deal."

She relaxed a little. "Oh." Looking up at him, Rachel frowned as a drop fell off the end of his nose. "You're wet."

"So are you." He added a deliberately suggestive curve to his smile. "Not that I'm complaining."

"Well, I am. I think we soaked the mattress."

"So we'll move to the guest room. Hang tight, I'll get you a towel."

\* \* \*

Half an hour later they were dry, and Nathan was watching her sleep.

Rachel had dropped off almost the moment her blow-dried head hit the pillow. Absently, he stroked a chocolate curl. It felt like silk under his fingertips, smelled of vanilla and her unique scent.

A line furrowed the fine skin between her brows, as if she were worrying even in her sleep. That precursor jolt had evidently brought home the risk she was running with the Gift.

Nathan's brows lifted as he realized his own fears had become a lot less acute. When had that happened?

Oh, yeah. The moment he'd seen her drive that spear down the raptor's throat. Any woman with that much self-control wasn't going to lose it even under a full-force blast from the Gift.

Absently, he stroked that gleaming curl again, wondering why he felt so damned sure of that. It wasn't as if the Latents who'd failed had been a weak-kneed lot. And yet, his instincts insisted Rachel would make it.

That very conviction sent a flash of unease through him. What was it about her that got to him so powerfully? He remembered his irrational terror when that simulated raptor tried to eat her. That hadn't even been real, and he'd still freaked the hell out.

It wasn't as if he was a virgin in this game. He'd long since lost track of the exact number of women he'd Gifted over a century as a Court Seducer. He'd even been mildly infatuated with one or two of them, charmed by their grace and intelligence. Which was no surprise; Majae candidates didn't come in "run-of-the-mill."

His feelings for Rachel were something different. Something more intense.

Maybe *too* intense.

Yet he couldn't believe a woman with so much strength and self-control would go insane from the Gift.

Staring at the ceiling, Nathan felt a smile spread over his face. He had the feeling it probably looked a little goofy.

*Rachel's going to be okay.*

When she woke up, he'd tell her they could forgo that final simulation. There was no point in putting either of them through the wringer again. And quite frankly, he had no interest in watching her endure another life-and-death struggle. He might have no choice except to deal with real-life shit storms, but that didn't mean he had to put up with simulated ones.

# Chapter Six

"You think you're leaving me?" a male voice snarled over the sounds of a child's sobs as Rachel eased through the small brick ranch's open back door. "Think again, bitch!"

Evidently Don Gordon had been drinking again.

She swore under her breath. She'd been called to the Gordon household three times in the last six months because Don was a very mean drunk. And when he got mean, he liked to use his fists on his wife and kids. She'd done her best to get Eileen to leave the abusive bastard. Sounded like the woman had finally had enough.

No surprise. The last time Rachel had answered a domestic here, it had taken her and two other cops to get the bastard under control, and she'd still ended up with a black eye. Gordon was big, and he was good with his fists.

She had the ugly feeling this was going to be worse. For one thing, her backup was still ten minutes away.

Ten minutes she probably didn't have.

"Put the gun down, Daddy! I'm live streaming this. Everybody will see what a jerk you are!"

Sounded like Amy, the fifteen-year-old.

"I don't give a shit," Gordon hissed. "Put that fucking phone away, or all your little friends will see you get your head blown off."

Luckily, one of those friends had called 911. Even more fortunately, Don didn't know it; Rachel had driven in with her siren off, afraid of triggering a tragedy. With a little more luck, she'd be able to get the drop on the son of a bitch and convince him to go quietly to jail. *Yeah, don't get your hopes up.*

"Put the phone away, Amy," Eileen snapped, her voice shaking.

"But Mom…"

"This isn't the time!"

Moving quietly on her rubber-soled cop shoes, Rachel ghosted through the painfully neat kitchen, her 9 mm Glock drawn.

"Now, Don, put down the gun," his wife said in the low, too-calm voice of a woman trying to deal with an unexploded IED. "You're going to hit one of the kids."

"I sure as fuck am. I'm sick of you making me look like a pussy, unable to control my own *wife*."

Rachel edged along the kitchen wall toward the doorway into the living room. Luckily, there was no door, so she could see Don standing in the middle of the living room. He held a pistol in a one-handed grip he'd probably seen in a movie.

The gun was trained on Eileen Gordon, a plump thirty-five-year-old who held four-year-old Emily in her arms. The child clung to her mother, crying stormily. Dark-haired Amy, fifteen, stood at her shoulder, cell phone pointed at her father.

*Way to pour gasoline on a situation, kid.* Rachel studied the scene grimly. *I've got to get this under control before someone ends up dead.* Mind working frantically, she tried to come up with some course of action that wouldn't end badly. Unfortunately, she didn't have a lot of options. *Just going to have to go for it and hope for the best.*

"Police!" She stepped into the living room, weapon aimed squarely in the center of Don's chest. "Put the gun down, Mr. Gordon."

As she'd hoped, Don jumped and swung the gun to point at her. Luckily, it didn't go off, which had been a calculated risk. He glared at her. "What the hell are you doing waltzing into my house? You didn't even knock!"

"You gave me probable cause with that live-streamed death threat on Facebook," she told him dryly. "Drop the weapon and kick it over to me."

His thin face flushed dark red. "Fuck you! You get outta here before I put a bullet in your brain!"

"Daddy!" The four-year-old sobbed, lunging toward him, forcing her mother to tighten her grip and sidestep to keep from dropping her.

"Drop the gun," Rachel said in the cold, steady tone she'd learned in the Academy. "I will not tell you again, sir. Drop. It."

"Daddy!" Emily wailed. "Don't hurt my daddy!"

"Dad, don't!" Amy yelled.

"Shut up!" Don screamed. "Just shut the hell up!" He swung his gun toward them, his red face rage-contorted.

Shit. They were too far away for Rachel to shove them to safety, and there wasn't time to grab him. She jumped in front of his gun -- and fired. The double reports of the two weapons sounded as thin as a pair of cap guns.

His bullet felt like stepping into the swing of a baseball bat, a brutal impact that drove the breath from her lungs. Her knees buckled, and she hit the carpet at the same time Gordon did. Gagging, she curled into herself, fighting to breathe.

A few feet away, the life drained from Don's eyes. The hole she'd put in the center of his chest looked far too small to kill a man. It barely bled at all before it stopped.

His heart had stopped.

As she crouched there trying to breathe, Emily began to scream, high-pitched and hysterical. "Daddy, daddy, daddy!"

Instead of the pain Rachel remembered, anger surged through her, building rapidly into rage that burst from her mouth in a furious torrent. "You ungrateful little *brat*. I took a bullet for you!"

*Wait, this isn't what happened*, a faint mental voice protested.

Snarling, Rachel glared at the three people whose lives she'd saved. Emily clutched her mother's neck as she sobbed hysterically. "She killed my daddy!"

Eileen curled her arms protectively around her child and shrank away from Rachel, much as she had from Don's gun.

Amy crowded against her mother, eyes wide and frightened, the phone now aimed at Rachel. Her voice sounded numb with shock. "She killed him. She really killed him…"

*This is not what happened.*

"I saved you!" Rachel snarled, as the storm of rage intensified until red began to cloud her vision. "I could've been killed doing it, and you have the gall to whine?"

Slowly, she rose to her feet. From the corner of one eye, she saw her lifted hand began to glow. A ball of fire ignited around her fingers, burning blue white with the heat of her rage.

*No!* Horror fought rage as she tried to stop herself, to regain control, but the fury only burned hotter.

So did the fireball.

With a screech of rage and madness, Rachel hurled the fireball. All three shrieked in terror as the blast hit them. They screamed even louder when they burst into flames and began to burn.

*No no no no*! a mental voice wailed in horror and disbelief.

She didn't care.

"Rachel!" Nathan charged into the room, only to jolt to a stop, staring at the three people who screamed and writhed, burning like torches. "What have you done?" He whirled toward her. "I told you what would happen! I should never have touched you!"

"Fuck you!" And she threw a ball of fire at his head.

He tried to leap aside too late. He bellowed in agony as he burst into flame. Somewhere inside her, a tortured mental voice screamed in grief and horror.

\* \* \*

"Rachel!"

Hands closed over her shoulders, and a body pressed against hers, containing her flailing struggles to escape. "Rachel, wake up!"

Her eyes snapped open as she sucked in a desperate breath. Her throat felt raw, as if she'd been screaming. "Nathan?"

"There you are." He smiled down at her, though his eyes were dark with concern. For a moment, she was afraid to believe he was even there. "You were having a nightmare. Sounded pretty nasty." He stroked a lock of hair back from her eyes, his touch soothing.

"That's putting it mildly." Shaken, she wrapped her arms around him, taking comfort in his solid warmth. The reality of him, here and safe.

It had only been a dream. *Thank God.*

But it had felt so fucking real. With a shudder, she pressed the side of her face to his muscled chest.

His heartbeat thumped, strong and steady. Listening to it, her own heart slowed its thunder.

Nathan stroked the line of her hair tumbling down her back. "Want to talk about it?"

"I dreamed about the shooting. It was all exactly the way it happened, right up until the end." Rachel swallowed as her throat went tight with remembered revulsion and fear. "Right up until Don Gordon died, and his little girl began screaming. Then suddenly I was a Maja, and I *blasted* them. They caught fire and started burning." She squeezed her eyes shut at the sick memory of screaming. "You came in, and I..." Her voice broke, shook. "... I blasted you too."

"Yeah, that does sound ugly." His hand stroked her shoulder and down her back, then up again. "But you're awake now."

*So why don't I feel any better*? A thought nagged at her, a niggling fear. Something Oriana told her once..."Gee said sometimes Latents get visions the second time." Her stomach gave a sick lurch. "What if it was a vision?"

"It wasn't."

"But..."

"The shooting already happened, Rachel." Nathan cupped the side of her face in one warm hand until she looked up at him. "Horrific as it was, it was only a nightmare."

"I... guess that makes sense." She remembered his hoarse screams, the stink of burning flesh..."But what if I do go insane?"

"You're not going to go insane." There was no doubt at all in his eyes.

"You've been telling me for the past two days that I could lose it and kill people. Kill *you*."

"And I was wrong. You're not going to hurt anyone."

God, she wanted to believe him. "So you're *sure* you can handle me?"

He snorted. "No, I'm sure you're not going to go crazy."

Frowning, Rachel studied his face -- and saw no doubt whatsoever. "What changed your mind?"

"Seeing how you handled Super Chicken. The idea of being eaten alive is a universal human nightmare, but you didn't even hesitate. You were completely cool under fire." He grimaced. "I, on the other hand, was ready to flip the hell out just watching you."

"But…"

Before she could finish, he leaned down and kissed her. It was a slow kiss, deep and gentle, almost iridescent with tenderness.

Despite her fear, she found herself relaxing into his hold, into the delicate pressure of his mouth. His tongue stroked along hers, feeling nubby across the top, slick and wet along the underside, a slow swirling thrust. When he drew back at last, his eyes were very dark. "Besides, I know you."

"Forty-eight hours isn't long enough to know anybody."

He smiled slowly. "Except for everything important: your courage, your intelligence, your strength of will. As for the rest of it, I'm looking forward to finding that out." His gaze was utterly steady, as if he meant every single word he'd said.

Rachel nibbled her lower lip as she studied him. God, she longed to believe he was right. "Look, I want to be a Maja. It's what I've always dreamed of. But I don't want it if it means risking your life."

"It's not a risk."

"You don't know that. You said yourself, there's no way to tell whether a Latent can withstand the Gift."

He hesitated a long moment. "Ultimately, no. Look, I have no idea how many women I've Gifted over the past century. Probably three hundred. Of those, five did not survive. The others did. The odds are in your favor."

"But all it takes is one," Rachel told him. "Any cop can tell you that. We do traffic stop after traffic stop until it's as routine as brushing your teeth. Until you pull over that one motherfucker who's got a body in the trunk. Next thing you know, he's going for his gun instead of his license. It's the routine that gets you. Routine makes cops careless, and then it makes them dead." She cupped his warm cheek. "I don't want to be the one who kills you, Nathan. I'd rather not try at all than take that risk with your life."

He snorted. "I'm a Magekind agent, Rachel. It's not exactly a desk job."

"I still don't want to take that risk." Which meant she'd never be able to sleep with him again. Jesus, that thought made her feel like her heart was being torn from her chest.

Nathan frowned, studying her. "I have an idea that may clarify things for you. May even help you process what happened with the Gordons." He grimaced. "Which, from the sound of it, you desperately need."

"What do you have in mind?"

"A simulation of the shooting. Oriana created it based on that Facebook video the Gordon kid shot."

She recoiled. "But we know how that turned out. And I have no desire to go through it again." Especially after that nightmare.

"Look. Morgana originally created the simulation circlets to give people a chance to examine what went wrong on missions. It lets you try other alternatives that might've worked better, maybe learn from your mistakes."

"So you *do* think I did the wrong thing."

He shook his dark head. "Fieldwork is never cut and dried. There are times we end up with results that aren't ideal, but still the best to be had under the circumstances. The simulation will give you the chance to either learn something or make peace with the outcome. Either way, I think it's worth it."

Rachel hesitated. He had a point. Besides, she'd do a lot never to have to hear *Daddy, daddy, daddy!* again. "Is there time before the sun comes up?"

He glanced down at his watch and shrugged. "It's 2 AM. There should be."

She took a deep breath and squared her shoulders. "Let's do it."

Ten minutes later, they stood in the dojo as they slid the circlets into place again.

\* \* \*

Rachel found herself in the Gordons' living room, Nathan by her side.

The Gordons all stood frozen, as if in mid-motion. She frowned, noticing none of them were in the positions she remembered. "I thought this was going to be like the thing with Super Chicken -- where I take part in the action."

"Not this time. I want you to see what actually happened."

The simulation exploded into movement. With a cry of pain, Eileen Gordon reeled back from her husband's brutal slap, her back hitting the living room wall.

Emily wailed as she clung to her sister's thigh. Amy fumbled with her cell phone, getting it up and pointed as Don hit his wife again. Tears ran silently down the girl's face, and her eyes were wild, but there was determination in the set of her lips. "Stop it! I'm live streaming this, Daddy!"

"Wait a minute," Rachel said, and the simulation froze. "This isn't what happened."

"This is before you arrived," Nathan explained. "You didn't see the whole video?"

"Just what was on TV."

"They must've edited it. The video ran for eleven minutes before you got there. One of Amy's friends called 911 five minutes in. You arrived six minutes after that."

When they fell silent, the simulation took up where it left off. Don whirled on his daughter and took a threatening step toward her, one big fist drawn back.

"No, Don!" Eileen grabbed for his forearm.

Without hesitating, he spun into a brutal roundhouse punch that slammed his wife into the wall behind her. Framed pictures fell with the sound of splintering glass. Rachel hadn't even noticed the debris when she walked in.

Eileen slid down the wall and landed on her backside with a bang. Don ignored her, trying to snatch Amy's phone. The girl pushed her little sister clear and ducked his clawing hand. Emily ran to the couch, kneeling to shove her way between it and the wall.

"Even if you break the phone, the evidence is online!" Amy yelled, darting away from his wild swings at her head. "Give it up and go sleep it off!"

*Amy has more guts than I realized*, Rachel thought.

He swayed there, flushed with rage and frustration, head down like an infuriated bull.

Even if Rachel hadn't known how this was going to turn out, she would've recognize the signs of a situation about to go critical. Don Gordon was like a lot of abusers -- a bully who took his sense of self-worth from his ability to terrorize anyone smaller and weaker than he was. And if those he viewed as his natural inferiors dared stand up to him, he wouldn't hesitate to kill to reclaim his sense of power.

Amy played a very dangerous game.

Don glared at her, his lips pulling off his teeth. "Who the fuck do you think you are? You fuckin' don't mouth off to me!"

"And you're not supposed to treat us like this!" Amy cried, backing away, the camera still aimed at him. "I hate lying about bruises or sayin' Emily fell out of the swing when you broke her arm!"

"If you little bitches did what I told you, I wouldn't have to teach you a lesson!" He lunged forward, swinging a fist at his daughter's fragile face.

Eileen grabbed his ankle as he went by. He crashed to the floor, cursing.

She scrambled up, yelling at her daughter. "Why did you do that? He's going to *kill* us!"

"You got that right, cunt!" He staggered to his feet again, eyes glittering, teeth bared, then turned and reeled off down the hall.

"We got to get out of here." Eileen looked around, her face white and tight with desperation. "Emily! Where's Emily?"

"Behind the couch, Mom." Amy wore a sick expression, as if it had finally dawned on her that she'd miscalculated.

"Emily, come out!" Eileen ran to the couch and pushed it aside so she could pull her child out from behind it. The sobbing child fought her hold, forcing her to bend over and scoop her into her arms. At four, Emily was no longer a lightweight, and Eileen had to struggle with her writhing weight.

"Daddy! What are you *doing*?" Genuine terror rang in Amy's voice.

Rachel jerked around and saw why. The big man stood in the hallway with his semi-auto in his hand and a twisted grin of fury and anticipation on his face.

"Put the gun down, Daddy!" Amy pointed the phone at him with shaking hands. "I'm live streaming this. *Everybody* will see!"

"I don't give a shit," Don hissed. "Put that fucking phone away, or all your little friends will see you get your head blown off."

"Put the phone away, Amy," Eileen snapped, her voice shaking, as she moved quickly toward the teen, Emily in her arms.

"But Mom…"

"This isn't the time!"

"Now, Don, put down the gun. You're going to hit one of the kids."

"I sure as fuck am. I'm sick of you making me look like a pussy, unable to control my own *wife*." He wore the frenzied expression of a man doing something he'd always fantasized about.

A slender figure stepped into the room, wearing a black Tayunita County uniform, a gun in her hand. Her expression was grim and cold. "Police!" she said in a sharp, icy voice, weapon aimed squarely in the center of Don's chest. "Put the gun down, Mr. Gordon."

Rachel drew in a breath. It felt fucking weird to look at herself, not in a mirror or recording, but as if she were someone else.

Don jerked around, pointing his gun at the simulated Rachel. "What the hell are you doing waltzing into my house? You didn't even knock!"

"You gave me probable cause with that live streamed death threat on Facebook. Drop the weapon and kick it over to me."

"Fuck you! You get out of my house before I put a bullet in your brain."

"Daddy!" The four-year-old sobbed, lunging toward him, forcing her mother to tighten her grip and sidestep to keep from dropping her.

"Drop the gun," the Rachel simulation ordered. "I will not tell you again, sir. Drop. It."

"Daddy!" Emily wailed. "Don't hurt my daddy!"

"Dad, don't!" Amy yelled.

"Shut up!" Don screamed. "Shut the hell up!" He swung his gun toward them, his face contorted with rage.

"Freeze it," Nathan ordered. Around them, all the figures stopped in mid-motion, like a freeze frame. For a long moment, he and Rachel studied the scene. "Doesn't look to me as if you had a lot of alternatives."

She moved from her simulation to Don, then paced the distance to his three targets. At last she shook her head. "I'm not seeing anything. I really am too far from him to disarm him, and too far from them to knock them out of the way. Which is pretty much what I thought to begin with, so at least there's that."

"Continue," Nathan said.

The simulation jumped in front of Don's gun. The double report as they both fired was deafening -- totally unlike the thin pops she remembered. Both shooters went down at the same time, Rachel's simulation hitting her knees as Gordon toppled.

Her gaze fell on Eileen and Amy, standing huddled together with the little girl. Both the woman and the teen wore expressions of disbelief that gave way to relief. Then, a moment later, to guilt.

"Daddy, daddy…"

"Freeze it," Nathan ordered, cutting off the child's scream.

"I didn't realize how fast it happened," Rachel said hoarsely. "It seemed to take so much longer than that."

"Adrenaline does that. It doesn't really slow down time, but it does give that illusion."

She moved to crouch over Don's crumpled body. "His mother told a reporter I could've shot him in the arm."

Nathan lifted a dark brow. "Funny, you don't look like the Lone Ranger."

"I sure hope not." Rachel snorted. "I aimed center mass because that's what we're taught in the Academy. Arms and legs are risky targets with lives on the line." She considered it, then shrugged. "What the hell, I've always been a good shot. Let me try it." She moved over to where the Rachel simulation had been standing when Don pointed his gun at his wife and kids.

There was a disorienting flash. Suddenly she found herself standing in the same location as the simulated Rachel a moment before, looking down the barrel of Don's gun.

"Shut up!" Don bellowed. "Shut the hell up!" He swung his semi-auto toward his wife and children, his face contorted and red with rage. Rachel switched her aim to his weapon arm, high on his shoulder. The two weapons thundered.

This time the little girl screamed. Her mother shrieked, "Emily!"

The man staggered with a shout of pain, clutching his wounded shoulder. The pistol tumbled from his hand even as Emily started to fall from her mother's arms.

"Bitch!" Don roared, and dove on the gun, grabbing it with his left hand and pointing it at her. Distracted by the sight of Emily limp and bloody in her hysterical mother's arms, she was too late bringing her gun up again.

This time the baseball bat hit her in the head.

* * *

When Rachel opened her eyes, she stood in the dojo.

Nathan looked disgusted. "And that, boys and girls, is why you don't shoot people in the arm."

"No shit." She probed her forehead gingerly, looking for the bullet wound. There wasn't one, of course.

He eyed her, visibly unhappy. "I trust that answers your questions."

"Is that really what would've happened?"

Nathan shrugged. "I have no idea. There are a lot of factors at play, and you can't really predict all of them. But those circlets act like magical computers -- they're designed to create the most likely result of whatever action you take in the simulation."

"In that case, I prefer the outcome I got in real life," Rachel said, pulling off the circlet and handing it over. He took off his own and put both back in the wooden case.

Watching him, she blew out a breath. She felt oddly… light, as if a weight had disappeared from her shoulders. She'd had to kill a man, yes, and she'd left a child without a father. She knew she'd carry the weight of that act for a long time, a reminder she could never make such decisions hastily. But the simulation had brought home that she could have made worse choices.

Ultimately, Don Gordon had forced her to choose between the lives of innocents and killing him. He could have surrendered, but he'd been too determined to make those who loved him pay for the slight to his ego. The responsibility for his death was his.

She took another long, relieved breath, and smiled. Really smiled.

She lost the relief when Nathan said, "We've still got two hours until dawn."

Time enough for the Gift. *Oh God.*

\* \* \*

As Nathan watched, Rachel's eyes widened, and the peace of a moment before gave way to anxiety. She glanced away, as if not wanting him to read her fear. He didn't tell her that her scent gave her away with its acrid tang. "I… uh… I need a shower." Her dark gaze slid to his, then away. "Alone. I need a little time to think."

"Sure," he said easily. "The house has more than one bathroom and a magical water heater. You can use the one in the master bedroom, and I'll take one of the guest rooms."

She nodded, turned, and strode from the room just short of running. He watched her go, then went to put the circlet box away in the armoire.

Actually, she wasn't the only one who needed time to think. He felt every bit as shaken as she did. He simply hid it better.

Nathan stood for moment, staring blankly at the selection of gleaming weapons. An image flashed to his mind: the bark of Gordon's gun, Rachel falling backward with a bullet hole in her forehead.

Just a simulation. And yet when the bastard bent and picked up his gun, it had been all Nathan could do not to leap on him and beat him like a drum.

The idea of the whole exercise had been to give her an opportunity to see what would have happened if she'd done something different. He was not supposed to interfere, but his instincts had howled in protest like starving wolves.

He'd never felt so damned out of control.

Nathan had trained plenty of rookie agents and never had any trouble whatsoever letting them handle their tests on their own.

Not that it was the first time he'd lost his shit when Rachel was endangered. Look at the way he'd hacked at Super Chicken after it tried to eat her. The idea of the simulation had been to see how she worked with a partner in a combat situation. Nathan had planned to hang back, observe what she did, maybe even make himself a target for the raptor to see how she handled it. Instead he'd gone after the creature as if it was a real threat.

It had been fucking irrational. He'd known that at the time, and yet he'd found himself doing it anyway.

Standing by and watching Gordon shoot her had been even worse.

It was only when Nathan heard the hiss of water coming from upstairs that he realized he'd been standing staring into the open armoire for several minutes. Prodded, he closed its twin doors and headed off in search of a shower in the nearest guest room.

*What the hell is she doing to me*? Never mind, the answer to that was obvious. *I guess I owe Galahad an apology.* He'd given his friend hell a decade ago when the knight had fallen like a brick for Caroline Lang, a brand-new Maja Galahad had only known a matter of days. Nathan had told him he'd mistaken infatuation for love.

Now Nathan understood just how far it was possible to fall, just how fast. This was definitely no infatuation.

He'd slept with too many women over the past four centuries to let his dick do his thinking for him. Known too many incredible Majae to mistake respect and friendship for love.

*I love Rachel Kent.*

Nathan stopped dead in the doorway of the guest room as the thought hit him with the impact of a bullet, shredding his old life, his old conception of himself. The shocking thing was that it didn't hurt at all.

His lips curved into a manic grin. *I love Rachel Kent.*

*And I just spent the last forty-eight hours demonstrating what an asshole I can be.*

The grin vanished.

# Chapter Seven

Rachel stared at her reflection in the vanity mirror. Her hair was still wet from her shower, and drops of water slid down her face like tears. *I did it. I'm about to become a Maja.*

When she'd been a little girl, she and the other Kent kids had played Magekind, the girls throwing imaginary spells, the boys swinging wooden swords and pretending to turn into wolves. Yet out of five generations of Kents, she was the only one chosen.

But all she could think of was that fucking dream -- of going mad and throwing a fireball at Nathan. Watching him burn like a torch. The other nightmares of the Gordon shooting had tormented her with horror and guilt, but none of them had triggered such cold, absolute terror.

*Don't be ridiculous. It's not going to happen. The Council chose me, and the odds are I won't go insane.* But when she pictured Nathan burning, those odds didn't seem nearly good enough.

Swallowing, she rubbed both hands over her face to wipe away the water as a cold realization rolled over her. *I can't do this.*

Aloud, she told her reflection, "Yes, you can. You're strong." She made herself remember the cool, determined face of the Rachel simulation. *That woman wasn't a coward.*

*That woman wasn't in love with Nathan Allard. I am.*

In the mirror, her reflected eyes went wide as the realization slammed into her. *No. Oh no. I'm not that big an idiot.* And as Oriana had told her more than once, only an idiot fell for a Court Seducer. Some of them were honest, but some, like Dominic Bonnhome, told whatever lie they had to do the job. Then after you changed, they dropped you and went on to the next sucker.

*Nathan's not like that.* He never lied. He was too brutally honest, and his sense of honor was too acute. Far from lying to get her to agree, he hadn't sugarcoated the cost of being an immortal: *You're going to end up fighting and killing. You're going to end up watching everyone you love die. Not only your mother and father, but your sister and your nieces and your nephews.*

Yet as painful as the thought of those losses were, the idea she might kill Nathan was worse. She knew -- really knew -- she wouldn't survive that. Not just figuratively, either; Oriana and half the Majae in Avalon would wipe her off the planet.

A thought she found perversely comforting. If she hurt Nathan, she'd need killing.

*I can't do this.* Rachel had never considered herself a coward, but when it came to Nathan... *I'd rather be a coward than Nathan's murderer.*

She was going to have to tell him. Him, Oriana, and her family. They were all going to be pissed.

And she'd never see Nathan again.

Shoulders slumping, she picked up the blow dryer and started getting her arguments ready for the conversation she dreaded.

* * *

Emerging from the master bedroom fifteen minutes later, she found Nathan waiting in the hallway, looking impossibly handsome in black slacks and a black silk shirt, open at the neck. Rachel, on the other hand, was still dressed in the same clothes she'd worn in the simulation because she hadn't brought anything else.

The vampire gave her a devastating smile and held a big hand out to her.

She didn't take it. "I... I need more time. I don't think I'm ready."

For a long moment he said nothing, his gaze steady on her face. It was all she could do not to shift under that challenging stare. "I don't think that's a good idea. You're not exactly the first Latent who's gotten cold feet over the third time. Almost all of them do. Considering they can end up dead, that's understandable."

"It's not dying I'm worried about. It's hurting you."

His expression softened, and his lips twitched up in a smile. "I realize that. But I've tried putting off the third time before, and I've found the longer Latents think about it, the worse their anxiety gets. Some of them even backed out completely without even trying."

She blinked at him. "That was what you were trying to get me to do."

"Yes, and I was wrong." This time when he reached for her hand, he didn't give her the option of refusing. His grip felt very warm and strong. "The Magekind need you, Rachel. I need you. And if you refuse the Gift, I'll never see you again."

Her fingers tightened convulsively on his. "I'm in love with you." The minute the words were out of her mouth, a wave of heat rolled up her face, and she knew she was blushing furiously. She tried to pull back, but he wouldn't release her. "I didn't mean that."

"Yes, you did." He let go only long enough to step in close, his arms sliding around her. "Like I mean this -- I love you."

She stared up at him in stunned disbelief. For a moment, a crazy joy started to bloom in her like an Amazonian orchid, exotic and delicately beautiful.

Followed a heartbeat later by anger. "Don't say that!" She planted a palm against his chest and pushed. He resisted her, only turning loose when she glared at him. "Don't lie to me so I'll accept the Gift. I know how this works." She sounded bitter even to herself. "I fall for it, then after I've changed, you just walk away, leaving me wrecked."

"Do you really think I'm that dishonorable?" There was more than offended pride in his eyes. He looked almost... hurt.

"Oriana says that kind of thing happens. Dominic Bonnhome..."

"Is an ass," Nathan told her hotly. "He thinks anything he does to get more Majae in the field is justified. I have never operated that way. I never led a Latent to believe I felt something I didn't." He caught her shoulders, his expression softening, the sincerity in his eyes seductive "If I tell you I love you, I love you. That's too important to lie about."

"There hasn't been time for either of us to fall in love. Infatuation, yes. Lust, yes. Love, no."

"Rachel, I'm four hundred years old. I know my own mind. I've made love to a lot of Latents -- beautiful women, intelligent women, accomplished women. But I never felt about any of them the way I feel about you. Yes, I fell for you hard and fast. But I have fallen, and I'm too much a realist to deny it." He reached out and cupped her face in his sword-callused hands, looking deeply into her eyes.

She stared up at him, feeling the magnetic pull of him -- not only his remarkable looks, but his intelligence, his strength, his indomitable sense of honor. Deep within her, the orchid burst into full bloom, delicate petals unfurling in his heat.

Joy. Anxiety. Hope. And...

"You know yourself too," he said softly. "Do you love me?"

She stared up into his handsome face as her heart beat hard in her ears. "If I didn't, the idea of losing control and hurting you wouldn't terrify me this much. You're right -- the odds are I'll survive the Gift. If it were only me, I'd go for it. But it's not only my life on the line. Even if I never see you again, I want to know you're alive. I *have* to know you're alive, or none of it means anything."

"God, Rachel, what you do to me." Nathan took her mouth in a famished pounce. His tongue thrust deep, swirled around hers, in a deeply erotic claiming. He kissed her until her nipples hardened, her knees went weak, and she clung to him as much to stay upright as anything else.

Finally he drew back and looked down at her, his gaze fierce. "Do you trust me?"

She swallowed, and tightened her grip on his biceps. "Yes."

"I would not do anything to put your life in danger," Nathan said, voice low and intense. "If I thought you wouldn't survive the Gift, I would tell you to go home and forget me. To find some young cop and settle down, because I can't stand the thought of losing you either." He stroked the hair back from her face. "You won't fail."

Somehow the certainty in his eyes made her anxiety lose its grip. She took a deep breath. "All right. But I think we should call Oriana for backup. Just in case."

"I am not making love to you with your great-whatever-grandma in the next room. Besides, she already gave me a gemstone to crush if I needed her. She could gate here before you'd have time to blink."

Nathan slid his hand down the length of her arm to wrap his fingers around hers, then drew her after him. "But we're not going to need her. Come on." Instead of guiding her back into the bedroom, he led her down the stairs.

"Where are we going?"

"I want to show you something."

Rachel blinked as she saw what was waiting for them on the kitchen table -- a bottle of champagne, two crystal champagne flutes, and two silver trays covered with fruit and canapés. "What's this?"

"Hey, don't look at me -- it wasn't my idea. Though it does look pretty good." He walked to the table, picked up the card propped against the bottle, and handed it to her.

Rachel flipped it over to recognize Oriana's flowing calligraphy. *I thought you needed a little something to keep your strength up -- Gee.* "Apparently Oriana's afraid I'm going to starve."

"Can't have that," Nathan said, and picked up both silver trays. "Get the bottle and glasses."

Laughing, she obeyed.

He led the way out the kitchen door and onto a broad deck that wrapped around the back of the house. Balancing the two trays with his usual effortless grace, Nathan descended a set of wooden steps that led down into a garden surrounded by a stone wall.

She blinked, taking in the surrounding garden. Rosebushes covered in white blooms vied with flowerbeds planted around massive oaks and magnolias. A sprawling water feature tumbled over stones into a pool inhabited by swimming koi in brilliant hues. At the center of the garden stood a padded platform, half-bed, half-couch, covered in red silk and piled with cushions. A red silk canopy covered it, lengths of scarlet spilling around the bed from a wrought iron pole at its head.

Rachel studied it, her eyebrows flying up. "Oriana again?"

"Nope, my idea. A couple of Majae created it for me."

"How did that silk survive the first rainstorm?"

He grinned at her. "Magic's a wonderful thing."

"I guess there are advantages to having a lot of witch girlfriends."

"Ex-girlfriends," Nathan corrected, putting the trays on a small table beside the platform. He gave her a gimme gesture, and she handed over the champagne. He popped the cork with a flick of one thumb, a trick she suspected no mere human could have duplicated. The champagne foamed, and he poured it into the two flutes she held out to him.

Setting the bottle down on the table, he took one of the glasses and raised it in toast to her. "To our newest Maja."

Rachel forced a smile, despite the jolt of anxiety the toast sent through her. "And to the Magus who plans to make me that way." They both sipped, and the champagne foamed cool and delicious over her tongue.

He gestured at the platform with his glass. "Have a seat. Let's see what goodies Oriana has provided for her favorite great-great-great-great grand."

"I wouldn't say favorite…"

"I would." He picked up something triangular wrapped in a perfect flaky crust and popped it into her mouth. "But then, you're easy to love."

The canapé seemed to melt on her tongue, tasting of cheese, chicken, and roasted vegetables. She moaned in delight. "Damn, it's too bad you don't eat. This is wonderful."

Nathan gave her a wicked little smile. "I'm sure I'll get a chance to dine on *something* delicious before the night's over."

She snorted. "I see what you did there."

"I do love a good double entendre." He contemplated the selection, plucked up a finger sandwich, and fed it to her.

As Rachel purred in pleasure at the taste, he leaned forward and kissed her. She melted against him, losing herself in the lush eroticism of his mouth. Against her lips he whispered, "You're right. That is delicious."

"Yeah," she croaked, as her head spun at the taste of Nathan and champagne, "it certainly is."

He pushed her gently down on the platform, and sat down to begin feeding her fruit, hors d'oeuvres, and swallows of champagne, kissing her between bites.

At first she was too distracted by the taste of him and the hot blue gleam in his eyes to think about how the night would end. Gradually, though, the thought of the Gift penetrated her sensual haze.

*Don't think about that.* She'd decided to trust Nathan, and she damned well wasn't going to back out now. Yet even as she tried to concentrate on the taste of the champagne, on the softness of his lips, the memory of him burning in the dream kept flashing through her head.

*Cut that out, damn it.*

He pulled back a fraction, staring into her eyes, a ghost of a frown playing around his mouth. His eyes narrowed, and she spotted a spark of anger, determination.

Ooops. He'd picked up on her mood. *Damn it, Rachel, don't ruin this! Nothing's going to happen...*

Nathan bursting into flames... *Stop that. Damn it, that's worse than "Daddy Daddy Daddy."*

He brought both hands up to tangle in her hair -- and curled them into fists. "I thought you said you trusted me." He tightened his grip until the hold stung.

Rachel licked her lips as the sheer dominance in the gesture gave her a little kick of arousal. "I do."

His smile was slow and deliberately nasty. "Maybe you shouldn't." Eyes narrowing, he curled one corner of his upper lip into a snarl. "You need to stop worrying about whatever you're imagining and start worrying about what I'm going to do to you." Planting a hand in the center of her chest, he pushed her down on the bed.

Slowly, he rose to his full height and started unbuttoning his shirt, opening a triangle of carved male flesh that grew wider and longer. He shrugged, and the fine black fabric slithered off his shoulders, revealing sculpted brawn.

*Oh my God, the vampire is doing a striptease.* The thought should've been funny, but the hot look in his eyes made her heart leap into a gallop.

Moonlight gleamed off the width of his shoulders, edged the rolling contours of his abdominal muscles and ribs, silvered the line of hair that led her gaze down...

A thick bulge began to harden behind the fly of his slacks. Remembering how it felt shoving its way to the balls, she licked her lips. Thick muscle worked in his biceps and corded forearms as he unbuckled his belt, the ring and click of the metal sounding very loud in the darkness.

The tenderness in his eyes had vanished so completely she almost wondered whether she'd imagined it. Instead, there was stark lust in the curve of his lips and the dark glitter of his eyes. The black goatee enhanced the seductive-bad-vamp he threw off, especially when his grin revealed the tips of lengthening fangs.

Rachel expected him to toss the belt aside, but instead he doubled it and reached for her. "Come here." It was unmistakably a command, but he edged it in a rough, erotic purr that aroused even as the order pissed her off.

She jerked back, dodging his hand. "Oh, hell no. I outgrew spankings a long, long time ago."

Nathan laughed, low and dark. "I have no intention of spanking you." The tip of a fang flashed. "At least not until you beg."

Despite the heat that zinged through her at that idea, she pretended to glare. "Then you'll be waiting a hell of a long time."

Now his smile was definitely taunting. "Maybe, maybe not." Nathan slapped the strap against his hand thoughtfully, then shook his head as if in regret. "But I have something else in mind for tonight."

And he pounced, springing onto the bed and landing astride her hips.

"Hey!" But before she could use any of the hand-to-hand techniques she knew, he captured one wrist in a loop of the belt. She tried to shove him away with her free hand, but he caught that too, wrapping the belt around it. As she sputtered in outrage, he looped the belt's end around the post that supported the platform's canopy.

Reluctantly intrigued, Rachel stared up at him as he knelt astride her. Moonlight edged his handsome face in silver, slid along hard male flesh until he looked like a marble Renaissance warrior come to life. The belt that circled her wrists felt warm from his body heat.

This really shouldn't be turning her on so much.

When he reached down, grabbed the fabric of her black tank in both fists, and ripped it as if it were wrapping paper, her arousal only grew. "Cut that out!" And couldn't she come up with a more convincing objection? Evidently not. Mostly because all the blood had left her brain, headed south for the evening.

"No." Nathan dropped the shreds of her shirt in the bushes. Sitting back on his heels, he admired the sight of her pinned in the grip of his thighs, his gaze blatantly possessive. "Now, that's much better,"

"I had no idea you were this kinky."

He flared his nostrils, as if breathing in her scent. "Says the woman wet as a peach."

Rachel looked down at the bulge behind his zipper. "Says the man who could choke a Clydesdale."

He flashed his fangs. "Why, thank you." He leaned over her, slid a finger underneath her bra between the cups, and ripped the fabric.

"Again?" she mocked, though her mouth was dry. "You are really hard on my clothes."

"Get used to it." He settled on the bed beside her, eyeing her tight, hard nipples. "That's much better." He aimed a glittering look at her face. "They were soft a minute ago. I was deeply offended."

"Can't have that."

"No." Slowly he leaned down to one erect tip, opening his mouth, revealing the tips of his fangs again. She expected him to suckle her, but instead he dragged one sharp point over her nipple. "Mmmmm," he murmured, his lids dipping as if he savored the anticipation of a bite.

Rachel gasped, the sound soft and strangled. He gave her a grin so taunting it was all she could do not to squirm in hot arousal.

A deliciously calloused hand covered the other breast, thumb stroking back and forth, each strumming contact sending another juicy, delighted jolt through her body. He teased her, swirling his tongue over her nipple, then closing his lips for a hard suckle as she grew wetter and hotter.

At last, Nathan lifted his head with a smile so wicked, she wanted to beg. "I'm feeling a little confined." Sliding off the bed, he reached for his zipper. It hissed, the sound erotic.

Rachel watched in hypnotized fascination as he slid the slacks down his hips. His cock sprang free, thick, flushed dark. Remembering what it felt like the last time he'd fucked her, she moaned in helpless anticipation.

The vampire grinned at the sound. "Now, that's what I like to hear." As she watched in shameless fascination, he slid the pants the rest of the way off, revealing the long, muscled power of his strong legs, the bunched muscle of his ass.

She swallowed, vaguely aware of the jangle of the belt buckle overhead. Her hands twisted and pulled at the leather, instinctively trying to get free. She ached to touch him. Taste him. Feel that thick cock driving to the balls into her slick cunt. It was frustrating as hell not being able to reach for him, yet the tight grip of the belt only drove her lust higher.

When he reached for the waistband of her leggings, she rolled her hips up to help him get them off. He promptly wadded them up and held them to his nose, breathing in deep. "Oh, yeah."

"Pervert."

"You bet your sweet, fragrant pussy." Sliding back onto the bed between her legs, Nathan grabbed her ankles in either hand. With effortless vampire strength, he planted a big hand behind each knee, bent her legs double, and pinned them against her chest. Rachel gasped, arousal increasing. Instinctively, she tried to push against his hold, only to discover she couldn't move at all.

"You're not going anywhere," he told her, settling on the mattress between her widespread thighs.

"This… isn't exactly comfortable," she panted.

"I don't care." Lowering his head, he licked. The sensation of his hot tongue scooping between her sensitive folds made her squirm with a helpless, high-pitched whine. The pleasure burned, intense as a shot of whiskey, flaming along her nerves.

Holding her legs helplessly pinned, Nathan settled down to feast, his wet tongue swirling and dancing over her clit, around the opening of her cunt, lapping back and forth between her swollen lips. Each pass of his tongue sent another fiery bolt burning its way through her consciousness, stoking her arousal into a forest-fire blaze.

She found herself fighting his hold, trying to straighten her legs, pushing not so much to get away as because she could not sit still under the lash of delight.

And every time she strained and struggled against his controlling hands, her lust increased another flaming degree.

He, meanwhile, completely ignored her muffled kicks, the writhing buck of her hips as he concentrated on licking and sucking and tasting her as if she was something delicious. Driving her out of her mind.

Rachel felt the climax winding tighter and tighter with every pass of his tongue, every delicate nibble of his teeth, each teasing press of his fangs against delicate flesh. Distantly, she was aware of her own cries, the moans and high-pitched whimpers, the gasped pleas.

The orgasm exploded over her like a tsunami crossed with a firestorm, drowning her in wave after wave of burning, helpless pleasure. When it finally subsided, Rachel lay panting and limp, thigh muscles twitching from the volcanic climax.

She was still quivering when Nathan rose from her pussy and sat up between her legs, spreading her captured thighs even wider apart.

"Nathan," she moaned, both helpless hands twisting at the belt.

"Don't you move," he snarled, and released one leg long enough to grab his cock and aim it for her pussy. Settling on top of her, he caught that knee again and slammed in right to the balls.

She screamed, a strangled sound of agonized pleasure. He felt huge in this position, and he wasn't small to begin with. It felt as if the entire massive width of him reached all the way into her lungs.

Nathan stared down at her, his lips peeled back from his fangs, eyes wide and fierce with lust. "Now," he rumbled, his voice hoarse. Bracing himself on her captured legs, he drew out and slammed in.

"Nathan!" She yelped, half in protest, half in unbearable delight.

He began to fuck her, riding hard, grinding deep, making her feel every single inch of him. She writhed, feeling the hot pulses begin again, throbbing and clenching deep in her sex. Each digging thrust made her breasts dance. Her hands twisted and jerked at the belt.

Another orgasm gathered, building like a storm, spurring her to grind against his working hips, chasing the taunting pleasure that seemed to race ahead of her.

Light flashed in the corners of her eyes, some illusion created by climax-battered senses.

Nathan threw back his head with a roar, his big hands clamping down on her knees, his handsome face contorting as he drove to the balls and froze. She felt the first pulse as he began to come, streaming hot into the depths of her cunt. The heat grew, brighter and hotter until it burned over the line into a pain so ferocious she screamed.

The lights she'd seen a moment before exploded across her vision, comets and wheeling stars that left glowing afterimages.

*The Gift. Oh, shit, it's the Gift!*

Stars spilled across the sky overhead, bursting into colors she'd never seen before, didn't even know the names of. Raining stinging sparks over her skin. The sting intensified into a fiery, whirling burn.

*It hurts! Gee never told me it hurt!*

The firestorm built, a tornado of energy that battered her senses until it seemed to sear the inside of her skull. *It's going to kill me!*

Helplessly, she writhed, lost in the pain. As if from a great distance, she heard Nathan's voice. "Don't fight it, Rachel! Let it come, relax into it, and it won't hurt you."

Sparks in a hundred shades of red and gold and blue whirled around her, pelting her like glowing hailstones. Ozone choked her with the stink of burned metal and lightning. She fought to breathe. *I've got to gain control or it's going to destroy me! Got to get it out!*

Her hands burned as she jerked at the belt, the pain intensifying until she felt it even through the blizzard of fire whipping her skin. Throwing her head back, Rachel stared at the belt wrapped around her wrists.

Magic bucked against the base of her skull, pushing, pushing as she stared at her hands, teeth clenched against the screams clawing her throat. *Pushing...*

Her hands burst into twin fireballs surrounded by a corona of sparks that rained over her arms.

The agony eased slightly, as if it had found an outlet. She threw more magic into her fingers, trying to bleed off the pressure. The rain of sparks intensified.

"That's it!" Nathan shouted. Or at least she thought he shouted -- she could barely hear him for the thundering magic. "Use it! Burn it off, gain control."

*Burn. Nathan, burning...*

The fireballs flared brighter, sparks spinning inside them like a cross between a snow globe and the Fourth of July. Brighter. Brighter. Panic raked her. What if she lost control altogether? "Oriana! Get Oriana! I'm losing it!"

He leaned over her, ignoring the terrifying globes of energy inches from his head. "It's all right! Rachel, it's all right. Listen to me. *Everything's fine.* You are still in control."

"I'm not! I can't hold it!" Squeezing her eyes shut, she fought the power, threw back her head and screamed, trying to reach Gee with a spell, a telepathic message. Something. "Oriana! *Gee!*"

"Rachel, you are not losing it." His voice cracked like a whip. "Look at the belt!"

At the hard command in his voice, her eyes opened, automatically going to the belt looped around her wrists. Except it was no longer a belt.

Thick steel manacles encircled her wrists, and chains bound her to the post that could have held a bull elephant. As she stared at them in shock, the storm of magic seemed to retreat. The fireballs died away from her hands, leaving her stinging hands whole, miraculously unburned. "Where the hell did those come from? They weren't there a minute ago…"

"You conjured them." He cupped the side of her face, drawing her attention. "You're not out of control, baby. Just the reverse. Your first instinct on receiving all that power was to protect me. That belt would never have held you, but your strength of will is more than up to the job." He bent and kissed her.

Rachel sobbed once in relief against his mouth and kissed him back. As her lips moved against his, she tasted salt from the tears sliding down her face. "I did it."

He drew back far enough that he could smile into her eyes. "You did. I knew you would."

She laughed, voice strained from screaming. "You did not."

"Maybe not at first, but as soon as I got to know you." He stroked her hair, the gesture infinitely tender. "You do realize Oriana is going to be insufferable for at least a month." Leaning in, Nathan gave her a slow, surprisingly sweet kiss. "I'm going to have to bear up. I owe her for giving you to me."

She grinned at him, suddenly giddy. "Did it ever occur to you she gave *you* to *me*?"

"As long as we're together, I don't care." He sobered, his gaze going solemn. "I think I need to warn you."

She blinked, exhausted, woozy, not sure she was tracking. "About?"

"I'm an asshole."

"What?" *Definitely not tracking.* "Where did that come from?"

"Because you're high as a kite on the Gift, and I have no business asking this question right now. But

I'm also too ruthless to wait for you to sober up." But he paused, hesitating, as an unfamiliar vulnerability filled his eyes. "Will you marry me?"

Rachel stared at him, incredulous. They barely knew each other. This was crazy. She…

Didn't give a damn.

And no, it wasn't because she was high on magic. Nathan, courageous, gorgeous, and occasionally an asshat, was the man she loved. "God, yes." Rachel tried to reach for him, wanting to slide her arms around his shoulders. Her arms jerked short, chains rattling. Craning her head back, she saw the manacles still encircled her wrists. "Oh hell."

Rich laughter boomed.

"Oh, shut up. You think I can conjure a key?" She sat up, trying to examine the cuffs. "Oh, crap, they don't have a keyhole!"

Nathan laughed harder.

"Keep it up, and I'll give you a pair of those donkey ears." Just when she was starting to feel truly desperate, sparks rained from her wrists. The manacles disappeared.

"Too bad. I think I like you in bondage."

"Keep it up, Eeyore, and you'll be the one in the chains."

Laughter faded from his eyes, leaving only tenderness. "As long as you're the one to put me there."

She was off the bed and in his arms without having any idea how she got there. The kiss he gave her made her see stars brighter than her magic.

# Master of Valor (Merlin's Legacy 2)

## Angela Knight

Handsome Afghan war veteran Duncan Carpenter barely survived a horrifying IED attack that cost him his legs. He gets a second chance at life when he agrees to become an agent of the Magekind -- a vampire sworn to protect humanity. The spell that transforms him also heals his broken body and gives him incredible new abilities. Now he must pay for that gift, because the Magekind is preparing for war with powerful magical enemies. But first he must complete his training with a Magekind witch, Masara Okeye. Problem. He's falling for his mentor, even as he struggles to deal with life as a vampire.

Masara finds her apprentice deliciously seductive -- a little bit too much so for her peace of mind, because he brings up memories better left buried. But when Duncan and Masara are asked to help a werewolf cop investigate the murder of a jogger, they're targeted by the same vicious killers. The fight for survival drives the couple together, despite Masara's determination to keep her distance. Then the case turns even more horrific and mysterious. What turned a couple of loving werewolf grandparents into vicious killers?

And what's with the flying rabid zombie rats?

# Preface

Jack Rand took one last look around his shop. The week's last client had picked up her laptop and paid her bill an hour ago, and he'd finished cleaning up. He pulled his cell off his belt and texted his wife. *On my way. We'll pack in the morning.*

Eleanor's reply came back a minute later: a puppy emoji with little red hearts popping around its head. *Yayy! Disney, here we come!*

Jack grinned. A whole week with the grandkids -- riding the *Tower of Terror* and taking pictures of Liam and Gemma posing with everyone from Mickey to Darth Vader. The kids were ten and eight, old enough that they wouldn't have to be carried everywhere, but young enough to be thoroughly entranced by the Magic Kingdom. It would be one of those golden childhood memories they'd remember long after he and Ellie were gone.

Jack armed CyberWizard's alarm system and headed for the door. Stepping out onto the sidewalk that ran the redbrick length of the Hollydale strip mall, he grinned up at the sky. It was a beautiful night, the full moon riding fat and white over the low, narrow skyline. Tyger River wasn't exactly the biggest city in South Carolina; the tallest building in sight was all of ten stories. He drew in a deep breath… And frowned. There was an odd, rank scent in the air, an odor of greasy fur and illness.

Something hissed, and he spun.

The biggest damned rat he'd ever seen crouched on the sidewalk five feet away, beady eyes glowing red, naked tail whipping back and forth as it glared up at him. He'd seen smaller cats.

"Beat it, Ricky." Jack's voice emerged in a resonant growl that sounded nothing like the middle-aged man he was most of the time. He made a mental note to call the exterminator when he got back from vacation. He started to turn away…

Something black blurred toward him. Pain knifed into his knee, and he leaped back, cursing. The rat clung to his leg, chisel teeth piercing his slacks to sink into his kneecap. "Shit!" Jack kicked out, trying to dislodge the nasty little bastard. The rat only clamped down harder. Blood rolled down his leg as the pain intensified, and he lost his temper. "You want a bite? *I'll give you a bite!*"

He grabbed for his magic and let it blast through him in a burning, foaming wave. Pain ripped over his body as muscle and bone contorted and swelled. A heartbeat later, he stared at the world from seven hulking feet of brawn, claws, and thick, graying fur.

He pounced with a slashing stroke of three-inch claws.

*Squeeee!* The rodent went flying to hit the building's brick wall. Its body thumped to the sidewalk in a bloody, disemboweled heap.

He curled his lip at it. *Should've known better, asshole.* Ten pounds of rat versus three hundred pounds of werewolf did not end well for the rat.

Claws scraped and clicked on pavement. *Hiiisssss, squeeeeeak!*

*Fuck, what now?* Jack whirled. A writhing black shadow rolled toward him, pocked with red, glowing eyes. A river of rats. "What the hell?" Fear made the fur rise on the back of his neck. Which pissed him right off. Jack Rand wasn't afraid of anything, especially animated cat food. "Fuck off!" he growled, his voice a saw-toothed, enraged-grizzly snarl. Any rodent with an ounce of self-preservation should have turned tail and bolted for the nearest rat hole.

They leaped for him.

* * *

Eleanor Rand paced her pretty living room, anxiety a cold buzz under her skin. She'd spent most of Saturday puttering in the garden that surrounded the farmhouse-style home she'd shared with Jack for twenty years, daydreaming about a whole week of grandchild spoiling. Now her instincts screamed something had gone horribly wrong.

As she pivoted to pace the other way, her gaze fell on the couch. She'd never noticed how much the cheerful poppy pattern looked like blood spatter. *Okay, Ellie, you've officially lost it.*

Where the heck was Jack? He'd texted her he was on his way home an hour ago, and it was only a fifteen-minute drive. Had something happened to him?

*Don't be ridiculous. The man's a werewolf. He could get hit by a truck, and he'd just heal.* But not even werewolves were immortal. They could die. It just took a lot to kill them.

*Maybe I should check.* Normally she and Jack were careful to respect each other's privacy, but she also knew her husband was obsessed with protecting her. If he'd run into something nasty, Jack was fully capable of keeping her in the dark to avoid scaring her. *A glance wouldn't hurt.* She opened the Spirit Link they'd established as newlyweds three decades ago.

A wave of churning emotion slapped her mind: pain, confusion, and a desperate need for her. *Jack! Oh, God, what's happening?*

Unfortunately, though their psychic link could communicate images and emotions, it didn't transmit thought. Ellie wouldn't find out what was going on until she could ask her husband in person. But whatever it was, it wasn't good. *What the heck should I do?*

Just as Ellie was working herself up into a genuine panic, her keen werewolf hearing detected a familiar rumble in the distance. Jack's Toyota Highlander had turned into the development two blocks away. Blowing out a relieved sigh, she hustled into the kitchen and down the short flight of stairs to the garage.

She raised the garage door just in time to see the SUV almost take out the mailbox turning into the drive. *Damn, Jack's lucky he didn't get pulled over driving home. Or worse.* What was wrong with him? She knew it wasn't alcohol. Dire Wolves couldn't get drunk.

"Jack!" Ellie called, hurrying to meet him as the SUV lurched to a stop in the garage's empty bay. "Are you all right?" The Highlander's door creaked open, and he reeled out under her worried stare.

Jack was a big man, with thick, curling gray hair, his hawkish features still distinguished after all these years. Tri-weekly sessions at the Tyger River Y had maintained the muscular strength he'd had when they married. One pocket of his navy blue knit shirt was embroidered with the CyberWizard's logo in metallic thread: a laptop surrounded by magical sparkles. Blue slacks made his long legs look even longer.

But the handsome husband she'd said goodbye to this morning now looked like hell, gray-faced and dazed. As his knees sagged, Ellie jumped to hook an arm around his waist. An ordinary woman would have gone down under his weight. "Jack! What happened?"

"Rats," he muttered. "Never saw so many rats…"

He leaned so heavily into her, Ellie gave serious thought to just picking him up and carrying him up the stairs. Though he outweighed her, she was still a werewolf. But he'd hate that, so she resisted the impulse.

Somehow she got him up the steps to the kitchen with his dignity intact. Easing him down into a chair, Ellie straightened to lay a palm against the side of his face. Direkind body temperature was normally a couple of degrees warmer than human, but Jack felt clammy and cold. Worse, the pupils of his hazel eyes were dilated as he stared at her in bleary confusion.

What the hell happened in the hour since he'd sent that text?

She hurried to the bedroom to retrieve the blue velour bathrobe her husband rarely wore. By the time she draped it around his hunched shoulders, he'd begun to shiver. If Jack had been human, she would have been driving him to the ER by now. Unfortunately, Direkind biology was just far enough off normal that no werewolf dared risk lab tests.

Not that weres needed medical care very often. Direkind magic made them immune to human diseases, even the most virulent. Poisons and drugs likewise had little effect on them, and they could heal just about any injury short of outright decapitation. So what the heck *was* this?

Ellie sat down in the chair opposite his and leaned her elbows on her knees to study his dazed eyes. "Jack, what happened?"

He blinked at her. "When?"

"Damn, you are out of it. With the rats, Jack. What happened?"

Jack stared at her a long moment before he said, "Parking lot. Big ol' rat just jumped up and bit me. Had to shift."

It took her the next half hour to get the whole story out of him. In a halting voice, Jack described being attacked by a nightmarish swarm of rats. The battle had left the strip mall's parking lot covered in pools of blood, rat corpses, and clawed footprints. "Couldn't leave it like that," he muttered.

Well, no. All they needed was for some cop to come by and find a wolf paw-print the size of a dinner plate. The kibbles would hit the fan. So Jack had dragged out the hose and sprayed down the parking lot before disposing of the bodies. "Why didn't you call me? I'd have helped. And you really shouldn't have tried to drive home."

Jack stared at her blankly for a long moment. "Didn't think of it."

He must have already been sick. "Let's get you to bed," Ellie told him at last, unable to think of anything else to do. If not for her werewolf strength, it would have been impossible to get him on his feet and down the hall to their bedroom. With a miserable groan, Jack collapsed on the bed, curled into a ball, and began to shiver.

Ellie undressed, flipped the floral spread over him, and climbed in, snuggling against his broad back to share her body heat. He sighed in relief and fell into a restless sleep. Maybe Jack's Dire Wolf immune system would burn through whatever this was by morning. If not… Ellie grimaced. She hated the idea of backing out on the Disney trip, but no way was she exposing the grandbabies to whatever this was. Which would screw up her daughter's long-planned second honeymoon to New York, but it couldn't be helped.

Amy and Tom would have to either cancel the trip or take the kids with them. At last, exhausted by worry, Ellie drifted to sleep.

* * *

The growl that woke Ellie sounded so deep and menacing, it vibrated the mattress. She pried her eyes open -- and gasped, jolting up in instinctive terror. Her husband loomed over the bed in Dire Wolf form, more than seven feet tall, a hulking lupine shadow in the dark. His eyes glowed, but instead of his usual Dire Wolf gold, they shone with a crimson, rat-like gleam. "Jack?" Her voice cracked.

His lips curled off the sharp white gleam of his fangs as he snarled again.

Eleanor fought to keep her voice calm as she edged cautiously back across the mattress, ready to roll off and run. When she reached for his mind through the Spirit Link, she was horrified to feel a malevolent alien presence. "Who the hell are *you?* And what did you do to my…"

He pounced.

# Chapter One

A globe of fire the size of a basketball flew at his face. Duncan Carpenter ducked behind his shield as flame splashed its tough, transparent surface. The magical attack triggered the shield's enchantment, and a ward sprang out to encircle him as the flame licked the barrier.

The fire cleared, and for a moment Duncan saw his opponent -- a towering teal blue humanoid whose three-fingered hands held a massive sword. The Fomorian's features were basically human, except for red irises rayed in veins of purple and gold -- oddly beautiful. His snarl revealed a mouthful of long, jagged teeth designed to tear flesh. The Fomorian charged, running silently on three-toed feet, insanely fast in enchanted leather armor engraved with protective spells.

Just as the sorcerer reached him, Duncan bounded five feet straight up and chopped down with his sword, aiming between the twin bony crests running over the top of the Fomorian's head.

The sorcerer shied back, avoiding the blow by a hair. As Duncan hit the floor, the Fomorian's hand shot into the air, a nimbus of light dancing from thumb to the two long, thick fingers. Duncan jerked his shield up...

Too late. The force blast hit him right in the face and knocked him across the room. He hit the wall so hard he saw a whole constellation of stars. When they faded, he lay on his back surrounded by smoke. Dazed, he turned his head -- to see the bloody remains of a leg clad in shredded camo pants. He knew it was his own...

*Fucking flashback. Get up and fight, Marine! Legs ain't free!*

Duncan blinked, and the illusionary leg vanished, becoming his sword again. He snatched the weapon off the ground as the Fomorian roared. Duncan threw himself into a roll. The sorcerer's blade cut so close, the breeze of its passage lifted his hair.

Springing upright, Duncan lunged at the Fomorian, shield still strapped to his left arm. Swinging his sword in furious arcs, he rained strokes at the sorcerer -- his head, his arms, thighs, abdomen. The seven-foot monster retreated, parrying, unable to launch his own attacks as he fought to block the thundering blows. Fear flashed over the sorcerer's face...

And Duncan really *felt* his own miraculous power, the speed and strength he couldn't have imagined six months before. Most of all, he felt every inch of his legs. The ones he'd lost a year ago on the worst day of his life. The ones that should be clumsy mechanical replacements instead of superhuman flesh and blood. He was the luckiest bastard on the planet. And he had to be worthy of his miracle. His lips peeled off his teeth in a bloodthirsty cross between a snarl and a grin.

Somewhere in the house, a clock struck midnight. The Fomorian threw up one hand and panted, "Lunch break."

*Ha!* He'd tired her out. Duncan straightened, breathing hard. As he watched, the Fomorian's body seemed to melt like wax, vivid blue-green skin darkening to something more human. A blink later, Masara Okeye stood there, no longer surrounded by the Fomorian illusion she'd worn for combat practice.

Masara was a head shorter than Duncan, but her lean body was as lithe and strong as a leopard's. Her long dreads swung as she walked across the room to retrieve a couple of towels from a shelf. She tossed him one and blotted her face with the other.

He caught the towel without really looking at it. She fascinated him, with those sculpted cheekbones, the full, deliciously sensual mouth, the exotic swoop of her nose, and her big, dark eyes. Not to mention all that skin, rich and brown and gleaming with sweat, barely concealed by a black jogging bra and leggings. Just looking at her made his upper jaw ache. Some air current brought the hot smell of exertion and woman to his sensitive nose, tinged with the seductive tang he'd learned to associate with witches. Lust flooded his blood and hardened his cock. And it wasn't the only thing growing, either. Judging by the ache in his upper jaw, his incisors had lengthened.

*Great,* Duncan thought, irritated at the all-too-visible reaction his instructor was bound to notice. *I'm getting a fang-on.* The spell that had healed Duncan had given him his legs back, but it had also made him a vampire.

*Yeah, well, legs ain't free.*

\* \* \*

*Good thing Duncan has no idea how tempting he looks,* Masara thought. *I'd be in trouble.* Bare-chested, sweat-slicked, wearing only a pair of loose shorts, her apprentice tested both her self-control and her ability to concentrate. He wore his curling chestnut hair tied back in a tight tail, calling attention to the brutal perfection of his features and the sensual mobility of his mouth. His eyes were a shimmering crystalline blue that turned dark when he was aroused and icy in anger. He reminded her of a young god.

He was certainly endowed like one. It took all Masara's considerable willpower to keep her eyes off the erection testing the soft blue nylon of his shorts. The deliciously long, thick shaft made her imagine all kinds of sensual possibilities. She really needed to take him to bed. If he'd been anybody else, she probably would have done so months ago. He needed to get his mind off what happened to him that nightmare day in Afghanistan, and a nice hot fling would probably do the trick.

Trouble was, he wasn't just another apprentice. She'd trained dozens of witches and vampires over the decades, but none of them had been as driven, as focused, or as haunted as Duncan. And none of them had such vivid blue eyes that took on that chill burn when he was frustrated or angry.

When Masara had been a child, a look like that in blue eyes meant it was time to find something else to do, as far away as possible. Even one hundred sixty-one years as a Magekind agent hadn't been enough to reprogram the reaction. Which made serving as Duncan's mentor a dicey proposition. She had psychic landmines of her own, and those eyes could trigger them.

Still, he was a hard man to resist. It just wasn't his looks or his formidable intelligence either; none of her apprentices had been homely, and they certainly weren't stupid. No, it was the man's stoic warrior attitude, his psychic wounds, his dogged determination to deserve the second chance he'd been given.

A second chance he'd needed because he'd sacrificed himself to save an Afghani child from an IED. The Magekind needed people like Duncan, and it was Masara's job to make sure he had the training to fight the Fomorians -- and survive.

They needed every warrior they could get to fulfill the mission Merlin had given them 1500 years ago. Keeping humanity from committing mass suicide through war or environmental catastrophe took a lot of manpower.

"After lunch," she told him as they caught their breath, "I want you to practice against a troll." Which meant another grueling hour maintaining an illusion spell, not to mention the physical effort of sparring with a vampire hand-to-hand. She'd be black and blue by the time they finished. Still, if it kept him alive, it was worth it.

"Trolls, centaurs, Fomorians, Merkind, giants…" He rolled his eyes and curled an expressive lip. "Why the heck do they all want a piece of us?"

"They don't like sharing Mageverse Earth with humans," Masara told him. "Or our Sidhe cousins, either. They want us all dead."

"An alien Axis of Evil." He shook his head. "My life is so damned weird."

"Welcome to the Magekind."

Side-by-side, they strolled across the dojo. Walls of ash-white wood curved up from the thickly padded floor between massive beams that jutted like ribs, meeting in an arch overhead. The effect was reminiscent of the hull of a ship lying upside down. It was a cavernous space, designed for no-holds-barred combat practice, whether hand-to-hand or using blades and magic. Masara had warded its thick walls to resist the most powerful blasts she could throw. It wouldn't do to blow a hole in the neighbor's French Château.

Unlike most of the homes in Avalon, Masara's owed little to traditional European architecture. The house's curving walls were built of laminated wood, so the whole building seemed to flow out of the earth. Cedar shingles covered its long, undulating body in an effect reminiscent of the scaled African anteater called a pangolin. Her only concessions to Avalonian taste were the oval stained-glass windows that filtered sunlight. Otherwise, a certain vampire apprentice might wake up with a very ugly sunburn. Not that he'd burst into flame -- Hollywood had gotten that wrong -- but such burns were nothing to take lightly.

They stepped out onto the deck that encircled the house, heading for the wicker and glass table where she had a meal waiting. Duncan slid into a hanging egg-shaped bamboo chair supported by a chain from one of the ceiling beams. As he settled down on the chair's thick cushion, he looked toward the lights of Avalon glowing through the trees. All those stained-glass windows gave the city a very different look from the white lights of Earth buildings. "It always blows my mind."

"What?" She picked up the bottle she'd left in the center of the table.

"That we're not on Earth." Duncan gestured at the city's exotic skyline. "That this is a whole different dimension. A year ago, I was in Bethesda..." He broke off, and an expression of loss and remembered pain flashed over his face.

"I know what you mean." She knew he'd spent months at Walter Reed, undergoing more surgeries than she wanted to think about.

Wrapping her fingers around the neck of the sealed bottle, Masara sent a little pulse of magic into it. The cork popped into her hand. She poured a brilliant crimson stream into his wine glass. "It can be strange to remember how far you've come." Though she usually found it best not to pursue that line of thought. Old rage at old wounds was pointless.

"Yeah." Duncan watched the glass fill, then flicked his gaze to her face. Something about his stare made the act of serving him a lot more intimate than it should have been. "That come from you?" The words emerged as a low, velvet rumble.

She hesitated a moment before shrugging and inserting the cork back into the bottle. An effort of will reactivated the stasis spell that preserved the blood. "A stroke would interfere with my career plans." Being a Maja -- a witch -- she needed to donate blood as badly as he needed to drink it.

"Yeah, starvation would pretty much suck too." He picked the glass up and lifted it to his nose. His striking eyes drifted closed as he inhaled, and he sipped slowly, as if savoring every swallow.

Tearing her gaze away from the sheer eroticism of his expression, Masara sat in the chair hanging opposite his. The meal she'd prepared waited on a stasis plate that kept the food hot until her fork broke the spell. Deciding she'd better concentrate on her stomach instead of another part of her anatomy, she took a bite of her omelet. The taste of eggs, chives, and cheese melted on her tongue, and she sighed in pleasure.

He smiled at her over the rim of his wine glass. "Good?"

She swallowed and used her napkin to blot her lips. "It's a good thing I'm a Maja, or I'd be the size of a barn. Too many years with my stomach empty most of the time."

"Yeah, hunger can be maddening." His gaze flicked to her throat, then met hers again. And blazed.

Masara cleared her throat and changed the subject. "I'm really pleased with your progress. Swordplay isn't an easy thing to learn, especially for someone from your generation." She gave him a smile. "You're the first apprentice I've had who doesn't complain about preferring guns."

Duncan shrugged. "Bullets don't do much good against sorcerers, but decapitation kills everybody." He took another tiny sip, his tempting lips parting to flash white teeth.

"You do realize you don't have to clutch that glass like Oliver Twist? You can have another."

His lashes dipped and his mouth curved in a sensual smile. "Some things deserve to be savored."

She swallowed. The notes of "Hotline Bling" trilled from empty air, breaking the hot mood. She gestured, and her enchanted cell appeared in her hand. "Masara."

"I have a mission for you and Duncan," Belle said in her liquid, French-accented purr. Besides being Masara's dearest friend, she and her husband Tristan ran the training program for the apprentices.

Masara straightened in alarm. "Have the Fomorians…"

Belle sighed. "No, Llyr and Arthur are still attempting peace talks with King Bres, though they're afraid he's just stringing them along." Her voice dropped to a mutter. "That bastard gives me Hitler flashbacks."

"The sociopathic glint in his eyes is familiar."

"Either way, Bres is a problem for another time. The current issue is that one of the Direkind has been a very bad werewolf. He attacked a mortal woman when she was out jogging this evening. Mauled her to death.

One of the local Dire Wolves -- who also happens to be a sheriff's deputy -- has requested our assistance."

Masara nodded. "Shouldn't be a problem."

"Not for you, anyway." Belle paused, then asked, "Do you think your boy is ready for his first mission?"

"He's not a boy. And yes, I have full confidence in him."

"Good." There was such satisfaction in Belle's voice, Masara wondered why her friend was so pleased she'd leapt to Duncan's defense. "I'm texting you the number. Good luck."

"Thanks. 'Night, Belle." A moment later a text alert chimed, and Masara looked down to find the contact information for someone named Brian Walker. She stroked her thumb over the contact and waited while the phone connected. Magic was a wonderful thing. It could even make cell service possible between two different universes, one of them with no magic at all.

A deep male voice answered in a crisp, professional tone softened by a rich southern accent. "Sergeant Brian Walker, Tyger County Sheriff's Office."

"Sergeant, Masara Okeye," she said, keeping her voice low. The Dire Wolf would have no problem hearing her. "I'm a Maja. Are you somewhere you can speak freely?"

He blew out an audible breath in relief. "Damn, I'm glad to hear from you. We've got a situation on our hands. And yes, I'm alone."

"My superior tells me you believe one of your people murdered a mortal."

"Seems that way. A lady named Crystal Martin went jogging this afternoon. She still wasn't back when her husband got home from work, so he started walking her usual route, calling her cell while he searched." His coolly professional tone went gruff with sympathy. "Poor bastard finally heard it ringing out in the woods beside the road. It was still in what was left of her pocket. The coroner's investigator thinks she was mauled by a black bear, based on the bites and claw wounds." His tone turned grim. "But that's only because he's never seen a werewolf attack."

"You get a lot of those?"

"God, no. This is the first rogue kill I've ever seen, and I hope it's the last. Fortunately, the pathologist and her staff are off the clock for the night. Unfortunately, the autopsy's scheduled for bright and early tomorrow morning, when she'll probably collect all kinds of evidence we don't want her to find."

"And you want me to make sure none of it points to werewolves."

"Yeah. After that, we'll have to swing by the sheriff's office evidence room and do the same with whatever our guys collected."

"Sounds simple enough." She winced as the words left her mouth, hoping she hadn't just tempted the God of Nasty Complications. In her experience, that never took much.

"I can meet you in the hospital parking lot."

"Make it the corridor outside the morgue. Just give me a call when there are no mortals around, and I'll open a dimensional gate." She hung up and looked at Duncan. "Be grateful you don't eat." Grimacing, Masara eyed her lunch. "I suspect I'm going to regret that I do."

* * *

*Witches, vampires and werewolves,* Duncan thought as he walked into the quarters Masara had assigned him. *Every time I think my life has reached peak weird…*

The room was furnished with a massive king-size bed covered with a bedspread in a geometric blue-and-white pattern. Built-in shelves held books and his growing weapons collection. But the thing that always drew Duncan's gaze was the huge stained-glass window depicting a male lion, gold eyes gleaming as he lay in thick savanna grass.

Masara had told him once she'd had no interest in Africa until she'd spent months spying on the Italians during the East African campaign of World War II. She'd spent most of 1941 working in Abyssinia, Eritrea, British and French Somaliland, and Kenya. She'd fallen in love with the wild landscape, the people, and their cultures. Duncan suspected her taste in décor was something of a "Fuck you" to the people who'd enslaved her.

A glance at the bedside clock told him he had five hours until sunrise. He'd better double-time it.

Ten minutes later he was ready, dressed in black slacks, a blue knit shirt, and a pair of Timberlands that reminded him of his combat boots.

Masara waited for him in the hall in an outfit that made his brows climb. A pair of black leather pants sheathed those long, delicious legs, tucked into flat-heeled riding boots. Her leather jacket was unzipped just enough to reveal a triangle of ribbed tank top. She'd gathered her dreadlocks into a bun on top of her head, spilling into a tail secured with gleaming gold bands.

Metallic green eye shadow and sweeping eyeliner enhanced her dark eyes, while burgundy lipstick slicked her full mouth. The whole effect was more "twenty-something about to go clubbing" than "immortal witch almost two centuries old." Until you met her gaze and saw the combat-hardened warrior looking back.

She eyed him up and down, and he had the uncomfortable impression she wasn't nearly as pleased with his appearance as he was with hers. "There are a couple of things to keep in mind when you're fighting werewolves."

"We're going to be fighting?"

There went that eyebrow. "Do you object?"

"I thought we were disposing of inconvenient evidence. Sounded pretty routine."

"Routine missions have a nasty tendency to erupt in blood and screaming."

*The boom hit his eardrums like a hammer as the world whirled around him...* He shook off the memory. "I've noticed."

Too much must have shown on his face, because her dark eyes warmed, and she reached out and touched him. Just a brush of cool fingertips on his forearm, but it made his whole nervous system reverberate like a gong. As if sensing the power of his reaction, she drew back, and her lovely face went cool and professional again. "Merlin created the Direkind specifically to wipe us out if we violated our oath to protect humanity, so magic has no effect on them. They're even stronger than you are -- they can bench-press a Ford pickup. And since they can heal any injury this side of decapitation, they're a nightmare to fight."

Duncan gave her his best cocky smirk. "So are we. Anyway, I can turn into a wolf too." It was the only real magic vampires could do, used primarily to heal injuries or track scents. He'd learned the technique during the six months of training he'd undergone before becoming Masara's apprentice.

"Not like this. A Dire Wolf is bipedal -- seven feet of fur and a whole lot of teeth and claws. Which is why I suspect you're a little underdressed." Slender fingers sketched an elaborate shape in the air. Duncan felt magic roll over his skin in a foaming wave as the scent of ozone flooded the air.

When he glanced down, his slacks and shirt had become a leather jacket and leather pants. Driving gloves covered his hands, and riding boots sheathed his shins to the knee. Basically, it was the male version of what she was wearing. Which was sexy on her, but probably made him look like somebody on a gay porn site. "If we're expecting a fight, shouldn't we be wearing body armor?"

"That *is* body armor. If a werewolf tries to bite you in that, he'll break his fangs. Plate armor would be even better, but since we don't want to look like we got lost on the way to Comic-Con, it'll have to do."

Duncan wasn't sure looking like a leather Dom was an improvement. *The cop's going to love this.* But all he said was, "Thanks."

"You're welcome. Touch your belt buckle with your right hand."

When Duncan obeyed, a longsword filled his palm. "Whoa!" He fumbled, barely managing to catch the three-foot weapon before it dropped out of his fingers. He gave it a testing swing. The blade was perfectly balanced, seeming to float in his hand like an extension of his arm.

When he started to test the edge, Masara caught his wrist. "Not unless you want your thumb sliced open. When you want to get rid of it, touch your belt buckle again."

Duncan obeyed, and sure enough, the sword disappeared. "Nice."

"Don't summon the sword unless you're under attack. The Direkind look intimidating, but for the most part they're the good guys. You don't want to trigger another Werewolf War by accidentally killing an innocent."

"Yeah, I definitely have no desire to do that." *I've got enough on my conscience as it is.*

She gave him a long, considering look. "Are you ready?"

Once again, Duncan flashed the cocky, asshole smile that had been a lie since that day in Afghanistan. "Oorah." Those dark, dark eyes locked on his with such intensity, he had to fight the urge to look away. *I'm not going to fuck up, damn it. Not this time.*

At last she nodded. "Let's go." Masara swept one of those elegant little Maja hand gestures. A glowing pinprick of light appeared in midair and began to expand to form a human-sized hole in the air. Beyond that, wavering like a desert mirage, lay the kind of brightly lit hospital hall he'd become far too familiar with at Walter Reed. She gave him a tight nod.

*Here we go.* His first mission since... He cut the thought off in a hurry. *Move your ass, Marine.*

Duncan cupped his hand over the magical belt buckle, not quite touching it, and stepped through. A cool, foaming tingle spread over his skin, the signature of Masara's magic. Then he was on the other side.

The world lost its vivid intensity, going flat and dull. It reminded him of the scene in *The Wizard of Oz* when Dorothy woke up back in Kansas to find the world black and white again after the Technicolor glory she'd discovered over the rainbow.

It took an effort of will not to stagger. *What the hell is this?*

Oh, right. One of his vampire instructors, Logan MacRoy, had warned the class that returning to Mortal Earth would suck the first time. "You're creatures of magic now, and there *is* no magic back home. It's like trying to breathe on top of Mount Everest -- the oxygen is just too damn thin."

The only way you could work magic on Earth was by drawing on the energies of the Mageverse.

*Get your head out of your ass, Carpenter. Protect Masara.* His muscles tensed as he scanned the hallway, acutely conscious of the soft click of boot heels as she stepped through after him. Masara made another of those fluid gestures, and the gate popped like a soap bubble, revealing the muscular man that stood just beyond it.

"Nice trick."

# Chapter Two

Duncan tensed, his hand tightening on his belt buckle. This time he managed not to drop the sword as it filled his palm. Fortunately, he spotted the man's badge a heartbeat before he could swing the weapon.

The cop wore the black uniform of a sheriff's deputy on a lean, tough body a couple of inches shorter than Duncan's. He was probably in his late 30s, with a long, angular face, a beak of a nose, and an unsmiling mouth. A neatly trimmed blond mustache framed his thin upper lip, and he wore his blond hair cut short. Duncan would have known he was a cop even without the uniform, just from the cool, measuring look in his gray eyes. Something about the way he held his body suggested he didn't lose many fights.

There was also a faint scent of fur and pine about him, a tang of magic that confirmed he wasn't entirely human. He raised a blond brow at Duncan's sword. "You planning on doing something with that?"

"Sorry." Touching his buckle again, Duncan banished the sword.

"Sergeant Walker?" Masara stepped forward, one hand extended, and Walker took it in a quick, professional handshake. "I'm Masara Okeye. This is my partner, Duncan Carpenter."

Walker's hand was strong, callused, and so warm it felt almost feverish as he gave Duncan's a single firm shake. The cop was either too confident or too adult to try to break another man's knuckles.

"Never worked with Magekind." The deputy studied Duncan, his gaze intense, measuring. "Never even met a vampire."

Duncan swallowed a smartass *"Don't worry -- I don't bite."* Probably not the kind of joke you made to a werewolf.

Masara gave the cop a reassuring smile. "We'll try to make it painless."

Walker's return smile lit up his face until it was almost handsome. Something about that look in his eyes sent a quick, hot snap of aggression through Duncan's blood. *Oh great. I'm jealous of Fido.* Which was just humiliating, considering his mentor's pointed professionalism.

The cop jerked a thumb at the massive set of double doors a few feet away. A small vinyl sign on the wall read *Morgue.* "How are you with locks? I don't have a key card."

Masara's dark eyes crinkled. "That is what I'm here for."

As she stepped forward and laid a hand on the card reader beside the door, Duncan drawled, "Do you really want to tell a cop you're skilled at B and E?"

"She's Magekind," Walker told him dryly. "I'd be shocked if she wasn't."

Duncan was wondering whether that was a slap when the double doors swung open with an electric hum. A wave of cold air rolled out, smelling of bleach, formaldehyde, and the faintest hint of decomposition. *Yeah, this is going to be awesome,* he thought, and followed them into the morgue.

As Masara strolled through, the overhead lights flashed on, presumably at her magical command. Duncan frowned. "Do they have security cameras here?"

She slanted him a smile over one shoulder. "Why, yes."

"And they won't show anything you don't want them to."

"I wouldn't be much of a witch if they did." To Walker she said, "Do you know where the body is?"

"The cooler." The deputy moved past her down the corridor and through another door wide enough for a gurney. A vinyl plaque on the wall read *Autopsy 1*.

Duncan's stomach lurched in unhappy anticipation as he followed them. *I won't see anything in here I haven't seen already,* he reminded it. *And I've probably seen worse.* Lights flashed on, revealing two long, stainless steel counters inset with sinks on either side of the room. Long metal tubes dangled over each of the sinks, with what appeared to be hand-held showerheads. There was no sign of the morgue drawers he'd seen on television cop shows.

"She'll be in here." Walker headed for a big metal door at the back of the room and pulled it open. Masara and Duncan exchanged a glance and followed him into the giant walk-in cooler. A wave of icy air smelling of decomposition and dried blood blew into Duncan's face, making him regret his vampiric sense of smell. He swallowed.

The Dire Wolf flicked on the lights, revealing a cavernous metal room lined with stainless steel shelving units. Several of them were occupied by white plastic body bags. Wheeled metal tables stood parked alongside the shelves, each holding a bagged corpse. There was no padding on the tables whatsoever, but then, he supposed it wasn't needed.

"There she is." Walker strode to one of the tables, took hold of one end, and wheeled it toward the door. He must have identified the victim by her scent. Masara stepped aside, giving him room, and Duncan pushed the door open for him. The table's wheels squeaked as they rolled over the tiled floor.

"Where you want her?" Walker asked.

"There, I think." Masara gestured to the center of the room. "I'll need plenty of space to work."

Walker positioned the table where she'd indicated and started to reach for the bag's zipper. The plastic vanished before he could even touch it.

Duncan recoiled despite himself. He'd seen some nauseating stuff during his tours, including a suicide bomber attack on a girls' school. This was worse.

The killer had taken bites out of Crystal Martin as if she were a chicken leg.

Dried blood soaked her pink running shorts and shredded T-shirt, and ragged wounds -- bites, claw marks -- marked her skin, white with blood loss where it wasn't livid from pooling blood. Duncan swallowed -- and tasted a hint of Masara's blood from lunch. That almost finished him off right there, but he clamped his teeth together and gulped his stomach back down -- only to forget his nausea as magic exploded around Walker like a bomb blast.

An eyeblink later, the cop was gone, replaced by seven towering, muscular feet of golden fur.

Duncan froze for a shocked, disbelieving moment. *Damn, Masara wasn't kidding. He's fucking huge.*

The Dire Wolf's head was distinctly canine, with a long, narrow muzzle and triangular ears tipped in tufts like a lynx's. A bushy blond mane surrounded his head and extended down his chest, reminding Duncan of a lion. Like vampires, Direkind clothing evidently disappeared during the change, but fortunately, his groin was covered by a thick furry ruff. *Thank God.*

*Some things I just don't need to see, and werewolf dong is high on the list.*

The claws on the monster's knobby hands were three inches long, matching the ones on his big feet. Getting raked by those suckers would ruin your whole day. Masara's hand wrapped around Duncan's wrist even as he reached for his sword. His dick, being his dick, wanted to sit up and beg at the feel of those long fingers. *Not the time,* he told it.

"It's okay." Her voice dropped to a mutter. "I think."

The werewolf looked at them and blinked gray eyes the same color as they were in his human form. "Oh, sorry." His voice had become a basso rumble. "I just want to smell the body. Which I couldn't exactly do at the crime scene."

Duncan recoiled. "What the hell for?"

The werewolf shrugged broad, powerful shoulders. "There are only ten werewolves in Tygerton, and we all socialize. Unless he's from out of town, I'll recognize the asshole's scent."

Masara nodded. "That would certainly simplify this job."

Feeling like an idiot, Duncan folded his arms, mostly to keep his hands away from his buckle. As they watched, Walker bent over one of the more revolting bites and drew in a deep breath. His head rocked back, and he straightened as if in surprise, staring down at the body. Then he bent again and began to sniff one bite after another.

Finally, he straightened again and stepped back. It was hard to read the expression on that inhuman face, but Duncan thought he looked unhappy. "That doesn't make any sense at all."

Duncan eyed him. "Want to share with the rest of the class?"

Walker gestured with a clawed hand. "This kind of rogue attack is normally committed by one person, almost always male. But there are two distinct scents here, and one of them's female."

Masara moved closer to study the body. "Do you recognize the scents?"

He bent and took another deep, drawing breath, then shook his big head. "I'm not sure. There's something there I almost recognize, but it's not quite right. It's got a weird metallic tang to it, plus this nasty, oily pong under that. I've never smelled anything like it on any Dire Wolf."

"Are you saying they're not werewolves?" Duncan bent and breathed in, forcing himself to control his revulsion. And frowned. "I see what you mean. Neither one of these bites smell anything like you."

Walker looked down at him from his greater height. "Glad to hear it." His tone was so dry it was almost arid.

Duncan moved to another bite wound and bent close, trying to parse the mélange of revolting odors. Vomit, old blood, and rot. Which he would have thought were the victim's, if Crystal's underlying scent hadn't been completely different. "Do the attackers smell sick to you?"

Walker hesitated so long he started to wonder if the man was going to answer. "Yes. And that doesn't make any sense either. We don't catch diseases. Our magic kills any bug that bites us."

Duncan nodded, unsurprised. He'd been told the same thing about vampires.

"Another thing," Walker continued. "While Dire Wolf males sometimes go rogue and start killing people, I've never heard of a Direkind *couple* committing this kind of crime."

"You don't even see couple murderers among humans very often," Duncan agreed.

"You'd be surprised what humans do," Masara muttered in a dark voice. "Was there a sexual assault?"

Walker shook his head. "No, thank God." He combed his blond mane with his claws, his expression thoughtful. "I'm going to have to talk to the Council of Clans about this. Something is badly wrong here."

"That's putting it mildly." Duncan, head lowered to inhale the body's scent, realized the arm he was examining was attached the body by nothing more than a flap of skin. The killer had ripped it out of the socket. Suddenly it felt as if both his legs were attached to a car battery.

Searing pain rolled from his toes all the way to the tops of his thighs. He had to bite back a scream. *It's not real, damn it. It's another fucking flashback.*

"Given all that," Masara asked, unaware of his reaction, "would you object to my trying a locator spell?"

Walker shrugged. "I doubt it'll work given our resistance to magic, but this case is so weird, who the hell knows? If you can figure out where they are, go for it."

"Then let's see." Masara spread her hands, her expression set with concentration. Duncan felt the familiar goose-bump-inducing sensation of magic, and the scent of ozone rose. Gold sparks gathered over the victim's body in a cloud, dancing and leaping over her skin. Masara frowned, and her lush mouth tightened as her elegant fingers curled into fists.

The sparks brightened until they blazed like an arc welder's torch. Duncan jolted back a step, half expecting the body to catch fire. The scent of ozone became a reek. The sense of her magic intensified until it was almost a physical pressure on his skin. Masara's face tightened with effort as a film of sweat broke out over her forehead.

Maybe it was the force of her magic. Maybe it was her intense focus and concentration, or the way her long body curved as she strained. But abruptly he was deeply aware of her -- the sensuality in the set of her mouth, the sweat dewing her cleavage in the opening of her unzipped jacket. His body stirred, and an ache grew in the roots of his fangs. The sparks brightened, becoming blinding as seconds became minutes and arousal became outright lust.

The sparks winked out. "Well, that answers that question." Sighing, she wiped her sweating forehead with the back of her hand.

Duncan started as the sensual spell broke. *For God's sake, get your head out of your pants, Carpenter. We're on the clock.*

"I won't be able to transform that fur either," Masara continued. "I'll have to wash the body to remove the physical traces, then conjure some fur more consistent with a bear attack."

He cleared his throat and tried to get his mind back on business. "What about the wounds? I don't know a hell of a lot about zoology, but I doubt a werewolf bite looks the same as a bear's."

"That I can fix. Her killers' genetic material may be resistant to magic, but her body isn't. I can change the physical imprint of the teeth and claws."

"They won't match the photos the coroner's investigator took at the scene," Walker told her slowly.

"But if all the test results come back saying it was a bear, the investigator will probably rule it an accidental death and close the case."

"Then let's get this done." Masara gestured the men to step back. A sweep of her hands created a huge basin around the table even as the woman's bloody clothes disappeared. A heartbeat later, an honest-to-God *rain cloud* appeared about a foot over the corpse, releasing a torrent that spilled over the body and swirled into the catch basin.

Duncan watched the water sluice over the victim as the last of his arousal vanished into sick pity. Crystal must have looked so vital and healthy when she'd gone running that afternoon in her pink shorts and tee, her long blonde hair tied back from her young face. Until her life had turned into a horror movie and everything ended.

When he looked away, his gaze collided with Walker's. "You haven't been doing this long, have you?" A note of sympathy softened his gravelly rumble.

Stung for no reason he could name, Duncan growled, "I served three combat tours in Afghanistan and Iraq." *I'm not a pussy, damn it.*

"Yeah, I was there during the Surge. But there's a big difference between war and somebody doing something like this for the sheer hell of it."

"Not sure it matters to the victims."

"No, probably not."

Duncan looked down at the toes of his boots and tried not to remember any fucking thing.

"How does this look?"

He glanced up -- and blinked, startled. If he hadn't known better, he would've sworn the body had never been touched. Crystal wore what appeared to be the same bloody shorts and top, with dried gore encrusting her body and hair. The basin had vanished, back to wherever such things went after Masara was done with them.

It was hard to tell given Walker's muzzle, but Duncan thought the werewolf looked impressed. "I can't tell you did anything at all, and I watched you do it."

Masara glanced at him. "What did the Direkind do in situations like this before we started working with you?"

The werewolf grimaced. "Obstructed justice like crazy. That's why so many of us joined our local police departments and first responders. We lost evidence, we destroyed it, and we hunted down the responsible parties. Sometimes we got caught tampering and went to jail." He gave Masara a *Jaws* kind of smile. "Which is why I'm so grateful for your help."

She smiled back, evidently unfazed by all those teeth. "Duncan and I have been assigned to work with you on this, so all you have to do is call." She conjured a new body bag to replace the original.

Walker wheeled the autopsy table back into the cooler, then reemerged a minute later. "I think we should…" The werewolf broke off, his eyes widening.

Duncan heard it even through the closed door of Autopsy 1 -- the sound of the morgue's hallway door swinging open and rubber wheels sighing over tile. "Masara!"

She was already conjuring a dimensional gate. Walker dove through before it was even open all the way, the two Magekind at his heels. The minute their feet hit the other side, Masara banished the gate, cutting off the creak of Autopsy 1's opening door.

"Oh, good God, that was close," the werewolf said, gray eyes huge.

Duncan glowered at him. "I thought you said the pathology department was closed."

"It is, but that's a hospital, and people die 24/7. Transporters bring the bodies up and put them in the cooler."

"You do realize it wasn't that big a problem anyway?" Masara asked, looking amused. "Even if we'd been caught, I would have simply cast a spell on the transporter, and he wouldn't remember we were ever there."

Walker eyed her. "Then why bother?"

She shrugged. "I don't like manipulating people's minds if I don't have to. It's delicate work, and things can go wrong."

"Yeah, I can understand that." This time Duncan saw the magic flare in the Dire Wolf's eyes a heartbeat before he transformed. Just like that, the cop was a foot shorter and back in uniform, complete with badge and gun. "Where the hell does it all go?"

"All what?"

Duncan gestured. "The hundred extra pounds of werewolf. I weigh the same in both forms."

"No idea. It's just mag..." He broke off, looking around at the house's curving walls as his jaw dropped. "Where the hell are we?"

"Masara's house," Duncan told him.

"No, why is it all so... vivid?"

The witch smiled slightly. "This is the Mageverse."

Walker turned in a slow circle, gaping. "It's like being inside one of those 3D superhero movies -- everything feels ten feet tall and glowing."

Which was when Duncan remembered having the exact opposite reaction when they'd gated to the hospital. Everything had felt so flattened and dull.

"Would you like a tour?" Masara asked politely.

The cop shook his head. "Love one, but we need to take care of whatever evidence my department collected at the scene."

Masara grimaced. "Oh, that's right. Can you show me where we'll need to go?"

Walker pulled up a map of the Tyger River Sheriff's Department on his cell phone, then pointed out the evidence room. "None of the evidence clerks are on duty this time of night," he told them. "The detectives and CSI would've put everything in the drop box in the hall outside the evidence room to be processed in the morning."

"Well, that simplifies things." She turned and cast a gate, which opened on yet another hallway. What appeared to be a curbside U.S. mail collection box stood against one wall, painted black with a gold Sheriff's star logo. The Maja frowned, considering the scene. She flicked her fingers -- probably taking out any cameras -- then stepped through. Walker followed her, Duncan at his heels.

Duncan shot an uneasy look around. "Do we need to worry about some cop catching us at this? Because a jail cell and sunlight would not do my complexion any good."

Masara shot him a raised eyebrow. "Now you're being insulting." She flicked her fingers, and the smoky scent of magic stung his nose. "Nobody will see or hear anything I don't want them to."

"Pop the lock while you're at it," the cop told her.

Another finger flick, and the drop box's metal door swung open. Walker knelt and began sorting through envelopes and boxes of evidence, putting some off to the side and tucking others back where he found them. As the werewolf worked, the Magekind knelt to help. Duncan started opening packages for Masara, who conjured replacements with duplicate evidence numbers. Their knees touched as he handed her a package, and she flashed him a smile. "Thanks."

He smiled back, enjoying the flash of warmth in those dark eyes. "You're welcome."

At last they were done. Walker stood and loaded the duplicates back into the drop box while the agents packed the originals into a conjured bag. "Mind if I take that?" The cop gestured at the bag. "I've got to interview the other werewolves in town, make sure none of them are involved. I don't really think so -- the scent's too far off -- but I can't afford to ignore the possibility. I'll give the ones I clear a sniff of the evidence and see if they can tell anything."

"Certainly." She handed it over. "I doubt I could do much with it anyway."

Five minutes later, they were back in the Mageverse. "Thank God that's done. Now I can check those weres and go home," Walker said, slinging the bag over one shoulder.

Duncan frowned at him. "You want backup?"

"I don't think that's necessary. I know these guys, and I can handle them. I'm not some helpless human. Besides, I'll scent them before I see them, so I can give you a call if I discover our assholes. You can gate over then." He frowned. "I just have to get back to my patrol unit."

Masara produced her cell phone and pulled up an image of the hospital on Google Earth. "Show me where you parked, and I'll gate you there."

Walker pointed out a corner of the lot, where a stand of trees blocked the illumination cast by nearby security lights. "It's pitch-dark there to normal humans because of the trees this time of night. I didn't want anybody looking too closely at my car."

"Probably wise." Masara flicked her fingers, and a wavering gate appeared. A big black-and-white SUV with a gold Sheriff's logo waited under the trees in lonely splendor.

"Thanks," Walker said. "After I ask around, I'll give you a call and let you know if I find out anything useful." He stepped through the gate and lifted the key fob. The SUV's headlights flashed...

Something huge slammed into the deputy like an NFL lineman sacking a quarterback. A thundering roar drowned out Walker's shocked yell as they both flew out of sight.

"Shit!" Duncan grabbed for his belt buckle, drew his sword, and leaped through the gate half a heartbeat before Masara.

Walker was pinned beneath another werewolf, the monster's fanged jaws snapping in furious clicks barely an inch from his carotid. The cop had both hands fisted in the rogue's mane as he strained to keep the knife-blade teeth from ripping his throat out. The rogue's lips peeled up as he snarled, "You are my meat, dog. I will rip you apart like a chicken." His voice was a rippling basso growl that made the hair rise on the back of Duncan's neck.

"Fuck! You!" Magic exploded, rolling over Walker's body... and two wolves snarled and strained against each other as the Magekind agents raced toward them. Which was when Duncan realized just how freaking huge the rogue was. A fuzzy Incredible Hulk of a werewolf, he made Walker look like a pup.

Duncan and Masara split up, him heading left, her running right, meaning to circle behind the combatants. Charging in to help the cop did no good if they got a face-full of fangs.

The attacking werewolf tore out of Walker's hold and lunged for his throat just as Masara sent a wave of magic rolling over the cop. Hulkwolf's teeth grated on the steel scales suddenly sheathing his opponent's neck.

Though the Maja couldn't cast a spell on a werewolf, it seemed she could cast one *around* him. She'd conjured Walker a suit of scale armor.

Red eyes narrowed in fury. "That won't save you, dog. I will chew you up and spit bones."

"Spit teeth!" Walker snarled, slamming an armored fist into Hulkwolf's muzzle.

And it was on, the werewolves kicking and clawing, fists swinging, blood and fur flying.

Duncan jumped back to avoid taking a huge clawed foot in the gut. Sparks swirled in front of his eyes, and something curved and reflective appeared before his face. Startled, he realized he now wore a helm with a transparent faceplate. The rest of his body was sheathed in the same kind of armor Walker now wore.

He glanced at Masara just as she sent another wave of magic his way. His sword's weight increased so suddenly, he almost dropped it on his foot. Steadying it with both hands, Duncan realized she'd turned the weapon into a battle-axe with a two-foot steel haft. Double-bladed, the head tipped with a long spike, it looked like it could put a hurting on a tank.

Which, given Hulkwolf, was about right. He hefted it, eyeing the snarling tangle of lupine rage writhing on the ground, looking for a pause in the action so he wouldn't hit the cop.

Masara spotted an opening first and swung her own transformed weapon in a horizontal cut. Hulkwolf saw it coming and rolled aside a heartbeat before she could cleave his head in two. Her battle-axe wasn't as massive as Duncan's -- she didn't have a vampire's strength -- but Duncan wouldn't have wanted to be on the receiving end of that swing.

The huge werewolf retreated from the furious arcs of Masara's blade, snarling. Walker scrambled up and leaped to help her. He broke step as an even bigger axe appeared in his hand, and he almost dropped it. *Glad I'm not the only one who fumbles Masara's passes,* Duncan thought.

Unfortunately, the rogue was a good foot taller than the Dire Wolf cop -- which made him two feet taller than Duncan. Hulkwolf had dagger claws and teeth like spikes, and the red eyes glowing in his massive head looked feral and mad.

*I'm going to get killed,* gibbered a voice from Duncan's mental coward gallery.

*Legs ain't free.* He threw himself at the monster wolf in a ten-foot vampire bound, axe raised in both hands...

Something clamped around his ankle and snatched him out of the air. Sky and earth wheeled around him as he flew like a tossed tennis ball. The ground seemed to explode in his face, slamming his head against the inside of his helmet. He bounced over the pavement like a rock in a blender, the ax flying. When the bouncing stopped, Duncan stared at the night sky, stunned and disoriented. *What the hell just happened?*

Which was when he realized the clicking he heard was the sound of claws running on pavement. *Toward him.*

*Oh, fuck.*

# Chapter Three

Even as Masara circled the Dire Wolf, she glimpsed a flurry of movement: Duncan leaping high, battle-axe raised. Something pale lunged out of the dark, grabbed him by one leg and sent him flying across the parking lot like a comet. He hit the pavement hard enough to kill anyone mortal. *Oh, sweet Lord Jesus!* "Duncan!"

"Help him! I'll take care of this bastard," Walker roared, as he ducked a swipe of the Dire Wolf's claws, then forced his foe to retreat with a flurry of axe swings.

She whirled and raced toward Duncan, who -- thank the Lord -- was up and scrambling across the pavement on his hands and knees, trying to recover his fallen axe. A second rogue werewolf ran after him, fanged maw gaped wide. This one's graying fur seemed to glow in the moonlight. "Avalon!" Masara roared, as much to distract Duncan's attacker as anything else.

"And there you are, my prey!" The Dire Wolf -- a female, judging by the breasts -- whipped around and slashed at her.

Claws raked across her chest, accompanied by cold, tearing pain. Jerking away, Masara saw deep gouges marked her armor. Blood oozed from the wounds. *My new armor!*

The female bared her teeth. "I have such plans for you." She lunged, snapping jaws splattering Masara's faceplate with saliva.

Masara swung the battle-axe up in a diagonal backhand stroke that forced the Dire Wolf to leap back. The rogue female circled, snarling, as Masara activated the communication spell on her helm with a shout.

"Belle! We need backup! We're under Dire Wolf attack." She felt the spell punch into the Mageverse, establishing a connection with Belle's spelled phone.

"What?" The French Maja's voice rang inside her helm, sharp with alarm. "Where are you?"

"Mortal Earth. Two big Dire Wolves, one male, one female. The third armored wolf is Walker. The rogues can punch through scale mail with their claws."

"Okay, okay, I've got a fix on your location. We're on our way. Hang on!"

"Hey, Hulkbitch!" Duncan yelled. He'd recovered his battle-axe and was on his feet, though he reeled a little, his face pale behind the transparent visor. Still, he wore a snarl of grim determination as he closed on the much larger Dire Wolf. "Back off, butt sniffer. You won't like me when I'm angry." He spun the axe between his hands, and moonlight glinted off its blade. "And right now, I'm seriously pissed."

"I quake." The big female crouched, watching him come with eyes that glowed crimson in her gray-furred lupine face. She snarled, deep and threatening, lips rolling back off her teeth.

*And if this fight keeps up, every cop in the county is going to be headed this way.* Masara paused to toss a concealing spell over the whole area, making sure no mortal heard or saw anything.

Duncan leaped for the werewolf, bellowing a challenge as he soared. The rogue female bounded to meet him as he swung his axe. Blood flew in an arc... but as his weapon scored her ribs, her huge fist rammed up into his gut, driving him upward. He tumbled, hitting the ground on his back.

"Duncan!" Masara shouted, and raced toward them.

"Now you die!" The Dire Wolf pounced, both fists crashing into his visor.

"Dream on, Fifi." He swung the axe at her, but she was inside his guard now and the haft thumped against her ribs. The rogue ignored the blow and started hammering punches into his visor. Duncan bellowed and tried to angle the axe to stab her with its spiked tip, but she pinned his arm with one hand and kept pounding his helmet with the other. His faceplate shattered, and his yell cut off.

"Duncan!" Masara darted in and swung her axe in a furious stroke at the female's huge, furry head. The monster rolled off Duncan, but Masara chased her, swinging the axe in a glittering figure eight. Blood flew as the axe sliced a furred shoulder. Roaring, the huge Dire Wolf raked her claws down the length of Masara's arm. She sucked in a scream as claws sliced steel and flesh. As her arm blazed, she almost lost the axe, but caught it in her left hand and swung it backhand.

Snarling, the Dire Wolf retreated, crimson eyes blazing, fangs bared. Masara gripped the axe in both hands and went after her, swinging in vicious arcs even as her injured arm blazed. "Shift, Duncan!" she yelled without looking away from her target. "You need to shift into wolf form!" If he was hurt as badly as she feared, transforming was the only thing that would save his life.

No answer.

*Oh, dear Jesus, is he dead?* Masara wanted to run to him, but the minute she turned her back, the female would be on her like a chainsaw. *"Duncan, shift!"*

No answer.

"If he's hurt, you're a rug," she warned the Dire Bitch, leaping into the swing, and this time her axe sliced the rogue across one breast. The monster yelped and danced back, raking the claws of her right hand across Masara's visor, gouging deep into the magical plastic. Masara instinctively jerked aside... just as the rogue's left hand whipped up and grabbed her head. All she could see was an enormous palm, fingers wrapping around her helm. The Dire Wolf hauled her skyward and jerked her back and forth, trying to break her neck. The magical armor snapped into a hard shell around her neck and torso, supporting her weight and saving her spine.

Masara swung her axe blindly, only to feel the Dire Wolf grab her weapon and jerk, twisting it out of her hand. She kicked out frantically. *Got to end this! Duncan needs...*

A dozen deep masculine voices bellowed, "Avalon!"

Masara recognized that chorus. *Oh, thank God -- the Knights of the Round Table!*

"Later, prey," the werewolf snarled, and tossed her aside like a discarded doll. Masara bit her tongue as she slammed to the pavement in a bone-rattling armored crash. For a heartbeat she lay stunned, tasting blood and listening to Dire Wolf roars blending with the bellows of a dozen furious knights, all retreating into the distance, as if the wolves had taken to their heels with the vampires in pursuit.

"Duncan?" She tried to move, but her armor was still spelled rigid. A muttered reversal chant made it release. Rolling over, Masara gritted her teeth against the pain in her abused neck and aching arm. She looked around blearily, but claw marks scored the visor. She muttered a spell at the enchanted plastic, and it cleared.

Duncan lay sprawled on his back twenty feet away, his faceplate shattered into a bloody wreck. "No no no…" Masara moaned, staggering to her feet and reeling over to him on legs that shook. This end of the parking lot was empty except for Walker's SUV, though she could hear shouts and roars from the woods. She hoped someone had thought to cast another cloaking spell, or 911 would be getting some very interesting calls.

Then she got a look at Duncan's face, and forgot everything else.

\* \* \*

Jack had died and gone to hell. And worse, he'd taken Ellie with him. Nothing made sense, and it was so hard to think. He and Ellie were running through the woods and men were chasing them. Armored men with swords.

Magekind. Why were Magekind chasing them?

*Because I did something horrible.* Or something had, using his body. Again.

At least Ellie was alive. He'd thought he'd killed her. He'd tried to scream a warning when he'd risen from their bed. Yesterday? The day before? He had no idea.

It had taken all his strength to force open his jaws as he loomed over her. He'd fought to make his fanged mouth shape the word, "*Run!*" But the only sound that had emerged was an inhuman roar. Then the thing that had stolen his body had fallen on Ellie.

Jack fought to keep from sinking his fangs into her delicate skin, but his body had gone right on attacking the woman he loved. She'd screamed the whole time, begging him to stop as his soul writhed in agony.

Until she'd shifted to Dire Wolf form, raked him across the muzzle, and fled. The usurper chased her into the woods and caught her again. She'd screamed, her eyes filled with horror and betrayal as she tried to fight the monster off. And failed.

The usurper ripped into her as Jack screamed helplessly in his head, unable to stop, unable to wake from this unspeakable nightmare. By the time *it* finished, she'd lost consciousness, covered in horrific bites. Jack had cried out to her through their Spirit Link, but all he'd felt was her life draining away. He'd waited for her death to kill him too. Prayed for it. But neither of them died. Instead she'd shifted and healed, and he'd thought for glorious moment she was going to be all right. Until he looked into her eyes.

Whatever looked back at him wasn't his Ellie.

Now the usurper controlled them both, piloting them like one of those remote-controlled drones he'd gotten the grandkids for Christmas. He could feel *It* in his head like a great spider, ancient and vicious and alien.

After Ellie had regained consciousness, *It* had let them sleep for a while, their bodies tangled together on a pile of leaves in the woods. Then at dawn *It* had forced them to go out hunting until they'd found that poor human girl. He'd felt the horror in Ellie's mind as they'd caught the girl, dragged her out into a nearby field, and killed her. She'd shrieked in pain and horror, Jack and Ellie screaming right along with her in their Spirit Link.

Now they'd attacked Walker and two people who smelled like Magekind, and armored knights were chasing them. None of it made any sense. As he ran, Jack prayed the Magekind would catch them and kill them before *It* made them do something even worse.

* * *

The werewolf's punch had caved in Duncan's visor, slicing up his handsome face. What Masara could see of his bloody features looked badly swollen and misshapen. He must have suffered major head trauma at the very least. With a savage gesture, she banished both their helmets, then disposed of her own gloves the same way. Groping for his carotid, she found it throbbing, too fast and too weak.

"Duncan. Duncan." She had to work to keep the panic out of her voice. *I've failed him. I've gotten him killed.* "Duncan, wake up and shift."

"Hey." Belle's husband, Sir Tristan, emerged from the woods. "Is he okay?" The Knight of the Round Table wore heavy plate combat armor worked with intricate spells.

Masara shot her friend a desperate glance. "No. He's not conscious and I can't get him to shift. Did you get the rogues?"

"The others are chasing them, but I had a feeling you needed help." The knight knelt on Duncan's other side, grimacing as he got a look. "Yeah, that's not good." He raised his voice, trying to rouse the unconscious man. "Come on, kid. You know how to do this. I taught you myself. Shift to wolf form, Duncan. Duncan, damn it, boy…"

His pulse was weakening under her fingers. Desperate, she grabbed for the Mageverse even as her skull screamed and sent power rolling into his poor battered head, trying to establish a psychic link she could use to drag him back to consciousness. And found nothing for so long, she wanted to scream in grief and fear. Until… *There you are!*

A ghostly hint of Duncan. But weak, far too weak. Masara threw herself wide to the burning lake that was the Mageverse and pumped its power into him, spinning a web of magic around him to support and strengthen his life.

As if from a great distance, she heard his mental voice through the link she was weaving between them. *Masara?* It sounded so horribly faint.

Dragging more power from the Mageverse, she fed it to him, working to pull him to full consciousness. *Duncan, come back to me! I need you!* She infused the demand with every bit of power she had, showing him the truth of it, the desperation.

Which was when she realized she meant every imploring word. *When did he get to me like this?* But she had no time to spare for the thought. All that mattered was saving Duncan.

Teeth gritted, she wrapped herself around that guttering spark of him, infused his mind with her magic, her will, her spirit, ignoring the burn of pain that warned she was pushing her power too far. *COME BACK!*

His eyes flew wide, and he jerked convulsively, his mind bursting through into full consciousness. Disorientation and pain triggered a flashback: *Smoke whirled around him as a wall of hurricane force blasted him off his feet…* "My legs!"

"Your legs are fine," Masara soothed. "They healed. Now you need to shift and heal this. You have severe head trauma."

He stared at her from eyes swollen half closed in a mask of blood, and she felt his bewilderment through their new link. "I'm… werewolf… now?" Given that he'd only recently turned into a vampire, she supposed it wasn't a ridiculous question.

"Different kind of wolf," Tristan told him. "Damn, you did get your bell rung. I covered this in class, remember? We use our transformations to heal. Watch…"

Magic exploded in a silent fireworks display, and a huge wolf sat where Tristan had been. Given his golden coat, he could have been mistaken for a dog if not for his distinctly lupine muzzle and jungle-green eyes. Not to mention the fact that he weighed every bit of two hundred pounds, though that no longer seemed quite as huge after the fight with the rogues.

"See? All you have to do is shift and your injuries will heal," Masara told Duncan.

"Oh…" But he looked vague, uncomprehending. Tristan was right, he wasn't tracking at all. She was going to have to help, though a brain injury so severe was beyond her healing abilities. Duncan had to do it himself.

Masara reached out and caught his face between her palms, ignoring the sticky, drying blood that covered his skin. Drawing furiously on the Mageverse -- it felt like inhaling fire because she'd used so much magic today -- she sent power pouring into him, strengthening the bond. *Getting too close to a Truebond…* And that psychic union of souls could not be broken.

She didn't care. Whatever it took. "Shift!" Masara put as much battleground bark into the command as she could. He was a Marine. Maybe spinal reflex would move him if nothing else did.

It worked. His face jerked between her hands, magic surging through him as he fought to obey… but the spell collapsed a minute later, leaving him lying there, bloody and dazed. *Please, Lord God, help him… Help me.* She grabbed for all the power she could command and sent it blazing into him. So much magic, it felt as if her brain would burst into flame…

Magic exploded between her palms, and she gasped, momentarily blinded. When she could see again, a big brown wolf lay on the pavement with his furry head between her hands and all four legs in the air. He yelped and rolled to his feet, his muzzle swinging as he looked wildly around. His blue eyes looked even bluer against his dark fur.

*Where'd the werewolves go?*

She heard the thought as clearly as if he'd spoken it aloud. Yeah, she'd definitely come a little too close to creating a Truebond. But he was healed and in one piece, and that was all she really cared about. Wrapping both arms around him, Masara buried her face in his thick fur. Her head throbbed viciously with the movement, but she barely noticed in her relief. "Sweet Lord, don't do that to me again."

He drew back, and she could feel how stripped naked and raw he felt. She suddenly realized the cocky persona that often irritated the daylights out of her was nothing but a mask. *I'm sorry I messed up.*

"You're still alive. That's all that matters."

He examined her, seeing more than she was entirely comfortable with. *You didn't mess up either.*

*I almost got you killed*, she argued.

*I almost got me killed.*

*Which amounts to the same thing, since it's my job to keep you alive.* Aloud she said, "Shift back. You need opposable thumbs and a larynx. I hear the Knights of the Round Table coming back."

She felt him reach for his magic, felt the strain of his effort... And nothing happened. *Oh God, am I stuck this way?*

She sighed and buried her fingers in his thick fur. "Don't let it bother you. It's never easy to work magic on Mortal Earth, and we've been doing a lot of it tonight. We'll gate back to the Mageverse and you can shift there."

"Hey, are you okay?" Walker padded toward them at Belle's side, still in Dire Wolf form and wearing the armor she'd created for him. He'd gotten almost as beaten up as Duncan, based on the gashes cutting across the blood-spattered scale.

"Fine, now." It wasn't quite a lie. "Are you all right?"

"Thanks to your armor. Without it, I'd have been meaty chunks. Thanks." He grinned, flashing more teeth than a sea monster.

Masara smiled wearily. "You're welcome."

"But, ah… can we get rid of it now? Because I'm not sure how to take it off, and whatever you're wearing when you shift, you'll wear when you change to that form the next time. And, well…"

Masara winced as her head gave a warning throb. "Ah."

Apparently reading her expression, Belle flicked her fingers and the werewolf's armor vanished. He gave her a very toothy smile. "Thanks." His own magic flared around him in a rain of sparks, and he was back in human form. Eyeing Duncan, Walker sniffed the air and blinked in startled recognition at his scent. "Wow, you really can shift."

Duncan barked -- and instantly looked so confused, Walker laughed. "Dude, no human vocal cords in that form."

Masara gave his thick fur a stroke and climbed to her feet, wincing as strained muscles protested. "I gather the werewolves got away."

"Unfortunately." Walker grimaced.

"One minute they were crashing through the woods ahead of us," Belle said. "The next they were just gone. If I didn't know better, I'd think they cast a dimensional gate."

Masara frowned. "*Could* they have cast a dimensional gate?"

"We don't work magic," Walker reminded her.

"Warlock did," she said, referring to the Direkind's immortal sorcerer. "So do his daughter Miranda and her husband Justice. It's possible, it just takes a lot of genetic tinkering."

Belle shook her head. "I didn't sense any magic. At all."

Walker grunted. "Thank God for small favors. There's something seriously wrong with that pair. I've never seen Direkind that size, and they sliced into armor my claws wouldn't have been able to cut. I think it's time for a long talk with the Wolf Sheriff. He'd know about this crap if anybody does." He looked around, spotted the pack of evidence lying on the ground next to his car, and ran to recover it. Anxiously, he unzipped it and sighed in relief. "Ah, good. Still got the evidence. I was afraid I'd lost it when that big bastard hit me."

Masara frowned. The Wolf Sheriff was the enforcer for the Council of Clans, the werewolf governing body. Walker was probably right. "When will you be able to talk to him?"

He shrugged. "Don't know. He's hunting a werewolf serial killer in California right now, which is why he isn't here running this case."

"If you need me to talk to him about what I found, I'll be happy to," Masara told him.

"I'll probably take you up on that." He thumbed his key fob, and the SUV's headlights flashed.

As he got in, Masara turned to Belle and Tristan. "What's the plan?"

"I think Arthur and Morgana intend to search for our furry friends a little longer." Belle gave her a long look. "As for you two, you need to get back to the Mageverse. You're running on fumes."

Masara sighed. "Yes, that would probably be best." Duncan looked up at her, and she realized she was resting one hand on the top of his big head. *I'm treating him like a dog.* She lifted her hand, but he settled one furry shoulder against her thigh. And for a moment, she felt his mind through the link. Felt the loneliness he was so damned good at hiding, the pain he worked so hard to ignore. She found herself stroking his thick fur again.

When she looked up, Belle and Tristan were watching her. The Knight's expression was knowing, while Belle looked weirdly pleased. "You did a good job today," her friend said.

"Thank you." The words sounded more clipped than she'd intended.

Belle must've read something she didn't like in Masara's expression, because she frowned. "Nobody died, Masara."

"And that includes the people we wanted to kill."

"There are two of them and ten thousand of us, plus a whole lot of werewolves," Tristan told her. "We'll get them."

"In the meantime, go feed your apprentice," Belle suggested. "He looks dead on his feet."

She glanced down to see Duncan staring up at her, his eyes longing. She could feel his craving vibrating through the link -- a need not only for her blood, but for her body. Her touch.

And all he expected to get was a glass.

*I want him.* The thought hit her like a thunderclap. She'd resisted that sensual hunger for months, wary of stirring old, bleak memories. But that was before she'd touched Duncan's mind, felt his courage and determination to be worthy of his miraculous second chance. *I'm tired of denying us both.*

His eyes widened as he read the thought through the link. Which was, she realized, entirely too active right now. His plumed tail wagged back and forth once, then stopped when he saw her looking at it.

"Debrief in the morning," Belle said.

"Yes, of course." As Masara started to reach for the dregs of her magic, the hot pinpoint of a gate appeared and dilated. She shot Belle a grateful smile over her shoulder, knowing her friend was responsible. "Thanks for the ride home."

"Go," Belle said firmly. "Sleep."

Smiling a little, Masara stepped through the gate, Duncan by her side, still four-legged. The minute they crossed over into the living room, magic flooded through her. She blew out a relieved breath and fell onto the couch. Thick padding gave under her back, and tight muscles began to loosen.

Light exploded. When the magic of the shift faded, Duncan was back in human form. He still wore his armor and the remains of his helmet -- not to mention the crust of dried blood that covered his features. The reminder of just how close she'd come to losing him made Masara's stomach clench. *I'm sick of regrets,* she thought suddenly. *And he was almost one of them.* There'd been so many things she'd wanted so desperately and feared to let herself have. *He's not going to be one of them anymore.*

She remembered the way he'd looked during combat practice that evening -- gloriously bare-chested, his cock hard and tempting, barely concealed by his thin shorts. Remembered how beautiful he'd been as he'd fought, muscle rippling along his chest and powerful arms. And during tonight's battle, his grace and power as he'd thrown himself at the werewolf in that ten-foot leap. So seductive.

Despite her exhaustion and throbbing head, magic came a lot easier here. The cleansing spell wiped away the blood and sweat of the fight, and left Duncan in a soft cotton tee and loose pants. On sheer impulse, she'd dressed herself in a crop top and shorts that were just a little tight.

Duncan sighed in relief and collapsed on the sofa beside her. She was instantly aware of his sheer muscled heat. "Thanks. Not to be greedy, but I hope you can spare a couple bottles of a nice Masara. I feel like hammered..." Pausing to censor the word, he finished... "Crap." He was always keenly aware of his language with her.

"Sorry, no bottles for you." When his eyes widened with a hint of hurt, Masara hooked a hand behind his neck and met his eyes. "But I do have some on tap."

Leaning forward, she took his mouth in a kiss as hot and wet as she could make it.

He made a muffled, confused sound against her lips, part moan, part growl of sheer need. *Do you mean that?*

In answer, she swirled her tongue between his parted lips, thrust slowly, deeply. *What do you think?*

*I think... I want everything you want to give me.* With a rumbling sound of gratitude, he kissed her back.

Duncan knew his way around a kiss. His tongue circled and licked at hers in a sweetly erotic duel, before taking her lower lip between his teeth for a tender, teasing bite. His hand came up to cradle her face in a big, warm palm, his thumb brushing over her cheekbone, the gesture tender. Wondering.

She could feel that wonder in his mind. Feel how much he wanted her, and how convinced he'd been that he would never have her. *Could* never have her.

*Tonight you can.* Masara lost herself in the kiss, one hand stroking through the rich, curling chestnut of Duncan's shoulder-length hair. By the time they both had to come up for breath, arousal curled hot in the pit of her belly, twin to the desire she could feel growing in his mind.

"This would probably be a lot easier without the clothes," he murmured, lust making his voice sound a little ragged.

"Not sure I'm up to another spell," she admitted.

"That's okay." He smiled, revealing the length of the fangs, which, like his impressive erection, showed just how hungry he really was. "I think we can manage."

"I think we can too." She rose to her feet, reaching down to take his hand. "Come on. I feel the need for a bed. We've got ninety minutes until dawn, and I've got a long list of things I want to do to you before then."

* * *

This was another one of those moments when Duncan wondered if he was hallucinating in his Bethesda hospital bed. Or hell, maybe he'd died and gone to heaven, and St. Peter had simply neglected to inform him. If so, he liked this version of heaven a lot more than the clouds and harps they'd talked about in Sunday school.

His eyes lingered on Masara's beauty as she preceded him down the hall. Her crop top showed several inches of smooth brown skin and the dip of her spine. Muscles worked in that perfect ass under those tight shorts as she sauntered along. Her legs looked longer than her long, long life, and her dreads swung with every step, the metal bands brushing her rump. His erection gave an approving little buck.

Duncan's mind drifted to the sight of her fighting the werewolf, a real-life Wonder Woman swinging a battle-axe as if it weighed no more than a feather. Her helmet's visor had framed a face both beautiful and merciless. His upper jaw ached ferociously, and he explored the length of his fangs with his tongue. *She keeps giving me a fang-on*, he thought, and grinned in giddy anticipation.

She looked back at him. Eyes twinkling, she said, her voice mock-stern, "I trust you're not laughing at me."

"You make me feel a lot of things, but an urge to laugh *at* you is not one of them."

"Then let's see what else I can make you feel." Reaching the end of the hall, she turned. Her hand wrapped around his cock, and he sucked in a startled breath as she towed him into her bedroom.

Though his room was located right across the hall from hers, he'd never been inside it. Now he realized he'd missed out. The entire room was curved, and so huge it must take up half this end of the house. But what really amazed him was the fact that both the curved right wall and the ceiling overhead were one enormous stained-glass window.

"Damn," Duncan murmured, gaping shamelessly as he turned, staring at his surroundings in awe. The massive window depicted the African savanna at sunrise -- giraffes, elephants, and zebra roaming under a sky blazing in shades of violet, rose, and orange as the huge golden ball of the sun rose over the distant trees. A lion crouched at the edge of the waterhole, eyes gleaming as he drank. A series of lights illuminated the glass from somewhere outside, making it glow against the darkness. "This is incredible," he breathed in awe.

"Glad you like it." Her face lighting up in a smile, Masara towed him toward a big circular bed in the middle of the room, piled high with pillows. The only other furnishings were a series of low chests that stood around the room. One ebony mannequin stood dressed in the same suit of scale mail she'd worn in combat, now repaired, the fine metal reflecting the light blazing from the windows.

He opened his mouth to ask her about it, but she turned to face him and pulled off her top, baring her lovely breasts as she tossed it aside and reached for the hem of his tee. Suddenly his entire consciousness was swamped with the sight of lovely muscle working as she tugged his shirt up. With a groan of raw need, he reached for the zipper of her shorts.

# Chapter Four

They fumbled as they undressed each other, tossing clothes aside in impatient haste, pausing only to kiss some tempting bit of anatomy -- her hard, dark nipple, his muscled biceps as they brushed her face.

Groaning around his aching fangs, Duncan cupped her cheek in one hand and used the other to do something he'd wanted to do since he met her -- he caught hold of a handful of her dreads. They felt cool and soft in his fingers. He savored the sensation as he kissed her, drinking in the intoxicating taste of her mouth. His fangs ached ferociously, shooting stabbing pains into his upper jaw, but he ignored the ache. All his focus was on her. He was damn well going to prove that while he might be a hundred and fifty years younger, he still knew how to make it good for her.

Leaning closer, he brushed his thumb over the silken angle of her jaw, kissing his way from the corner of her mouth to the curve of her ear, exploring the contours of bone and silken flesh. All the while, she touched him, her elegant, tapered fingers dancing over his skin, until his every muscle drew hard and eager.

It had been six months since he'd made love to the Court Seducer sent to transform him into a Magus. Since then he'd been utterly consumed by the need to learn everything an agent of the Magekind needed to know. The closest he'd been to a woman had been drinking blood from a bottle. The only female touch he'd experienced had been when Masara demonstrated the proper way to handle a sword.

Now her hands caressed his aching cock. The scent of her rolled over his head, sex and woman and magic, but more importantly, Masara. Masara, whom he'd craved like a junkie craved a fix for months, even while believing she'd never let him touch her. Now that he could, he was going to make it last.

His mouth found the throbbing pulse of her carotid, and the scent of her flooded his skull until it seemed he tasted her on his tongue. The delicious aroma sent two needles of sweet pain driving from the tips of his fangs all the way to their roots. His stomach cramped as though he were starving. *I could taste her*, wheedled a desperate, hungry voice from the depths of his brain. *Just one small bite. She won't mind.* Duncan jerked his head up, away from that tempting throb. *I mind. I'm going to make this good for her.*

He realized the hand that gripped her dreads had tightened until he was pulling her head to one side, exposing her pounding pulse. He released her hair as if it had burned him. The pain in his jaw intensified…

A warm, smooth palm curved around his cheek, and Masara's dark eyes met his. "Hey. Duncan, hey." He could barely hear the words over the deep throb of her heartbeat. It had quickened with excitement. Or was that fear? *God, I hope it's not fear.*

"Stop that." Her fingers tightened on the curve of his cheek. "I brought you here to feed you, remember?"

The inside of his mouth had gone so dry, he had the ugly suspicion he needed to brush his teeth. "Maybe it would be better if you just gave me one of those bottles, let me take the edge off." He forced his mouth into a smile he didn't feel. A quiver ran through his legs, and honesty forced him to add, "Or maybe two bottles."

"A bottle will not give you what you need. Not considering how much magic you had to use healing that head injury." She tangled her fist in his long hair.

"I want you to drink from me." And she tilted her head back and a little to one side, pulling his head down until his lips brushed the silken curve of her throat.

Lust and hunger leaped so high, it scared him. He tried to jerk back, but she held fast. He remembered a horror story his Court Seducer had told him about a Latent who'd been unable to control his hunger. She'd had to kill the poor bastard to keep him from ripping her throat out. "I don't think I'd better. A bottle…"

"You won't lose control," Masara interrupted, her voice steady, confident. "If you didn't lose control when you became a Magus, you won't lose it now. That's not the way it works."

"But…"

Her magic brushed his consciousness again, reopening the psychic link she'd established. And he felt what she was thinking. Masara believed in him. Believed absolutely that he would not lose control, that he would take no more than she wanted to give him. *I'm safe with you. And you're safe with me. Do it. I want this as much as you do.*

With a groan of surrender, he opened his lips against her silken skin and bit deep. His fangs sank into the soft, thin flesh, and her blood flooded his mouth. She groaned, the sound sensual with arousal.

Her blood tasted completely different from the meaty copper tang he'd tasted whenever he'd split his lip as a mortal. The flavor was even more intense than her bottled blood. Masara straight from the vein was sunlight, sex, and woman, overlaid with a smoky scent that reminded him of sparklers on the Fourth of July.

*Magic.*

He heard her groan with pleasure, felt her enjoyment flood his mind. Her lean, muscled arms wrapped around him as he drank, and every inch of her body pressed against his. One smooth leg slid up his, hooking around the back of his thigh until he could feel the soft hair of her pussy, the press of plump lips, already growing damp. The hot intimacy of her hold sent a shudder rolling through his body. He paused to draw his fangs from her, but she cupped the back of his head and whispered, "Don't stop."

"Just for a moment," he murmured, and bent to sweep her into his arms, then carried her to the bed, her body feeling weightless as a feather as he lowered her to the mattress. Dark eyes met his, and she tilted her head back in invitation. With a groan, Duncan took her throat again, and the raw sex taste of her flooded his mouth. He moaned in pleasure.

With every swallow, magic flooded his body until it felt as if he could bench-press a tank. Her hips rolled against his, her flat, silken belly stroking the hard jut of his cock as her nipples teased his chest with every breath, until the clamor of his cock was louder than the roar of his hunger. With exquisite care, he drew his fangs from her throat. Looking down, he saw blood beading, bright crimson against her dark skin. He bent his head and licked the tiny wound, so that the magic in his saliva would induce it to heal. By tomorrow, no one would even know she'd been bitten.

Something told him the mark she left on him would last a lot longer.

* * *

Duncan's eyes looked very blue in the frame of wild chestnut curls as he met her gaze, licking a bead of blood away from his full lower lip. Memory reared up, jabbing fear into her mind. That shade of blue was just too close to *his*. She buried the thought hastily, knowing she and Duncan were still linked. He was too vulnerable for that revelation, too raw and uncertain in their relationship. Whatever that relationship was -- she wasn't sure she knew herself.

To distract them both, Masara danced her fingertips along the ridge of muscles of his back, to the dip of his spine, then traced its hollow downward. There was nothing at all soft about the man, not in his body or his mind. Anything pampered had been driven out by the Marine Corps and Afghanistan. She brushed his thoughts in the link. He was utterly enthralled by the feel of her body, her scent, and her taste and her touch.

Duncan considered her the most beautiful woman he'd ever seen, though he'd never said the words to her aloud. She'd been told she was beautiful before, but his mind held none of that greed she'd experienced from other men, no edge of possession or entitlement. There was something incredibly seductive about seeing herself through Duncan's eyes.

*You really don't know me very well,* she thought, more to herself than to him.

*I know you better than you think. I know what counts.* One big hand slid from her waist, tracing teasing patterns along the ridges of her ribs. She could see his goal in his mind -- her dark, stiffened nipples. Which grew even harder at the thought of his touch. Every inch of her body felt sensitized and eager as his fingers caressed her with such exquisite care.

Hungry to give him the same pleasure, Masara began to explore. He was plated with slabs of muscle, the powerful shapes nested together like puzzle pieces over his big bones. Soft hair grew on his chest, stretching from one nipple to the other before narrowing down into a thin trail leading to the ruff surrounding his erect cock.

"Do you want me to shave it?"

"Don't you dare. You're a man, not a Ken doll." She stroked the soft, springy curls. "Besides, I like how it feels."

"See if you like this too." He pushed her over onto her back and began to kiss his way down her neck. Her breath roughened as she anticipated the touch of his mouth on her nipples, so hard and aching... but instead he kept kissing down the length of her sternum, pausing here and there to nibble a rib, or swirl his tongue around some freckle he found particularly erotic.

He paused at her belly button, licking its outer rim, the ticklish sensation making her squirm. He thrust his tongue in and out of the little dip. When she giggled and tried to twist away, he caught her hips in both big hands, holding her down.

The memory burst from the psychic closet she'd locked it in: *hard hands pinning, pain ripping as he...* Masara stiffened, fighting the rise of cold panic.

Duncan instantly released her and jerked back, eyes widening with shock and horror. "Sorry! I'm so sorry..."

Masara grabbed his face in both hands to keep him from retreating further. "Don't be. It was a long time ago and you're nothing like him." She jacked up into a sitting position and kissed him so hard her lips ground against his erect fangs.

At last he groaned and kissed her back. He started to reach for her, then froze.

"Don't you dare treat me like I'm any less," she growled.

To her surprise, his lips twitched in a smile. "You're the most *more* woman I've ever known." Gently, Duncan took her face in both hands and kissed her again, first a slow, tender brush of the lips, a delicate apology for stirring such horrible memories. When she swirled her tongue around his, he opened his mouth and his mind to her completely, showing her exactly how he felt. Let her see how often he'd watched the curve of her backside as she walked away from him. How he'd been hypnotized by the elegant fluidity of her every movement, whether she was swinging a sword or pouring him a glass of blood.

Beneath that, she felt his longing for her, his belief that he had nothing to give her that she could possibly want. Because he was broken.

"You are not broken."

He recoiled, as if he hadn't intended to reveal quite so much. Planting both hands on his shoulders, Masara pushed him back on the bed and swung a leg over his hips. She bent to kiss him, intent on showing him with her mouth and her hands just what she thought of him. Showed him the memory of watching his big body move, all power and grace even when he was struggling to learn some sword technique alien to his experience. Showed him she'd wanted him even when she'd thought she should be nothing more than his teacher.

Masara no longer cared what she *should* be. She wanted him as much as he wanted her, and their relationship had nothing whatsoever to do with coercion. *And believe me, I do know the difference.*

Duncan went still, half afraid to believe she meant it.

To prove she did, she started licking and sucking her way down his chest. Found his tight, tiny male nipple, rosy against his pale skin. She sensed his embarrassment at his pale skin, a product of his hospital stay, preserved by Merlin's Gift. *There's nothing sickly about you.* Masara flashed him an image of himself as he leaped at the werewolf, swinging his axe in a great arc.

With a growl, Duncan jackknifed off the bed and wrapped both arms around her. "Let me..."

So she did. Duncan bent her back against the hard brace of his arms while his mouth closed over a stiff nipple. Pleasure poured through her as he laved the eager point, raked it with delicate passes of his teeth. She felt the curve of his fangs against her breast, felt how he craved her even after feeding so deeply. Not because he was hungry, but because she was Masara. And he craved her. Needed her.

He kissed his way to the other breast to lavish attention on it, and she heard the purr of thought in his mind. *Beautiful, so beautiful and sweet, a Hershey's kiss of a nipple...* Followed by a guilty, *Not supposed to compare you to food...*

"Don't care," she growled, her hands fisting in his hair, pulling him tight against her skin. "More!"

Duncan gave her what she asked for, suckling and stroking, finding the perfect pressure from listening to her mind, to her body's hot response to his touch. He started exploring every inch of her he could reach, seeking out each sensitive spot -- here behind one bent knee, there under her arm, exploring. Listening to her body through the link with absorbed attention.

It was surprising how much intimacy their psychic link gave to making love. Her pleasure fed his and his arousal fed hers, each touch and kiss and taste amplifying their need. Duncan leaned down, spread her legs, and breathed deep, inches from the heart of her pussy. She was surprised at how erotic he found the scent; she'd never much liked the odor of her body.

Blue eyes blinked up at her. "Are you kidding? You're the most delicious thing I've ever smelled." And he caught both legs under each knee and draped them over his broad shoulders. His mouth covered her pussy, and the first slick slide of his tongue made her eyes roll back.

He made a deep, purring sound. "So that's what that feels like. I see why you like it." Then he began to lap at her in quick, thirsty strokes that maddened her, made her writhe and roll her hips against his face.

Masara had been eaten out before, of course, but there was something so different about the way he did it. It was no polite tit-for-tat service. It wasn't just a stop on the way to his orgasm. For him, cunnilingus was a profound erotic experience all by itself. It made her want to suck him off.

"Later," he growled against her pussy, though his cock jerked at the thought of sliding into her wet mouth. He closed his lips around her clit in a deep, drawing suckle and slid two fingers between her wet lips. He ate her greedily, piling pleasure upon pleasure, until he had to stop, gasping, too close to the edge himself.

Masara took ruthless advantage of his distraction, wrapping her magic around him and pulling him up off her and onto his knees. And ignored the protesting twinge from her brain's overused magic centers. Duncan gasped in shock, tried to struggle, only to discover even vampire strength couldn't break the bonds magic created.

She sat up and gave him a deliberately wicked smile. "You look a picture," she told him, admiring the straining arc of his powerful body, the deep bow of his erect cock dewed in pre-come.

"Don't," he groaned, seeing in the link what she intended. "I won't be able to…"

"You underestimate yourself. And me too." Leaning down, she wrapped her fingers around his thick shaft and stroked, enjoying the way he writhed, the way his hips bucked even as he fought the need to come. Opening her mouth, she engulfed him in a long sweep, shuddering as the link showed her just how incredible that felt to him -- the delicious heat of her mouth sliding along the exquisitely sensitive skin of his shaft. Up. Down. Using all the skills she learned even before she became a Maja.

As the dark memory rose, he stiffened, appalled, but she shut it away fast and lifted her head. "This is for my pleasure as much as yours," she told him fiercely and then took him as deep as she could with a slow, wet slide of tongue and lips.

The stark power of the sensation brought him so close to orgasm, his entire body seemed to vibrate like a struck tuning fork. He fought the building pulses, trying to hold onto his self-control, determined not to disappoint her.

*You won't disappoint me,* she thought at him, taking him deep again, slowly sliding down the wet shaft. *I can make you come as many times as I want, and my magic can still make your body harden with a touch.*

*But I want the first time to be* in *you.* The hot intensity behind the thought drove right through her absorption with the sensual elegance of his body. Looking up into those fierce blue eyes, she realized he meant it. He needed to come inside her with the desperation of a man who'd been helpless, who'd seen himself as crippled and less.

She released him. With a moan of gratitude that morphed into a growl of hunger, he snapped forward, pouncing on her and tossing her to the bed on her back. Grabbing her behind each leg, he spread her wide and entered in a long, driving thrust that ripped a cry from her mouth. She knew she must have had lovers as well-endowed as Duncan, but none of them had ever felt like this.

He froze, staring into her face, letting them both adjust to the feeling of him so deep in her wet, tight heat. She rolled her hips against him, opening her mind to his, wanting to feel how he felt taking her. Hungry to feel his body respond to hers, to share his delight and hunger.

"God, yes." He began to fuck her, sliding out slowly, carefully, and then in again, teeth clenched as he fought his pleasure and hers. His eyes were wide with wonder, as if he was once again that sixteen-year-old virgin jock making it with a cheerleader in the back of his dad's SUV…

She carefully suppressed the memory of her own first time. To make sure it stayed buried, she tightened inner muscles around his thick cock. Duncan made a strangled sound in his throat. He began to pump, driving deeper, harder, sensation piling upon sensation, her pleasure upon his, intensifying each other.

Masara hunched up at him as fiercely as he drove down at her. She could feel how desperately he strained to contain the orgasm even as his body screamed for release. "Let go!" she gasped in his ear, grinding up as he plunged in and out. The pleasure gathered in a ferocious, towering wave that hung over them, defying gravity as it built.

"I love you!" he gasped, and she saw he meant every word.

The fire crashed down on them, drowning them in flame and wet heat and blinding magic. He roared in her ear as she screamed, coming, driving her nails into the thick muscle of his shoulders.

When it was all over, they lay there, hearts thundering in a ragged chorus. Duncan had collapsed beside her, both arms wrapped around her, and she could feel how wrung out he felt, how breathless and exhilarated.

Then he said it again. "I love you."

*No, you don't,* she thought.

His head jerked up off the pillow and those blue eyes met hers. Hurt and anger lanced through him. "I know how I feel."

"I'm not rejecting you," she told him quietly. "It's just easy to get carried away." And she knew he heard the rest of the thought flashing through her mind. He was young, and he'd never known the intensity of a battlefield psychic link. That, combined with the importance of a mentor's approval, then fighting beside her against monsters trying to kill them both... It was easy to misread that kind of relationship and make it into more than it was. "I just don't want you hurt."

He stared at her, his blue gaze cold. "I can take care of myself." There was no wounded male vanity in his tone, only a kind of icy dignity. Duncan rolled out of bed and stalked from the room.

* * *

Pissed, aching, he strode into his bedroom and closed the door, resisting the savage urge to give it a thundering slam. "You dumbass," he raged at himself. "You had to go and open your mouth." Though wasn't sure it would have mattered if he had kept quiet. Masara had been in his head just as he'd been in hers. The problem with telepathy was that it stripped all illusions away. He couldn't even tell himself she didn't mean what she'd said. She damned well had.

Stilling his thoughts, Duncan reached for her. But she was gone, the link shut down. *Thank God. I can bleed in peace.* He stomped across his bedroom, paused just long enough to slide into a pair of blue jeans, then made for the French doors that led onto the veranda. Over the past month, he'd discovered nothing leveled him out like staring across the multicolored skyline of Avalon.

He needed to get Masara's scent out of his head, her taste out of his mouth. He was going to have a hell of a time breaking his addiction to her. *And I only had her once.*

Opening the doors, Duncan stepped out onto the redwood deck. The cool night air smelled of the exotic African flowers Masara cultivated in those elaborate gardens of hers, mixed with the scent of her neighbors' roses. If it was green, the witches grew it, then magically shaped it into topiary elephants or some damn thing.

Duncan leaned against the thick wooden railing, wrapping both hands around it. The wood gave a loud warning creak, and he hastily loosened his grip. He'd spent his first couple of weeks as a vampire breaking damn near everything he touched before he'd finally learned to moderate his strength. It didn't help that tonight he badly *wanted* to break something.

Duncan sucked in a deep breath, staring out across Avalon. All that stained glass gave the skyline a Christmas-tree quality he'd seen in no other city. That -- combined with a funky blend of architectural styles ranging from Gothic to Frank Lloyd Wright -- made the town look more like the Magic Kingdom than twenty-first century.

With a sigh, he dropped into one of the wicker chairs, propped his bare heels up on the railing, and settled in for a good brood.

Duncan had known for weeks he was falling for her, though at first, she'd just intimidated the hell out of him. He'd had good reason to find her overwhelming. One of his instructors had told him he was damned lucky to have her. And it was true.

As Logan MacRoy said, Masara might not be the most powerful Maja in Avalon, but she'd become legendary for her icy daring as a spy during the American Civil War. She'd spied in countless wars since then -- whenever the Magekind decided the fate of humanity depended on it. "She's one of the most driven people I've ever known," MacRoy told him. And coming from the son of King Arthur, that said a hell of a lot.

So when Duncan had realized he was falling for her, he'd dismissed his feelings as infatuation. It hadn't even occurred to him that he had a prayer of so much as kissing her. Then she'd opened that psychic link, and he'd learned her feelings for him were a lot more complicated than he'd known. Not necessarily in a good way, either.

He hadn't been pleased to discover his eyes were evidently the exact same shade of blue as whatever son of a bitch had given her those psychic scars. He'd seen only a flash of the memory he'd triggered when he'd held her down, but it had been enough to horrify him. He'd have left her bed right then, but he'd felt how desperately she needed him to drive the flashback away.

And Masara did feel something for him. Duncan had sensed the strength of it when he'd been on the verge of dying. She'd been wide open to him in that moment, terrified at the thought of losing him. It felt a lot like outright panic, which shocked him considering her reputation for icy courage. Would she have felt that for just anybody?

Then again, he'd been willing to die for Farijaad. Sometimes you did desperate shit because you couldn't live with yourself if you didn't. Besides, ultimately it didn't matter whether Masara felt anything for him or not. If she was determined to keep him at a distance, there was nothing he could do about it. If there was one thing his mother had drummed into his head, it was that no most definitely meant *no*.

Especially if the one saying no could turn you into a frog. He…

Agony flashed across his back in a flaming line of blinding pain. Duncan convulsed and leaped out of his chair, whipping around to hit the werewolf who'd just laid his shoulders open.

There was no one there.

Another line of fire slashed from his right shoulder to his waist. He felt skin split and blood spurt. Duncan twisted around, one hand groping, but his back was whole under his fingers, and there was no sign of the blood he could feel rolling down his spine. Terror rang through him, so intense it made his entire body recoil. *Emily! Don't*!

Masara. It was Masara's terror, Masara's pain. Something was killing her.

# Chapter Five

Duncan bolted through the balcony doors and raced across his bedroom to throw the door open and charge across the hall. Fire raked his back again as he seized the doorknob. It was locked. Pain sliced him again, and he knew the werewolf must be tearing her open. Rearing back on one foot, he slammed the other to the door. It shattered like balsa wood. Duncan bulled through the fragments, ignoring the rake of splintered shards across his skin.

Masara lay curled in a ball in the center of the bed, naked and alone.

Duncan scanned the room wildly, looking for whatever had attacked her, but there was nothing there. "Masara?" he asked, his heart still pounding. *What the hell is going on?* Then in the light pouring in through the shattered door, he saw something rip across her back. The link blasted him with such pain, he had to clench his teeth against a shout of pain.

"Arrh!" Masara writhed, and he saw that what he'd thought were shadows shone wet in the light from the hall.

*Jesus, that's blood. Those are wounds!* Deep cuts slashed across her skin from shoulders to hips. Staring at her in horror, he spotted a rib shining white through torn, bloody flesh. "Masara!" Duncan reached for her through the waves of pain blasting through the battlefield link. "Masara, what's…"

"Emily!" She twisted, rolling onto her stomach. "No, stop!"

An image flashed through his mind -- a pale woman with a startling resemblance to Masara except for the thick blond hair piled high on her head. Her blood-splattered face was twisted in rage and hate.

*What the fuck is this? Is it an attack, a dream, what? Something's sure as hell hurting her.* "Wake up! It's me, Duncan!" His first impulse was to shake her, but he himself had been known to come out of a nightmare swinging. "Masara…"

"Emily!" She screamed and threw herself off the bed to land facing him, twin fireballs floating above her hands.

*Oh, shit!* He took a hasty step back. "Masara, it's Duncan. Are you all right? What's going on?"

She stared at him, her dark eyes huge with rage and terror as the globes of flame swelled, growing larger, hotter. Duncan tensed to duck. Vampires might be a hell of a lot stronger, but the real heavy hitters of Avalon were the witches. She could fry his ass without breaking a sweat. "Masara! You're dreaming! Wake up!"

Her rage turned to confusion. "Who are…" She broke off as recognition flared in her eyes at last. The fireballs winked out. "Duncan? What are you… Ow." Wincing, she twisted her head around to look down over one shoulder. And hissed a word he hadn't thought she knew.

"Are you under some kind of magical attack?" He'd thought it was a nightmare, but in the Mageverse, anything was possible.

"In a manner of speaking." Masara probed at her ribs, flinching as if it hurt. "But it's my magic doing the attacking." She moved to the full-length cheval mirror and turned her back to it, twisting around to examine herself.

Flipping on the overhead light, he took a step closer. And swore. The wounds raking across her back did indeed look as if a werewolf had ripped into her. Blood rolled from a dozen long slices, tracing crimson streams over her dark skin. "Oh my God." He started to reach for her, only to draw back, afraid of hurting her any worse.

"Actually, this isn't too bad," she said, appraising her injuries with surprising detachment. "You woke me up before she really got going."

He stared at her, sickened. "She?"

"Emily. My sister. Technically, half-sister."

"What?" And he remembered the flashing memory he'd seen of that face. "She did look a little like you."

"You saw that? Of course, our link's open. Sorry about that."

"Yeah, I thought a werewolf was attacking you. Scared the crap out of me."

"No werewolf, just Emily."

He folded his arms and eyed her. "Your sister could give a werewolf a run for his kibble in the bunny-boiling-crazy department."

"Emily wasn't crazy. Just spoiled."

Duncan gestured at her shredded back. "That's not spoiled, that's attempted murder."

"Oh, it was more than attempted." When he looked confused, she added in a cool, too-controlled voice, "I was pregnant. The beating was so severe, I miscarried."

He stared at her, completely at a loss. "I'm... so sorry."

"It was a long time ago, and Emily has been dead for most of it." She walked over to the dresser and picked up a bottle, then poured the amber contents into a crystal tumbler. She drank it down in one long draft. Magic flared, rolling over her in a glowing wave, swirled around her, and vanished. Her back was unmarked, as if the dream attack had never happened.

Reading the question in his mind, Masara lifted the bottle and shook it to make it slosh. "One of the healers gave me this for nights like this, when I'm too fried to work magic. Which always seems to be when I have that dream." She turned to the armoire in the corner, reached inside, and pulled out a long red robe. Sliding into it, she said, "Let's go to the great room. After that, we both need a drink."

He blinked at that. The most alcohol he'd ever seen her drink was a glass of wine at dinner. Apparently, this was going to be one hell of a conversation.

As they left the room and headed down the hall, he ventured a question. "This Emily -- was she a Latent too?" If Emily had been a descendant of one of the original knights and ladies of Camelot, she, like Masara, could have become a Maja.

"Yes, although we didn't know about the Magekind at the time. A few decades ago I got curious, so I did some scrying into the past. It seems our father descended from Galahad, who'd slept with one of our ancestors some generations back."

The great room was a cavernous space, lined with bookshelves stuffed with leather-bound volumes and paperbacks of every kind. A conversation pit held a semicircular wicker couch upholstered with an orange and red geometric African print. A magical fire burned in a huge copper bowl in the pit's center, producing light, but no heat or smoke. Masara headed for the elegant ebony bar. Duncan followed and leaned an elbow on its gleaming surface.

She grabbed a couple of cut crystal glasses, then poured each of them two fingers of from one the bottles on the bar. Curious, he picked the bottle up. Its label described it as a fifty-year-old single malt Scotch whisky. "Damn, this stuff is my mother's age. Do I want to know how much it cost?"

She smiled at him and lifted her glass in a toast. "Nope."

"It's good to be friends with a witch." Taking a reverent sip from his own glass, he discovered the whisky was delightfully smooth, with a rich, smoky taste. *Not as good as Masara, though...* He squelched the thought. He really didn't want to go there just now.

When she headed for the couch carrying the bottle and her glass, he followed. "I loved Emily when we were kids," Masara said after another meditative sip. "She was my big sister. My mother, who was her nursemaid, raised both of us -- that was how it was done then. I didn't realize Emily owned me until I was eight years old."

He stared at her. "I can't even imagine what that must've been like."

"Many of us worked very hard to ensure you can't." She took another sip and held the whisky in her mouth for a long moment. "When she was young, she wasn't so cruel. Spoiled, yes, not to mention convinced she occupied the pinnacle of creation. Just under her daddy."

"Sounds delightful," Duncan said dryly.

"My mother tried to warn me. 'Betsy, you can't trust them. You can't love them. You don't mean anything more to them than a hound. Less, because they're not afraid a hound is going to poison them or rise up in the night and murder everyone in the family.' And she was right."

His brows shot up. "Betsy?"

"We changed names frequently back then. Every time you got a new master, he changed your name.

When I became Magekind, I changed my name to Masara. It's Swahili for sorceress."

"It's pretty."

"Thank you." Masara stared into the fire a long moment. "I thought my mother was wrong. True, Emily hit me occasionally, but she always said I'd given her no choice."

Duncan scowled. "And you bought that?"

"I loved her. And I saw myself as…" She shrugged. "… less."

"You weren't."

"No, but it took me a very long time to realize that. The light dawned soon after Emily married Robert Townsend. She was seventeen, I was fifteen, and he was a handsome thirty-five year-old widower. Since I belonged to her, I went with her. She worshiped the ground he walked on." Masara's lip curled as her eyes blazed with old rage. "She had no idea. Me, I knew exactly what he had in mind."

"He raped you." His own fury began to rise.

"Robert wouldn't have described it in those terms. It never occurred to him I had the right to say no." Her dark eyes narrowed as she stared into a past he didn't even want to think about. "I knew better than to even try, though I quoted the Bible at the bastard at every turn, trying to remind him he was committing adultery. I did everything but try to fight him off." Her voice dropped into a deadly growl. "I didn't want to die, and he was a killer. All slaveholders were ruthless, but he was a sadist. Of course, when you have three hundred people in the middle of nowhere, how do you get them to work if you don't pay them?"

"By beating the fuck out of them."

"Yes. And they got away with it because on their plantations, they were gods."

Duncan wasn't sure he wanted to hear this, but he felt driven to learn as much about her as she could. "I never understood how anyone could do what they did."

"Money. Lots and lots and lots of money. They were the richest men in the country, and they did whatever they wanted to whomever they wanted. And they made sure the law was on their side." No matter how long it had been since her enslavement, the rage was still there. It had just gone deep and cold and glacial. "You could breed your slaves, sell them, and get even richer."

"So Robert got you pregnant."

"And Emily noticed the way her husband watched me."

He studied her. "I take it he wasn't exactly subtle."

"Of course not. It never dawned on him that she had any say about what he did."

He made himself ask the question. "When did she go after you?"

"After the fourth time I cast up my breakfast into a chamber pot." Masara grimaced. "Emily realized it was morning sickness and lost her mind. Dragged me out to the barn and laid into me with a strip of cowhide. After she was through with my back, she hit me across the face and sliced me open, temple to chin. And told me, 'He won't want you now.' I lost the baby and very nearly my life." She drained the glass in one long pull. "The horrible part was that I was relieved, though I knew it was a sin."

Duncan blinked. "Wait, what?"

"I'd seen what happened to my mother when Emily's father sold my older brother. It crushed Mama. I didn't want to suffer the same fate. But most of all, I didn't want my child to be a slave." Her eyes narrowed in an expression so cold, Duncan was glad it wasn't directed at him. "But Emily didn't gloat for long."

"Do I want to know why?"

She poured herself another glass and topped his off as well. "When Mama came to take care of me afterward, she said Robert had beaten Emily soundly." Glancing up, she caught his expression and snorted. "Not out of concern for me, I assure you. He could have sold our child for a thousand dollars as an adult, which translated to roughly the price of a new SUV today." He could feel the rage boiling just under her iron control. "Raping slaves wasn't just allowed, it was highly profitable."

The rage under that controlled surface seemed to burn him. He wanted her to let it out. To trust him that much. "You don't have to pretend with me, Masara."

She looked up at him. "Pretend what?"

"That this is an academic discussion of your dead child's financial value. It was fucking horrible, and you're entitled to be pissed."

"I know." She drained the glass. "But whenever I talk about those days, the old habits come back. Showing anger was a good way to lose the skin off your back." She stared at the stained-glass window. "Whites saw us as weak and contemptible for allowing ourselves to be slaves -- that's why they didn't want to let black men enlist in the Union Army. Now even our descendants see us that way. 'I'm not like them. I'd have kicked their asses.' Easy to say when you've never felt the whip."

He shifted, suddenly, painfully aware of the color of his skin. "I'm sorry." The words felt pitifully inadequate.

"You have nothing to be sorry for. You didn't do it."

"But I'm the beneficiary." The memory of Emily's jealousy-twisted face flashed through his mind, accompanied by the white-hot agony of her whip. Rage flamed up in him, hot and all consuming, until he wanted to go back in time and beat the shit out of Robert. But he couldn't. There wasn't a single fucking thing he could do for her.

"You know," Masara said, her tone musing, "I honestly thought the scars would keep him away. I guess I didn't understand any more than she did, because it was never really about sex. He wanted to breed me. And maybe teach Emily her place. He took me again as soon as I healed enough not to bleed." She paused to refill their glasses. "I knew he'd get me pregnant again, so I ran the minute he left. Just headed into the woods and took off. No plan, no money, not a thought in my head but rage. I was lucky I wasn't caught and hauled back to be beaten to death." She settled back into the couch cushions. "And I was running from one of the worst places in the country to run from -- South Carolina, hundreds of miles from the Mason-Dixon line. And me a woman on foot. Even if I'd made it to the North, they'd passed the Fugitive Slave Act, so the odds were some slave catcher would recapture me. I didn't care. I was headed to Canada."

"How'd you survive?"

"I'd heard a rumor about a woman who lived up in the North Carolina mountains, about a hundred miles from the plantation. They said she was a conductor in the Underground Railroad, meaning she helped slaves escape. Turned out, it was Belle."

Duncan turned to stare at her. "Tristan's Belle?"

"They weren't together then, but yes. She'd had a vision that a Latent they badly needed to recruit was going to stumble out of the woods." She shrugged and tipped her glass at him. "And so here I am."

His control shattered, and the words exploded from him in a snarl. "That was nice of them."

Masara eyed him. "I thought so."

"Why the fuck didn't they do something sooner?" He set the glass down and lunged to his feet. "Why the fuck did they let those bastards enslave you? Enslave *all* of you for all those centuries? They could have stopped it, and they didn't!"

She sighed. "Yeah, it infuriated me too for a very, very long time. It's only been in the past twenty years that I realized why someone couldn't just wave a magic wand and end slavery. Why we had to endure the enslavement of countless millions. Why we had to engineer a war that cost 620,000 lives."

He stared. "Wait, the Magekind engineered the Civil War?"

"Perhaps 'engineered' is the wrong word, but we did encourage it. Visions suggested slavery would endure for centuries otherwise. Too many people were making too much money. They were going to take it industrial."

"So why let it get started to begin with? There must have been another way."

"There wasn't." She watched as he turned and began to pace, trying to burn off his anger. "Merlin's law allows us to guide the people who fight evil, inspire them, help them with material assistance. We can work behind the scenes to defeat movements like the Confederacy, the Nazis, or the Taliban. But we can't force justice down humanity's throats. If we do that, we become dictators, not saviors."

He turned to pace again, trying to burn off his frustrated rage at what she'd suffered. "What did you do to Emily? After you became a Maja?"

"Nothing. Oh, I won't deny I dreamed of feeding her a fireball and castrating Robert. But I couldn't misuse the power I've been given." She smiled faintly. "I didn't want to take the chance."

"I'm not as evolved as you are," he growled.

"If you weren't, you'd still be in a wheelchair. They don't give people the Gift who indulge in petty revenge."

"I guess not." He paused to study her. "Belle's little job offer must've seemed unbelievable, given your background."

She lifted a dark brow. "Did *you* have the option of not believing when they offered you the Gift?"

"Good point."

"Besides, Belle had already demonstrated her abilities." Her expression went grim. "My wounds had become infected. I collapsed in the woods feverish and out of my head. Belle had a vision I was dying, and she gated directly to me. When I saw her step through that hole in the air, I thought she was a hallucination."

He laughed, though there was no real amusement in it. "I know the feeling."

"By the time I woke up, she'd healed me, and I knew all about the Magekind. Knew about them the way I knew my own name, because Belle had implanted the knowledge in my mind. I also knew I could become a witch like her. All I had to do was sleep with a vampire three times to activate Merlin's Gift." Masara sipped her whiskey. "But the most unbelievable part of it was that I was needed." To his shock, her voice cracked "The idea that they needed me to help free my people, that I could actually serve such a purpose…" She looked away.

He reached out and wrapped his fingers around hers, offering what comfort he could. "After what Robert had done… I mean, it couldn't have been easy to trust a man again."

"Belle brought in a Court Seducer." One of the Magekind who specialized in triggering Merlin's Gift in Latents. "He was from the African line of champions who aren't related to Arthur at all. He was very skilled, very kind. It was the first time I'd slept with anyone who cared about my pleasure."

That stung, never mind that it was years before Duncan had even been born. "I care."

"I know. I can feel it." She managed a smile for him. "It must've been even more of a shock for you. Your generation doesn't believe in magic at all."

Maybe it was time for a change of topic, at that. He wasn't sure he could take any more of Masara's straight-razor memories. "My doctor at Walter Reed told me I was being transferred to a private hospital in California." The Magekind had established Elysium Sanctuary to treat Latents who'd never received the Gift. "Confused the hell out of me. My dad's a construction worker and my mother's a librarian. We didn't have that kind of money or connections, but the doc said I had an anonymous benefactor. I'd been hospitalized for four months at that point, and I was still having surgeries." He sipped his Scotch, remembering the pain and despair of those days. "So they flew me to California. This Maja healer, Estelle, came into my room the next day. I thought she was some kind of nut when she started chanting over me. Then it started to hurt. A lot. I grabbed her hand and demanded what the hell she thought she was doing.

Estelle looked at me and shook her head. She said, 'Well, this isn't going to work.' I don't even remember passing out, but when I woke up, my dick was back."

Masara flinched.

"Yeah, I was leaping when I hit that second IED, so my legs were apart. That didn't end well."

"That's worse than my whipping story."

"Hardly. I was in Afghanistan because I wanted to be." He swallowed another hot mouthful of Scotch. "I woke up like you did, knowing it all. And then Estelle asked me what I would do if I could go back in time, back before the explosion. And I asked, 'You can do that?'"

"She couldn't. Even we can't time travel."

"No, but I didn't know that. The next thing I knew I was standing right there with the team of Afghan Army recruits I'd been helping train. Everything felt absolutely real. I thought it was real."

Masara winced. "At least they didn't make me relive that whipping. You really thought she'd sent you back in time to change your fate?"

"Estelle didn't actually say that, but it was the impression I got. We'd found this IED, and we were guarding it while we waited for EOD to come disarm it. Farijaad comes darting out of a side alley. His father was on the team, and the boy hadn't seen him in a month. The IED was between us and the kid. I saw the look of horror on his daddy's face. Everybody was yelling, but Farijaad didn't stop. I don't think he understood -- he was maybe six."

Masara shook her head "I read your file, but I didn't know the details. This is worse than I thought."

"I assumed someone else would save Farijaad. See, I'd second-guessed myself a lot, wondering if his dad could've gotten to him in time, or maybe just told him to stop. But then I realized that no, that child was going to die. I fucking couldn't let that happen,"

"Of course not."

"I jumped a hell of a lot farther, trying to clear both pressure plates -- the one we knew about and the one I'd come down on." He drained his Scotch, remembering the deafening sound, the smoke, the pain. Lying in the dirt street. Turning his head to see one of his legs a few feet away...

"Then BOOM -- I was back in bed with my legs gone. I thought I'd fucked up my one chance, but Estelle told me it had all been an illusion -- a test to see if I was worthy. I was furious. But before I could tell her what I thought of her, this gorgeous woman walks through the door. The Court Seducer. Estelle left, and we spent the next three hours making love."

"Given that you didn't even have a cock an hour before, that must have been some experience."

"Oh, God, yes. I was a hell of a lot more upset about losing my dick than my legs. There are surgical interventions, but it's not the same. The third time the Seducer came, Merlin's Gift hit me like a lightning bolt. It felt as if every cell in my body was exploding. Hurt worse than the IED. Next thing I knew, I was back. *All* of me."

Silently, she leaned in and filled his glass again. He lifted it to her in a toast. "To second chances."

"May we not screw them up."

They drank.

For a long moment, they sat in silence. "Getting close to dawn," Masara said quietly.

"I remind you of him, don't I?"

Her eyes slid away from his.

"I'm not like that, Masara."

"I know you're not. Otherwise I'd never have slept with you."

"What can I do?" He reached out and took her hand in his and met her eyes. "How can I help you heal?"

She smiled, but it looked forced. "I am healed, Duncan. It was fifteen decades ago, and Robert is dust in his grave."

"Then why did I see his eyes in your dream?"

"It was just a dream."

"'Just dreams' don't cut your back to ribbons." He stroked his fingers across her knuckles, trying to see to the bottom of those dark, dark eyes. "The last thing I want to do is tear into old scars."

"Duncan, any wounds I've suffered, I healed." Gently, Masara pulled her hand away from his. "You do realize that you've only got a few minutes to get to bed?" She flashed him a smile. "I can carry you with my magic, of course, but…"

It was a dismissal, and Duncan knew it. "Yeah, I'm not sure my fragile male ego would survive the trip." He put the glass down on the table with a clink. *Fuck it*, he thought, and leaned in slowly, giving her plenty of time to object. When she didn't he kissed her, making it as tender and sweet as he could. "With me, no always means no," he whispered against her mouth.

She smiled and laid a hand against his cheek. "I know, Duncan. Sleep well."

\* \* \*

In his room, he lost no time skimming out of his jeans. Flipping the covers down, he crawled into bed. At least he didn't have long to brood before the sun came up and put him out of his misery. It was sickening to realize that his eyes reminded Masara of slavery and brutalization. *Do I have any hope at all?* And yet, he couldn't seem to give up. He wanted her. Wanted to be with her. If she'd have him. If he could make her forget Robert. If not...

*Damn it, sun, would you rise alr...*

\* \* \*

The roar sent his hindbrain in a convulsion of terror. *Oh, Christ, what now?* Duncan grabbed for the sheathed sword hanging from his bedpost, and his feet hit the floor before his eyes were even open. He drew it as another roar sounded. It was coming from outside. "Masara!" Lunging for the veranda doors, he threw them open.

A huge shape flew past, blocking out the sky. Duncan thought it was an airplane until the wings beat, and he realized it had a beak. Moonlight rolled across fur and feathers as the creature spiraled in for a landing on the wide swath of rolling grassland that surrounded the city. *Damn, that's a griffin.*

He'd heard all kinds of weird shit lived in the Mageverse, but how was a cross between a lion and an eagle even possible? Especially given that the thing must be the size of an elephant... As the griffin touched down, something even bigger tipped up a triangular head and breathed a gout of flame. "Holy shit." Other huge heads turned to watch.

Dragons. There must be dozens of them out there.

Duncan had met a dragon once during training. Kel was a Knight of the Round Table, but he was also the only member of the shapeshifting Dragonkind who lived in Avalon. So where had all those others come from?

"You do realize you're standing there stark naked?" Masara asked from the doorway, sounding amused. "And that sword you're holding is a practice weapon."

*Crap.* Before he could retreat into the house, a wave of magic rolled up his body. When he looked down, he saw he was wearing the same leather garb he'd worn the day before. Even his scent had changed; evidently she'd cast one of those cleaning spells she used when there was no time for a proper shower.

"Not that I disapprove of the view," Masara added, one corner of her lips lifting in a smile.

Duncan relaxed. If the shit had truly hit the fan, she'd have looked a lot more concerned. "What's going on?"

"The Fomorians have attacked Llyr's palace." Llyr was king of the Sidhe, Mageverse Earth's version of humanity. He was also Arthur's ally. "Evidently King Bres was indeed using the peace talks to buy time to get his forces into position. We're officially at war." Her mouth flattened. "Which means you and I will have no backup at all." She turned and walked back into the bedroom.

"Wait, we're not joining in the fighting?" Duncan followed her.

"No," Masara told him as they walked into the thoroughly twenty-first-century kitchen, where she had a meal waiting in the breakfast nook. Evidently, they wouldn't be eating on the veranda tonight. "Walker found out who the werewolves are, and he needs our help taking them down before they murder another mortal. We're going to grab breakfast and gate over there."

"How did he figure that out?"

"A Direkind woman named Amy Harrington went to check on her parents and found their house empty and splattered with blood. Judging by the scent patterns, she thinks her father attacked her mother Friday night. Walker believes they both killed the jogger Saturday morning." She poured him a glass from a bottle, handed it to him, then sat down at her place at the table. "We're supposed to meet him at the Harrington house and try to get a lead on where they might have gone and what caused them to do this."

Duncan took a sip from his glass. It tasted flat and unsatisfying after the memory of drinking from Masara's throat. "How did you spend the day? Because I can tell by looking at you it wasn't sleeping."

She shot him a cool glance over a bowl of what looked like oatmeal. "Flatterer. And anyway, I did sleep."

"Let me guess -- about three hours. You worked a lot of magic yesterday, Masara. You're probably going to work more today. You can't do that running on fumes."

Masara snorted. "I was fighting wars a century before your great-granddaddy was born."

"Did you know your southern accent gets thick when you're tired?"

"You're one to talk, Magnolia Mouth. Drink your breakfast."

He obeyed, but he watched her as he did so -- the graceful, precise movements of her right hand as she ate, the little frown line between her brows. The way her full lips closed around her spoon, long lashes casting shadows on her down-turned, angular face. The bands on her dreads glittered as she moved her head. Desire rose in him, even hotter for the taste of her on his tongue. He shifted, feeling his cock harden. Good thing the table concealed his lap. He wanted her so badly his fangs ached.

*Patience, Marine. It's her call. After what happened to her, I'm damned if I'm going to push.* All he could do was wait and hope that she was willing to look past her ghosts.

# Chapter Six

It didn't look like a werewolf's kitchen, not that Duncan had any idea what a werewolf's kitchen was supposed to look like. The cabinetry was white, with dark green marble countertops, potted plants sitting here and there between stainless steel appliances.

A woman sat on a barstool at the kitchen island, looking stunned as the dimensional gate vanished behind them. Her hazel eyes were so red and swollen from crying, they clashed with the bright copper of the long hair she wore in a messy knot on top of her head. She wasn't particularly tall, but her body looked lean in black leggings and a long, sky-blue tunic. Duncan thought she'd probably be pretty if she didn't look so devastated.

"Good of you to come," Walker said, giving them a nod from the opposite side of the island. "I've got a feeling we're going to need all the help we can get. We found a key piece of evidence, but I wanted to brief you before you take a look."

"We're glad to help," Masara told him. "The last thing we want is for someone else to die."

The woman rose from her chair, moving like someone who'd taken a beating. Walker turned to her with a compassionate smile. "This is Masara Okeye and her partner Duncan Carpenter of the Magekind. Folks, Amy Harrington. She needs some help with her parents."

Masara extended a hand, sympathy softening her gaze. "I'm so sorry. I can only imagine how painful this must be for you."

"Yes." Amy's voice cracked, and she visibly fought grief. "Dad's not like this! He'd never hurt anyone, especially not my mother..." She choked back a sob.

Duncan's heart seemed to contract in his chest. He'd seen that dazed expression too many times overseas on those who'd just watched family members die. Cut adrift, flailing in a world plunged into chaos and blood.

"I understand," Masara said, laying a hand on the woman's shoulder.

"He's never been violent to my mom. He's just not like this. I don't understand. Something's wrong here!" She stared up and Masara, her gaze pleading for understanding, for belief, for some explanation for what had happened to her family.

Masara sat down at the island, facing Amy, so their knees brushed. Duncan and Walker exchanged a silent glance and eased backward to lean against the kitchen wall, giving the Maja room to work.

Duncan's gaze fell on the bay window beyond them. It was a glorious fall night, the trees awash with moonlight. A huge cedar play set dominated the yard, an elaborate cedar structure with swings, a slide, and a rock-climbing wall, topped with a sturdy fort. *Oh great. She's got kids. Kids whose grandparents have been murdering people.*

"What can you tell us?" Masara asked softly.

Amy looked blindly around. Walker straightened, lifted a box of tissues off the countertop, and handed it to her. She took a Kleenex and blew her nose. "Tom and I are celebrating our fifteenth anniversary this week. We were supposed to fly to New York tomorrow night. Mom and Dad were taking the kids to Disney World -- they were going to swing by and pick them up this morning." A tear rolled silently down her cheek, and she paused to pluck another tissue and wipe her eyes. "We were all busy packing, and I knew Dad was trying to wrap things up at his shop. When I didn't hear anything from them, at first I didn't think anything of it. But after they didn't show up this morning, I decided to drop by and check on them." A spasm of grief and horror twisted her face. "I smelled blood when I walked in the door."

Her hand tightened hard on the wadded Kleenex, and Duncan was startled to see a crimson stain spreading through the tissue. Her fingernails had lengthened and curled into claws on her human fingers, cutting into her palms. She didn't appear to notice.

"I thought someone had... attacked them, but the only recent scents were Mom's and Dad's. But he didn't smell right. He smelled... sick. And really pissed-off." For a moment, anger broke through her grief, and she straightened, her tone going fierce. "Jack Rand never lifted a hand to my mother, ever. Would never. Something made him do that. Some spell or sickness or... I don't know. But it wasn't his fault."

*It never is*, Duncan thought.

Hunching in on herself, Amy began to cry. Masara slid from her seat and pulled the woman into her arms. Amy clung to her as the Maja stroked her hair, her face compassionate. The witch looked up, her gaze meeting Walker's in a silent request for information.

"She called her husband and he called me," the cop said quietly. "I met them at the scene. The initial attack took place in the bedroom. The bed..."

"It was a wreck," Amy said, blotting her eyes. "They'd fought and clawed it up, and she bled... I think he must've bitten her. There was a lot of blood." Her eyes went unfocused. "There's a blood trail all the way through the house where she ran from him. He bled too -- she did fight back -- but it didn't smell right. It... We followed the scent trail out into the woods. She stopped fighting him. I think maybe she lost consciousness. It smelled like they stayed there together overnight. We went to CyberWizard's..."

"CyberWizard's?" Duncan asked

"That's Dad's shop. He repairs computers." Amy frowned. "There were some really weird scents there. Animal smells. Blood and sickness, but faint, as if it had been washed away. I think he must have hosed down the parking lot. We followed his trail to a grave in the field behind the strip mall where he'd buried something. We dug it up. I was afraid it might be..." She broke off, blinking hard. "But there were thirty-four rat corpses."

Masara's brows climbed. "*Rat* corpses?"

She nodded. "Big ones, too. Tom said he thought they were Norwegian wharf rats. I didn't even know we had any of those around here."

"Rand had killed them all." Walker put in. "Ripped some of them to pieces, bitten others. And they all smelled of his blood. They must've attacked him, and he had to fight them off. From the scents, it happened several hours before he went after his wife. He didn't smell sick at the time of the rat attack, but all the rats stank."

"So it's possible they're the source of the infection." Masara straightened, her gaze going focused and intent. "What did you do with these corpses?"

"I bagged one of them for you. It's in the back of the SUV. I reburied the others, since I was afraid they were contagious."

"Good thinking. I'd like to see this rat."

Amy reached out and caught Masara's wrist. "Do you think it was a spell? Or some kind of disease?"

She hesitated. "I don't know. It could be, but we'll need to learn more."

Amy bit her lower lip. "If it is, will you be able to cure it?"

"I don't know." Masara gave her shoulder a comforting squeeze. "I will certainly do everything I can."

\* \* \*

The four of them walked out to Walker's sheriff's department SUV. Walker pulled his keys from his pocket and thumbed the fob. The trunk popped open. "It's right in... Holy shit!"

Among a neatly organized collection of police gear lay the remains of an empty plastic bag and shreds of duct tape. "What the hell? My car was locked!" The sergeant started to snatch up the plastic bag. "How did somebody get in to steal..."

"Don't touch it," Masara ordered. She gestured, and the bag floated upward. Amy gasped at her, eyes huge. Duncan realized it must be the first time she'd seen a witch work magic. "Let me check that bag first."

Walker stepped back from the SUV as he stared around warily, scenting the air. To Masara, he said, "Hey, would you cast one of those invisibility spells of yours? I want to sniff around."

She nodded. "Of course." She gestured and the smell of ozone filled the air like smoke, magic flared around the cop as he shifted.

The big werewolf sniffed the SUV, then the bag still hovering in the air. "Nothing on the truck. Not smelling anything on the bag either. And if Rand ripped it open, his scent should be all over it. I'm not smelling anything but rat."

Amy recoiled, her eyes going wide. "Do you think it... escaped?"

Walker frowned down at her -- at least, Duncan thought that was a frown. "It was dead. Disemboweled. I may not know what the hell is going on, but I know dead."

"Maybe another rat got it," Duncan suggested.

"The SUV was locked," the cop protested. "How the hell would it have gotten in?"

"Is there such a thing as shape-shifting rats?"

Walker glowered. "Don't be ridiculous."

Duncan pointed a finger at each of them in turn. "Hey, vampire, witch, werewolves. Why not shape-shifting rats? Or, hell, zombie rats?"

"Because it's bullshit. I'm going to look for a scent trail."

"I'll help." Drawing on the Mageverse as he'd been taught, Duncan shifted to wolf form -- and so did Amy, to his surprise. She was a delicately built Dire Wolf next to Walker's muscular bulk, with fur as red as an Irish Setter's. Together they searched the entire area, but they found nothing.

"Maybe whoever took the rat drove away in a car," Masara suggested after they all shifted back.

"They would still have had to walk to the car," Walker told her. "There's no scent trail at all. It's as if it just flew away."

*Flying zombie rats*? Duncan kept the thought to himself. He had the feeling no one would appreciate the joke. He eyed Masara, whose attention had returned to the hovering plastic bag, her long fingers flicking to turn it this way and that. "Anything?"

"Whatever was in this bag was definitely dead. Now, whether it was dead when it left the bag is a different question."

"Are you saying it got out of that bag under its own power?" Walker demanded, a definite canine rumble in his voice.

"I don't know, but it does appear the bag was torn open from the inside."

Amy stared at her. "So we *are* dealing with a zombie rat?"

"Not necessarily. Could be a spell." She flicked a hand, and a box appeared in her palm. It flipped open and the bag floated into it. The lid snapped closed and she gestured. The box vanished with an audible pop. "I'll take a look in the Mageverse where the magic's stronger. There are a few spells I can try there I can't work here. Whatever that rat was, I don't think it's immune to magic."

"First good news we've had all day," Walker growled.

* * *

As they returned to the kitchen, Amy caught Masara's arm. She looked very young. Very vulnerable. "Can you help them? If it's a black magic spell, can you break it? Can you heal them?"

*Not if spells don't work on them,* Duncan thought.

Masara wrapped her strong fingers around the other woman's and gave her a comforting squeeze. "We'll do everything we can. Do you have any idea where they might have gone?"

Amy shook her head. "We looked everywhere we could think of."

Duncan caught a flash of movement out of the corner of one eye. He turned to see a young boy hovering in the doorway, looking tense and frightened.

The kid had a head full of dark curls and big brown eyes, and though he was older and his skin paler, something about him reminded Duncan of Farijaad.

The kid saw him looking and retreated quickly. The fear and vulnerability on the young face made Duncan long to comfort him. He found himself following. He rounded the corner to see the child perched on the flight of steps leading to the second floor, hands twisted together in anxiety. "Is my granddad dead?" Enormous dark eyes stared pleadingly into his.

A lie leaped to Duncan's mouth, but he swallowed it. "We don't know. We don't think so." He dropped to one knee in front of the kid and offered his hand. "I'm Duncan Carpenter."

The boy hesitated a moment, then solemnly took his hand, squeezed, and shook once, as if following parental instructions. "My name's Liam Harrington. I'm ten. And a half." He bit his lower lip. "Grandpa did something bad to my grandma, didn't he?"

"We don't know that either. Not for sure."

"Mama picked up the scents. I heard her and my dad talking. She said it smelled like Grandpa bit Grandma. Bit her bad." In a rush he added, "But he loves my grandma. He wouldn't do that. Did witches put a spell on him? Did y'all do something to him?"

"We don't do things like that. We're the good guys." Duncan managed a reassuring smile. The suspicion in those brown eyes reminded him far too much of Afghanistan.

"I heard the policeman say my grandma and grandpa killed a jogger lady. Did a bad witch turn them into serial killers?" His lower lip trembled. "Are they going to kill me too?"

"Of course not. Your grandparents love you. They'd never hurt you." Never mind that he didn't know what the hell he was talking about. "We'll find your grandparents, and we'll do everything we can to help them."

"Are you really a vampire?"

He blinked. "Well... yeah."

"If you try to bite me, my momma will turn into a werewolf and *eat* you."

"I don't bite little boys." *I save my bites for grown witches. Preferably Masara.* "We're the good guys, remember?"

Liam eyed him suspiciously. "The vampires on television are evil."

"Television people also think werewolves are evil."

Liam considered that solemnly. "Mama says they make stuff up." He appraised Duncan. "You promise you'll save them?"

Reaching out, he gripped the kid's knee, gave it a little squeeze. "We'll do everything we can." *I just hope it's enough.*

A tall, dark-haired man stepped out into the hallway, carrying a red-haired little girl in one arm, though she was well past the age of being a comfortable burden. Tears tracked the child's face, and her big blue eyes were swollen and red.

"Time for bed, Liam." Tom Harrington was muscular, with a long, bearded face and dark eyes that matched his son's. The boy nodded and scrambled up the stairs ahead of his father. The two men exchanged a nod as Duncan stepped back, giving the children's father room to pass.

Heading back into the kitchen Duncan found Masara still talking to Amy.

"It would be best if I cleaned your parents' house sooner rather than later," the witch said. "Eventually someone's going to go by and check."

"You can... you can do that? There's so much blood. I was dreading..."

Masara's eyes were warm with compassion. "I can take care of it all with my magic. Even the smell will be gone."

"Thank you. That'd be a big help." But she didn't smile when she said it.

Duncan didn't blame her.

\* \* \*

He'd seen some gut-twisting shit overseas -- hell, he'd been directly involved in some of it. But there was something about the Rand house that made his hair stand on end.

That was partly because of his new vampire senses. He'd known terror had a scent -- the jogger's body had reeked of it. But there was so much sickness, fear, and desperation hanging in the air at the couple's home, it made him want to jump out of his skin.

A couple of days before, the place must have looked like somebody's Pinterest page. Except for the blood trail, it was perfectly clean and beautifully decorated, with care in the selection of every photo, houseplant, and stick of furniture. All of which made the pall of blood and horror more gut wrenching.

Masara, Duncan, and Walker searched the house, the cop in Dire Wolf form, the Magekind with swords drawn. Though Walker had already been through once with Amy and her husband, there was always the possibility Jack and Ellie had returned.

Moving through the kitchen and down the hall, they carefully sidestepped the dried blood trails, dark brown against the pale hardwood of the hallway. Some of those paw prints were only a little smaller than dinner plates.

The cop and the two Magekind examined the trail grimly. "We definitely have to clean this up," Duncan said.

"That's putting it mildly." It was obvious neither the victim nor her attacker had been human.

They followed the trail to the Rands' master bedroom to find the splintered door hanging from one warped hinge. "See the way it's smashed?" Walker said. "I think she broke it down trying to get away from him."

Glancing inside, Duncan swore. The king-sized oak bed looked as if a pig had been slaughtered on it. The mattress and comforter were covered in blood and clawed to ribbons. A bedside lamp lay on the floor, shattered, and the oak bureau lay on its side, half crushed, as splintered as the door. "Looks like she tried to block his path with it, but he crashed right through."

Masara studied the scene grimly. "I'm going to have to burn that bed and create a new one. Magic is not going to get that blood out."

Walker shifted back to human. When he saw Duncan's questioning glance, he explained, "I don't think we're likely to be attacked here. Judging by the scents, they haven't been here in a couple days."

"What did you learn when you searched the house with Amy and her husband?" Masara asked.

The deputy shoved his hands in his uniform pants. "It's a little hard to tell because of the way the scents are layered, but I don't think she was sick when she lay down with him. She was worried as hell, though."

"She had good reason to be," Duncan said.

"Sometime during the night, he attacked her." Walker gestured at the wall, where blood splattered a framed wedding photograph of a lovely redheaded woman in what looked like a mile of white silk, lace, and seed pearls. Her green eyes sparkled as she smiled up at a tall, handsome man in a white tux, who grinned down at her, obviously besotted. Duncan winced. *Poor fuckers.*

As he studied the wedding photo, he felt an uncomfortable combination of pity and a kind of aching envy. No matter how it had gone bad at the end, at least they'd had that radiant love for more than thirty years. He and Masara had barely managed a single night...

"Here's what I think is the timeline," Walker said, jolting Duncan out of his moment of self-pity. "Sunday night infected rats attack Jack Rand as he's leaving his business. He fights them, kills them, and buries them in a hole behind the shop, then hoses down the parking lot so his neighbors won't see the blood everywhere when they come to work the next morning. By the time he gets home, he's already sick. He and his wife go to bed. Sometime in the middle of the night, Jack attacks her. He chases her through the house and out into the woods, where she collapses. He doesn't attack her again, just stays with her. Judging by the scents, she starts getting sick. By ten o'clock the next morning, she's as crazy as he is. They both kill the jogger."

"And it starts with those rats," Masara said.

"Killer rabid zombie rats," Duncan added.

"Not funny," Walker growled.

"Nope," he agreed, and turned to Masara. "What kind of *Night of the Living Dead* crap is going on here?"

"I have no idea." She glared at the bed. "But I'm going to try a scrying spell and see what I can find out."

Walker frowned. "Scrying spell?"

"A spell to see the future, past, or something some distance away in the present. I don't know if it'll work, given that we're dealing with werewolves, but if they interact with humans, I may be able to see the mortals." She shrugged. "It's certainly worth a try, and it's not as if we have a lot of other leads." Masara began to pace around the room eyeing the arrangement of furniture. A gesture sent a rocking chair sliding into the corner, followed a moment later by the chest that stood at the end of the bed. A wave of sparkles splashed over the bed, lifting it as if it weighed no more than a paperback and wafting it into the middle of the room. Duncan and Walker stepped hastily out of the way.

"What the hell is she doing?" Walker asked Duncan as she began to walk a slow circle around the bed. Where she stepped, a line of something that glittered appeared on the hardwood floor.

"Casting the most powerful spell she can."

Walker frowned, watching lit candles appear around the circle's perimeter. "I thought all they had to do was wave and point."

"Usually, but when things get hairy, they use rituals to amplify their power, especially in this dimension. My instructor said it's kind of like directing sunlight through a magnifying glass to set something on fire."

Masara sent them an irritated glare. "Would you be quiet? I'm trying to work."

"Fair enough," Walker said. "While you're doing that, I want to search the rest of the house again. See if I can find any indication this isn't rabid zombie rats." He grimaced, then looked at Duncan. "Want to give me a hand?"

"Can't. I have to be her spotter in case something goes wrong."

Walker snorted, watching Masara climb up on the bloody bed and sink into a Lotus position. "Yeah, I can see how that might be a concern. Better you than me. This witch stuff freaks me right out." Shaking his head, he went off to conduct his search.

Duncan moved closer until he stood at the edge of the circle. The smell of incense from the candles rose in the air, competing with the stench of dried blood and horror.

"Don't break the circle unless you think it's an emergency," Masara told him.

"Yeah, I remember the class." He also remembered some of the hair-raising stories about what could go wrong in a ritual. He just hoped none of it would happen today.

Masara closed her eyes, and magic rose up, the circle beginning to glow around her. Her dreads stirred as if in a wind as she sat in a Lotus Position, her feet hooked over her thighs, her palms resting open on her knees. She began to chant, the candle flames stretching upward, though by all rights the wind whipping through the circle should have put them out. Her dark face seemed to glow.

Duncan had no idea what language she was speaking. He didn't think it was the Latin many Majae used in rituals; the cadence sounded more musical than that. Could be an African language, like the Swahili she'd used to name herself.

The smell of incense and ozone grew more intense, overwhelming even the smell of decaying blood. Her chanting picked up speed, growing louder, as her expression tightened with effort. Her eyes flew open. They were completely black, the sclera gone, tiny points of light sparkling against the utter darkness.

*Stars.* Hair rose on the back of his neck.

The psychic link snapped open between them, and she thundered into his mind. Duncan staggered as they fused until it was hard to tell where he left off and she began. Images and emotions swamped him even as he realized she didn't even know he was there. She was totally focused on her fight to see the future -- to keep anyone else from dying. To prevent more victims from suffering as she'd suffered. Her soul still reverberated with grief for people who'd died fifteen decades before he was born.

Time ripped around him like rotten cotton. Fire exploded across his shoulders and down his back, and a horrible pressure ground between his legs, forcing its way into his body. *Hurts, oh God, it hurts…*

*Christ, it's a penis. Robert. She's remembering Robert…*

And then, thank God, the tearing pain was gone. A hand hit his face so hard he saw stars. A female voice shrieked, *"Who do you think you are? You're nothing! I'm no blood of yours. You're cursed like the rest of your kind, you little slut!"*

Then that too was gone, swept away as she fought to see the werewolves' next victim. See them so she could save them…

And prove *her* wrong. *You're nothing!*

Masara knew she wasn't the most powerful Maja. She certainly wasn't the most experienced. But she was, by God, the most stubborn. She would not fail these people. That would be the same as if she'd killed the victims herself. She had to find who was doing this and stop them, no matter what it took. Even if it meant dying…

*Oh, fuck no, you don't!* Denial rang through Duncan's soul like a scream. *I'm not going to let you die. I'm not going to lose you!*

*Duncan? What are you…?*

*You pulled me in.*

Horrified embarrassment swamped her as she realized how much he'd seen. An answering guilt stung him, as if she'd caught him peeking through her bedroom window. *Hey, it wasn't my idea…*

She thrust him out of her mind so hard, he staggered and almost fell on his ass. "Damn it, Masara!"

Masara blinked, and the magic vanished from her eyes. "I didn't know you were there. I'm sorry you…" She broke off and rubbed both hands over her face. "I couldn't see a damn thing." She clamped her mouth shut as the fine muscles of her jaw worked. At last she said, "But I don't think anything's going to happen tonight." Rolling off the bed, she gestured. The candles disappeared, leaving behind a faint tang of incense and ozone. The smell of decaying blood rushed back, so intense it was all Duncan could do not to gag.

Walker stuck his head in the door. "Everything okay in here? I thought I heard someone shout." His gaze flicked to Duncan, who realized it must've been him.

"Everything's fine," he said shortly.

Walker just looked at him, one eyebrow climbing.

"Do we have everything we need out of this room?" Masara's tone sounded cool and clipped.

The sergeant frowned. "I think so. The Harringtons and I searched it earlier. Didn't find anything beyond that." He gestured at the bloody bed.

"Then I'm going to take care of this mess."

They all retreated out into the hallway. Masara gestured, and a glowing barrier appeared over the door. She muttered something under her breath, and the bed ignited, blazing up like a torch. Walker hissed a curse as the ceiling caught. The whole room flashed white and the floor vibrated under them with a muffled *whooooom*! When the light disappeared, the walls were charred, the furniture little more than blackened sticks.

"Shit!" Walker sounded appalled. "Those are load-bearing walls! Do you want the house to collapse?"

"Please, give me a little credit." Masara indicated the barrier over the doorway. "That barrier surrounds the room, including the floor and ceiling. It contained the blast." Duncan felt the surge of magical effort a heartbeat before another blinding flash. A glance through the door showed the room looked complexly untouched, the walls white again, the bed whole and neatly made under a cream comforter covered in tiny blue wildflowers. Even the pictures on the wall were back, the Rand family smiling out at the world as if their lives hadn't gone to hell forty-eight hours before.

The werewolf blinked and shot her a respectful glance. "It's a good thing you're one of the good guys, because we'd never catch you."

Her lips twitched at the grudging compliment. "Come on, I need to take care of the rest of the house."

They turned down the hallway, following the blood. Walker paused to stare at the huge bloody paw print on the floor. "Here's what I don't get. I've been around Jack when he shifts -- we used to hunt deer in Dire Wolf form. He's maybe two-thirds this size normally. This isn't just some kind of disease. It didn't just drive Jack and Ellie crazy, it altered them." The cop shook his head. "He spoke to me during that attack at the hospital. Didn't even sound like him. Not just physically, either. The word choice was seriously weird... All that stuff about dogs and meat."

"Which begs the question, what the hell is doing this?" Duncan said, rubbing a hand over his jaw.

Walker eyed Masara. "You guys sure you killed Warlock? Because this is the kind of shit he did. Like the guy he turned into the giant snake, or that centaur thing who killed those humans."

Masara frowned. "Walker, I saw Arthur take the wizard's head. Warlock's as dead as it gets. Besides, none of the people he transformed into those creatures were werewolves when he created them. Even as powerful as Warlock was, he couldn't cast a spell on people who were already Dire Kind. His magic didn't work on you either. Merlin designed them that way so the Magekind couldn't cast spells on them. And if magic didn't work on them, they couldn't cast spells either."

Walker flicked a finger at the paw print. "Then what's doing this? Diseases don't make you eight feet tall or talk like something out of a horror movie."

Propping her fists on her hips, she stared down at the bloody prints. "I have no idea."

# Chapter Seven

When they gated to the Harrington home half an hour later, they found Amy sitting on the couch with her husband. She rose to her feet, her gaze measuring and wary, with painful hope beneath. "How did it go?"

*Not good. I don't think we can save your parents.* But Masara couldn't bring herself to say the words aloud. "I cleaned the house. Everything is back to rights."

A fraction of the tension left Amy's shoulders. "Thank you. Do you have any idea what caused them to…" She broke off, as if unable to finish the sentence.

"I'm still working on it. It's not a spell, that much I know. The only magic I detected is werewolf magic."

"What about Warlock's daughter, Miranda Justice? And her husband. Maybe they could help."

"Yes, and I'm sure they will. But the Magekind are in the middle of a battle right now, and they're too powerful to be spared."

"An actual battle?" Amy stared at her. "Who are they fighting? Nobody human is a match for…"

"The war's on Mageverse Earth. There's this race called the Fomorians, and their king is intent on conquering…" It was too complicated to get into. "Never mind. They're tied up right now, but I'm sure they'll help when they can."

As if trying to help smooth things over, Walker said, "I issued a BOLO for your parents' SUV. We know they took it. Once someone spots it, that should give us a place to look. In the meantime, you and I need to fill out a missing person's report."

"Yes, of course."

He nodded. "The paperwork's in my SUV. I'll go get it."

Fifteen minutes later, Masara watched as the cop and the Harringtons worked their way through the report. A headache throbbed behind her eyes, a warning that she'd worked far too much magic today.

"So," Duncan murmured, "if I were a mutated werewolf bitten by rabid zombie rats, what would I do next? Who's my next target?"

Masara blinked as cold realization struck, abrupt as a bullet. She lifted her voice to catch the cop's attention. "I need a word with you, Sergeant."

Walker looked up at her, then told the Harringtons, "Give me a minute. I'll be right back."

Masara, Duncan, and the werewolf stepped out into the hall. "Somebody needs to watch this house," she told them in a low voice. "If Jack attacked his wife so he could infect her, he might come after his daughter and her family next. That may be the reason why I couldn't scry anything. If his next targets are werewolves…"

"That's a damned good point," Walker said. He fell silent a long moment, frowning as if considering the angles. "Normally I'd try to get my lieutenant to assign someone to keep an eye on things, but that's obviously not an option with this."

"We're going to have to do it ourselves," Masara agreed. She studied the big cop. "How long has it been since you had any sleep?"

He sighed. "About forty-eight hours. Not the best circumstances for a stakeout."

"I've had more sleep than either of you," Duncan said. "I can take the first watch."

"And I could put a ward up around the house," Masara said thoughtfully. "Something to alert us and delay them from getting inside until we can put a stop to it."

"Would that kind of magic even work on them?" Walker asked.

"The Direkind may be immune to magic, but you're not immune to electricity. A ward designed to generate an electric discharge when it's broken would stop you in your tracks."

"It could also prove an ugly surprise for the garbage man."

"Not if I key it to respond only to those with magic. Besides, the idea isn't to kill anyone, just slow them down long enough for us to mount a defense."

"That might work. The problem is, I'm on duty from eight a.m. to six p.m. I could be here by six-thirty, but that leaves you alone for several hours while Duncan is in his Daysleep. You can call me if there's an attack and I'll come running, but it would still take me time to get here."

"Didn't you say there were other werewolves in town?" Duncan asked. "Couldn't some of them back her up?"

Walker rubbed his chin, considering it. "Maybe. There are ten of us, counting me, our bad guys, and the Harringtons. Two others are elderly. Another is a single mother with kids, so she's out. There are a couple of single guys, though. I could call, see if they can give us a hand."

Duncan looked back into the living room, where Tom sat with his arms around his wife, whispering into her hair. "We'd probably better give the Harringtons a head's up too, especially if we're going to be hanging out in the yard and setting up electricity-generating spells."

"I'll take care of that," Masara told him.

"Good. I'll make those calls."

While he walked off down the hall, Duncan and Masara started hashing out the details of the plan. He wasn't particularly pleased when she told him he'd have to gate back to the Mageverse during the Daysleep.

"If you're in a coma, you're nothing but a hostage," she argued. "We did that when Warlock invaded Avalon. A swarm of werewolves grabbed Arthur and his knights and hauled them around like sacks of flour. If a fairy goddess hadn't taken an interest, we'd all be dead. So, no, not doing that again. You're sleeping at the house in the morning."

"What if you're butt deep in werewolves by the time I wake up, and I'm stuck in the Mageverse? I'd have to go find someone to gate me."

"I'll put a gate spell on your armor. It'll transport you wherever I am."

"Jesus. Would you at least try Belle again?"

So she did. And once again, got nothing but a blast of mystical static.

When Walker stomped around the corner wearing a pissed expression, Duncan swore in sheer frustration. "That about sums it up," the cop said. "According to their grandma, both those idiots are in fricking jail in Daytona Beach. Got drunk and disorderly and busted up a bar. And to put the cherry on the shit sundae, they put another guy in the hospital, so they're charged with aggravated assault. Only decent part of the whole thing is at least they weren't furry at the time. They won't even be able to see a judge until sometime tomorrow afternoon. No way are they going to be back in time to do us any damn good." He scrubbed his hands through his hair. "Then I tried to call the Wolf Sheriff." Whom he'd said was the enforcer for the Council of Clans. "He's currently in California, hunting a werewolf serial killer there who's murdered six women, which is why I couldn't get his help with this to begin with. Only I couldn't get through, not to him or any other werewolf I know."

Masara frowned. "That's… odd."

"It's more than odd," Duncan growled. "It reminds me of something my old CO used to say: 'Once is bad luck, twice is coincidence, but three times is enemy action.'"

Walker looked at him. "Flying rabid zombie rats who own stock in Verizon?"

"*You* explain it."

"Fuck me," the werewolf groaned. "What are we going to do?"

Masara sighed. "Go get some sleep. I've got to think about this. If it is enemy action, there's got to be some way to figure out who, what, where, and why."

Duncan swore some more. It didn't help.

* * *

Thoroughly disgusted, Walker headed home to catch what sleep he could while Masara and Duncan briefed the Harringtons. She explained what she had in mind as the couple looked increasingly worried. "If you hear the wards go off, grab the kids and run. In fact, I think it would be a good idea if you arrange to be elsewhere until this is over."

"You really think my parents are going to come here and infect us?" Amy looked pale, clinging to her husband's hands as if he was the only stable thing in her world. "Infect my kids?"

"I don't know. But given what happened with your mother, I don't think we can afford to assume they won't. If somebody designed this to be spread by biting, werewolves are definitely the way to do it."

Amy nibbled her lower lip. "I want to tell you that's nuts, but with everything going on… you're right, we can't assume anything." She turned to her husband. "That credit we got on the canceled flight. Could we rebook and add the kids?"

Harrington frowned. "We can try. We'll have to book another hotel too, but I'm sure there's something available in New York, of all places. But…" He looked at Masara. "I should stay and help fight. Amy can get the kids to safety."

"And if they get through us and you get yourself killed, what happens to your family?" Masara asked. "I've fought them. They're a foot taller than Walker, and whatever's happened to them has made them incredibly vicious. Do you have any combat training at all?"

"No," Amy said. "He's an accountant."

Tom shot her a dirty look. "I'm still a werewolf. I can defend myself. And you need all the help you can get."

"Not if you end up getting infected. The last thing we need is more werewolves spreading this."

"And if you get killed, you're not going to be able to stop anything."

She sighed. "Look, we'll have backup. If someone is blocking our communications, I can gate to the Mageverse and get reinforcements. We'll have all the help we need."

Tom hesitated. His wife gave him a look that was just shy of wild-eyed, and he sighed. "I don't like it, but I see the point. I'll make the reservations." He pulled out his cell phone and hunched over it.

Amy looked equally relieved and guilty. "We can't thank you enough for everything you're doing. I realize you're taking a big risk to protect us. I want to tell you we can take care of ourselves, but…"

"You've got your kids to worry about, and your kids are more important than your pride."

"Yes. If something happened to Gemma and Liam…" She shook her head. "I can't let that happen."

"Of course not. And we're going to do everything we possibly can to make sure you're all safe."

*Here's hoping we don't get killed doing it,* Duncan thought grimly.

\* \* \*

"The wards come first," Masara told Duncan as they headed outside. "I need to make sure the werewolves don't hit us while we're dealing with the other issues." Her voice dropped to a mutter. "While I'm at it, I should add something to the spell to make sure none of the humans shoot cell phone video of us fighting eight-foot werewolves."

Duncan followed as she began walking a circle around the house. Every few feet, she paused, conjured a metal stake, and sank it into the ground. "These will sense werewolf intruders and zap them with an electrical charge." It took her another twenty minutes to close the circle. Finally, she stepped back, gesturing Duncan to come with her. Closing her eyes, she murmured a soft chant. Through their bond, he felt the surge of effort and concentration…

A glowing blue hemisphere sprang up silently around them, encircling the house like something from a science fiction movie. "Good thing ordinary humans can't see that," he told her. "Because Morgana would kick our asses."

"With the spells I've cast, we could stage the climax of *Lord of the Rings* in the front yard, and no one would see or hear a thing." Next, she conjured a dome-shaped tent off to one side of the spell circle, so it had a good view of both the back and the front of the house. No sooner had she created it than she gestured again. It vanished.

Duncan frowned. "Did you change your mind about the tent?"

"No, just rendered it invisible."

"But won't the werewolves be able to see through the spell?"

"The spell isn't on them. It bends the light around the tent, which makes it invisible."

He frowned. "They'll still be able to smell us, though."

"Yes, and since they're able to sense magic, they'll be able to figure out where we are. But by the time they have a chance to do all that, they'll have tripped the wards. We'll be awake and waiting for them. Point is, they're not going to be able to sneak up on us." Masara gestured again with a weary wave of one hand and their armor disappeared, replaced by jeans and knit shirts, both in black. At the same time, a dark opening appeared in the air -- the open tent flap.

Duncan watched as she dropped to her knees and crawled in. The delicious, rounded curve of her ass sent his mind wandering into territory he needed to avoid if he didn't want to spend the night acutely frustrated.

Putting a chokehold on his libido, he dropped to his knees and followed her into the tent. A thick pad of what felt like gel gave beneath his hands and knees. When he looked upward, he didn't see the dome of the tent at all. The starry sky sprawled overhead, the moon hanging full and white over the tree line.

"Now let's tackle the communication problem," she told him. "Fortunately, this isn't the first time we've run into some variation of this issue, though we usually encounter it with Mageverse enemies rather than the ones here." She held up one hand, and light flared. When it faded, a golden globe the size of a tennis ball rested on her palm.

As Duncan's brows lifted, she began talking to it like someone recording a livestream video, laying out all the information they'd collected over the past couple of days. Her voice as she spoke was brisk and stripped of emotion. And she spoke in such detail, he realized she was making sure the Magekind would know everything in case Masara, Duncan, Walker, and even the Harringtons ended up dead.

"I think we must consider the possibility this is some kind of attack by the Fomorians, possibly intended to out us all to the mortals. I'm requesting that you send as many teams as you can as quickly as possible, so we can contain this before it gets worse. Otherwise I'm afraid the situation will spiral completely out of control. Not only could this blow the collective cover of the Magekind and the Direkind, a great many people could end up dead."

He felt her magic crest, and the orb vanished in a flare of light. Masara sighed in relief. "That's done."

"What if the Fomorians intercept it?"

"They'd have to know it's coming to intercept it. Why do you think I recorded it in here? Even if Bres has someone watching this house, we couldn't be seen in here. Anyway, we've used those messengers on Mageverse battlefields for centuries. They're fast, surrounded by an invisibility spell, and they find whoever they're sent after. Which in this case is Belle, Tristan, Morgana, or Arthur. We'll get our backup."

"What leads you to believe the Fomorians are behind this?" He frowned. "What the hell are they trying to accomplish? I thought they wanted us off Mageverse Earth. Why infect a couple of werewolves and kill a jogger here, for God's sake?"

Masara collapsed back on the mat and sighed, rubbing her eyes. "I don't know. I do know that rabid zombie rats don't own stock in Verizon. On the other hand, Bres is fully capable of *creating* rabid zombie rats -- and blocking our communications. He's the simplest explanation for this tangle."

"Nothing about this is simple."

"Which is probably why it feels as if someone is beating my temples with hammers."

"No wonder, considering all the magic you did today. Why don't you get some sleep?" he suggested. "You really do look fried. And I'm good for the rest of the night." As a vampire, he wouldn't get sleepy until he passed out at dawn.

Masara gave him a stern look. "If you see anything suspicious, wake me. Do not go out there to fight whatever it is by yourself."

"Yes, Mother."

"That's 'yes, instructor,' to you, apprentice."

"Yes, Master Masara. Your Padawan hears and obeys."

Her lips twitched, but she pretended to glare. "See that you do." She rolled over on her side, back to him, conjured a pillow, and curled into a ball.

Duncan folded his legs to sit tailor fashion, braced his elbows on his knees, and scanned the darkness around them. This wasn't the first time he'd stood watch in hostile territory. But though the walls of the tent were invisible, the air inside was warm and close. And entirely too full of the delicious female scent of Masara. He found himself growing sharply aware of her heartbeat, which showed no sign of slowing into sleep as the minutes passed. As worn out as she looked, she should have dropped off almost immediately.

Gazing down at her elegant profile, he saw the gleam of her dark eyes staring into the woods. There was something grim in the set of her soft, tempting mouth. And God, he wanted to kiss her. Wanted to taste the salt on her skin, breathe deep of that intoxicating Maja scent. And yet...

Duncan remembered that searing moment when she worked the scrying spell and he'd touched the core of her. He'd thought their link had been deep before, but now he realized it had barely scratched the surface. He knew exactly how it felt when Robert had attacked her, not to mention that Christ-awful whipping at Emily's hands...

Masara lifted her head and glowered over her shoulder at him. "Would you quit thinking so loud?"

Heat flooded his cheeks. "I thought you'd blocked me out."

Masara was silent for a long moment. "I can't," she growled at last. "That circle I worked strengthened the bond even more." She groaned. "I can't believe I Truebonded us."

"What's a Truebond?"

"A very deep mental link, usually forged between people who are married." She scrubbed at her eyes with one hand. "Most people have better sense than to form one by accident."

Duncan frowned. Concentrating, he realized he could indeed sense her in the depths of his mind. "Can't you break it?"

She sighed. "Yes, but it would take a full circle. Besides, we may need it. We're just going to have to ignore it." She squeezed her eyes shut.

He sat still and stared into the dark, trying not to think. Waiting for her heartbeat to slow. It didn't. In fact, he thought it might be speeding up a little. So was his. Even though he could see the moonlit darkness all around them, the air in the invisible tent felt warm and close, and full of the scent of her. That wonderful fragrance that was Maja, a combination of woman and magic and sex. And the faintest tang of blood.

His fangs gave a warning twinge. *Don't start*, he told them.

They didn't seem to be listening. Neither was his dick. It was lengthening, pressing against his fly. *Damn it, stop that. She needs to sleep. She'll be all by herself tomorrow, and I won't be there to help her. The least I can do is not lust at her.*

"Or maybe lusting at me is exactly what I need." She rolled on her back and looked up at him, her eyes glittering in the moonlit dark. "Maybe what both of us need is to burn some of this off."

Duncan started to lick his lips and stopped when he hit a fang. "But the wolves --"

"-- are on the other side of that ward, and they can't get in." She gave him a slow, sensual smile. "I, on the other hand, am right here. And so are you."

He stared at her as his heart began to hammer. "Are you sure?"

"What do you think?" Masara dropped all her mental barriers, and let him see her, feel her.

She needed *him*. Needed to burn off her clawing feeling of being so utterly alone for the first time since Belle had found her, feverish and sick, in those South Carolina woods. In all these years since, in all the battles, all the wars, she'd known she had the Magekind at her back. All she had to do was call, and they'd be there for her. Now they might not be. The messenger might fail to find them in time. She might die tomorrow. Or far worse to her, he might.

But he was here now. A memory flashed through her mind -- the feel of him sliding into her, the glory of his pleasure feeding her own, the frantic gallop to completion. He caught his breath as her emotions stormed over his mind. The desperation, the need to forget, if only for a few moments. The pain on Amy's face, her children's fear and bewilderment, her husband's frustrated helplessness. The face of the girl on the autopsy table. *What if I can't do it?* The thought rang in the bond. *Belle should've assigned this case to someone who could do the job.*

Duncan had heard enough. "You helped kill American slavery, for God's sake -- something that had infected this country since the sixteenth century. A couple of Dire Wolves don't stand a chance. Even if Bres is pulling the strings, we've got this."

Masara stared at him. "You believe that."

"Well, yeah. It's true."

She reached out, grabbed a fistful of his hair, and dragged him forward with that astounding Maja strength. Then her mouth was on his, hot and desperate and devouring. The smell of her filled his senses, as his fangs instantly lengthened. He groaned in hot need against her mouth. Her tongue thrust deep, licking the sharp tips of his fangs in a sweet, erotic promise. He shuddered as a wave of lust rolled over him.

\* \* \*

Masara felt his hunger explode, rolling over her with a startling intensity. Hunger not just for her body, not just for the flashing release of orgasm, but for *her*. For everything she was.

She also felt him grappling for self-control, afraid to trigger memories of Robert.

Pulling back a fraction, she tightened her grip on his hair. "Don't hold back. Let go. Make us both forget." With that, she threw open the link completely, dropping all her defenses. They snapped together like two magnets, gasping as the link amplified even the simple kiss into deep, spinning pleasure.

Duncan stared into her face, eyes wide. She realized that regardless of color, they were nothing at all like Robert's. That man had never seen her as anything but a sheath for his cock.

"Screw Robert. He was an asshole, and he's dead," Duncan growled. "And he deserves to be." His hands wrapped around her shoulders and pulled her onto his lap. She saw what he wanted in his mind, and she flicked her fingers. Their clothes vanished in a swirl of hungry magic.

He angled an arm behind her back, lifting her so his mouth could cover one breast. His teeth closed around her nipple, not quite biting as he suckled. Every long pull shot pleasure into her brain as his fingers caressed and explored. This wasn't going to be slow or sweet. And that was good, because hot and fast was exactly what she wanted.

Masara had never really considered herself beautiful. Her body had been shaped by grinding work as a child, and as an adult, by war. Yet to him, she was beautiful. He loved even the dark skin she'd been told was ugly, the nose that was too wide, the mouth that was too full.

He released her breast. "You could never be anything but beautiful to anyone with eyes." It wasn't just empty flattery. She could see the stark honesty in his mind.

Just as she saw his doubt. Not doubt of her, of himself. His worst fear was that he would fail her when she needed him most. That his courage would fail at the next IED, figurative or literal. *You won't. You saved Farijaad the second time even knowing what would happen.*

*That wasn't real.*

*It was to you. And so is this.* She dragged his head down for a ferocious, biting kiss, sucking his lower lip hard. He groaned, and his hands skimmed down her body, tracing the line of her ribcage and the curve of her hip. She released his hair and he drew back, breathing hard, trying to control his need. His parted lips showed the tips of his fangs, and she remembered the hot pleasure-pain of his bite.

He groaned and grabbed a fistful of her dreads, pulling her head back, arching her body upward. His lips tasted the line of her jaw, nibbled and sucked, exploring the muscles and veins and tendons under her skin.

Masara sensed his fierce need to sink his fangs into her throbbing pulse, yet he squelched it. He wanted this to be for her, to show her she mattered, that she came first. Would come first. The unintentional pun made her smile.

Duncan lifted her off his lap and laid her down on the thick mattress. And began to feast. His hands and mouth explored her, seeking out the sensitive places, the ones that would make her pleasure spike. The hollow between her collarbones, the bend of her elbow. He located a particularly sensitive bundle of nerves under her armpit and licked and suckled it, drawing the scent of her deeply into his lungs.

That would've made her feel self-conscious -- it had been hours since her last shower -- if it hadn't been clear how much he loved that scent, that taste. How he wanted to roll in it like a cat in catnip.

"Charmer." Masara laughed, threading her hands into his curls as he nibbled his way to the rise of her hipbone, then sought out her belly button. His tongue thrust in and out of it, flickering until she giggled.

*I didn't even think you could make that sound,* he told her, a smile in his mind. *Let's see what other sounds I can make you make...* Long fingers found her ribs and dug in, tickling ruthlessly. She squirmed, laughing as she slapped at his chest. "Quit that... Or I'll... turn you into a frog!"

*As long as you're my lily pad...* He went right on tickling her until, with a mock growl, she grabbed his hands and jerked them away from her hapless ribs, then muscled him onto his back. Pinning his hands to the mattress over his head, Masara grinned down at him. "My turn."

He tilted up his chin, seeing what she wanted in the bond. She dipped her head to nibble, stringing tiny bites along the angle of his stubborn jaw and along his throat. Duncan pulled his hands free -- there was no way she could really hold him -- and traced the long line of her spine down to the dimple over her buttocks. The whole time, he kept his head tilted back, enjoying her mouth as shamelessly as a cat enjoying a stroking hand.

Masara explored the broad plates of his pecs, suckled small male nipples, tasted and savored the sweat on his skin, that dark scent that was vampire and Duncan. God, how she loved that smell. Loved... she cut the thought off.

Duncan's eyes went wide, and he jerked his head up to stare at her, stunned. *What did you say?*

She froze, knowing precisely what word he wanted her to repeat. The one she wanted to say, would have said if she hadn't been afraid to lay herself so open. Loving anyone had never brought her anything but pain. Her mother had died a slave, her brother vanished, sold down the river. Emily had beaten her so badly she'd lost the baby she hadn't dared even want. *I can't.*

For an instant anger and frustration flashed through him, so hot it was almost frightening. But before she could pull away in alarm, Duncan's big hands caught her hips and lifted her off him.

*What are...* Then he sat her down astride his face. Duncan's tongue flicked hot across her clit. Masara stiffened, startled, as a hot, stark pleasure she wasn't expecting stabbed into her brain. *I think... you skipped a step... Or twelve.*

His only answer was a growl against her soft, wet flesh, as his tongue swirled over her clit, dancing hot patterns. He reached one long, muscled arm up, caught her breast with his fingertips, and began to pinch and tug as his mouth fed on her pussy.

Masara jerked in his grip at the erotic assault on her nerves. He held her still with effortless strength. She felt no fear at all. He wouldn't hurt her. Wouldn't...

Before she could track the implications of that thought, his lips engulfed her clit and sucked, fierce and merciless. His tongue lashed the nubbin in burning flicks that shot bolts of pleasure from her groin to her brain. Masara stiffened at the sudden pounding delight. His free hand clamped on her hip, holding her in place, refusing to let her retreat from the overwhelming sensations.

She heard herself gasping, high, desperate little sounds, hips dancing against his mouth. Grinding as if she had no self-control whatsoever. His fingers tugged her nipple harder as he ate, sending the delight to blazing new peaks. She could feel him struggling to concentrate through the waves of her pleasure pounding his mind. Duncan was determined to drive her into a fierce climax. Suckling, stroking, the curve of his fangs pressing against her delicate flesh...

The climax hit like an explosion in her brain, and she shrieked, her body writhing in his ruthless grip. Helpless and overwhelmed and lost. Her body was still twitching when he spilled her off him onto the gel mat. Her elbow hit the fabric of the tent, but she didn't care. He reared up and jerked her beneath him. His head smacked the top of the tent, but he didn't even pause, rolling her facedown and lifting her hips high.

His cock slid into her, and she squealed in delight, a sound she couldn't remember ever making before. His reply was a growl as he pushed, shoving all the way to the balls. Thick, so deliciously thick... And she could feel how wet she felt to him, how perfectly she gripped him. The bond let her experience the penetration from his angle, the pleasure so deliciously, erotically alien.

He pumped, deep, in and out and...

Masara yowled her pleasure into the tent pad as she felt the climax building. Before it could crash over her, Duncan pulled out and sat back. Ignoring her moan of protest, he wrapped his sweat-slicked arms around her and pulled her astride his lap. One big hand closed around her jaw, tilting her head to the side. Then his fangs sank deep. She cried out as he drank in hard, deep swallows. And drove into her again, impaled her on his cock. Held her there, deliciously trapped.

Masara wanted to buck against him, but his free hand gripped her hip, holding her still. *No*, he growled in her mind, and she froze. He wanted to drink from her like this, joined but unmoving, in some kind of vampire version of Tantric sex.

One hand slid between her thighs, found her clit, and stroked it. Maddening. She couldn't move -- he wouldn't let her -- so instead she tightened her muscles on him, gripping hard, then releasing, gripping and releasing, until he groaned against her skin. He fed as he stroked her pleasure to blinding heights with ruthless fingers. Until he slid his fangs free with delicate care. Duncan wrapped one arm around her torso and lifted her off his cock, just far enough that he could grind up into her. Thrusting hard, he growled in her ear, his free hand riding her clit.

Her throat stung from his bite, and his cock felt huge, bucking in and out. She came, screaming, high and helpless, sweet pulses blazing through her. Her climax fed his, his fed hers... And she screamed until her throat hurt.

* * *

Masara hung limp in his arms in the aftermath, deliciously wrung out and exhausted as he licked her, tonguing the tiny wounds left by his fangs, healing them with his saliva. Encircled by his body, she floated in peace. It felt as if all her haunting grief and loss had been driven into the distance by his ferocious passion.

And he felt that peace, took pride in giving it to her, because as far as he was concerned she deserved it. In his eyes, she was powerful, competent, and professional. A hero.

"You're the strongest woman I've ever known," he told her softly, running his fingers through her dreads. "And if you knew my mother, you'd know what a compliment that is."

"I do know your mother." Knew her from his memories, from his love for both his parents. It made her remember her own mother, long dead. The two women had been nothing alike in many ways. Duncan's mother was a librarian, a thoroughly twenty-first century woman who considered herself the equal of anyone and never backed down from a fight. Masara's mother had been a slave who'd never been permitted to learn to read, whose life had been marked with tragedy and injustice. And yet both women had been fiercely dedicated to nurturing and protecting those they loved.

Funny how so much could change over fifteen decades, yet love was the same.

# Chapter Eight

Duncan held her as Masara slipped toward sleep, her head resting on his chest as he stroked the silken curve of one shoulder. He tried to remember the last time he'd felt such sweet peace. And couldn't think of a thing.

Masara spoke, her voice a little slurred and sated. "I need to move. You've got to…" She yawned. "Keep watch." She rolled off him.

He wanted to pull her back, but instead he sighed and sat up. "I'm also going to need armor."

She lifted her head and frowned, flicking her fingers. Sparks flowed over him, leaving scale mail behind. She nestled down again, and he listened as her heartbeat evened out and slowed into sleep.

He felt… happy. So happy his heart seemed to float in his chest. Happier than he'd imagined he could be since that day in Afghanistan. Even after he'd received Merlin's Gift and learned he wouldn't spend the rest of his life as a double amputee, he'd been relieved, but not happy. Certainly not Masara happy.

He'd been too damn busy trying to earn the blessings he'd been given, too deeply aware of all the other wounded warriors who weren't blessed with Merlin's Gift in their DNA. He'd known he had to deserve that gift. Later, he'd been driven by the compulsion to earn Masara's approval. Her love hadn't even been on his horizon.

Suddenly he could see a faint outline glowing against the shadowed woods -- the shape of the tent opening. It hadn't been there before. Evidently, he sensed it with Masara's magic.

Carefully he eased away from her, pushed the tent flap aside, and crawled out. Straightening, he scanned the darkness around him, breathing deep as he parsed the air for scents. There was no trace of werewolf on the evening breeze.

For the next few hours, Duncan alternated between walking the perimeter of the ward and retreating into the tent with Masara, to breathe her scent and bask in the peace, while the night remained stubbornly werewolfless.

Meanwhile the sun edged closer to the horizon. At last, he knew he could wait no longer and leaned over to touch the curve of Masara's delicate shoulder. "The sun's coming up."

Dark eyes flew wide, and she jerked upright, looking around wildly. Her gaze fell on the pinkening sky through the invisible tent roof. "Why did you let me sleep so long? I need to get you out of here." She gestured, conjuring clothing for herself and banishing the tent.

He longed to stay with her, but a glance at the sky told him they'd just run out of time. Again, he felt the pressure of her will as she drew on the burning power of the Mageverse. She gestured, and a gate bloomed open.

He grabbed her and pulled her into a ferocious kiss, letting her feel his need, his love. She kissed him back, just as fierce, until he forced himself to pull away. "Damn it, Masara, stay alive for me!"

She gave him a brilliant smile and a little push toward the gate. "I will. Now get your tempting backside to bed before the sun knocks you out cold."

With a muttered curse, Duncan turned away and stepped through. And found himself in his bedroom. Since he had no desire to wake up with his face in a puddle of blood from another split lip, he stomped to the bed and threw himself down on the mattress fully dressed. And prayed for the first time since he'd regained consciousness to find his legs and cock gone. "Please, Lord God, keep her alive until I can…"

The sun cut off the rest of the sentence.

\* \* \*

The Harringtons left for the airport, leaving Masara alone behind the wards, watching the house.

Of course, there was no guarantee Jack and Ellie would take the bait and show up here. They could be anywhere, attacking anyone. Unfortunately, this was the only hunch she had to play. She had to hope she'd get lucky.

Or very, very unlucky. What was she going to do if they showed up before Walker returned for his watch, or before Duncan woke? What if Belle didn't get her message? She'd hoped her friend would have arrived by now.

But there were things Masara could do while she waited. Things she was going to do now that everyone was gone. She'd better prepare in case she did end up fighting them single-handedly. But she'd rather they came after her than some poor mortal who wouldn't have a prayer. At least she had some hope of defending herself. But what if she failed?

Her sister's voice hissed from the depths of her mind, *You're nothing! You're a stupid, ugly little slut!*

*Shut. Up. I'm not going to fail. I will not.*

Well, she knew how she needed to spend the next few hours while she waited. She had to make sure that the next time the wolves attacked, they'd find it a lot harder to get their claws through that magical armor. She definitely did not want to get bitten. Were the claws infectious too? Probably not -- both she and Duncan had gotten scratched up through the armor. They'd have been infected by now if that was a vector.

All of which meant she needed to reinforce their armor to make sure the werewolves' fangs didn't pierce skin.

She also needed a more effective weapon. The Direkind were immune to direct magic, but not natural forces like electricity or fire. Fire was a possibility, but a fireball needed a magical fuel source to keep it burning in flight. That was probably why fireballs hadn't been effective during the Werewolf War.

Besides, there was too great a chance any fire would spread and destroy the house. Which made throwing actual lightning around problematic, since it could easily start a fire. A better bet would be a weapon that generated electricity along a metal surface like a blade. Stalking into the living room, Masara gestured. A wave of force pushed the furniture aside, clearing a space. She had a lot to get done.

\* \* \*

It was almost six o'clock before Masara got the call. "I am outside the ward," Walker said, his deep voice rasping, with a strained note that made her wonder if he'd gotten any sleep. "Let me in."

"Give me a minute." She'd spent the day designing armor, and she felt blasted. Thank God it was almost sunset. She hung up and tucked the phone back into her pants' pocket. Wearily, she contemplated the two suits of armor in the living room. As massive as they were, they were going to be a bitch to fight in, but at least they should prevent any of them from being bitten.

She'd taken the scale mail she'd already created and added a cuirass -- a heavy chest plate -- pauldrons to protect the shoulders, gauntlets, cuisses to protect the thighs, and armored boots with knee plates, all engraved with protective spells. She just hoped they'd be enough.

With a sigh, she headed out to the driveway. The deputy sat in a blue Toyota just outside the wards. She sensed no one else inside his car.

Masara gestured, and the wards dropped. Walker parked behind the Harringtons' vehicle. He got out, moving a little stiffly, as if sore. His face was drawn, and his eyes looked hollow. For once he wore jeans and a sweater instead of his uniform. He must have gone home to change and get his personal vehicle.

Masara studied him. "Did you get any sleep at all last night?"

"I couldn't sleep."

She sighed. "There's a lot of that going around. Come on, let me show you the armor I've been working on. It should do a better job of protecting us from bites." She led the way into the living room, where the two armored suits stood waiting in the magic circle she'd used to amplify her magic while conjuring. Duncan already had his. Masara had gated to the Mageverse to conjure the suit around the comatose vampire, in case everything went sideways and she didn't get the chance to do it later.

"I want to try it out, see if you can get your claws through it," she told Walker. "I hate going into combat in armor I haven't worn, at least in practice."

In the back of the house, something screeched, sounding like a window sliding up. Masara's head jerked toward the sound, her body tensing. Magic exploded directly behind her, accompanied by a greasy, sickly reek.

And she knew.

Masara threw herself forward, heard the snap of jaws, felt whiskers brush the side of her cheek as Walker's bite missed by inches. She twisted aside, narrowly avoiding the Dire Wolf's second lunge. *Oh, Lord, they got him!*

"You will not escape me this time, prey!" Claws raked across her shoulder as she dove over the coffee table and sent her power shooting toward the two suits.

Magic surrounded hers like a cloud, disassembled it, and materialized it around her. She grimaced as its weight crushed down on her. Blood poured down her left arm as the battle-axe filled her hands. She grimaced as she tightened her grip on the weapon.

Claws raked the floor. Masara ducked, whirling aside as something huge and golden flashed past. The house shook as Walker hit the ground and spun toward her.

She recoiled in horror. Where before his Dire Wolf head had been sleek and wolfish, now Walker had the misshapen face of a nightmare. His teeth were long and jagged, curving outward, so even when his jaws were closed they protruded on either side of his muzzle. If anything, he was even bigger than the infected Jack, muscle bulging obscenely from a body well over eight feet tall. His snarl revealed an inner row of teeth lining his gums, like those of a shark's.

*I should have known they'd target him,* Masara thought, feeling sick. *But no, I was focused on the Harringtons, convinced they'd come after the kids because that was my personal nightmare.* And Walker had paid the price for her arrogance.

"I am so sorry." Sorry she'd failed him. Sorry she had to kill him now or die herself.

"Save your pity for yourself," he rumbled, stalking her, his eyes gone rat red.

Retreating, she rotated her wrist, feeling the axe's charge activate, crackling softly. Normally, she'd worry about frying herself, but the spell on the weapon would kill the charge when it sensed the blade was in contact with her flesh.

Heavy clawed feet hit the hallway floor running from the rear of the house. Jack and Ellie must have slipped past the ward when she dropped it to let Walker in.

Walker leaped at her, so she ducked and ran. Claws raked over her armor as she passed him, but she kept going, sprinting across the kitchen for the far wall. There was no way she could fight in here. There wasn't room to swing the axe.

Desperately, Masara sprang for the window over the kitchen sink, knowing it was far too narrow for her armored shoulders.

A blast of magic vaporized the window and a chunk of the wall around it, creating a perfectly round hole just as she dove through headfirst. She hit the ground hard, gritting her teeth against the weight of the armor slamming into shoulders and arms as she tucked and rolled to her feet.

The Dire Wolf roared as his massive shoulders rammed into the edge of the hole -- and didn't quite break through. Mortar cracked, broken bricks pelting the ground around her. "You die this night, prey!"

"Hardly." Masara took a running step forward and whirled her axe at his head. He ducked back with something that sounded like a curse in some unfamiliar language. She spun and raced off again, aiming for the wards. If she could just get through them, she could feed them enough power to trap the werewolves inside.

Behind her, Walker hit the wall again. Bricks rained to the grass as the werewolf broke through and thudded to the ground, roaring. The other infected wolves howled from the inside the house. They'd be out in a heartbeat.

Masara poured on the speed, though the armor felt like lead weight. She'd been afraid she'd made the suit too bloody heavy, but she couldn't risk infection. God forbid she lose control and carry whatever this was to Avalon.

Behind her, the werewolves roared, massive paws hitting the ground.

Twenty yards to the ward. Ten. Five. She shot a magical order to the nearest generator spike, and the ward vanished. If she could get through and trap the werewolves inside the ward, she'd have all the time in the world to wait for Belle. They could figure out how to do to cure the captive wolves at their...

Walker hit her like a subway train. They went down in a rolling tumble of armor and hair-covered brawn. The impact jolted the axe from her hand, and it spun into the gathering twilight. *Get up get up get up!* She squirmed free of raking claws and scrambled over the ground, looking for the ward so she cross it and could bring it up again... *Where the devil are the spikes?*

Walker's jaws clamped over her forearm, the pressure agonizing even with the armor. Masara turned and hammered her free fist into his muzzle. He let go with a vicious alien curse. She surged to her feet, back-peddling desperately as she looked around...

And spotted the ward -- *between* them and the oncoming werewolves. *He knocked me right past the spikes!*

She lifted her hand, but before she could throw the spell to reactivate the ward, a clawed fist slammed

into her helmeted head, sending her staggering.
Catching herself, she blasted power into the ward,
reactivating it and increasing its power even more. If
one of the wolves hit it now, the barrier would damn
near fry them.

But even as the ward activated in a cold blue
flare, Masara realized she'd been too slow. Ellie and
Jack were already past it and heading right for her. She
turned to run, but Walker pounced on her like a wolf
on a rabbit, knocking her on her back. Flattened under
his massive bulk, she stared up into gaping jaws and
double rows of jagged teeth.

"You gave me a good chase, but the outcome was
fated." A fist slammed into her visor, and she tasted
blood in a blinding burst of pain and light as her head
jolted inside her helmet. Something seized both her
legs and jerked viciously. She caught a glimpse of Jack
and Ellie, hands clamped around her ankles, heaving
as Walker knelt astride her chest.

*Christ, Our Lord and Savior!* They were trying to
rip her legs out of their sockets! Masara threw out an
arm, reaching desperately for the axe that lay on the
grass a few feet away. She hissed a spell, and it flew
toward her hand…

Walker hit her so hard, she missed the catch. He
started punching her like somebody working a speed
bag, bouncing her helmeted head on the ground. Each
blow snapped her teeth together. She threw up both
arms to block, screaming as Jack and Ellie heaved at
her ankles again. Flame licked the length of her legs
from foot to hip, bones and muscles howling in protest.

"Belle!" she yelled into her helmet. The
communication spell activated…

The only reply was the discordant shriek of
magical interference. *Damn it, where are you, Belle!*

A hissed spell popped razor-sharp claws from her gauntlets, and she slashed upward at her captor as he leaned down to hit her again. The blades raked across Walker's muzzle.

"This is pointless." His eyes blazed red as he caught her arm and twisted it savagely.

She bit back a scream of pain, only to lose control of the shriek as Jack and Ellie wrenched so hard, she felt the joints start to give… Until the spelled scale mail beneath the plate went rigid at last, protecting her legs.

She gasped in relief as the frustrated wolves snarled.

"I will pry you out of your shell, snail." Walker drew back and slammed his fist into her faceplate so hard, the impact rattled her head in her helmet. Pain spiked behind her eyes.

Even if he didn't manage to break her visor, he could kill her just by slamming her brain against the inside of her skull. She grabbed for the axe with her magic, and drove it through the air, straight at the werewolf's head. He ducked, and it sailed harmlessly by. Snarling, he slammed both fists into her faceplate again, and the world broke into dancing black sparks. The pain dimmed…

A crunching, shrieking sound knifed her ears, jolting her back to full consciousness. Dazed, she looked up as Walker drew back his fist as Jack and Ellie punched and clawed at her armored boots, trying to crush them and the legs beneath. *Sweet Lord, Duncan! I need you!*

\* \* \*

Duncan screamed into the luminous sky of Afghanistan, his body on fire with the worst pain he'd ever felt. Lifting his head, he stared down the length of his torso. His legs were gone, his groin a gory ruin, and the remnants of his bloody pants were on fire... Bellowing in pain and confusion, he threw himself out of the bed, though his body felt impossibly heavy. One shoulder slammed into the bureau so hard, wood cracked as it crashed into the wall, which crunched under the impact.

Confused, frantic, he caught a glimpse of himself in the cracked mirror that hung askew from the bureau. And stared. He wore a combination of scale and heavy plate armor. *Where the hell had that come from?*

*Masara. Masara must have sent them to me before I woke up. But what the fuck's wrong with my legs?* They felt like they were being crushed in a vise...

Something slammed into his head so hard he reeled into the wall again. *Not a flashback.* The pain was real, but it wasn't his -- it was Masara's. He was feeling her pain through their psychic link again. *The fucking werewolves are doing something to her.*

Backup. He needed backup. He looked around wildly for his magic cell phone, then caught sight of his own reflection again. He was wearing a helmet -- and the Magekind always spelled helmets for communication. "Belle!"

Interference shrieked.

"Goddamnit!" He didn't have time for this. *Masara* didn't have time for this -- not the way she was hurting. What had they done to her? And where the fuck was his sword? There was no sign of it... But a massive double-headed battle-axe lay on the bed, its blade heavily engraved. Duncan snatched it up.

"Duncan," Masara's voice said in the air, sounding impossibly calm given the agony he could feel radiating through the link. It must be a magical recording, a spell she'd laid on the axe before they attacked her. "The axe blade emits an electrical field whenever you hit something with it. It should act like a Taser, stunning the werewolves. The new armor I've created should protect you from their bites. It's much heavier than I would like, but we can't afford to be infected by whatever this is. When you're ready to gate, say 'Take me to her.'"

"Masara!" he howled in the depths of their link, reaching for her desperately.

All he felt was pain. Cold spread over him. He had to save her, even if it meant going up against the two Dire Wolves alone. He didn't give a fuck.

Focusing on the vicious psychic burn coming through their bond, he snapped, "Take me to her!"

The white-hot point of the gate appeared directly in front of him, expanding to full size in a blink. All that was visible through its wavering frame was a view of moonlit woods. He thought he recognized the trees behind the Harrington house.

A roar sliced through the night, echoed by a chorus of snarls. *What are they doing to her*? Raising the axe in both hands, Duncan leaped.

# Chapter Nine

The minute Duncan touched the ground, the gate vanished. He looked around -- and swore. Three enormous werewolves had pinned a small armored female figure to the ground, one kneeling astride her hips, the other two beating and clawing her legs, trying to crush the armor. *Three? Where the hell did the third...*

The wolf's gold fur was the same shade as Walker's, though the enormous deformed creature looked nothing like the cop's Dire Wolf form. *Shit.* They'd infected Walker. Horror chilled him. *You poor bastard...*

But he didn't care if it was Walker. Duncan wasn't going to let them infect her. If that meant he had to kill them all, he'd do what he had to and deal with the consequences later.

The gold werewolf lifted a huge fist and brought it slamming down on Masara's faceplate.

He remembered the sensation of enchanted plastic shattering, the shards cutting his own face. *I don't fucking think so!* He threw himself into a run, rage boiling through him as he raised the axe. The female wolf saw him coming and leaped up, releasing Masara's ankle to backpedal away. The other two wolves scattered, snarling, glowing ruby eyes focused on him with murderous intensity.

Masara sprawled unmoving in the grass. He reached for her through the Truebond and hissed a relieved breath. Alive, just out cold.

He planted himself between her and the three wolves, his axe raised.

The Dire Wolves spread out, as if to encircle him. He moved to the right, trying to lead them away from her. *Masara?* he called into the link. *Get up. I need you,*

*Masara!* If anything could bring her around, that would do the job.

There was no answer in the mental link. She wasn't dead -- he'd know if she was dead -- but she was so deeply out he couldn't even feel her mind at all. *Fuck shit piss!*

Christ, all three of them had at least a couple hundred pounds on him, including the female. He was so dead.

*Shut up*, he growled at the treacherous mental voice. If he lost, Masara was dead too, so he fucking well wouldn't lose.

The thing that had been Walker moved toward him. Where the cop's eyes had been gray in werewolf form, now they were a rat-like ruby red. But even without the color shift, Duncan would have known the thing looking at him wasn't Walker. Its stare was too cold and soulless to be the cop's.

Walker's mouth opened, revealing a forest of deformed, curving teeth. "Leave or die with her." It didn't even sound like the deputy anymore, the voice grating and rusty, even deeper than Walker's had been.

Well, *that* didn't sound like magical rabies. Duncan forced a nasty smile despite the little voice screaming *I'm fucked* in his head. "Yeah, no. You're about to find yourself ass deep in Knights of the Round Table, hairball. They're going to chop you into meaty chunks."

Lips peeled back from malformed teeth. "You look all alone to me. And by the time help arrives, you will both be mine."

There was such utter certainty in the thing's words, fear iced his stomach. He forced a smirk anyway. "Sorry, we're not into threesomes." He caught a blur of gray from the corner of one eye. Ducking, Duncan swung the axe at the wolf as he spun away. The blade bit into flesh with a savage crackle. He jerked it free, slinging an arc of wet droplets through the moonlight. The thing that had been Jack hit the ground and rolled with a high-pitched yip of agony. Ellie echoed the sound, taking a half step toward him, only to freeze a heartbeat later. Behind her, Walker's head jerked as if in pain.

Duncan recognized that reaction. He'd found himself flinching from Masara's pain the same way. The three were mentally linked somehow, feeling each other's pain the way he and Masara did. Could he use that?

Ellie charged him, moving with such impossible speed he had no time to react. Claws dug into his left pauldron. Duncan pivoted, swinging the axe, but the angle was bad and the flat of the blade hit her in the temple. The axe discharged with a loud electric pop. This time it was no glancing blow, and she flew ten feet to hit the ground in a tumble. Before he could move in on her, Walker bounded at him, fanged jaws gaped wide. Jack lunged from the other direction.

*Shit.*

\* \* \*

Even as her skull rang with pain from the electric blast, Eleanor's mind cleared. The invader was gone. *Jack!* she screamed in her mind, reaching for her husband along the Spirit Bond.

Her gaze fell on the huge, grotesquely distorted figure that had been the man she loved, stalking the young vampire. The thing that had been Walker closed in from the vampire's other side.

They'd spent days trapped in this hell, watching in helpless horror as their bodies did unspeakable things. The infection, and the delirium that followed, had given the invader an opening he'd used to seize control of them. Yet somehow the vampire's axe had broken the bastard's hold. *Jack?*

Fortunately, the usurper was concentrating so hard on controlling all three of his puppets' bodies, he was paying no attention to her thoughts.

The witch was the key. Everything the usurper was doing was about the Maja, about luring her here and infecting her. They could see that much from the bastard's thoughts. Why infecting her was so important wasn't as clear. But they had to protect her. Using the Spirit Link, Ellie flashed an image at her husband: the witch's axe, the pain of the electrical shock, that glorious moment she'd been free. *The shock disrupts his control. Not for longer than a few seconds, but maybe long enough.* Too bad the damned Link couldn't communicate verbal thought.

She could feel Jack concentrating fiercely on the images she sent, trying desperately to decipher them.

Until understanding dawned. Along with pain and resignation.

And in the midst of all that, she felt the warm bloom of his love. Ellie's werewolf eyes stung even as the usurper curled her lips in a snarl.

* * *

Duncan's fury and desperation drove Masara back to consciousness. Instinctively, she tried to go to him, but just lifting her knee sent agony bolting the length of her leg. She jerked, triggering another savage blast of pain. Freezing, Masara stared wide-eyed at the starry sky. Remembered the werewolves trying to wrench her body apart.

Somehow Duncan had saved her. She reached out to his mind, opening her consciousness to his, until she could see through his eyes. He leaped at Walker, the axe a crackling streak of light. The big werewolf ducked under his attack, claws flashing upward to grate furrows across the plate armor.

And it wasn't the first time they'd caught him. His armor was dented, scratched, gouges cutting through the plate to penetrate all the way to flesh. Pain sliced him with every move he made, and exhaustion and blood loss rode him hard. Sweat rolled into his eyes, but he kept fighting, kept swinging the axe despite his aching muscles and countless injuries. Knowing if he stopped, the werewolves would tear him apart. And she'd be next.

Alone. Duncan was all alone against the three of them, grim and terrified and determined to save her. And they'd hurt Masara so damn badly, she wouldn't be able to do a thing to help him unless she could heal herself.

So she threw herself open to the Mageverse, dragging in every ounce of power she could reach, and sent it boiling the length of her body.

Mangled ligaments and muscle and fractured bones itched and burned as they healed, the pain almost as brutal as the original injuries. Masara clenched her teeth and fought not to scream. When the agony faded, she tried to move again, but her armor was still locked down, rendered rigid by the protective spell. A whispered chant released the spell, and she cautiously rolled over. To her relief, she managed it without drowning in fire again. But when she tried to stand, the world spun around her, and she almost vomited inside her helmet. She staggered and fell to her hands and knees.

*I've got a concussion.* One so severe she hadn't been able to heal it completely. She needed a healer. *Yes, well, Duncan needs* me.

Spotting her fallen axe, Masara crawled over and picked it up, planted its head on the ground and used the haft to lever herself to her feet. Leaning on the axe like a cane, she fought dizziness as the world revolved drunkenly around her.

Duncan whirled and leaped as he fought the three werewolves, swinging the battle-axe in great arcs that forced them to keep their distance. Despite her savage headache, pride shot through her. Damn, he was good. When he'd come to her six months ago, he could barely control his vampire strength as he tripped over his own feet. Now he was all smooth agility and blinding power.

As Duncan charged, Jack leapt aside, a huge clawed hand raking across his armored chest. Walker slammed one huge fist into his gut, sending him staggering back. Duncan almost fell into the ward, but Jack grabbed him by one pauldron and jerked him into the air.

*Oh no, you don't.* Masara staggered forward, ignoring the vicious pounding of her headache. Gathering her magic, she prepared to send her axe flying toward the werewolf.

Something rammed into her from behind, smashing her into the dirt. Her face smacked against her visor so hard she saw stars and her mouth filled with bile. Something wrenched at her back. *Not again!*

From the corner of one eye, Masara saw Ellie kneeling on top of her, hooking both claws under the edges of the back plate of her armor. Deformed muscle surged, and the plate tore free, half lifting her off the ground.

The werewolf slung the back plate like a Frisbee, then slammed both clawed hands down between her shoulder blades. Jerking upward, Ellie ripped the scale armor like paper. Pain blasted through Masara's back as the werewolf's claws dug into skin.

For a heartbeat, she was back in the barn, feeling rawhide slice her flesh as Emily whipped her in a frenzy of jealousy and rage. *"You're nothing, nothing, nothing!"* Above her, the werewolf's jaws gaped wide as the monster prepared to sink her fangs into bare flesh.

"Fuck! You!" Masara screamed as she shot the axe toward the werewolf's head with a blast of magic. The blow landed badly, the edge missing, yet the impact still snapped her foe's head back so hard, it knocked her off her perch.

Masara leaped upward, throwing out one hand. Her magic brought the axe flying back to smack into her palm. "I'm *not* nothing! *I'm a Maja!*" She swung the axe at the werewolf with every ounce of her strength.

* * *

The blade sliced toward Eleanor. The usurper started to throw her backward, but Ellie saw her chance and struck, locking the muscles of one knee. For a single glorious instant, her body obeyed. The axe bit into her chest in a blast of white-hot agony, and its electric charge went off with a crackling SNAP.

Every muscle in her body seized, and Ellie toppled into the blue glowing barrier of the ward.

Just as she'd intended.

The blast of electricity seared her with the worst physical pain she'd ever felt.

She embraced it as she flung open her Spirit Link to Jack -- even as he reached for her, accepting her pain. Deliberately magnifying and weaponizing it against the usurper.

The invader howled as their joint agony ripped through him. Recoiling, he lost his grip on their minds.

Jack released the vampire's axe arm and arrested the punch he'd been about to throw. He met the young warrior's gaze. "Take my head!"

The vampire hesitated, eyes searching his...

*No, you will not!* the usurper hissed, flooded back into his mind.

"Now!" Jack howled.

The vampire swung the axe in a hard, fast arc that cleaved through Jack's neck in a single stroke.

As her husband's soul ripped free of his body, the Spirit Link did exactly what it was designed to, dragging Eleanor with him. With a cry of joy and relief, she exploded from her body the moment before the witch's axe sent her head tumbling.

Ellie swirled up to meet Jack's spirit, and they streamed into the light.

Together.

* * *

Axe in hand, Masara whirled at the sound of Walker's howl of agony as Jack and Ellie died. The werewolf's rat-red eyes went wide and round with pain, his malformed face contorted. Duncan cleared five feet in one leap, swinging his axe up and around in a backhanded diagonal chop that cleaved into the werewolf's chest. And lodged there.

Walker gasped, his tone desperate, "I'm free! Oh, thank God! Take my head before he regains control or he'll..." He jerked backward, tearing the blade from Duncan's hands and whirled to flee, only to topple to his hands and knees as if something had tripped him.

"For God's sake, do it!" It was a howl of anguish and rage.

Masara tossed her axe to Duncan, who caught it and brought it down in one smooth, fast strike. The werewolf's head hit the ground and rolled in an arc of bright blood. His body collapsed.

"Jesus Christ!" Duncan stared down at the severed head, his expression sickened. "Did he say he was possessed?"

"Wait," she snapped. "Let me make sure they're actually dead." Masara sent a wave of magic dancing over the three bodies. There was none of the hum of magical energy she associated with werewolves. "I don't sense any life force." She blew out a breath, wincing as she looked down at the cop's body. "God, Walker, I'm so sorry." Guilt rose, choking her. She remembered the big werewolf's dedication, his compassion for the jogger, his sense of duty toward his people. He'd deserved so much better.

Duncan blew out a breath and moved to join her, the axe in his hand. "Even if you'd known they'd been possessed by something, what could you have done? They're still immune to magic."

"Yes, they are," Masara said, thinking out loud. "If it was the Fomorians, how did they do it? And where did the rats fit in?"

"What the hell happened before I got here?"

She described Walker's arrival, and his request she let him in. "His voice sounded a little... off, but I thought he was just tired. Lord knows I am." Her body felt impossibly heavy in what was left of her armor. With a gesture, she banished her helmet and dragged in deep lungfuls of air. "Jack and Ellie must have ambushed him somewhere. Probably at his home, since they all knew each other."

Usually there was at least some sense of exhilaration whenever she'd survived such a close call. This time, she felt nothing but a kind of shell-shocked exhaustion. "They helped us. Somehow at the end, they helped us. Dammit, I wish we could've saved them. They weren't responsible for any of this."

Duncan shook his head. "No, but I don't see what we could have done." His eyes narrowed. "But if it is the Fomorians doing this, we need to kick some teal-blue ass."

Masara's gaze fell on Walker's severed head, and she knelt, meaning to cast a stasis spell over it. She reached down…

Black, ropelike tentacles exploded from the sides of the severed head and shot upward, wrapping around her neck. They tightened, jerking the head up toward her face, jaws gaping wide to bite…

Something silver flashed past her face, and the grip on her head was gone even as she threw herself backward. Sliced tentacles fell from around her throat. She landed on her ass as Duncan reversed his stroke to hack the werewolf's head in two. Roaring in rage, he struck again and again, sending bone fragments, blood, and bits of brain tissue flying. "What the…" Chop! "FUCK…" CHOP! "… does it take to…" CHOP! "… kill you…" CHOP! "… you possessing motherfucker?"

By the time he stopped, the grass was covered in blood and gore.

"Oh, holy Christ, our Savior," she croaked.

Panting, he looked up at her, white-faced. "I thought you were dead. I thought it was going to kill you."

"So did I," she whispered. And she still wanted to run screaming. "Thank you. I'm impressed. I doubt

I'd have been able to cut those tentacles without hitting me."

He gave her a wild-eyed look through a badly clawed visor. His hands were shaking. "I was just thinking that if this was a horror movie -- and what with the flying zombie rats, it's been that kind of week…" Duncan shook his head. "So when it actually *grabbed* you, I already had the axe lined up." Glancing down, he leaped back. "Fuck me!"

Following his gaze, Masara too, jolted away. The bloody fragments of Walker's head *moved*. Something black and heaving covered it, beginning to hum with a high, insectile buzzing. Glittering in the moonlight, it launched skyward on countless beating wings.

Flies? Flying roaches? It was impossible to tell. Acting on sheer reflex, Masara shot a fireball at the stream of insects. Even as the blast left her fingers, she remembered werewolves were immune to magic. But when the fireball hit the swarm, it ignited. Ash rained to the ground.

Still the hum continued. More swarms rose like smoke from the bodies and severed heads. Cursing, Masara started blasting fireballs at them. Another swarm ignited, but the rest of the insects shot off in a thousand different directions. A heartbeat later they'd all vanished.

"What the hell?" Duncan demanded.

Masara gaped at the night sky, blinking in shock. "I've fought dragons, demonic aliens, werewolves, giant snakes and fairies, and I have *never* seen anything like that."

Magic exploded in her senses, and she wheeled around, dragging in her power and preparing to fight.

"Fuck," Duncan swore, raising his axe. "What now?"

But to her relief, Masara saw the hot point of a dimensional gate expanding. A moment later, Arthur Pendragon strode through, followed by Belle, Tristan, Guinevere, Morgana Le Fay, and the Knights of the Round Table. They all had their swords drawn, and they looked bloody and battered.

The former king broke step, studying the bodies. "Well, hell. I take it I'm not the only one who's had a bad day." He flashed them one of his sudden, surprisingly boyish smiles. "But I'm delighted you survived. What the hell happened?"

Masara sighed as she looked down at what was left of the werewolves. "We lost some very good people who damn well didn't deserve it."

"I'm sorry it took me so long to get your message," Belle told her as they all scanned the area. "We've been gating all over Mageverse Earth chasing King Bres and his bloody army. We were still trying to catch him when your messenger found us."

"At least you're here now," Masara told her friend. "We've got to get those bodies into containment bags. Now, before anything else comes out of them."

Arthur raised his dark brows. "Anything *else*?"

* * *

King Bres swore, his three-fingered hands curling into massive fists. He'd *had* the little Maja whore. He'd been so close to sinking his she-wolf's fangs into her, he could practically taste the bitch's blood.

The next moment, the witch had torn free and hit his puppet with that axe, and the wolf bitch had sacrificed herself to break his grip on all three of them. The whole situation had blown up in his face.

He'd never felt such pain in all his long life. He'd been so incapacitated, he'd almost lost the Contagion to her magical blasts, which would have truly thrown his plans into chaos.

Two years of planning, painstaking negotiations to build alliances with the trolls, the Jotung, the Centauri, and the Mer. The creation of the Contagion and infecting the two wolves... It had gone so well at first. The Contagion had overcome the Direkind pair's natural immunity and provided a conduit he could use to possess his victims. He'd been able to use them to kill the mortal bitch with no difficulty at all, despite their stubborn attempts to resist his control.

Just as Bres had expected, the werewolf officer had called in the Magekind to assist in a cover up of the mortal's murder. He'd then staged the attack on Llyr's palace as a feint, and seen to it that his victims couldn't call for help. This should have isolated the two Magekind agents and left them vulnerable to infection. As an added benefit, the attack on the palace had given Bres an opportunity to study Arthur Pendragon in action.

Then, after all that, the attack had failed, so frustratingly close to victory. Because of three stubborn dogs and a pair of Magekind who didn't know when to lay down and die. Still, he'd preserved the Contagion. The plan could still go forward.

It had to. He'd spent years studying the wards around Avalon, and he was convinced there was no other way to penetrate the city's magical shields. No one could get through the wards except the Magekind agents they'd been designed to recognize.

Which meant he had to infect one of the Majae and seize control of her once the Contagion had cracked her mental defenses. A Magus wouldn't do; vampires couldn't create magical gates. Once he had her, Bres could walk her right through the city's defenses and pry Avalon apart like an oyster.

And kill every single member of the Magekind.

The very thought soothed his frustrated fury. Bres smiled in cold anticipation. *Soon, prey. Very soon.*

\* \* \*

Masara touched Duncan, and his battered armor dissolved into sparks and vanished, replaced with the leather he'd worn at the beginning of the evening. Hers did the same. Next began the cleanup. They didn't relax until all three werewolf bodies were enclosed in magical stasis units they wouldn't be able to escape even if they somehow came to life again. Belle transported them back to Avalon to be examined by one of the Maja healers, this one a former pathologist.

In the meantime, they had to come up with some way to explain Walker's death to the Tyger County Sheriff's Office without raising questions nobody wanted to answer.

In the end, it was decided that the best solution was one the Magekind had used many times before. Morgana conjured three "corpses" identical to Walker, Ellie, and Jack, but for the fact that they would pass as human. Conjuring a car for the Rands identical to their missing vehicle, the witch staged a head-on collision with Walker's Toyota, added appropriate injuries to the bodies, and called 911 before gating away.

Meanwhile, Masara repaired the damage to the Harrington's home, then called Amy's cell.

"Hello?" Amy said, sounding hesitant.

"It's Masara," she said. "Is it all right if Duncan and I gate to your location? We'd like to talk to you."

There was a long, painful silence before Amy asked, sounding numb, "Is it over?"

She exchanged an exhausted glance with Duncan. *Lord, I hope so.* "Yes."

"All right." The Dire Wolf's voice sounded choked. They said goodbye and hung up.

Masara sighed and turned to Duncan. "Let's get it over with." They owed Jack and Ellie this.

* * *

They stepped through the gate to find Amy huddled in the circle of her husband's arms. Tom was dressed in a pair of pajama bottoms and a T-shirt, while his wife wore a top and shorts. Both looked as exhausted, as pale and hollow-eyed as Masara felt.

Nearby, a pair of small figures lay in one of the two king-size beds, dark hair and red curls peeking above the navy-blue comforter.

"We'll need to talk out on the balcony," Amy told them in a hoarse whisper as her husband moved to open the room's sliding glass door. "The kids are asleep, and I don't want them hearing this."

Masara and Duncan followed them out into the brisk evening air. The brilliant skyline of Manhattan towered around the hotel. The fall air was cool as it blew around them, carrying the sounds of honking horns and the smell of gasoline. There was barely room on the balcony for all four of them, but it was better than waking up the children.

Amy sank down into one of the two plastic chairs and huddled there, wiping her eyes with a balled-up tissue. "What... what happened?"

Masara straightened her aching shoulders, grateful for Duncan's quiet presence at her side. She described the events of the night in a few terse sentences. "I wanted you to know your parents helped us. Ellie didn't just fall into that ward. She threw herself into it, and the pain seemed to break the puppeteer's control. Your father cried out to Duncan to take his head. So did Walker, who said to strike before 'he' could regain control. Possibly Bres or one of the Fomorians' allies, though we don't know for sure. Either way, they all fought hard against whoever it was. Without their self-sacrifice, I doubt we'd have survived."

"That sounds like my folks." Some of the horrible grief lifted from Amy's face. "My parents did have a Spirit Link."

"What?" Duncan asked, confused.

"It's a kind of psychic bond Direkind couples form," Tom told him. "Not everyone does it, because if your partner dies, the psychic shock kills you too."

"Like the Truebond?" Duncan asked Masara.

"It is similar, but as I understand it, it communicates sensation and emotion more than thoughts." She brushed her thumb over her lower lip. "I did have the impression they seemed to feel each other's pain."

Duncan's dark brows rose. "If that was what was going on, maybe they used the pain to break the puppet master's control."

Amy frowned. "So the rabies theory is definitely out."

"We thought so." Masara grimaced. Apparently, there was no way out of telling them the ugly details. "But it seems to be more complicated than that. When I bent over Walker's decapitated head, tentacles shot out of it and wrapped around my neck. It would've bitten me if Duncan hadn't cut me free."

The two werewolves stared at her in startled revulsion. "My God," Tom said.

"It gets worse. After it was over, a cloud of insects appeared around the bodies and flew away. I fried some of them with a fireball, but the rest escaped."

"Where did they go?" Amy demanded.

Masara shook her head. "Again, no idea. The other Majae attempted tracking spells, but nothing worked. They're gone."

A horrified silence ticked by. "You do realize they'll be back?" Tom asked at last.

"That's what we're worried about," Masara admitted.

"Look, I can't..." Amy wiped her eyes again and blew out a breath. "What's going to happen to my parents' bodies? How are we going to explain this?"

Masara described the simulated car crash with its simulated bodies. "You'll probably be getting a call from law enforcement once they find your parents' IDs."

"Well, at least we'll be able to have a funeral." She frowned. "What about the real bodies?"

"We're conducting autopsies on them to try to determine what was done to them and how. Normally I'd be optimistic, but as we've discovered, werewolf magic seems to trump ours." Masara sighed. "Either way, we'll cremate the remains and return them to you."

"That probably would be safer," Amy scrubbed a hand over her eyes. Her husband wrapped his arms around her, and she leaned back against his body.

"You think this thing will come after us and the kids?" Tom asked.

Masara hesitated a long moment. "I don't think it's particularly likely. From what he said, I was his main target. Why, I don't know. But until we take care of this, we're going to have agents keep an eye on you. I'll maintain the ward around your house and provide you with a panic button you can activate if you need to call for help."

Amy dredged up a smile with obvious effort. "Thank you. For everything."

Masara shook her head. "I only wish I could've found a way to free your folks and Walker."

"Considering everything you've told me, I can't imagine how that would've been possible. That thing…" Her lip trembled. "Just catch it for us. I don't want any other family to go through this."

Masara leaned forward and squeezed her hand. "We're going to do everything in our power. Besides, this thing has made a very bad mistake." She smiled grimly. "It's pissed off Arthur Pendragon."

# Chapter Ten

Duncan stepped through the gate Masara created without even noticing where it led to. Then he stopped dead, blinking as he gazed around in wonder. "Where are we?"

"Home," she said, with an exhausted sigh as she stepped through behind him. "After all that, my heart is hurting. And I desperately need time to rest and heal and be with you."

"I can't think of a prettier spot."

It looked as if they'd stepped into a fairyland. Directly in front of him, a waterfall danced and leaped down a rock cliff to splash into a ten-foot pool that steamed gently in the moonlight. Exotic scents filled the air from the flowering bushes, trees, and draping vines that surrounded it -- African daisies, King Protea, Impala Lily, Ixia. Flowers he'd never even heard of until he'd encountered them in Masara's garden. Though he knew it was fall, the air felt deliciously warm and springlike.

When he turned, scanning their surroundings, he spotted the undulating shape of Masara's house covered in the countless cedar shingles that made it look like an exotic African animal. A stained-glass window depicting a lion glowed through the darkness in a thousand colors, and recognizing it, he realized they were in the garden behind her house. "I never knew this pool was here." They'd walked in the garden many times before, but the mounds of greenery that surrounded the pool must have concealed it.

"I was saving it for a surprise." She touched him, and his leather street clothes vanished.

Glancing around, he froze, staring, breath caught in wonder as hers vanished, as well. Masara looked like a goddess, her body lean and muscular and very female, her pretty breasts tipped by hard, dark nipples. She hooked her hand behind his neck and pulled him down for a kiss so hot it curled his toes.

He groaned against her mouth as his cock instantly hardened and his upper jaw took on a furious ache. He wanted to grab her... but, remembering Robert, he kept his hands where they were.

"You are not Robert," she growled.

Duncan's throat tightened, and he wrapped his arms around her. The feel of her, warm and naked against him, reminded him of that horrible moment he thought he'd lost her. Breaking the kiss, he pressed his head into her hair and squeezed his eyes shut. "When I saw that werewolf tear your armor off and rear back to bite, and I knew there was no way I could get to you..."

"I handled it."

He lifted his head and managed a smile. "I noticed. And I also heard you drop the F bomb. You've never done that before."

Her white teeth flashed at him. "You're a bad influence on me, Marine."

"Yeah?" Duncan stroked his thumbs over the regal rise of her cheekbones. "Let's see just how bad an influence I can be." Leaning in, he kissed her again, licking her lips, tasting the perfect heat of her mouth.

Masara caressed him in return, her fingers tracing the breadth of his chest, dancing over the rise and ripple of muscle. Through the link, he could feel just how much she liked his body, the way arousal clenched like a hot fist in the pit of her belly. He also saw what she intended the moment before she did it. Duncan grabbed her wrist just as she gave him a hard shove. A tug pulled her after him as he plunged into the pool with a huge splash.

For a moment they sank together into the deliciously hot water, their bodies twining around each other, until his backside hit the pool's smooth stone floor. They came up together, their heads breaking the surface, spitting water and grinning at each other like a pair of kids. The steaming water seemed to fizz over his skin in a way he recognized. "This feels really good. Is it enchanted?"

She leaned against him lazily. "Yes. The stones that line the pool are spelled for healing. That way if I'm too magically drained, a good soak will take care of the worst of my bruises and cuts."

Duncan grinned wickedly. "Ever made love in here?"

She wrinkled her nose at him. "Water, oddly enough, generally isn't the best thing for nice slippery sex."

"Why don't we try it and see?"

He dipped his head and kissed her, long and slow, until she purred into his mouth, "You talked me into it." Lifting her right leg, Masara wrapped it around his hip. Duncan caught her under the thigh as she coiled the other leg around him and hooked her arms behind his neck. For a long, sweet moment, they did nothing but kiss.

And for that moment, kissing was enough. There was so much pleasure to be found in the taste of her velvet lips, the slick texture of her teeth, the strength of long, smooth legs gripping him as soft breasts pressed against his chest, while his thick cock nudged her belly in stark erotic promise.

That was her perception, not his. He blinked at how intoxicating he felt to her. She drew back to grin up into his eyes. *You even turned me on in combat.* A memory flashed through her mind -- Duncan leaping through the air at the werewolf, swinging his axe, fierce and agile and impossibly male.

*That's how you see me?* Another memory flashed: This one of staring at himself in a mirror in his hospital room, painfully thin and hollow-eyed. *Less than a man.*

Anger spiked through her. *You've never been less than a man. Not even then. You were what you've always been -- a warrior and a hero.* Her lips curled off her teeth in a fierce little snarl. *Just as I am what I've always been.* And she showed him the werewolf's claws ripping into her back, throwing her into a flashback of Emily's whip.

The moment Masara saw herself for what she was: A Maja, powerful and driven.

"A warrior and a hero," he murmured. This time when Duncan kissed her, there was nothing sweet about it. Not with the memory of how close they'd come to losing each other. This kiss was all frantic hunger, teeth and tongue and fierce hands gripping thighs and shoulders.

He bent her backward in his arms, supporting her spine as he found her nipple and sucked hard, drinking in the delicious female scent of magic, sweat, and sex. His fangs ached in his jaw, throbbing almost as hard as his cock. Suddenly ravenous, he carried her through the water and spilled her onto the thick grass. Eyes hot, Masara watched as he braced his arms on the pool's edge and scrambled out to join her.

Through her eyes, he saw water stream down his muscled arms as his body steamed in the evening air. His cock jutted at her, bobbing and eager. And his eyes seemed to glow, impossibly blue.

With a hot feline purr, Masara flicked her fingers, conjuring a pile of pillows. With a happy growl, they fell onto them -- and into each other's arms. Drunk on one another's scent and taste, on the wet heat of each other's bodies. His fangs aching fiercely in his jaw, his balls aching just as hard, Duncan tasted his way down the length of her throat. *Shut up,* he told his growling libido. *I'm going to make this good for her…*

Duncan's cock felt hot and solid against Masara's belly, and she gloried in the hard weight of him as he braced above her on his elbows. She could feel his need for her. The feral vampire craving for her blood, yes, but even that was dwarfed by something deeper and more elemental: yearning. The need to connect with her, to touch her soul as well as her body. To find an end to his loneliness.

A need she shared.

Taking his time, he licked and nibbled his way down her sternum to the rise of her right breast. Long, warm fingers encircled soft skin, cupping and squeezing until her nipple jutted, eager for his mouth. He rewarded it with a burning lick that sent pleasure jolting through her. Closing his mouth over the erect nub, he suckled in eager pulls that made her want to writhe. Groaning, she threaded her fingers through his thick curls, arching her back to lift her breasts in invitation.

Duncan took her up on it, raking each little bud with his teeth, then drawing so hard she gasped in pleasure. Rolling onto one elbow, he sent a big hand stroking down her body, tracing the line of ribs, pausing to tease her belly button. She squirmed, huffing a laugh. And felt the echo of his pleasure at the smooth warmth of her skin, the entrancing curves of breasts and hips. At the taste of her, woman and magic and the scent of blood so close to the surface. Making his fangs ache.

He was working far too hard to control himself. Masara didn't want him to hold back. She wanted all of him, the fierce vampire warrior as well as the careful lover. When he felt that desire through the link, his arousal spiked even hotter, harder. She also knew he wouldn't do it unless she was sure that was what she wanted. *And if you change your mind, I'll stop,* he thought. *It might not be easy, but I'll do it.*

*I know.* She dug her nails into the tight, hard muscles of his biceps, inflicting a deliberate sting of pain. *But we don't need to be careful.*

A growl rumbled through him, deep and hungry and joyous. He bent his head and bit her nipple just hard enough to inflict a quick, hot sting. Masara sucked in a breath as her arousal spiked. The grip of his hands strengthened in a way that might have frightened her -- if not for the link reminding her with every heartbeat that this was Duncan and no one else.

Duncan, who loved her. Because he did. It was there in the link, as naked as he was, and just as unblushing. It wasn't a crush, or simple admiration for a teacher. It was a man's love for a woman, fierce and dark.

Just like the love burning in the depths of Masara's mind.

Never mind that she was a hundred and fifty years older. War and suffering had stripped any traces of boy from him, had left him hard and capable, with no illusions about himself or anyone else. Duncan froze against her as he shared the realization that had just rolled over her. His eyes jerked up to search her face. *Do you mean it? You love me?*

*Yes. Sweet Lord, yes. I've protected myself from everyone and everything so long, it was like living in a suit of armor. You've made me want to love.* Because he wouldn't betray her. That just wasn't in his nature. She was safe with him.

His eyes glowed in the dark, and she saw the flash of his fangs in the moonlight as he smiled. *Are you sure you* want *to be safe?*

The darkness in the thought spread a smile over her face, hot with anticipation. Duncan pounced on her, his hands strong and rough as they squeezed, caressed. His fangs raked gently across her skin with the perfect, stinging pressure to send her arousal spiking. She could feel him listening to her mind, reading her pleasure, intuiting her desires. His hands slid between her legs, obeying her wordless need. He made a rough sound when he found her wet and swollen, and she felt the delicious alien jerk of his cock, so heavy between his thighs.

Masara also wanted to give him the same feral erotic pleasure. As he stroked and bit, his big hands delightfully rough, she sent her magic teasing over him. Licked at him with phantom mouths even as her flesh-and-blood hands stroked the hard breadth of his shoulders, the ridges of muscle and bone lying beneath his skin. Each pleasure they gave each other rang through their bond like a carillon of great bells. Pleasure magnified pleasure.

Duncan reared off her, meaning to throw himself between her thighs and eat her. She showed him her craving for his taste. He grinned at her. "You talked me into it." Throwing a leg over her torso, he bent head down between her thighs, giving her pussy a slow sampling lick. Her pleasure dragged a tortured groan from his mouth.

Masara reached between his legs and grabbed the thick, veined length of his cock. It felt so deliciously hot, skin like velvet in her hands. Stroking slowly up and down its length, she sent her magic kissing and biting the length of his body. Until it felt as if a dozen Masaras sucked and nibbled and licked him. *This is turning into an orgy,* he thought, amusement warring with lust in his brain.

*I wouldn't know. Never been in one.*

*I'd say I had...*

*But I'd know you're lying.* Laughing, she traced elaborate patterns on his muscular ass with the fingers of one hand as she stroked his cock with the other. The thick head was tipped with a shimmering pearl of arousal. He angled his head to find the bead of her clit, then swirled his tongue around it. Her whole body vibrated in delight, which intensified as Duncan slid a forefinger deep, spiking quivering, eager pleasure up her spine.

"God, Duncan!" She imagined his thick cock replacing that finger...

And he showed her how that would feel -- how tight she was, how perfectly she always gripped him. So wet and slick, it was all he could do not to pounce on her and pound into her like a barbarian. His fierce need stoking hers, she wrapped her magic around the head of his cock. Imagined stretching her mouth around his width, straining to accommodate his length...

Duncan shuddered, wildly excited at the images in her mind. Abruptly, Masara had no patience for foreplay anymore. Her magic swept over him, scooped him up, and flipped him onto his back. His eyes widened in shock. "Masara!"

Before he could finish the protest, she grabbed his cock and aimed it for her mouth. And sucked him down, angling her head so she could slide him as deep she could get him. As she swooped down the length of his shaft, their bond reverberated with the sensation, so deliciously exotic.

Masara drew slowly off him, sucking hard, careful of her teeth, and the feeling of her mouth was so arousing, he had to clamp down hard on the need to come then and there. She didn't want to wait any longer. She wanted to fuck him, drive them both out of their minds.

Masara pulled off him and flung one leg over his hips. Grabbing his shaft, she pointed him toward her wet, aching depths, and impaled herself hard and fast, the grind of his hard cock over sensitive tissues tearing a muffled scream from her mouth.

"Not that fast! You're hurting yourself!" he gritted, though she could feel how delicious it felt to him.

"I don't care!" The pleasure he felt overwhelmed the ache and sting in her pussy. Bracing her hands on his flat, muscled belly, Masara began to rise, taking it slow. Making it last. Loving the sensation of his cock sliding through tight, slick, silken flesh. It was if her clit was a foot long, being sucked by an impossible mouth.

He laughed, breathy and tight. "I'm not quite... that big," he panted.

"Feels like it to me," she gasped back, and slid down again.

Each entry and retreat felt exquisite as she rode him, pleasure building on pleasure. Her breasts bounced with the motion, and he caught one to tease the nipple with a callused thumb. The other hand slid between her legs, finding her clit and teasing it every time she rose and fell. The erotic sensations intensified, growing more soul shaking than anything she'd ever known before, and suddenly she couldn't hold back any longer, couldn't take it slow. Any lingering discomfort was gone, banished by the hot, wet grip of her pussy around that incredible cock.

Masara began grinding hard as he pushed back, picking up a rhythm easily through the link and matching it so that each stroke was a perfect dance of hip and hip.

The storm of orgasm gathered as delight fed delight. So close, right on the edge...

Duncan's eyes blazed up at her, wild and wide, and she saw what he wanted. Masara flung herself down full-length against him, giving him her throat.

He sank his fangs deep even as he rolled his hips, thrusting into her. Her blood flooded his mouth, blasting his senses with her taste and scent. The sting of his fangs felt impossibly erotic, just as each swallow of her blood tasted like distilled delight.

It wasn't possible to tell who came first.

Masara screamed for both of them as they catapulted into ecstasy.

* * *

They lay entwined together, catching their breath as their heartbeats slowed. Absently, Duncan picked up one of the thick, heavy ropes of her hair. It was still dripping wet, though he knew she could dry it in an instant. A thought flashed through his mind: *What does it look like without the dreads?*

Masara grinned and gestured. The dreadlocks vanished, replaced by a gold band that pinned her hair flat to her head before it flared around her head in a dark corona. Sprawled against the pillows, her face surrounded by all that magnificent hair, she lay framed by exotic flowers, her wet skin gleaming in the moonlight.

Words came out of his mouth with absolutely no forethought whatsoever. "Marry me."

Masara stared at him in shock. "What?"

Oh, fuck, he'd just blown it. *Perfect*, he snarled at himself. *Way to ruin the mood, you ass. Now she's going to back the hell off.*

Her eyes narrowed dangerously. "Now that, to quote a certain Marine, is bullshit. If you want to know what I think, all you have to do is look." And she threw herself open to him, nothing held back.

*You're fierce and male and so courageous you terrify me. And you know what it's like to suffer, know what it's like to survive even when you're not sure you want to. Know what it's like to heal even when it hurts so badly all you want to do is die. And you know what it means to sacrifice for the good of other people.* "Yes, I will marry you," she told him aloud, a huge smile spreading across her face, her dark eyes lighting with joy. "And that's no sacrifice at all."

They were in each other's arms without knowing who'd moved first. All they knew for sure was that together they were so much more, and without each other they'd be so much less.

# Master of Fate (Merlin's Legacy 3)

## Angela Knight

Alys Hawkwood is the most powerful seer among the witches of the Magekind. She's seen a lot of horrors in her visions, but this is the worst: the destruction of the Magekind. The only way to prevent the deaths of everyone she cares about is to allow their worst enemy to kidnap her. Her only hope of rescue is her vampire partner, Davon -- the man she loves -- and the one she can never have.

To carry out her plan and save them all, Davon must pull off the impossible: take on a dragon and countless alien enemies alone. But his most deadly opponent is Alys herself...

# Chapter One

Davon Fredericks watched the rich crimson liquid swirl in the cut crystal glass as he rotated his wrist. The roots of his fangs ached.

He took a sip, and the taste exploded on his tongue, sending a jolt of magic lancing the length of his spine. Heat streamed into his groin at the flavor, the scent, the sheer, erotic essence of Alys Hawkwood's blood.

His gaze slid over to her as she sat next to him on the dark tufted leather of the couch, watching Netflix on an enchanted tablet. Alys looked barely twenty -- quite a trick for someone born when Shakespeare was writing *Hamlet*.

Twelve years ago, if someone had told Davon he'd be partners with an Elizabethan, he'd have put that idiot on a psych hold. He'd considered himself a thoroughly rational man, a believer in science and logic. He'd had to be. He was a twenty-first century African American trauma surgeon in Chicago, a city where it wasn't easy to be either black or a doctor. He hadn't had time for woo-woo crap -- until a witch offered him the chance to become a vampire and save humanity.

Now here he was, immortal partner to another beautiful witch.

And Alys *was* beautiful.

Her skin was a couple of shades lighter than his own deep bronze, since she was the daughter of an African vampire father and a Caucasian witch. Her lean, muscled body was a product of centuries of fighting for the survival of humanity -- and a tendency to forget to eat unless Davon nagged her.

A riot of gleaming midnight curls sprang from her elegant head, framing a delicate, angular face. Huge eyes of a deep cinnamon brown balanced the swoop of her wide nose and the lush curve of her mouth. Soft, vulnerable lips parted as she laughed at something on her screen, showing the white edges of her teeth.

God, Davon hungered for that mouth. He'd wanted to kiss her the first time he met her, and he still wanted it ten years later. And he wanted to taste a lot more than her mouth, starting with the smooth length of those golden thighs, only partially concealed by a tiny pair of yellow shorts. A matching silk shirt bloused over her pretty breasts, drawing his attention to the hard nipples tenting the thin fabric.

Davon's fangs gave another throbbing pulse as his cock hardened. *Yeah, no.*

He dragged his gaze away by sheer force of will, focusing his attention on the oak wainscoting that ran around the house's library. That section of paneling was intricately carved with magical symbols designed to amplify Alys's magic. Though they'd shared the big Tudor-style mansion for ten years, he was still finding new flourishes in the decor.

Whenever Alys felt anxious, she conjured something beautiful. The unicorn tapestry that covered one of the library walls had appeared following the last battle with King Bres. Davon's near death at the hands of a troll had resulted in a stained-glass portrait of Merlin. He suspected every statue, rug, and carved ceiling beam in the house owed its existence to post-battle anxiety.

The whole place was the three-dimensional equivalent of Pinterest page therapy -- lovely, whimsical -- and ever so slightly OCD.

Aaand his erection had finally deflated, thank God. He blew out a breath in relief. He and Alys didn't have that kind of fuckbuddy partnership. Damn it.

Mostly to keep his mind off his dick, he asked, "Any word on what Bres is up to?" Nothing could kill an erotic mood quite like a magic-using psychotic who wanted all humans dead.

Alys looked up, intelligence burning like a flame in cinnamon eyes. "The Fomorians have gone quiet. I have a feeling he's up to som…" Her voice trailed off.

What looked like a wave of ink flooded Alys's sclera and irises, drowning her eyes in black. Points of light burst against the darkness, stars igniting in the eternal night. *Oh, hell.* She was having a vision.

Though his heart had begun to pound, Davon didn't move, didn't do anything to interrupt. Alys was the most powerful seer among the Magekind's witches. They all got flashes of the future, but no one else saw as clearly. More importantly, she could often predict how to avoid a horrific future, a talent not even Morgana Le Fay had.

So no, you didn't interrupt one of Alys's visions.

Not that what she learned was always welcome. Sometimes preventing one ugly future would trigger something even worse, so they couldn't do a damn thing.

Which didn't do a lot for her mental state. There was a reason they called her Mad Alys. Davon's mission in life was making sure that shitty nickname didn't become a reality.

He watched her expression, trying to determine whether this one was going to be another one of *those* situations. At least there were no flickers of terror and despair on her face, though the tightening line of her jaw suggested growing anger.

A kid must be involved in this. Nothing pissed Alys off like some asshole hurting a child. Often the asshole in question ended up very, very dead by the time she and Davon finished teaching him the error of his ways.

The blackness drained from Alys's eyes as if someone had pulled a stopper in her skull, revealing her normal irises. She blinked at him, her gaze a little confused.

"Alys?" he asked.

The vague air vanished as her eyes snapped into focus. "We've got a mission." Surging off the couch as if she'd been launched from a catapult, the Maja flung her arms wide.

Magic flooded the room in response to her will, rolling over Davon's body. The foaming wave of sparks condensed into the new suit of armor she'd conjured last week. Its gleaming chest plate, groin protector, gauntlets and boots were intricately engraved with protective spells. Fine scale mail, as light and flexible as his own skin, covered everything the plate didn't. The suit's helm looked more futuristic than medieval, with a transparent faceplate designed to allow maximum peripheral vision.

Davon thoroughly approved. It was much lighter than the old armor, easier to move in, more resistant to magical blasts. Unlike the previous kit, nothing would be able to penetrate it with fang, claw or blade. Not without a hell of a lot of work, anyway.

A familiar weight hung against his back. He turned his head to see the hilt of his sword protruding over his left shoulder, the blade sheathed in a diagonal scabbard.

When Davon glanced back, armor had replaced Alys's shorts and shirt, covering her lean, elegant body in gold plate and scale mail.

She drew her longsword from its back scabbard and tossed it onto the couch with a soft thump. "I'm going to need something with a little bit more buzz for this job." She raised both hands, and light blazed between her palms, solidifying into a weapon.

The two-handed great sword shone with an unearthly blue light, magic spiraling in hair-thin lightning forks from pommel to point and back again. The blade smoked as she held it, filling the air with the smell of ozone.

"Oh, shit!" Davon took an instinctive step back. "Reaver? We need *Reaver* for this?"

She shrugged. "It's going to get a little dicey."

"How dicey? What's going on?"

"King Llyr's kid has been snatched by his own bodyguard. The traitor's going to hand the boy over to the Fomorians, who are meeting him for the handoff."

"Fucking Bres." She'd been right about the enemy king being up to something.

"Exactly. Your job is to grab Prince Dearg. I'll be the big, loud distraction with a side order of flaming death."

Davon grinned. "You do play to your strengths."

"Yep. I'll call King Llyr and Arthur, but the vision says it'll take our backup eight minutes to arrive. If we don't have Dearg in four, he's dead. We've got zero wiggle room on this mission, 'Von." Her gaze burned into his, fierce and level. "Do not leave that boy. Even if I go down, you're to protect him above everything else."

He gave her a crisp nod. "I'll take care of it."

Alys smiled. "I know." She flicked her long fingers, and he felt the communication spell sizzle through the air, off to alert Arthur and the child's father. "I'll take this gate, you take the next."

She gestured, and a white-hot point appeared in midair. Normally it took a moment for a dimensional gate to stabilize, but this one expanded to human-size in a heartbeat. She wasn't fooling around.

"Avaaaaalonnnnn!" Howling the Magekind's battle cry, Alys leaped through the gate, tossing a spell over her shoulder as she went.

Another blazing spark ignited before Davon's face, swelling out into the wavering oval that was his own magical doorway. Drawing his sword, he slipped through like a shadow.

Magic rolled over his skin as his booted feet came down on a thick carpet of leaves. Massive oaks and maples the size of redwoods loomed around him, branches so thickly intertwined, they blocked the star-flecked Mageverse sky.

A mortal wouldn't have been able to see a damn thing. Luckily, Davon hadn't been mortal in eleven years.

A clearing lay ten yards away, illuminated by Reaver's blue fire. High, feminine laughter rang out over the sword's menacing crackle. His partner was giving the Fomos the full Mad Alys floorshow.

The Fomorians cursed, and something that sounded like a troll roared as hooves thumped on the loamy forest floor.

Where the hell was Dearg?

Davon edged closer until he glimpsed Alys charging the band of armored warriors, swinging Reaver in crackling arcs. The Fomorians wisely recoiled. He scanned the group, but there was no sign of the Sidhe traitor and his captive. Aside from a centaur and a troll, the other twelve warriors were Fomo, judging by the blue skin, three-fingered hands, and the way they walked on their toes like dogs.

The troll towered over them all, eight feet of massive green shoulders corded with muscle beneath chain mail and enchanted leather armor. Tusks distorted his snarling mouth, thrusting up from his jutting bulldog jaw. He carried a battleaxe in one huge hand and a kite-shaped shield in the other.

"Great," Davon muttered. "She's picked a fight with the Incredible Hulk and a team of psychotic Smurfs." And as if that wasn't bad enough, a centaur stalked Alys, his hair a wild tangle, bloodlust contorting his face. His humanoid torso was only a little smaller than the troll's, while his horse half was easily the size of a Clydesdale. Dressed in plate armor and carrying a pike, he pawed the ground.

On the Mageverse's version of Earth, humankind wasn't the only intelligent species. From tiny demi-Sidhe to dragons, they all used combat magic, rendering guns and other mortal tech useless.

The centaur spat something guttural, making a lewd gesture with his spear. The communication spell on Davon's helm whispered an English translation: "Whore, I'll savor your screams while I bugger your ass and impale your cunt on my pike!"

Fury peeled Davon's lips back from his teeth, but he didn't have time to show that horse fucker where the pike *really* belonged. He had to find the prince.

The thud of hooves on the leaves announced the centaur's charge. Alys spun aside like a bullfighter, dodging a pike thrust by millimeters.

As the 'taur thundered past, she raked Reaver's enchanted blade along his ribs. A thunderous crack sounded, and the centaur howled as the wound exploded with leaping bolts of mystical energy. His deep voice spiraled into the high-pitched shriek of a dying stallion as the magical fire spread, and he reared, screaming, flames leaping twenty feet in the air. A moment later, his huge body toppled, already black with char as the enchanted flame winked out. The smoky air reeked with the smell of burned meat.

"Who's screaming now, pony boy?" Alys laughed, one of those high-pitched cackles guaranteed to rivet everybody's attention on the crazy lady with the blazing sword.

Rather than, say, her sneaky vampire partner lurking in the woods.

Something moved in the darkness off to his right, and Davon snapped his head around. *There.* The familiar curving contours of Sidhe armor gleamed in Reaver's blue shimmer.

The traitor stood on the edge of the clearing, about twenty feet away, the limp body of a young boy draped over one armored shoulder. Though he couldn't see the boy's face, he didn't like the way the prince's head dangled. His mane of straight black hair hung past the Sidhe's ass, swaying with his captor's movements. *Definitely unconscious,* Davon thought.

At least, he hoped the kid was just out cold.

Davon moved toward the two, ghosting around a huge tree. He normally hated killing an enemy from behind -- it made his gut heave with bad memories. But *this* kidnapping motherfucker deserved whatever he got.

The trick would be taking the Sidhe out without hurting the boy. If Davon tried to run the abductor through, he risked hitting Dearg. Beheading him was out for the same reason...

*His sword flashed in a gleaming arc, severing the thin neck. The dark head tumbled, blood spraying in a crimson…*

*Shut. Up.*

An upward thrust on the traitor's right side wouldn't injure Dearg, who hung over his left shoulder. But it was tight, and if the dickhead…

The warrior spun, hurling a fireball at Davon's face.

But Alys had spent ten years teaching Davon to fight, and he was moving before the Sidhe completed the turn. The blast missed his head by inches. Nasty one, too. He felt the heat even through his helmet.

Davon charged, swinging his sword in a diagonal upward slice at the right side of the Sidhe's chest. His blade rammed into something that flared with blue light. The weapon rebounded so hard, it almost flew out of his hand.

Fuck. Shield spell. He'd dealt with enough of those to know this one was damned powerful. He wouldn't be able to just batter at it until it fell.

"One of Arthur Pendragon's more insignificant vampires." The traitor sneered through the transparent visor of his helm, malevolent pleasure in his eyes. "And you without a witch to work magic for you." His lip curled. "Pray to whatever God you worship."

"Big talk, Tinkerbell." Alys had said he had four minutes to rescue Dearg. *How long does the boy have left? Two minutes? A minute and a half?*

Beyond him, Alys shouted in pain and rage. Davon gritted his teeth. He had to trust her to do her job as she trusted him to do his. He circled the kidnapper, who pivoted to follow him. Given the traitor's shield, he couldn't do much else. On the other hand, the Sidhe would have to drop the barrier to hit him. Davon could strike while the shield was down, assuming he could avoid getting fried in the process.

Dearg stirred as the two fighters circled. He abruptly jackknifed upright, rearing against the Sidhe's hold on his hips, straightening to look down at the man in confused terror. The side of his face was black and blue.

Rage stabbed Davon, and he glared at Dearg's abductor. *You're a dead fairy, Tinkerdick.*

Dearg blinked in shocked recognition and said something Davon couldn't hear. The traitor spat a reply. Fury joined fear on the boy's face as his irises blazed white-hot.

Dearg's magical shield slammed outward, ramming Tinkerdick against the inside of the traitor's barrier. With a yelp, the Sidhe dropped his shield -- it was that or be crushed between it and Dearg's.

Even so, the expansion of Dearg's shield smashed the traitor face-first to the ground and flung the child through the air. The prince hit the ground five feet away with a cry of pain.

*Shit,* Davon thought. Pouncing on Tinkerdick, he drove his blade down at the man's chest. The Sidhe brought up his own weapon in a frantic parry, but Davon flicked his around it, avoiding the block even as he rammed downward. His sword punched through the traitor's cuirass, driving right through the warrior to stake him to the ground.

Gasping in agony, the Sidhe stared up the length of Davon's blade. Shock and pain turned to outrage. "You will pay for this, vam..." His fury abruptly drained, leaving the traitor gasping. He blinked. To Davon's amazement, his eyes filled with a bizarre kind of gratitude. "You... freed me... Tell my king... Didn't betray… him. Bres… It was Bres…" His voice faded into a rattling wheeze as his eyes went fixed.

Dead.

"Fuck." Davon had killed an innocent. Again. Just like Jimmy Sheridan…

*I don't have time for this.* He shook the guilt off and ran for the boy, who still lay on his back.

Dearg saw him coming. Iridescent eyes widening in fear, he tried to stagger to his feet. Magic ignited above his palm, becoming an impressive fireball. "Who are you? What do you want?"

"Magekind agent -- name's Davon Fredericks. My partner and I are here to protect you until your parents arrive."

"You… are?" He stared at Davon until whatever he saw reassured him. Both fireball and shield winked out. "I thought Erim was going to…" His lips trembled, and he bit them hard, visibly fighting to hide his fear and pain.

"You're safe now. Are you all right?" Davon dropped to one knee by his side. Trauma doc training demanded he check Dearg out -- even as combat experience told him the middle of a battle was no place to do it. He pacified his inner M.D. by studying the boy intently.

Despite the bruises, Dearg was a good-looking child, with the pointed ears and handsome, angular features of the Sidhe. Like most Sidhe males, he wore his black hair long, though leaves and twigs were tangled in its snarled length. His doublet, hose and knee-length boots were dirty and blood-splattered. Davon hoped none of the gore was his.

But his pupils were even, and his gaze was alert, if bright with the tears he was fighting. "Any broken bones? How's your head? You hit the ground pretty hard."

"I'm okay." Must have learned English from his American mother, though his accent held a Sidhe lilt that sounded faintly Irish. "I thought Erim... Why would he... he was my friend." His breath hitched, and a single tear rolled down the prince's bruised cheek. "When I woke up, he was standing by my bed. He hit me so... *hard*! I tried to block, but..." He broke off, staring toward the clearing, where Alys was beheading the troll. The huge body exploded into flame and toppled. "Who the heck is that? What's happening? Where *are* we?"

"My partner." Davon laid an armored hand on the child's shoulder and gave him a comforting squeeze. "She's taking care of the Fomorians while I keep you safe."

"The Fomorians?" The kid stared at him. "Erim was going to give me to the Fomos?"

"I think Bres was controlling him." Where the hell was their backup? Davon cast an uneasy glance at the clearing. The troll lay smoking, looking like a blackened hillside surrounded by four smaller, equally crispy corpses. Probably Fomo warriors. The centaur's ashy remains were flaking away on the wind.

The eight survivors circled Alys warily, understandably in no hurry to get within range of Reaver. Davon badly wanted to dive in there and help before they evolved balls and overwhelmed her. Alys was damned good, and Reaver scared hell out of anyone sane, but eight-to-one odds...

*"Do not leave that boy. Even if I go down, you are to protect him above all."* When Alys gave that kind of order after a vision, you damned well listened. Or

wished to fuck you had because of the resulting body count.

"Look," Davon told the boy, "Alys is doing a good job keeping the Fomos busy, but one of them may decide to come after us. Can you conjure a shield?"

Dearg wiped his nose on one loose, flowing sleeve. "Oh, yeah -- Dad said you vampire guys can't do that kind of magic." He gestured, and a shimmering translucent dome appeared around them both.

Davon eyed it. The magical glow was strong and even. "Nice work."

"Better be." The prince scrubbed impatiently at his wet eyes, smearing dirt over his bruised face. "My father's been training me for this sort of stuff since I was five. He'd be pissed if I screwed it up." His face turned grim. "He had ten kids before me. My uncle killed 'em all. Dad doesn't need to lose me too."

Alys began to laugh in that high, shrieking cackle again. Somebody must be getting ballsy.

Dearg cast her a wary glance as she charged a warrior, her sword blazing blue. The Fomorian skittered away from Reaver's crackling point. "Your partner's creepy."

"Nah, that's an act." *Mostly.* "She's making sure everybody's too freaked out to…"

"Crap, here comes one!" Dearg pointed. Sure enough, a Fomorian slunk toward them, rose eyes cold and murderous against the blue of his skin. "Want me to drop the shield so you can…"

"No, we're better off letting him beat on it until your parents and the Knights arrive." Still, Davon fell into guard, sword ready to attack or parry.

But instead of charging them, the warrior bent, seized Erim's corpse, and heaved it across one shoulder. A dimensional gate flared wide and the Fomorian vanished through it with his burden.

"Damn it!" Davon spat. "Look, can you track where that gate…"

Before he could finish the thought, magic roared in his senses. A *lot* of dimensional gates were opening all around them. He blew out a relieved breath. "Damn, that was a long eight minutes." Sparks flared in the surrounding darkness, expanding into wavering doorways.

"Avaaaaalon!" Arthur roared as he plunged through the nearest gate, a brawny figure in the same kind of armor Davon wore. Excalibur in one hand, a ferocious glower on his bearded face, he paused just long enough to evaluate the situation before charging the Fomorians.

His wife Guinevere raced in his wake, blond and beautiful, a pair of conjured fireballs ready to go. Morgana le Fay was the next agent to appear, magic boiling around her like a storm, Percival, Marrok and Cador behind her. Kel, Lancelot, Galahad, Gawain, Tristan, Lamark, and Badoff popped out of the other gates, accompanied by their Majae partners.

The Knights of the Round Table had arrived, ready to kick Fomorian ass.

Which weren't in any hurry to get kicked. One Fomo shouted to the others, yelling something Davon's helmet translated as, "*Retreat!*"

Sparks flared, only to instantly wink out. A Maja must have cast a blocking spell.

Howling, the Fomos turned to meet the Magekind charge. Steel rang on steel, accompanied by the boom and crackle of magic. The Fomorians fought like berserkers, apparently less afraid of dying than of what their leader would do to them if they were captured. No surprise. King Bres was a sociopathic son of a bitch who showed his own people as little mercy as he did his enemies.

Davon ached to join the fight now that reinforcements were here, but he had his orders. He could only watch as Alys went after every Fomo she could, her sword a vicious blaze even the Knights eyed with caution.

Watching the Magekind take the Fomorians apart, Davon realized they didn't need his help. He was a good swordsman for his generation, but Arthur's immortal crew had more than fifteen centuries of combat experience.

"They're pretty good," Dearg said, sounding surprised. "Almost as good as my fath…" He broke off as a wild-eyed Fomorian raced toward them, sword lifted.

A roar rang through the clearing, sounding like a seriously pissed lion. Something black barreled out of the melee to leap on the Fomo, smashing him to the ground. The furred figure tore off the gorget protecting the warrior's neck, slashing three three-inch claws across his throat. Blood flew and the Fomo convulsed, gagging, dying, as the Dire Wolf spun, scanning the clearing, pale eyes narrow slits of ice and rage.

A broad grin lit Dearg's face, and he waved like the kid he was. "Hi, Mom!"

# Chapter Two

*Mom?* Davon thought. Taking another look, he realized the werewolf was indeed female, judging by the full breasts under all that thick black fur.

But Carol Brady, she was not. Snarling lips peeled back to reveal more teeth than a crocodile. A long mane surrounded her lupine head, making her well over seven feet tall.

"Well, shit." She straightened out of her crouch with a disappointed grunt. "They're all dead."

Arthur and Excalibur had just parted the last Fomorian from his head.

"Mom!" Dearg yelled again. He banished the shield around himself and Davon, then raced toward the Dire Wolf.

Magic flared, and abruptly the werewolf was a foot shorter. Now a slim, lovely woman, she wore a blue velvet gown in an elaborate Sidhe style shimmering with sapphires and silver embroidery. Her black hair was swept into an intricate updo of woven braids, revealing ears that lacked her son's elegant points. No surprise, since she was human.

More or less.

"Dearg!" As the prince threw himself into her arms, Queen Diana Galatyn swept the boy off his feet. Her pale eyes glittered with tears as she clutched him in frantic joy. "Oh, God, Dearg! I thought I'd lost you!"

"Ouch! Ribs, Mom! They're kind of bruised."

With a soft cry, the queen put him down and drew back to study him, her expression more than a little wild. "What did they do to you?"

"Nothing much," Dearg said. Probably lying, judging by his pain-tight lips. "Dad's done worse in combat practice."

"Yeah, right. Llyr!"

A man looked toward them from the other side of the clearing, where he stood wiping his bloody sword and talking to Arthur. King Llyr Galatyn was a tall, handsome man in the elaborately engraved armor of a Sidhe noble. Evidently Davon had missed seeing him and his queen gate in. A relieved grin flashed across his face, and he started toward them in long strides.

It looked like the kid was in safe hands, so Davon stepped aside to give them some privacy.

"Good work."

He turned to find Alys sheathing Reaver in her back scabbard. The sword had gone dark, its blade no longer crackling; she'd ceased feeding it her magic. Sweaty and exhausted, she was smeared with soot and blood in various non-human shades. But her mail seemed to be in one piece, without any visible punctures or slices. Which was something of a miracle, considering the odds she'd been facing.

"I had the easy job." Davon shrugged. "Dearg basically saved himself. I'd have had a hell of a time getting through Erim's shield if the prince hadn't forced him to drop it."

"Don't kid yourself." Alys's expression turned grim. "I saw a future where you left Dearg to protect me. One of the Fomos ran the kid through."

Crap. He remembered the warrior who'd grabbed the Sidhe's corpse and gated. That was probably the one who'd have killed the prince if Davon hadn't obeyed orders.

"In that future, Llyr turned against us for failing to protect his child. Without him…" Alys swallowed and looked away. "It… would have been bad."

He squeezed her armored shoulder, wishing he could touch skin. "You told me not to leave him. I've learned to listen."

Her dark mood lightening, she gave him a smile. "Best partner I've ever had."

*I'd like to be more than your partner.* But he didn't say the words, silenced by a decade of romantic inertia.

Across the clearing, he heard Llyr's furious Sidhe-accented rumble. "I cannot *believe* this. How did the Fomorians get to Erim? Of all my men, I'd have sworn he was the least likely to betray us."

Davon turned to find Llyr and his wife huddling protectively around Dearg as they spoke to Morgana, Gwen, and Arthur. The boy looked much better, bruises gone, eyes no longer tight with pain. The king must have healed his injuries, though the prince still looked thoroughly miserable. Probably as upset at his bodyguard's betrayal as Llyr was.

Reminded of his opponent's last words, Davon walked over. "Your Majesty, I don't think Erim acted of his own accord."

"Indeed?" Llyr lifted one golden eyebrow, watching coolly as he and Alys approached. "What leads you to that conclusion?"

Davon described his fight with the Sidhe bodyguard. "One minute Erim was snarling threats. The next, he got a relieved expression on his face. The last thing he said was, 'You freed me. Tell my king I didn't betray him. It was Bres.' One of the Fomorians grabbed the body and gated out."

After a thoughtful silence, Arthur said, "That sounds similar to what two of my agents experienced with those werewolves last month." To Llyr he explained, "We think Bres infected three werewolves with a contagion he used to gain control of their minds and turn them into puppets. Maybe he possessed Erim the same way."

The queen frowned. "A contagion? What kind of contagion?"

"We're working on that." Morgana le Fay moved to join the group. The leader of the Majae was tall, dark-haired, and impossibly beautiful in her armor. As always, her raw power danced ghostly fingers over Davon's skin. "Do you know if your man was bitten by anything? The first of those werewolves was infected when he was attacked by a swarm of rats."

Llyr shook his head, his long white hair swaying around armored shoulders. "Not that I know of. Erim was on leave this past week. I believe he planned to visit his brother in my Morven territories."

Arthur's dark brows lifted. "Could have been attacked on the way. Maybe you should ask his brother if he actually made it there."

Davon frowned. "If he did arrive, find out if he was ill. I discussed this with Masara Okeye -- she's the Maja agent who handled the werewolf case. She said the man's daughter believed he was sick for several hours before he savaged his wife, infecting her too. The two of them then attacked a third werewolf before all three went after Masara."

"We'd better make sure none of our people go anywhere alone," Arthur said grimly. "We can't afford to lose anyone else to this thing."

"Which means we need to get our hands on a blood sample as soon as possible," Davon suggested. "We might be able to vaccinate our people if we could capture someone who's been infected."

"Bres probably thinks so too," Morgana speculated. "I'll wager that's why he makes sure to remove the bodies." She described the swarm of black insects that had emerged from the werewolf corpses and flown away. "There was no sign of any disease or virus present in their cells afterward. It's almost as if the insects *were* the contagion."

"That sounds like magic," Diana protested. "We're immune to all magic except our own."

Morgana shrugged. "Well, something sure as hell is possessing people."

Diana shuddered and pulled her son close. "Now, *there's* a subject for my next nightmare."

\* \* \*

After the royal couple, Dearg, and their guards gated back to the Sidhe lands, the Majae began magically examining the enemy dead for any sign of the contagion. None were infected, so they started disposing of the bodies.

As the last corpses vanished in a storm of sparks, Alys made some slight sound, almost a moan. Davon glanced away from the magical bonfire to see ink swirl through one of her eyes. Terror flashed across her face. The hair rose on the back of his neck, but he kept his mouth shut, not wanting to interrupt the vision. She blinked and the ink drained away.

"What'd you see?" he demanded. The look on her face… "Was that a vision?"

"No, I…" Alys frowned. "I'm not sure. For a minute, I thought…" Shaking her head, she gave him a tight smile. "It's gone now."

He frowned. *Yeah, that's not ominous at all.*

\* \* \*

It took the last of Alys's strength to open a dimensional gate back to Avalon, the Magekind's home city on Mageverse Earth. Though the fight with the Fomorians had been relatively brief, eight minutes swinging Reaver was the equivalent of running a marathon wearing lead shorts. Powering the magical blade was a bitch, even without the physical effort of fighting fourteen opponents at once. But she'd had no choice. Her visions had predicted she wouldn't last three minutes without Reaver.

The effort of creating the magical doorway sent a dagger of pain shooting into Alys's skull. Even as she stepped through the gate, the room spun around her. Her knees buckled.

Powerful arms wrapped around her as Davon scooped her off her feet.

"I can walk!"

"Yeah, right." Ignoring her glower, he carried her through the house, his arms warm and strong.

Arguing with Davon in this mood was a waste of effort. She found herself relaxing into his muscular body with an exhausted sigh. When they reached the kitchen, he deposited her on one of the barstools at the central island. Alys planted both elbows on the table and let herself slump.

Most of the house did a reasonable imitation of Tudor architecture -- high ceilings, exposed beams, oak wainscoting and paneling. The kitchen was the exception. The two story high ceiling was supported by the house's usual thick oak beams, but the walls and cabinetry were a gleaming white, while the floor was covered in rust brown ceramic tile. Where a Tudor kitchen would have had a fireplace, Alys's featured a huge stainless steel stove that looked like a Mortal Earth appliance, though powered by magic rather than electricity. There was no refrigerator or dishwasher -- spells kept the dishes clean and the food in the cabinets fresh.

Thinking of food made her stomach growl.

Davon laughed softly. "Give me a minute, witch." He shed his gauntlets, then dropped them on the island's gleaming oak top. He reached for her helmet, which reacted to his touch, disengaging from the rest of the suit. Lifting the helm off her head, he put it down beside his gloves.

Alys considered protesting that she could undress herself, but when she sought her magic to send the armor swirling back to the mannequin in her room, her head produced nothing more than an angry throb. She gritted out an involuntary groan between her teeth.

"Yeah, you did fry yourself, didn't you?" His deep voice seemed to stroke along her skin like the brush of velvet. "You let me take care of the armor. I have opposable thumbs for a reason."

He was right. Alys had tested her limits often enough to recognize the cold pit where her magic should be. She made no protest as he brushed his fingers over her gauntlet. Her arm's scale mail retracted into the glove, and he pulled it off and dropped it beside the helm.

His hands felt deliciously warm and sword-calloused as he stripped her. Alys sighed in relief as cool air breathed over her body, then grimaced at the liberated stink of fear sweat clinging to her flesh under her one-piece tank suit. "I smell like a goat."

"But a very pretty one." He started removing his own armor, its assorted pieces rattling down on top of her own.

As Alys slumped in weariness, her stomach produced a growl that would have done Diana Galatyn proud. Davon laughed, the sound so rich and masculine, the deep inner muscles of her sex clenched in reaction. Even as exhausted as she was, he affected her.

"I can see I need to feed my witch. Just let me get my Spam out of this can and I'll get right on that."

The prospect of watching Davon undress made Alys open eyes she hadn't realized she'd closed.

He popped open the chest plate, revealing rich, bronze skin sliding over rolling muscle. Her body warmed as he stripped down to a pair of skintight gray briefs, purring approval at his muscled ass, the strong contours of his upper thighs, the generous bulge of his cock and balls.

Heat rolled through her, until she suspected she was creaming her suit's cotton crotch.

"How does a steak, a salad and a baked potato sound?" Davon asked.

"Delicious." The word emerged as a purr that had more to do with the view than her stomach.

"Give me fifteen and you'll have it." 'Von smiled at her, brown eyes crinkling in his long, handsome face. He wore his hair buzzed short on the sides, with long curling locks tumbling over his intelligent forehead. Like everything else about him, she found the style ridiculously sexy.

Turning, he started moving around the kitchen, all sensual male grace. Being a vampire, Davon no longer ate, but his mother had taught him to cook when he was a kid. He still knew his way around a kitchen, and he seemed to enjoy feeding her.

Unlike most Majae, who turned food production into a competitive sport, Alys had never enjoyed cooking. She was happy to let him do it. She could have conjured a meal, of course, but food always seemed to taste better when Davon prepared it.

He rummaged in the cabinets, pulling out a thick rib eye and a selection of vegetables in stasis packs. He dropped them on the island and wrapped a baked potato in magical foil designed to speed heating then popped it into the oven and pulled a ceramic knife from a drawer.

As Davon went to work slicing veggies with skill and concentration, she watched the smooth slide of tendon and muscle in those clever surgeon's hands. Heat and sweet longing rolled through her like a tide of sun-warmed honey. "Do you ever miss it?"

He looked up. "Miss what?"

"Being a doctor." She grimaced. "Instead of partner to a witch half of Avalon thinks is mad." The words sounded more bitter than she'd intended.

"Only the idiots think any such thing." His dark gaze met hers. "How many did we save today?"

She shrugged. "Thousands. Arthur would have pulled it out in the end, but the death toll…"

"Exactly." He put on a pair of oven mitts and got the potato out of the stove, replacing it with the steak. "I became a doctor to save lives. But I could never have done as much good in the ER as I have working with you."

The compliment made her feel oddly warm -- probably because Davon never said anything he didn't mean. Alys smiled at him in genuine pleasure. "Thanks."

One raspberry vinaigrette preparation later, he presented her with a salad bowl, silverware, and a linen napkin. Alys picked up a fork and speared a crunchy bite. It was every bit as fresh and tangy as she'd known it would be, and she purred in pleasure. "Delicious, as usual." She was only halfway through the salad when a plate joined it in front of her. The potato steamed under a small mountain of butter and sour cream, and the steak was cooked medium rare and juicy.

Davon smiled at her, lazy sensuality lighting those warm velvet eyes. "*Bon Appétit.*"

She cut a bite of steak and forked it into her mouth. A rich, meaty taste hit her tongue, and she moaned. "Oh, God, that's good." Her voice sounded throaty.

He watched her lips, heat flaring in those dark, dark irises. "Glad you approve." His voice dipped into an even deeper register than usual.

As she tucked into the meal, Davon headed to the wine rack and selected a couple of bottles. He got a pair of glasses out of the cabinet and filled one of them with something deep and crimson -- her blood. The bottle's stasis spell kept it as warm and fresh as the moment it left her veins.

Davon topped off the other glass with the merlot and put it down by her plate, then slid into the chair opposite hers with his own. His lids lowered, dark lashes casting shadows on his cheeks as he drank. Just a sip first. Taking her into his mouth and holding her there. His big, half-naked body shuddered in pleasure.

*I can't have him,* Alys reminded herself, watching him. Remembering.

They'd met at a party to celebrate the end of the Werewolf War. Davon had been standing on the edge of the drunken, happy crowd, his handsome face grim, his dark eyes bleak. He'd had good reason to be depressed; his first partner had just died, and he still blamed himself for the boy he'd killed under the influence of an enemy's spell.

Alys had taken one look at him, and a voice spoke up from the back of her brain. *Him. He's the one.*

That voice had been right. As it always was, even when she wished to fuck it was wrong. With a frustrated sigh, she went back to her dinner.

Halfway through the meal, Alys realized her right hand had developed a persistent ache. She'd just finished the last forkful when the muscles of her forearm knotted. "Shit!" Pain stabbed viciously to her shoulder, and she grabbed her wrist with her left hand, feeling her fingers seize and jerk.

Davon caught her forearm in one warm hand as he wrapped the other around her own, thumb digging in to the knotted muscle until the cramp began to ease. "Using that damned sword always kicks your ass."

"Reaver... isn't that well-balanced," she gasped, arching backward in her chair as waves of agony rippled up her arm. The savage pain retreated as his skilled fingers pressed and kneaded, working the knots until they released. She moaned in relief. "You are definitely the best partner I've ever had."

His gaze flicked up to hers as his lips curled in a wry smile. "That bar's set pretty low."

"Having Mad Alys for a partner isn't exactly a party, either." Then again, sometimes *being* Mad Alys sucked even more.

Like the hours she'd spent crying on September 10th, 2001. She'd seen it all -- the way all those people would die. Some crushed, some burning, some throwing themselves to their deaths.

She could have saved them. It would have been so easy to prevent the terrorists from boarding those planes. A handful of agents could have killed all the bastards as they so richly deserved. No innocent deaths. No wives, husbands, children, parents, families left grieving.

Davon glowered. "You always have a damn good reason for everything you do."

"Maybe, but people tend to get a little pissy when you don't prevent the catastrophe you know is coming. Or worse, tell them they can't prevent it, either."

Without those three thousand murdered innocents sending America to war exactly when it went to war, five years later Osama bin Laden would have gotten his hands on a nuclear bomb. And used it on Washington, D.C.

In every potential future Alys had seen, preventing 9/11 would cause the nuclear destruction of a major American city. It didn't matter what she did to avoid the bombing, who she warned, or who she killed, millions were going to die. In the initial blast, in the fallout, in the resulting world war.

The only way to ensure the survival of those millions was to do nothing to save the Twin Towers.

So Alys had done just that: *nothing.* But she still had nightmares about those three thousand people she could have saved. Her nasty little nickname was a lot closer to coming true than anyone knew. Even 'Von.

Alys gave him a smile and lifted the glass in a toast. "To partners," she said.

Davon clicked his own against it, making the fragile crystal chime. "To partners."

\* \* \*

Insomnia was never a problem when you were a vampire. The minute the sun came up, it snuffed out your consciousness with the Daysleep. Some days that was a curse. Some it was a blessing. Tonight, Davon wished it would hurry the hell up.

He lay staring up at the four-poster's intricately carved wooden canopy. Although it was in the style of the Tudor era, the bed was as wide as a California King, with thick wooden posts carved in twining rose vines. A close examination revealed dragons, fairies, unicorns, and lions lurking among the greenery.

The rest of the room was just as beautiful. A massive armoire stood opposite an equally huge bureau, both in pale carved oak. A tall mannequin stood radiating magic in one corner, dressed in Davon's enchanted armor and wearing his sword. It waited for Alys's magical summons to dematerialize the gear and reassemble it on his body.

The engraved metal glittered, backlit by the enormous stained-glass window that took up one wall. Exterior lights illuminated the countless pieces of jewel-toned glass, splashing a rainbow glow over every surface in the room.

The image the glass portrayed was just as beautiful. An armored knight sat astride a huge roan warhorse as a woman in a crimson gown offered him a golden cup. She was obviously Alys, but the knight's visor was down, hiding his identity. Which was probably intentional.

The window always made Davon wonder how many journeymen vampires had stayed in this room, struggling with whatever impossible choices Alys had given them. Whatever grinding need she inspired.

That thought triggered a memory of Alys in those shorts, her legs long and bare and lean, her breasts riding high beneath that yellow silk top.

Heat flooded Davon's balls, and his cock rose above his belly, tenting the sheet. He gritted his teeth and looked away from the window.

*If I had any sense, I'd go find a lover.* Other Majae had offered Davon sexual companionship in the past decade. He'd even accepted a few times, hoping to avoid another disastrous obsession with a partner.

*Jimmy Sheridan's head pinwheeled off his shoulders, blood spraying the living room and the game controller in his lap.* Davon flinched in sick horror.

He'd murdered that boy.

True, he'd been under a spell at the time, part of an elaborate plot to trigger a war with the Direkind. A psychotic werewolf sorcerer named Warlock had attempted to frame Arthur for ordering Jimmy's murder.

The plot cost the life of Davon's then-partner Cherise Myers. Trying to atone and defuse the war, Davon had surrendered to the werewolves. He'd have been executed if Arthur hadn't staged a rescue. The whole mess came to a crescendo when Warlock invaded Avalon and Arthur killed the furry bastard.

So when Davon was assigned to work with Alys soon afterward, he'd fully intended to keep his distance. He didn't want another partner's death on his conscience.

They'd become friends anyway.

*Friends, hell. I'm in love with her. I've loved her for years.*

Alys had helped him deal with his guilt over Cherise and Jimmy. Helped him build his strength, speed, and skill with a sword. Their partnership might be frustratingly celibate, but it was also more emotionally intense and satisfying than any other relationship he'd ever experienced.

Which still didn't make celibacy fun. Unfortunately, the last time he'd tried to make love to someone else, his body had flatly refused to respond. If he hadn't indulged in a fantasy of Alys out of sheer desperation, they'd be calling him *Limp Dick Davon.* Majae gossiped.

Davon had decided then and there never to try extracurricular fucking ever again. One, it was an insult to the woman making love to him, and two, he had enough reason to feel guilty as it was.

Glancing down, he saw his erection had deflated under that barrage of unpleasant memories. He sighed in relief and closed his eyes. How much longer until sunrise?

*Alys purred in pleasure as he massaged her forearm, chasing the huge knot in the muscle. Her skin felt like silk under his fingers. The sound of her low moan was more erotic that another woman's climactic scream.*

*She smiled, her eyes warm with approval. "Best partner I've ever had…"*

Aaaand there came the hard-on again, rearing up under the sheet for another try.

With a groan of surrender, he reached over his head and opened a drawer in the massive headboard, then groped for the tube of lube he'd bought on a trip to Mortal Earth. He squeezed out a generous amount, slicked his right hand, and settled back to give his dick what it wanted.

His mind slid to his latest favorite fantasy -- that lesson in hand-to-hand grappling a few months ago…

*Alys's lean body twisted against his as he struggled to pin her to the mat. She wore only a pair of boy shorts and a sports bra that showed every delicious curve of her body. He felt the slide of her long, long legs around his back.* She'd been preparing to flip him off at the time, but his dick hadn't cared. Still didn't.

Now, as his hand gripped his cock in long, slick strokes, he fantasized about doing what he'd longed to do then. Rolling his hips, he strained…

*He lowered his head and took Alys's delicious mouth in a deep, slow kiss.*

*She froze against him. Instead of flipping him, her legs curled tighter around his waist. Then she moaned in that throaty Alys voice, lips parting under his, her mouth sweet and tart, tasting of lemon drops.* He could almost feel the warm strength of her thighs riding his ass as his hand jerked his cock faster and faster. His breath caught as he imagined Alys tasting her way down the curve of his throat.

Their clothing vanished in a foaming wave of magic, leaving her long, beautiful body exquisitely bare and hot beneath his. She arched, straining against him. "Davon… God, Davon…"

*He took her nipple, sucking the hard, dark peak, drinking in the rich taste of Alys's body. Skating his fingers down over her lean elegance, he found the tight heat between her thighs. She was slick for him, and when he looked up, she watched him, her gaze fierce and hungry.*

His balls tightened at the tight grip around his dick, and he let himself imagine it was her hand stroking him. *"Fuck me, 'Von,"* fantasy Alys gasped.

*God, yes!*

Davon slid between her legs and thrust deep into her. Impossibly slick, incredibly eager, she rolled against him as his fangs slid from his stinging gums.

He found the vein throbbing fast in her throat and bit deep as he pumped into her. Her heels dug into his ass, her thighs gripping him with her surprising Maja strength. Urging him on. Her pussy felt like a wet, silken fist, so hot and impossibly tight…

The orgasm shot from his balls to his brain like a burning arrow. Davon arched as a hot spurt of come splattered his belly and chest. He tasted blood -- his own bitten lip -- and the throb of his fangs added a delicious zing to the orgasm.

With a relieved groan, he sagged back into the mattress.

But even as he lay there, his thundering heartbeat slowing as his hot skin cooled, Davon felt utterly alone. And wondered how long he'd be in love with a woman who didn't want him.

# Chapter Three

As the sun came up, Alys envied Davon the Daysleep. She knew she was going to have a much harder time dropping off. She could feel a nightmare gathering on her mental horizon like tornado storm clouds. *This is going to be a bad one.*

Unfortunately, avoiding the dream wouldn't keep it from coming true. She'd just deprive herself of the warning her power could give her -- the opportunity to prevent whatever God-awful thing was about to happen.

So, she went to bed.

Which was not, unfortunately, the same thing as going to sleep. She lay there in the huge king-sized bed, watching the sunlight illuminate the stained-glass skylight as anxiety gathered in the pit of her stomach.

She *had* to sleep. Had to find out what was coming.

Eventually she headed downstairs, poured the rest of the merlot into a glass, doctored it with her favorite sleeping potion, and headed back upstairs.

Only to find herself walking into Davon's room. She stood there at the foot of his bed for a long moment, the glass in one hand, staring at his handsome face. He looked so still and peaceful as his powerful chest rose and fell in sleep.

"Fuck it," Alys muttered, and lifted the sheet to slide in next to him. "I'll get up and leave in a minute." Curling against his warm side, she listening to him breathe as she sipped the potion.

God, she wanted to make love to him so fucking badly.

When she began to feel sleepy, she pressed a kiss to his chest, right over his heart. With a sound somewhere between a sigh and a groan, Alys drained the glass and rolled out of his bed to go crawl into her own. Curling into a miserable ball, she waited to find out what fresh hell awaited. She was fantasizing about making love to him when the potion dragged her into the sleep she both needed and feared.

* * *

Sunlight poured like honey over Avalon's central square, heating the cobblestones and casting dappled shadows through the oaks and magnolias that grew among massive stone buildings in a dozen architectural styles. Topiary knights and ladies engaged in leafy green flirtations, while butterflies the size of robins fluttered around huge stoneware pots of roses, pansies, tulips, and daffodils.

The spark of a dimensional gate appeared amid all that calm beauty, swelled outward. Kept swelling until it was the wide enough for an army.

Morgana Le Fay was the first one through, tall and slim in armor that cast blinding reflections in the morning light. For a moment, the witch's face filled Alys's sight, and a chill rolled over her. There was something wrong with Morgana's eyes. Normally there was cool intelligence in her gaze, or at worst, a certain calculation.

But cruelty filled those green eyes now. Cruelty, malice, and a horrible anticipation.

*That's not Morgana. That's Bres.*

Bres/Morgana stepped aside, making way for the enemy army who marched through the gate after her. Ranks of armed and armored Fomorians, trolls, centaurs, giants -- even a huge green dragon. Thousands of enemy warriors.

A female voice shouted in alarm, followed by a pulse of magic as the Maja warned the city with a spell.

Or at least, everyone who wasn't in the Daysleep.

Majae came running, hurling magical blasts, swords ready. The shadows of great wings fell across the square as Kel roared overhead like a fighter jet. The enemy dragon leaped to meet him, breathing fire.

Kel's wife, Nineva, shifted to dragon form and hurled herself into the sky, obviously determined to help her husband.

Avalon's Council of Majae gathered in a circle -- Guinevere, Grace, Caroline, Lark, Eva, and Miranda, along with the two Avalonian males who weren't vampires, Smoke and William Justice. Smoke was in his warrior form -- nine feet tall, his thick ebony fur striped across the haunches in silver. He attacked the nearest troll, his roar thunderous. The troll roared back, swinging a mace at Smoke's big feline skull.

Justice and Miranda shifted to Dire Wolves, almost as big, his fur midnight black, hers fox red, both of them lithe and deadly with their claws and fangs and magic.

As their defenders ringed them in a protective circle, Guinevere, Caroline, Eva, and Grace linked hands and closed their eyes, mouths moving in a chant. They cried out, and a huge shaft of magic speared skyward... only to splash against what appeared to be an invisible bowl high overhead: the great magical shield of Avalon, which prevented invaders from gating into the city.

*They're trying to polarize the shield so the vampires will awake,* Alys realized. It was the spell created by Maeve, the Mother of Fairies, when Warlock and his Direkind had tried this a decade ago. Back then, the men had awoken with the artificial nightfall and had helped beat off the attack.

This time nothing happened.

Morgana/Bres stepped from among the Fomorians, her mouth curled into that vicious smile. *Bres did something to the shield*, Alys realized, her heart sinking. Of course. Though Merlin had created the magical barrier to begin with, Morgana had crafted the spells the Majae used to strengthen and improve it.

Once Bres gained control of her, he controlled the shield.

Terror and despair rolled over the faces of the defenders as they realized they were doomed. Then with cries of defiance and rage, every one of them lunged for the nearest Fomorian.

The dream dissolved into chaotic images of blood, blinding bolts of magic flying like lightning strikes, accompanied by the clash of swords, axes, and spears. Screams, curses, and battle cries rang out as buildings caught fire -- chateaus, villas, Gothic and Georgian mansions alike, blazing out of control.

The vision seemed to wrench, and Alys realized she was looking into Arthur's sleeping face as he lay comatose in the Daysleep. She found herself screaming at him to wake up, even knowing he couldn't. Couldn't hear her. Couldn't wake so long as the sun was up. That was the way vampire magic worked.

A three-fingered armored hand closed around his wrist and jerked him brutally out of bed. As his helpless body slammed to the floor, a sword rose and fell.

And the head of the Once and Future King rolled away from his body.

The image wrenched to Guinevere's face in the frame of her visor, her mouth drawing into a silent rictus of agony. The sword tumbled from her hand as her magical shield winked out.

And she fell dead, slain by the wrenching shock of Arthur's death. Killed by the Truebond, the psychic union she'd had with her husband for fifteen centuries.

Gwen wasn't alone. More Majae dropped, slain as the Fomorians murdered their helpless husbands even as the witches struggled to hold off the invaders.

The women who were left fought on, outnumbered. Growing more outnumbered as the minutes passed. Doomed.

Nineva fell, burning, from the sky. Kel roared in anguish and agony, tumbling after her, dead from their psychic link before he hit the ground. The falling dragons crushed a group of Majae unable to gate away in time.

Alys saw a dark-skinned figure racing down a cobbled street, swinging Reaver in great flaming arcs. With a sick kind of horror, she realized the figure was herself, striking down every Fomorian in her way, merciless in her rage and terror. "Davon! Davon, wake up!" Alys knew even as she howled that he couldn't wake, not with the sun up.

But they didn't have a Truebond. His death wouldn't cause hers. She sprinted up the stone walkway toward the front door, praying she'd get to him before…

A troll stepped out of the house, carrying Davon's decapitated head by the hair.

* * *

Davon woke to the sound of Alys's terrified screams. The house was dark. He catapulted out of bed, naked, his bare feet hitting the cool wooden floor as he lunged for his sword. He jerked it out of the scabbard that hung from the armored mannequin, then bolted from the room and across the hall. Throwing Alys's bedroom door open with one hand, he spun to the side and snapped a glance inside. He saw no one. Davon charged into the room and stopped dead at the foot of her bed, staring in sick, growing fear.

Alys writhed under the quilt, staring at the stained-glass skylight, her face contorted as scream after scream ripped from her mouth. This was no ordinary nightmare. Her open, staring eyes were awash in inky black, stars glittering in the dark.

Davon froze in indecision. Grabbing her now would be a good way to get a fireball in the face. Besides, he didn't want to interrupt the vision before she'd seen whatever she needed to see. Yet as her screams stabbed his eardrums, he longed desperately to wake her. Standing around while she endured such terror made his every protective instinct howl.

But if there was one thing a decade as Alys's partner had taught him, it was the ability to ignore his own needs. She and her visions came first.

With desperate self-control, Davon put the sword aside on the bureau. *Good thing she's got soundproofing spells around the house. Otherwise every vampire and witch for blocks around would be banging on the door, trying to find out what's killing Alys.*

At last the black rolled away from her eyes. Her face contorted in anguished grief as she rolled over onto her side and huddled there, as if curled around a mortal wound. Davon moved to bend over her, laying a hand against her shaking back. "Alys." He had to work to keep his voice steady, despite his own anguish. "Alys…"

She lifted her head, staring at him. With a tearing sob, she hurled herself into his arms. He caught her automatically and drew her close, realizing only then that he held a naked Alys against his equally nude body. But for once, even his self-absorbed cock showed no interest in sex. Not with her shivering in his arms, her nails digging desperately into his biceps as if he was the only solid thing in her drowning world.

Slowly, gently, Davon began to smooth one hand over her mass of springy curls. "What do you need me to do?" he asked, keeping his voice soft, calm.

"Hold me," she whispered, her voice a raw croak. "I need you."

He didn't hesitate, drawing her closer until every inch of her silken skin was pressed against his. And thought a mental threat at his dick in case it got the wrong idea. He had never seen her like this. No matter how ugly things got, no matter how bad the future her visions predicted, she'd never... *shattered*.

True, this wasn't the first time he'd awakened to the sound of her screams. But once awake, her response was always to clamp down on her emotions while she decided how to prevent whatever her visions had predicted. *What the fuck had she seen?*

He couldn't ask. If Alys didn't tell him, it was because anyone else knowing could trigger whatever she most wanted to avoid. And in this case, whatever she wanted to avoid was obviously pretty fucking bad.

Davon held her until she abruptly pulled out of his arms. Conjuring a handkerchief, Alys wiped her nose and closed her swollen eyes. She spent several nerve-wracking moments just breathing, in through her nose and out through her mouth. The hand holding the handkerchief shook.

*What the hell is going on?* It took all his self-control keep the impatient demand from bursting from his mouth.

They stood quietly while she worked through the techniques she'd taught him to control an adrenaline dump.

At last Alys looked up at him. Her slight smile showed a hell of a lot of effort. "Thank you. I need my lab."

She started from the room, only to hesitate in mid-step as she looked down at herself. "I'm naked."

"Noticed."

Alys glanced at him, and for a moment he thought she was going to give him a genuine smile. "So are you." Her lips flattened and she threw up a hand. Magic sparked and swirled around her, leaving behind a white gown that seemed to glow against her golden skin.

The sparks streamed to him next, whirling around his body in a miniature glowing storm. When they vanished, he found himself wearing loose cotton pants and a T-shirt, both black. His feet, like hers, were bare.

Alys was already striding from the room. He hurried after her as she swung into the wrought iron spiral staircase and headed downward to the lab far beneath the house. Deep enough to protect the neighborhood if the wrong thing exploded.

The stairs rang and clattered with their footsteps as they descended past the library, down into the earth.

The lab was a huge stone room lined with floor-to-ceiling shelves that held books, magical objects, and neatly labeled jars of powders, liquids, and enchanted organic materials. She'd told him once that creating a powerful magical object required the physical act of making it with your hands and imbuing it with your magic over a period of hours, even days.

Now, as Davon watched, Alys moved to a section of the shelves packed with a huge selection of beeswax candles, many flecked with magical herbs and powders. She gathered fistfuls of them and loaded them into his arms. They made an awkward burden as he followed her along the aisle.

Next, Alys chose a golden orb from among a collection of assorted magical objects. Sinuous holes pierced its top, while its heavily engraved bottom was inset with gemstones in a rainbow of colors. Taking the top off, she cupped both halves in one hand and headed for a section of shelving lined with labeled glass jars. She spent the next several minutes adding assorted powders with measuring spoons hanging from hooks on each jar.

Davon's brows flew up as he read the label on one. It was a Sidhe hallucinogen designed to intensify visions. The contents of the next jar were even stronger. He'd never seen her combine the two. "You sure about that?"

Alys shot him a cold look and snapped, "Yes."

*All right then. Not in the mood to be questioned.*

"You can wait upstairs if you'd prefer."

"Don't be insulting." It was his job to be her spotter in case something went wrong during a difficult spell.

She grunted and reached into a drawer to lift out a string of moonstones, then dropped them around his neck. "Charm against poisons. It will block the effect." Her voice dropped. "Mostly."

"That's encouraging," he muttered.

"Hey, at least *you* don't have to inhale it." She put the lid back on the incense burner and carried it into the next room.

Davon followed her slim back, his arms full of candles. This was her scrying room -- the chamber she employed when she needed to ride the currents of possibility, looking for a way to avoid some particularly black future that was bearing down on them like a nuclear cruise missile.

The walls were thick, smooth granite, the better to insulate her from random magic. The floor was a solid sheet of gleaming black onyx inlaid with a silver ring fifteen feet in diameter. Intricate glyphs, carved from gemstones, were inset in the floor within the circle, creating an amplification spell.

Alys stopped just outside the ring and closed her eyes. When she opened them again, black swirled within their depths. Lifting her voice in a soft, rhythmic chant, she began to walk around the circle, planting candles along its edge.

Davon retreated to brace his back against the nearest wall. Still chanting, Alys cupped the incense burner in both hands. Smoke began to pour through the holes in its lid, smelling of sandalwood, exotic Mageverse herbs, and magic.

She walked to the circle's center and sank to the floor, curling her legs into the lotus position, each foot resting on the opposite thigh as she cradled the censer. The smoke wafted around her in long plumes.

Every breath he took smelled of that exotic, drugging incense. Once he thought he saw something moving out of the corner of his eye, but when he whipped around, there was nothing there. And that was *with* the moonstone charm. God knew what he'd be seeing without it.

In the circle, Alys's voice edged toward a shout. It sounded ragged with despair.

Leaping to her feet, she dropped the censer. As it bounced on the floor, she screamed something, a cry of anguish. A great wind whipped through the room, extinguishing the candles and sending them rolling across the floor to the chiming ring of the tumbling incense burner.

For a moment Davon stood frozen in a darkness complete even to vampire eyes.

Then came a soft, strangled sound.

Alys was crying.

The candles ignited again with a soft *phut*, revealing her lying in a ball on the floor.

*Help her, dumbass.* Jolting from his paralysis, Davon hurried over to kneel beside her. "Alys?" He laid a hand gently on her shoulder.

She turned her head to look up at him, her huge, beautiful eyes swimming with tears. "Davon... God, Davon!" And she threw herself into his arms, hers wrapping tight around him. Her entire body shook, quivering like something small and wounded.

His heart sank as he lifted a hand to stroke the back of her head. "So, there's no way out of it -- whatever you saw?"

She laughed, the sound bitter. It broke somewhere in the middle and became a sob. "Oh, there's a way out. I'm just going to have to pay for it. So will you. It may not be death, but the price... God, I'm sorry. I'm so, so sorry."

Davon's arms tightened convulsively around her. *Oh God, what the hell is coming?* "There are no other options?"

"I searched every future I could find. I went as deep as I could. And in every case, it was the same. If we fail, the Magekind will die and that Fomorian bastard will grind humanity under his boot."

"What do we have to do?"

"No, the question is, what do *you* have to do?" Alys looked up at him, her gaze steady and hard even as a tear rolled down her face. "Everything rests on you. You're going to have to do it alone."

His hands tightened around her upper arms as an icy blade of terror stabbed him. "Are you going to die? Is that what you're telling me?"

There was that horrible laugh again. "I'd almost prefer that." Her gaze slid away from his to fix on something impossibly distant. Fear contorted her face. He'd never understood the phrase "thousand-yard stare" until now. "I may die." She shrugged. "Or I may just wish to hell I had."

"Christ."

"Tell me about it." She wiped her eyes with angry, impatient swipes of both hands. "I do understand a lot of things I didn't until now. Things I sensed I had to do without knowing why. Like why I couldn't be with you." Alys looked up at him, her gaze suddenly fierce. "I also know that reason doesn't apply anymore. I need you tonight. Please don't tell me no."

Davon stared down at her, his jaw dropping. "Wait. Isn't all hell breaking loose?"

"It is. Just not tonight." Her gaze softened, and she reached up to brush his curling locks out of his eyes. "We have an hour before we have to start getting ready. And I know how I want to spend it."

"I…" She meant that. His heart began to hammer in his chest. God, he'd *hungered* for her, a craving that had grown stronger with every year he denied himself. "Are you sure?"

"Yes." The word seemed to hang there, naked.

It gave him courage. "I've wanted you from the first time I saw you." He lowered his head.

"And I've wanted you." Alys rose on her toes to meet his mouth. Her lips tasted salty as they trembled against his.

Hunger rose, sudden and hot, forcing him to grapple for self-control. *Not like this.* He was damned if he was going to make love to her in a frenzy of fear and desperation. They deserved better after a decade of frustration. He'd make it good for her, if it was the last thing he ever did.

Because it just might be.

Yeah, she thought they'd survive, but he'd learned things could go wrong that her visions didn't predict.

Banishing his fear and doubt, he focused on Alys, on the feel of her body pressed tight to his as their lips met, pressed, pulled apart. Their tongues danced, the sensation jolting lust into his balls at the witchy taste of her he knew so well.

God, he'd wanted her for so long, it was all he could do not to throw her up against the nearest wall and rip her dress off. And yet at the same time, he felt an aching tenderness as he looked down into those cinnamon-brown eyes.

It seemed his entire life had revolved around Alys's eyes. Watching them for visions. Watching them for cues as she taught him a parry or attack. Watching the play of emotion in their expressive depths. Now they were almost black with need, her pupils dilated until only a thin ring of the cinnamon remained. Each breath carried the scent of her arousal.

And Davon was every bit as turned on. His body hardened even more as she touched him, skating delicate fingertips along the line of his jaw, her thumb tracing the cleft of his chin.

She'd touched him a thousand times, but that had been to demonstrate some combat technique. Or maybe as a gesture of friendship -- a squeeze of the shoulder, a pat on the back.

Did she realize how much those touches had meant to him? How he'd fed them like scraps to his starving, unrequited love?

Now he could feast.

Davon groaned and crashed his mouth down on hers again. She leaned into him, warm and solid, one slender hand tracing the muscles of his biceps beneath his T-shirt as the other stroked the indentation of his spine through the cotton. Made him fight the urge to grind his erection against her soft belly.

Alys closed her teeth on his lower lip in a gentle bite that made him shudder. His fangs ached, and his cock bucked in the confines of his pants. His need felt huge, an aching pit she alone could fill. With her body, her scent. Her wet heat.

Davon slid his hands into the cool silk of her curls. He fingered one springy coil, pulling it straight. It was surprisingly long.

She kissed him, slow and hungry, her mouth pressing softly against his. His tongue slid out to trace the line of her lips, tasting her skin, filling his skull with the delicate, smoky scent of Alys.

Yes, she also smelled like sweat and desperation and grief, and, God help him, Sidhe hallucinogens. It was a good thing he was still wearing that necklace of hers, or he'd be high about now.

*But it'd be worth it*, Davon thought as he bent his head to the fragile line of her jaw. His fangs throbbed. He forced himself to concentrate on tracing his fingers around the shell of her ears as he tasted her, pressing deep, then withdrawing, swirling his tongue against hers. His free hand slid down the warm curves of her body to cup the firm flesh of her ass. He almost moaned at her lush warmth.

Gasping, Alys drew back. When her eyes met his, there was a wild, glittering desperation in their depths. "Make love to me." The words hung naked in the air.

Davon smiled. "I thought you'd never ask."

She laughed, the sound a little wild as she grabbed his hand and raced for the stairs. He loped in her wake as they took them two at a time, the wrought iron ringing.

# Chapter Four

Davon was tempted to sweep her into his arms like a bridegroom, but he felt so damned shaky, he feared he'd dump them both on their heads, vampire strength or no.

Magic swirled around them as they reached the first-floor library. Davon stopped, surprised. The library furniture had either vanished, or she'd transformed the bookshelves, couch, and desk into one enormous bed. Draped in white satin and covered in drifts of rose petals, it looked surprisingly romantic, given her usual hardheaded pragmatism.

"Come. Here." Alys's small, strong hands wrapped in the fabric of his black T-shirt and pulled him closer.

They kissed again, slower this time, though an undercurrent of desperation still flavored the way she cupped his erect cock through the soft fabric of his pants. Groaning into her mouth, he slid his hands down her body. Found the soft curves of those sweetly tempting breasts under the fabric of her nightgown. Her little nipples felt tight under his stroking fingers. Erect and eager. And oh, so tempting...

Davon wanted her naked. He ached to see the lush body he knew so well from so much maddening combat practice. He knew the shape of her -- the long legs and slim, muscled arms, the fighter's balance and grace. And yes, he'd seen her naked more than once, but never in a situation he could enjoy the view. Usually one or the other of them had just come too damned close to dying for him to find the situation erotic.

So he was Goddamn well entitled to *look* at her.

He realized he wasn't the only one who felt that way when she ripped his shirt right off his back. The cotton tore like tissue paper under her Magekind strength.

As she dropped the shreds on the floor with a feral grin of triumph, Davon's brows climbed. "A little impatient?"

"More like too fucking patient. That's over tonight." Alys dropped to her knees before him.

Davon almost stepped back in shock. While he'd certainly fantasized about Alys taking him in her mouth, he'd never imagined she'd go on her knees to him. Then she demonstrated that being on her knees just put her closer to what she wanted. Grabbing the waistband of his cotton pants, she jerked them down to free his cock. Her eyes dropped to the thick, impatient shaft, throbbing with his heartbeat. Pretty lips curled into a wicked smile. "Mmm. I knew you'd be delicious. And look at that -- you are." Leaning forward, she grabbed his width in one hand and sucked him in, so deep, so hard, so...

*Jesus!* Davon jolted at the astonishing heat and warmth of her wet mouth as she began to suckle in deep, drawing pulls that made his knees go weak. "I want to make love to you, too," he managed, his voice shaking with the furious lust blazing through his blood.

Alys released his lengthening cock to flash him a white, toothy smile. "Oh, you'll get your chance." Then she angled him up and began to tongue his harp string, licking up and down over the gathered flesh before engulfing him again. As he quivered, her lips encircled his length and tightened, pulling hard.

He threw his head back, gasping at the ceiling as she rolled her tongue around his shaft. Almost swaying at the intensity of his blazing arousal, Davon looked down at her as she knelt there in that virginal gown with his cock halfway down her throat, one slim hand tugging and working him. He had never seen anything so intensely erotic.

Dropping his hands to the shoulders of her gown, Davon hooked his thumbs into either side of its lacy neckline. It was his turn to rip. The cotton shredded from top to bottom in his vampire grip, and he dropped the pieces on the floor.

He drank in the sight of her kneeling there, long and lithe and naked, all slim brown curves in the moonlight pouring in through the library's stained glass window.

Alys drew her mouth off his erection with an erotic pop and caught hold of his shaft, angling it upward so she could lick her way up the underside, tongue flickering along the thick veins running from his balls to his cock head. With a feline little purr, she sucked his balls one by one into her mouth. Rolling them back and forth with her tongue, she sent even more rich pleasure raking his spine.

Breathing hard, he watched her suckle him with slow, intense concentration. It had never even occurred to him that she'd serve him on her knees.

*She doesn't belong there.* Davon reached down and cupped her face in his hands, urging her to meet his eyes. Encouraging that devastating mouth to release him. "Let me," he managed, his mouth dry, fangs aching. "I want to taste you."

"Well, then." Alys drew back, releasing his captive genitals as she shot him a hot look. "I don't want to be greedy."

Davon picked her up in his arms like a child. It always astonished him how little she weighed, considering how much mass she had in his life.

She wrapped her legs around him, griping him with those strong thighs, and cupped his face, staring into his eyes. As he lowered them both to the mattress, he groaned at the feeling of her silken belly stroking his aching cock. Davon pressed soft kisses to her cheeks, her eyelids, her gasping mouth. Tasted the salt of her tears. "I'm going to make this good for you," he muttered, his voice guttural. "No matter what else happens, neither one of us is going to regret this."

Kissing his way down to the elegant, fragile line of her jaw, he followed the tendons of her throat. Her heart pounded in his ears, her pulse beating against his lips. He fought the need to bite, despite the ache and sting of his fangs. *Later*, he promised them.

Davon paused to explore her collarbone, acutely aware of the scent of her flooding his mouth with every breath. Her fists closed tight in his hair, pulling just short of pain as her hips rolled against his, stroking her lean abdomen over his aching cock. His balls gave a fierce, urgent throb.

*Not yet.* He'd damned well build her arousal as high as she'd stoked his. She was probably dry even now, thanks to whatever she'd seen in that God-awful vision.

Stroking, kissing, he lifted a hand to cup her breast with careful fingers. God, the flesh was soft as kitten fur. Her nipple puckered as he stroked his thumb over it, teasing it even harder. She groaned, the sound breathy as she hunched harder against him. Davon inhaled, drinking in the erotic, salty fragrance of her need.

At least her arousal was beginning to bloom. *And she'll be even hotter.*

"Oh God, I knew you'd be like this," she hissed through her teeth.

He shot her a surprised glance. Had she fantasized about this as often as he had? She returned the glance with a hot stare before the fists in his hair dragged his head lower. He needed no further encouragement. His mouth surrounded her nipple for a deep, fierce suckle.

"God, Davon!" Alys cried out, arching upward against him so strongly, she lifted his two hundred pounds right off the bed.

The sweet triumph of that reaction made him smile.

\* \* \*

Davon's mouth felt every bit as good as she'd always known it would. His clever lips tugged, spinning sweet starbursts of pleasure through her body in his own erotic magic.

There was a delicious intensity to 'Von's lovemaking, an intense focus on her pleasure. She'd always known he'd be like that. The man was a born caretaker.

She let her hands drift down his flexing body, enjoying the muscle sliding under rich bronze skin as he nibbled his way from one breast to the other. Each tug and lick spilled pleasure through her nervous system in luscious waves. Alys shuddered as she remembered the feel of his cock filling her mouth until her jaws ached. Such sweet pain.

There would be no other man for her. She knew it as she knew too many things, though she couldn't tell whether that was because of love or death. If he survived, she'd have no regrets.

Davon stopped at her bellybutton. His tongue stroked in and out in tiny licks. The ticklish sensation made her giggle, and he responded with a deep purr of pleasure.

He'd always treated her approval as a prize.

Alys lay back, focusing her senses on him, the feel of his mouth, the velvet lips, the gentle scrape of fang points against her belly. Oh, he *was* aroused.

Wrapping her arms around him, she savored his hot warrior's weight. He'd been leaner when he'd come to her a decade ago, but she'd sensed he needed more brute strength. She'd driven him to pile on muscle, obeying those seeress instincts. Now she knew why he needed so much power.

*Don't think about that. Keep your head in the now.*

Davon helped. He'd reached the soft thatch between her thighs and paused to nuzzle. Lifting her head, Alys watched him, admiring the roll of those muscled shoulders, the corded neck, the clever, pointed tongue. He slid a hand up between her legs as he kissed her. When his eyes rolled up to meet hers, they looked completely black, with no hint of brown iris, as fully dilated as if he were drugged. His nostrils flared, breathing her in.

Sword-calloused fingertips probed, and his eyes widened as he traced her plump inner lips, realizing how wet she was.

Davon bent to devote his attention to her pussy, sliding two fingers deep until he found an exquisitely sensitive bundle of nerves. Sensation bolted through her like lightning as he strummed her G-spot like a lute string. Gasping, Alys threw her head back, arching her back, her breasts pointed at the painted cherubs lurking on the plastered ceiling.

One big hand claimed her right breast, teasing and tugging the nipple, piling pleasure on pleasure. Alys threw her legs wide, shameless with need. God, she needed!

He went on playing inside her, outside her, teasing sensitive nerves with exquisite skill, unbearable patience. *If I'd known how good he'd be, I never could have kept my hands off him.*

Davon found her jutting, hungry clit and began to suck, drawing hard, then more gently, skillful and unpredictable. Meanwhile, one hand continued to torment her breast while the other fingered her G-spot. *Dr. Fredericks definitely paid attention in anatomy class,* she thought, writhing as he toyed with her, wrenching more pleasure from her straining body. The delight intensified until it grew breathtaking edges. Alys clawed for the orgasm just out of reach. Almost... *almost...*

She dug her nails into his back and fought the urge to rake.

It wasn't enough. It wasn't enough to just take from him as she so often took from her lovers, seeking the forgetfulness she could find in a big cock or a good spanking. She wanted more from him. Needed it. Needed him inside her. To the balls. "Enough!" she gasped.

But his dark eyes only narrowed as his tongue flickered over her clit, driving her another bright fraction closer to that orgasm. God, she craved the hot oblivion of it, the utter exhaustion... if only for a moment...

*Not... enough!* She sent her magic swirling over him, spinning glittering strands around him in an erotic web. His muscled body rolled in her magical grip as her power curled from her soul to his body. He made a low rumble of pleasure against her pussy, the deep vibration pulsing through her as he lapped and suckled.

Alys spread her fingers, kneading the magic like a cat, enjoying his warrior's strength as she caressed him. Slowly, carefully, she closed her fingers -- and her magic tightened, lifting him off her -- and into the air.

Dark, startled eyes met hers. "Don't... I want..."

"I know what you want. You'll get it after I'm done."

With a wrench of will, she flipped him on his back and pounced. His dark eyes narrowed in that stubborn determination she knew so well from a hundred training sessions. He surged upward, trying to get to her, and if it hadn't been for her magic there was no way Alys could have held him down.

But she did have magic, and he stayed where she'd put him. She reached down, grabbed his cock, and sent her magic pouring into it. Now it was his turn to jerk as her power found every nerve he had and played on them all at once.

And stopped, in the very instant before he could come.

He writhed, all fierce grace and lethal power, his cock so thick she could fit barely close her fingers around it. God, she was starved for him. The need clawed through her, born of ten years of self-denial, fed by the way he looked with a sword in his hand and sweat streaming down his muscled chest and long bronze thighs.

He shouted, his fangs white and long against the red of his mouth. A little pre-come spurted from his cock head, drew a gleaming white line down his belly. She tightened her magical grip, stopping his orgasm dead. For the moment.

Davon gave a guttural, outraged curse, and she grinned at him. "Patience, darling." Bending over him, she aimed his cock upward.

"Oh God, don't. I'll lose it…"

Merlin's Silver Cup, she loved listening to the man beg. "I won't let you."

His mouth pulled into something between a grin and a grimace. "That's what I'm afraid of," he gasped. And cried out, sounding strangled as she swooped down over his hard, smooth shaft, angling her head to take him as deeply as she could. She couldn't quite manage to engulf him all the way to the balls, so she moved around until she could, taking it slow, enjoying his gritted teeth and wild eyes. Enjoying the velvet slide of his skin over her lips, her tongue.

*He won't forget this.*

Even if she had to.

She began to slide him slowly, *slowly* out of her mouth.

"Alys! Ahh… You're killing me!"

*Not today.* She cut the thought off.

Alys gripped his shaft with one hand as she rolled his balls with the other, admiring the flexing play of his abdominals, his thighs straining as he fought to control the need to thrust deep. He was always so damned careful with her, no matter how she provoked him.

She sensed the hot spill of energy through him as his climax tried again to break free. A flick of magic arrested his orgasm again. He cursed with such surprising invention she had to grin. "Why, 'Von, I didn't even know you knew those words."

He hissed something rude through his teeth. Then she was on top of him, swinging one leg over his hips. Rising high, she angled his length to the opening of her pussy. Biting her lip, Alys began the long, delicious slide downward over him. Down, down and *down*. He filled her so completely, so sweetly, taking her to the straining verge between pain and pleasure.

Davon stared up at her, nothing of the calm, disciplined surgeon about him now. There was only a wild male animal straining to get loose in those black eyes. His long white fangs cemented the impression of a wolf on the verge of escaping a snare. "Let *go*!" he demanded, straining against her magical grip.

"In a minute." She rose again slowly, taking her time. "Oh God, you feel so fucking good!" The words sounded ragged, half-hissed through her teeth.

"Let me play with your clit!" His lips pulled off his teeth as he said the words.

Staring down into his feral gaze, Alys realized she wanted to let him take the lead. She released the grip of her magic. One of those big male hands found her nubbin as she began to jog on him, slowly, spinning out every single glittering moment, devouring each straining instant. She stretched herself along his sweating body, her eyes slitting in pleasure as the angle of the penetration changed. "Take it. Take me!"

Swearing, Davon started pumping his cock in long, digging thrusts. Every one of them seemed to ram a sweet spike through her, jolting her deliciously. She clung to him, moaning without shame as he took her hard, fierce and driving. If she hadn't been so wet, it would have hurt. Instead she savored every instant, teeth clenched, eyes squeezed shut. Felt him cup her breast, the flesh dancing in his hold as he teased her nipple and plowed her deep.

Alys stretched her head back, angling it so her throat pressed against his open lips. "Bite," she hissed.

He hesitated -- probably afraid he'd hurt her in the violence of his thrusts.

"Damn it, 'Von! Bite me!"

His fangs sliced into her throat with a delicious, silvery pain that met the piston pleasure of his cock. The building climax coiled tighter and tighter and... slammed into her in an explosion of blinding, white-hot sparks that made her toes twitch and curl. The orgasm was so overwhelming she thought she was having another vision.

But when she blinked away the sparks, she saw only the spill of light from the stained glass as 'Von's mouth worked her throat, drinking hard, cock pumping.

Gasping, Alys shivered as another wave of orgasm spilled over her, shaking her body and battering her nervous system. Followed by another, and then another, rattling her brain in her skull like a pebble in a Coke can, until Davon finally froze, his cock buried deep. He bellowed, the sound muffled against her throat as his bowing body lifted hers off the mattress. His cock jerked, flooding her with pulse after liquid pulse of come.

When he collapsed under her at last, she curled her shaking arms around him. His skin felt sweat slick, almost steaming against her body.

She grinned, more than a little smug. *Well, it took us long enough to get around to it -- but by Merlin's hairless chin, we finally did it right.*

Davon pulled free and began to lick the little puncture wounds, healing them with his vampire saliva.

"Don't stop..."

"I have to," he muttered into her neck. "I don't want to take too much."

Alys considered protesting, but her spinning head told her he was right. She'd need a healing potion as it was if she was going to get through the rest of the night.

* * *

Davon lay with his arms wrapped around her, barely resisting the impulse to clutch. He could feel the stolen seconds ticking away as they lay listening to each other breathe. "God," he murmured, "I've dreamed of this. Not just making love but... holding you."

Alys swirled long tapering fingers through the curling hair on his chest. "Me too. I can't tell you how many times I lay in bed waiting for the sun, wishing I could go to you."

He looked down at her, blinking in shock. "Then... why didn't you? You must have known I wouldn't have turned you down."

"I knew. But something in the back of my head told me I had to keep my distance."

"And you don't ignore that little voice."

"No. Not even when I wish I could." Alys sighed, warm breath gusting across his skin. "And now it's telling me we're running out of time. We've got too much to do between now and sunrise." She rolled off the bed.

As he started to follow, magic rolled over him. He found himself wearing a long-sleeved Henley and blue jeans, a pair of low-heeled boots on his feet. He grinned at her, tossing the hair out of his face. "Thanks."

She gave him a lazy smile. "Baby, that was pure self-interest. I'd never be able to concentrate with all that on display." A wicked flick of her eyes from head to foot revealed what "that" she referred to.

"I could say the same about you."

She glanced down at her glorious nudity, and her fingers moved one of those graceful weaving patterns. A heartbeat later, she wore a T-shirt and cotton sweats that hung low and loose on her hips. The iron steps rang under her feet as she started down. "We need to get to work. We have a hell of a lot to do and very little time to do it in."

As Davon followed her into the lab, she conjured a backpack, of all things, then walked over to a shelf and pulled out four metal discs about the size of hockey pucks.

"What the hell are those?" He moved closer to eye them.

"Gate generators," she said, dropping the discs into the pack.

Davon was familiar with the concept. Vampire agents used gate generators when they didn't have a Maja partner so they could go back and forth to the Mageverse. You needed two for each gate -- one to create it wherever you were, and another for your destination. Which, now that he thought about it, sounded damned handy. "So I can just carry them around and jump where I need to go?"

"No, generators don't work that way. They take time to establish a stable gate between points, so you need to set them up and give them plenty of time to create a wormhole."

Which probably explained why the vampires who used them generally had one set up at their Avalonian home and another wherever they were working on Mortal Earth. He frowned. "What keeps mortals from wandering into them?"

"They don't respond to mortals." Alys headed for another set of shelves and spent several moments sorting through magical equipment. At last she pulled out a metal case only a bit larger than a shoebox. She carried it over to the lab table and flipped it open, revealing a pair of armored gauntlets far more elaborate than his current set. They were heavily engraved with Sidhe sigils, and the back of each glove was embedded with three huge fire opals. Smaller opals were inset along each of the glove's fingers, also in sets of three.

Alys pulled the gauntlets out of the box and handed them to him. "Put these on. I have to key them to you, or you won't be able to use them."

He eyed him dubiously. "I doubt they're going to fit." They looked far too small for him.

She smiled. "They'll fit."

Surprisingly, they did. He had to struggle a bit at first, but then they seemed to expand to accommodate his hands until they felt made for him. "Will they work with my current armor?"

"With some adjustments." Alys laid a hand on each glove. "Brace yourself. This probably won't be fun."

He sensed the pulse of magic -- and was instantly glad for her warning. A fiery sting ignited up and down his forearm, as if the gauntlets had bitten into him with tiny teeth. "The hell?"

Each of the gemstones flashed with a bright pearlescent glow, and his arms seemed to vibrate with a disturbing magic. It felt... *alien* somehow. And not at all friendly. The back of his neck prickled. "What the fuck is that?"

"Elementalverse magic," Alys told him, her gaze going a trifle grim.

Davon stared at her. There were an infinite number of universes, and in each of them the laws of physics were a little bit different. In that of Mortal Earth, magic didn't exist at all. If you wanted to work spells there, you had to draw on the Mageverse, where magic was a physical law.

Magic was even more powerful in the Elementalverse, where the physics were so different, nothing that evolved in the Mageverse could live there, and vice versa. The only life forms were non-corporeal energy beings. If Elementals tried to come here, they had to find a living host to inhabit if they wanted to survive.

Davon eyed the gloves and fought the impulse to snatch them off his hands. They'd probably eat him. "Where the hell did you get them?"

Alys shrugged. "Maeve."

He digested that a moment. It made sense. Maeve, also known as the Mother of Fairies, was a Sidhe demi-goddess known for creating powerful weaponry. "And she gave them to you?"

"Maeve owed me a favor. I had a vision that an Elementalverse predator was going to possess her dog."

"Bet Guinness loved that." Despite his looks, Guinness was no ordinary Chihuahua. Like the rest of Maeve's menagerie, he was inhabited by an Elemental who gave him enhanced intelligence and the ability to talk. He was also the most beloved of Maeve's beasts.

"It got worse," Alys told him. "My vision predicted the predator was going to kill Maeve and feed on her and her pets. I warned her, and she was able to capture the predator before it could attack Guinness. As a gesture of gratitude, she gave me Reaver and the gloves, which were supposed to let me use the sword without getting so drained."

"Really?" His brows lifted. "I've never seen you wear them."

"Something told me to save them. And it's a good thing I never keyed them to myself, or you wouldn't be able to wear them. Now you can use them to work spells as if you're a Maja. Not for very long -- the opals will probably burn out quickly, considering the way you're going to use them."

"Which way is that?"

"In a minute. I want you to think of claws."

"Claws? You mean like a werewolf's?" As the image flashed into his mind, three-inch claws slid from the glove's fingertips. Davon blinked down at them, impressed. "That's convenient. I'm supposed to fight with these?"

"Not... exactly."

He flexed his fingers, watching the light slide up and down the gauntlets. "Then what do I use them for?"

"Getting to that. Besides the claws, the gauntlets will let you produce a magical shield. Don't do it more than once, though, because you'll drain power you're going to need."

He looked up, frowning. "What do I do the rest of the time?"

"Duck." When he snorted, she grinned at him. "Between that and your armor, it should be enough."

"*Should* be?"

Alys shrugged. "There are an infinite number of possibilities in the future. I can see the most likely ones, and I can see how to get to the one I want, but changes in timing and action affect the outcome." She tapped one of his gauntleted forearms. "Focus on the gloves and will them to release your arms."

He obeyed. Instantly the opals went dark, and the stinging faded. Gingerly, he pulled the gauntlets off and returned them to the box, then tucked it into the bag. Examining his skin, he saw that his forearms were covered with tiny pinpricks that bled sluggishly. They stopped a moment later.

"Now let me show you what we're dealing with," Alys told him, heading for the room she'd use to scry earlier that evening. "You need to know what to look for when it happens."

Instead of stepping into the inlaid circle, she made a fluid gesture, pouring magic into the air. Mist swirled into a three-dimensional image of Davon and Alys, standing in some sort of moonlit room. "This is what I saw during my vision."

The image widened, and he saw they were standing inside the garage of a thoroughly middle-class Mortal Earth brick ranch. In the yard in front of the house, a dimensional gate bloomed open. Four Fomorians stepped through it.

Future Davon and Alys immediately attacked.

At first the fight looked no different than their usual Fomo brawls. Right up until Future Alys went into a showy figure-eight stroke as she attacked two Fomorians at once.

The image froze as Alys pointed at her future self. "See that move? That's your cue to run."

"Run?" He stared at her, his jaw dropping. "Wait, what?"

# Chapter Five

"Watch." Alys flicked her fingers. The image rolled forward again. Future Davon broke off his fight with a Fomorian and raced away toward the woods that bordered the backyard. Even as he ran, more dimensional gateways opened, disgorging a dozen Fomorians.

But future Alys was staring after Davon in shocked confusion. "'Von? Where the hell are you…"

As future Davon disappeared into the trees, Alys cursed and turned back to the fight -- right into the magical blast that detonated in her face. She toppled, knocked cold. The Fomorians pounced on her, picked her up, and opened a gate. A heartbeat later, they all vanished.

Davon stared at the image with his jaw hanging open. "I'm supposed to just run out on you?" He shook his head hard as his bewilderment turned to outrage, then to outright fury. "No. Fuck no! Forget that!"

"You have to." Alys stepped right up to him, shoving her face up to his, her dark eyes hot. "Because if you don't, we're all fucked. If Bres does not infect me, he's going to infect Morgana."

He stared at her, feeling a wave of icy shock roll down his face. "Bres is going to infect you?"

"Better me than Morgana Le Fay." Her gaze was haunted. "If he gets Morgana, we're all screwed."

Davon listened in sick horror as she related everything her vision had revealed: Morgana leading the Fomorians into Avalon, followed by the systematic slaughter of the sleeping vampires and their Majae defenders. "Which is why we have to let Bres infect me."

"But what happens to *you*?"

"You're going to cure me."

He blinked at her, stunned, struggling to come up with a coherent list of reasons that idea made no sense. "How the hell am I supposed to do that? I was a trauma surgeon, Alys. For something like that, you need an epidemiologist."

"I don't mean researching a cure, Davon." She made a dismissive gesture. "I've got a knife we can use."

"A knife? How the hell is a knife supposed to..." He threw up a hand. "Never mind. Look, if Bres controls you, won't he know what you know?"

"Yes, which is why I'm going to have to forget this. I won't remember any of this. Not the visions, not the plan for the cure, nothing." Pain lit her dark eyes. "Not even us making love. I have to wipe it all from my memory. I can't even know what day it is." Her mouth hardened as her brows dipped. "And you can't tell me *any* of it. Can't act as if anything is different, because if you do and there's the slightest suspicion in my mind, Bres will realize it's a trap and go back to his Avalon plan."

Davon swore and spun away to pace several frantic steps before whirling back. "But how can you make yourself forget all this?"

Alys shrugged. "I've got a circlet we use to learn new languages and particularly complicated spells. I can alter it to block my memories of tonight and implant a replacement scenario. I'll wake tomorrow night and think I've had a vision. Which I have -- I just won't remember all of it. Obeying that vision, we'll show up to spring the trap Bres has planned."

"So he'll get you instead of Morgana." The words emerged in an acidic snarl.

"Yes."

"Fuck me." Davon stared at her in frustration. "And I'm supposed to know all this and hide it from you? Christ, Alys! What's Bres going to do to you?"

"You don't need to know." Her expression went so flat he knew it was bad.

Davon exploded into movement, stomping around the lab and cursing in the vilest terms he knew. Alys stepped into his path, forcing him to stop short. Resting a slim hand on his cheekbone, she stared up into his eyes. "I know this is going to be difficult for you…"

"Me? You're the one that fucker's going to kidnap!"

"Yes," she said steadily. "And you're not going to want to let it happen. Every protective instinct you have -- and you've got a lot of them -- is going to scream in outrage. You've got to ignore them, Davon. Otherwise we're all fucked. Anything else will not save me or yourself."

"I don't give a shit about myself! I care about you!"

Her calm cracked into a snarl, revealing the fear and anger beneath. "Then Goddamn do what I tell you! I have one chance -- humanity has *one* fucking chance. And that's for you to follow the plan. I'm not saying it's going to be easy. I know it's going to rip your guts out. And it could end up killing you. I may not make it either, but it's the best chance any of us have."

They stared at each other, Davon fighting rage, despair, and pain.

Finally she blew out a breath, "Come on, we've got a lot of preparations to make. And you have to memorize some combat sequences that could kill you if you screw them up."

"That's encouraging," he muttered. And followed her.

* * *

They spent the next several hours in a frantic rush, gating back and forth to Mortal Earth as they scrambled to get the plan in place. The whole time, Davon was acutely aware of the fear in the depths of her dark eyes. He wanted to rage at her. Or God, or Satan, or Bres, or whoever the fuck was responsible for this hell they were trapped in. But it wouldn't do any good.

When they finally returned to the house, Davon made one final trip to the lab with her. He watched while she searched the shelves, finally pulling out a small flat box. "I think I'll have it teach me the Fomorian language, and maybe some Dragon," Alys said, her voice a little too bright. She handed the box to him and turned around to rummage in a second, larger container. Its contents rattled. Looking over her shoulder, he saw it held a selection of gemstones in small containers. She plucked out an emerald and a topaz, then gathered a handful of opals and led the way over to the lab table. He put the box on the table, and she flipped it open.

Inside sat a silver circlet of twining ivy leaves, each curled around an empty set of metal prongs. He realized they were gemstone settings when she pushed the emerald into the setting. The prongs promptly tightened around the stone, which flared green in response. "I want to understand the bastards when they talk to me," she said, feeding the topaz to a second setting opposite the first.

Davon frowned. "Won't you notice you're suddenly speaking languages you don't remember acquiring?"

Alys snorted and began popping opals into the circlet's remaining settings. "I doubt it'll register. I'll have other things to worry about." Spreading her hands over the circlet, she began to chant. The gemstones started to glow, their light flaring until it was almost blinding.

"What did you just do?" Davon asked as she dropped her hands with a tired sigh.

She twisted from side to side, stretching as if to relieve tight back muscles. "Bespelled it to block my memories of today. It will leave part of the vision of Carilla and her kids, which the spell will make me see again in the morning. It will also plant a false vision that will surface after I'm in Bres's hands. According to what I saw in the circle, that one will convince him to launch an alternate attack, rather than the assault on Avalon he has planned."

The more Davon thought about all this, the less he liked it. "And I can't let on about anything I know. Not to you, not even to Arthur or Morgana."

"Exactly." She pushed her corkscrew curls back off her forehead. Her hand trembled. "I saw what happens if you attempt to warn any of us. Each and every time, it ends in disaster."

He rubbed the aching spot between his eyebrows. His every bone and muscle ached after the hours he'd spent struggling to memorize those damn combat sequences. Alys had pronounced herself satisfied, but he wasn't exactly confident. Too fucking much could go wrong.

The two of them stood looking down at the circlet for a long moment. Finally, Alys shook her head and closed the box, then tucked it under her arm. "Sun'll be up in about half an hour. We've got to get to bed."

They started up the stairs together. Davon tried not to think of people climbing the steps to the guillotine. When they reached the top floor, he stopped to meet her gaze. Aching. Longing. "I guess I'll have to sleep in my bedroom. Otherwise you'll wonder…"

Her hand locked in his hair and dragged his head down for a kiss that held tongue, teeth, and raw desperation. When Alys finally drew back, she rested her forehead against his. He spotted the shine of tears on her eyelashes. "I need you," she said in a ragged voice. "I don't care if it's the world's shortest quickie. I need… Not to think for the next thirty minutes." The cinnamon eyes lifted and caught his. "Can you do that for me?"

He reached up and cupped her face in both hands. "I'll do my damnedest."

A tear rolled down her cheek, and she nodded and turned toward her bedroom door as if unable to speak.

They entered together. Like the rest of the house, it was a beautiful space. A glorious stained-glass skylight depicted a wreath of intertwined roses, irises, lilies, and bluebells, fairies playing among the blooms. An enormous bed, this one lacking a canopy, lay centered beneath it. A magnificent tapestry bedspread repeated the floral pattern against a background of white silk.

Usually Davon liked to take his time examining the room, checking to see what new magical decoration had appeared since the last time he'd entered. This time he was too busy aching to care as he followed her to the bed.

Alys put the circlet's box on the elaborately carved oak nightstand. The click of wood meeting wood rang like a gunshot.

Davon caught her shoulders and spun her around, hauling her into his arms. She moaned, the sound desperate and grieving, as his mouth came down over hers, his tongue thrusting in to stroke and circle hers.

They stood there eating at each other in kisses fueled by anxiety and helpless need. Finally Alys dragged her mouth away and stared up at him, breathing hard. "Oh God, help me forget. Help me think about something else."

Davon reached for the sundress she'd worn during that last trip to Mortal Earth, but Alys gestured. Light flared, and every stitch they were wearing vanished.

Her abrupt, graceful nudity took his breath away. He took an instinctive step back so his gaze could slide down the full length of Alys's body, taking in the round, high breasts, the slim waist, the lean, muscular grace. His fangs began to throb in time to the pulse in his dick. Every inch of his body clamored for the taste of hers, the smell of her, the velvet press of her skin.

"I don't want slow," she told him, a ragged note in her voice. "I don't want gentle. I need hard and fast and mindless."

"I can do that. Will do that. Exactly the way you need it." It was a vow. Davon moved back in, pulling her close to kiss his way down the line of her throat, tracing the delicate veins with the tip of his tongue, listening to her heart thunder more in despair than desire.

It was up to him to change that. To make sure she wanted him as something more than a distraction.

She looked up at him, her eyes eating the rainbow light. "Now's good."

He grinned. "Yes, it certainly is."

Davon bent, swept her off her feet, and tossed her lightly onto the bed. Her laughter sounded a little too tight.

And became a startled gasp as he landed on her a heartbeat later, flattening her beneath his male weight. Deliberately letting her feel just how much bigger he was. How much stronger he was.

He met her gaze. And for the first time in all the years he'd known her, he let the predator show, abandoning his careful self-control for once in his damned life.

* * *

Alys gasped as he rolled over her like a storm, his mouth hot and greedy. The sting of his fangs raking across her skin was just the perfect pain to jerk her out of the spiral of fear.

His fangs scraped her skin as he nibbled and sucked his way down her belly, drawing blood. He muttered a rough apology and stopped to lick and suckle that tiny wound, cleaning it with wild circles of his tongue. As he caressed and stroked with skillful hands, he squeezed just a bit too hard, moved just a little too fast.

And it was just right. Just exactly what she needed to empty her mind of everything else but Davon.

His mouth found her nipple, sucking, fierce, each hot tug sending a comet of pleasure flashing through her body.

She watched the roll of muscle underneath his smooth brown skin. And stroked him, loving the feel of him under her hands, the strain and stretch of his powerful body as he worked to build her need.

Rearing in his arms, Alys found his shoulder with her mouth, tasting hot sweat. Drinking in that intoxicating vampire musk. "Let me taste you," she panted, suddenly dying to stuff her mouth with cock. To give him the same pleasure he was giving her.

"No." His eyes lifted to meet hers, narrow, fierce, brooking no opposition.

"But…"

Before she could do more than yelp, he dragged her hips up and draped her knees over his shoulders. Instinctively, Alys tried to struggle, but she had no more chance against that vampire strength than she did against a runaway stallion's.

She jerked as Davon's mouth found her pussy and began to lick. His tongue flickered over and around her clit as one finger slid into her pussy. Pushed deep, pulled out, scissoring and stretching her as he ate her with dark male greed. Fangs scraped that most delicate flesh. Not in a bite -- exactly -- more like a teasing sting. A reminder that for all Davon's good soldier instincts, there was a predator just beneath.

She'd assumed they'd have to use lube, given… well, everything. But as that long tongue tormented her clit in rhythm with his working fingers, her pussy swelled and grew slick. She cried out into the mattress, bright piercing streaks of delight racing through her body. The muscles of her thighs began to shake.

Davon went right on feasting. The tip of a fang caught her again, and he rumbled a rough apology, closing his mouth over it -- and engulfing her clit at the same time. He suckled so hard she dug her nails into the mattress and yowled like a cat.

"Yeah. That. I want more of that sound." He jerked up away from her, lifted her by the hips, and tossed her to the middle of the mattress. She jackknifed up, but he landed between her spread legs, grabbed her by the thighs, and flipped her onto her face. One hand closed on the back of her head, holding it down as he hooked an arm around her waist and dragged her ass into the air.

His thick cock brushed her juicing slit. Found the opening. And pushed, filling her in a hard, merciless rush. And God, he felt huge and delicious and she screamed as he kept coming and coming, stretching, pulling, pain and pleasure and...

"Mine. Mine, mine, mine," he chanted, punctuating each word with another thrust, circling his hips, making her feel every glorious inch of his cock screwing in and out of her pussy.

Alys had never felt so turned on, not even by lovers with centuries more experience. *I didn't love any of them.* Crying out, frantic in her arousal, she slid a hand between her legs and found her clit. Stroked it as he pounded, his thick cock raking slick walls, every thrust wringing more and more pleasure out of her body. Her orgasm barreled closer, fierce as a solar storm.

Hooking an arm around her chest, Davon dragged her up and the back until she was kneeling upright, changing their position. Then he hauled her onto his lap and impaled her on that thick cock again.

"Merlin's beard!" she gasped.

He laughed in her ear. "Merlin didn't have a beard. Merlin looked fifteen."

"Who the fuck cares?" she hissed as he began to pound her with a delicious lack of mercy.

Alys tossed her head back, half-blinded by the waves of sensation he exacted with every stroke. Davon nuzzled her arched throat and chuckled, à la Bela Lugosi, "I vant to drink your blood."

"Take it!" Alys spread her legs and angled her body until she could impale herself again and again on the rigid jut of his cock, crying out in agonized pleasure, loving the raw intensity of the penetration.

He didn't bite.

She wanted him to. Desperately.

He reached between her legs to find her clit as he hunched fiercely up into her. She felt the hot, wet stroke of his tongue as he licked the line of her throat, tasting the veins there. "Jesus, Davon, would you just fucking do it?"

"You sure?" There was a taunt in his voice.

"Yes!" It was a scream, a plea, shameless and hungry.

Davon bit deep, his fingers dancing over her clit. That delicious pain was just what she needed to hurtle her into a ferocious orgasm. She screamed as he drowned her in fire, the pleasure rolling on and on as he drank, her pleasure-tormented body writhing in his arms.

He bellowed as he came.

\* \* \*

Davon gathered her back against him, cuddling her in his arms. "God, I wish I could go to sleep with you."

"There isn't time." Her voice sounded harsh, hoarse.

He wanted to ask if he'd ever have a chance to do this again -- if they'd die tomorrow. Shuddering, he remembered the hours of practice -- and how many times he'd fucked up the timing of a sword stroke or a leap. If he did that tomorrow...

His arms tightened convulsively. "Jesus, I hope I don't fuck this up."

She turned her head, angling it to look up at him. "You won't."

"You don't know that." When she opened her mouth, he said, "Yeah, you saw it, but something could go wrong."

"It won't. Kiss me."

With a deep groan, he leaned forward to take her lips, swirling his tongue around hers. Feeling his chest ache even as he gave her all the heat and hope and fear in him. Finally, she lifted off his lap, pulling free of his softening cock. It felt as if something tore. She pivoted on her knees to face him, taking his face between her palms. Cinnamon eyes stared deeply into his. Demanding belief. "I love you."

He froze, and for a moment it seemed his heart stopped.

"You look so shocked." She stroked his hair back from his forehead, toying with the longer curls at the crown of his head.

Davon licked suddenly dry lips. "When did that happen?"

Her lips twitched, and for a moment the warmth in her eyes overcame the pain and fear. "I'm not quite sure. I think you've been sneaking up on me for a while now."

A memory rose, and he smiled. "I remember the first time I saw you. It was at the party to celebrate Warlock's defeat after the attack on Avalon." Reaching up, he stroked a hand through her wild black curls. "There was so much power around you, you made my skin tingle." His smile widened. "Then again, the tingle may have been because you were the most beautiful woman I'd ever seen. And you scared the hell out of me."

She snorted. "The Mad Alys rumors probably had something to do with that."

Davon shrugged. "Maybe a little. But I started falling in love with you then. I've never stopped."

She gave him a smile, though he could see the effort in it. "We'll get through this. Trust me."

"Trusting you has never been the issue."

"Then trust *you*. I do." She tilted her head back to look at the skylight and sighed. "And we've just run out of time."

Alys crawled across the bed to the nightstand where the box waited. Flipping open the lid, she looked down at the gleaming circlet for a long moment. A shudder ran the length of her body. "Let's do this."

*Let's don't.* But he didn't say it.

Alys squared her shoulders, took the circlet out of the box and slipped it on, adjusting it until the curling vines framed her face. Blowing out of breath, she lay down, stretching out on the big bed.

Davon eased down beside her, encircling her in his arms, needing to hold her. Because this might be the last time.

"I love you," she said again.

"And I love you." His arms tightened convulsively. "I won't fail you."

"I know you won't." The circlet began to glow, dim at first, then brighter and brighter as the magic built. Her eyes met his, and for a moment he saw her terror. Then they rolled back and her face went blank as her eyes closed.

Davon lay staring at her, battling a suffocating wave of fear. At last he pulled the circlet off her head and tucked it back in its box. He picked the box up and carried it downstairs, where he returned it to its place on the lab shelves.

That done, he dragged himself back up the stairs to his bedroom and climbed into bed to wait for the sun to put him out of his misery.

* * *

Sunset liberated Davon to jerk awake in a rush of fear and adrenaline.

He shuddered, remembering his nightmares. Most of the time the Daysleep was like being hit with a hammer -- you went down hard and didn't wake up again until the sun went down. If he had dreams, he usually didn't remember them.

Today, he'd dreamed of watching Alys die.

It was a good thing vampires didn't have prophetic visions -- that was the Majae's burden.

He hoped.

Davon rolled out of bed, battling yet another wave of anxiety. No sooner had his feet hit the floor than Alys called through his bedroom door, "Davon, we've got a job. Come on."

Davon grimaced, hoping he'd join her to find he'd dreamed the whole terrifying thing.

He knew better.

Carefully, he arranged his features into an expression that would hopefully pass for alert rather than devastated and terrified.

When he stepped into the hall, Alys waited, fully armored. She made a graceful, swirling gesture and magic rolled around him, a spill of effervescence tingling across his skin to become his own armor.

Automatically, he put a hand back to feel the hilt of his usual sword in its back scabbard. "What's the mission?" he asked, knowing exactly what she'd say. Hoping he sounded normal.

"Bres is sending a team to hit a Maja who's gone on sabbatical to raise her children on Mortal Earth. We're going to get there first and tell her to gate for Avalon with the kids." She bared her white teeth. "Then we're going to kick Fomo ass."

Davon nodded and asked, because he normally would, "Are we calling for backup?"

She shook her head. "There are only four of them. We can handle them without breaking a sweat."

It would be a lot more than four, but he didn't tell her that. The taste of betrayal burned his tongue like acid. He hoped to God nothing of what he felt showed on his face. Luckily Alys was already turning away, sweeping one hand in an oval, her fingers shaping some tight bit of magic to direct the gate.

It instantly bloomed outward, and she stepped through. Davon strode after her, his belly tying itself in a sick, writhing knot.

His booted feet came down on a gleaming wooden floor. Glancing around, he saw they were in a bedroom that belonged to a pair of small boys, judging by the twin beds shaped like the Batmobile standing against opposite walls.

A Latina woman sat with the children in her lap, staring at them in frozen astonishment from one of the beds. The kids were ridiculously cute, maybe four or five years old, so close in age they look like twins. Both had enormous brown eyes and tousled chocolate curls, and both wore matching Captain America jammies.

Their mother had been reading *Where the Wild Things Are.* Appropriate.

The witch's dark eyes narrowed, taking on an enraged glint as a shield popped up around the three. She looked barely twenty-five -- but then, she'd look no older if she were Arthur's age. For a moment, he thought he and Alys were about to get force-fed a fireball. Then she blinked and visibly relaxed. The shield winked out. "Alys? What are you doing here?" A faint Spanish accent softened her vowels.

"I had a vision, Carilla. Bres is sending an attack team to grab you and your kids. You need to get them to safety in Avalon. Now." She gestured toward the gate she'd left open.

"Bres?" The witch's eyes went wide and appalled. "You have got to be kidding me!" She looked back at her children, and instantly her expression smoothed as she forced a smile. "Come on, boys, we're going to Mommy's house in Avalon." She lifted the younger of the two and put him on his feet beside the bed.

The other scrambled to the floor. "But I thought we were going to go to the movie tomorrow!"

"I'll take you to see Smoke instead. If you ask him nicely, maybe he'll turn into a tiger for you and let you ride him around."

At that, both boys' faces lit. They made no further protest as she guided them toward Alys's open gate. Before they started through, Carilla paused and shot them a look of concern. "Have you called for backup?"

Alys made an airy gesture. "Not necessary. Davon and I can handle it."

"You sure about that?" The Maja frowned deeply, her gaze sliding to Davon, who tried not to look as grim as he felt. Her lips tightened. "If you're not back in fifteen minutes, I'll call backup *for* you."

*And she will, too. It just won't do any damn good.*

Carilla disappeared through the gate with her kids, thus ensuring their survival. They'd have all been dead in ten minutes otherwise. Alys turned and gave

Davon a Mad Alys smile. She did love a good fight. "Let's throw our blue friends a surprise party." Then her gaze narrowed and went sharp, staring at him. "What's wrong?"

*Crap.* "Nothing."

"Yeah, right. Look, I've seen this. They're not going to lay a hand on either one of us."

Davon gave her the confident smile he'd once employed to encourage parents, even when he feared their kid would die on the table. "Of course not. I have faith in us."

She grinned back. "You should."

He followed her out of the bedroom and down the hall, through a den strewn with Legos and action figures. The kitchen they passed through still smelled of garlic and spaghetti and a hint of the cleanser the Maja had made obvious use of. She was serious about pretending to be a "normal" mom for her kids. At least all three would survive this. He and Alys had accomplished that much.

Davon had never been so terrified, including the night he'd expected the werewolves to execute him for Jimmy Sheridan's murder.

Of course, he'd been suicidal then. Tonight was going to make that little disaster look like a party.

Alys led the way out into the two-car garage that had been seared into Davon's memory. Carilla's brick ranch didn't look like the kind of place where you held a fight to the death. The surrounding Atlanta neighborhood was thoroughly middle-class.

A sturdy wooden play fort stood in the backyard, not far from the stand of oaks, maples, and pines that lay cool in the evening dark. Davon's mouth tightened as he remembered the preparations he and Alys had made in those woods the night before.

Christ, he dreaded this.

Moonlight glinted on Alys's golden armor as she swept one hand in an intricate gesture. A pulse of magic flashed over the area. Catching him looking at her, she misinterpreted his expression. "I'm casting a cloaking spell to make sure the neighbors don't call the cops when all hell starts breaking loose. The last thing we need is someone shooting cell phone video of me hurtling magical blasts at big blue aliens."

"Yeah, we definitely don't want that." He tried not to wonder what Bres was going to do to her.

Goddamn it. He ached to scream the truth. *"We've got to get the hell out of here -- now! We've got to just fucking leave!"* Maybe her visions were wrong and there was something he could do that wouldn't leave her in Bres's hands, suffering God knew what...

"Davon?" Alys's gauntleted hand landed on his shoulder as he stared blindly into the night. He resisted the urge to turn and look at her. He wasn't sure he trusted his face. She peered at his profile, frowning. "Are you feeling all right? Do I need to conjure you a quick glass of blood?"

He forced a smile, hoped it was too dark for her Maja eyes to see how false it was. "No, I'm fine." *I drank from you last night.*

The memory smashed into him -- the feel of her silken throat against his lips, the taste of her blood pouring into his mouth. He'd rarely tasted it in anything other than a glass. And every other time he'd drunk from her vein, he'd been mortally injured and in no shape to appreciate it.

*And she doesn't remember.* It was as if it hadn't happened at all. That thought was inexpressibly lonely. He hoped to hell he had the chance to drink from her again -- or even just kiss her again. For a moment he stared at her mouth through the transparent visor of her helmet, craving the taste of her so badly, he ached from his cock to the root of his fangs.

His hand lifted, reached toward her, but before he could touch her, she snapped around, her lean body tensing. "There they are."

# Chapter Six

Davon's stomach seemed to drop as if he were in free-fall, and a wave of ice rolled to the top of his head. He must be going as pale as his complexion would allow.

Through the open garage door, he saw sparks bloom as the dimensional gate expanded. Four Fomorians stepped through. The sizzle of alien magic rolled over him, and he heard Alys make a soft, purring hum. She stepped forward, drawing her sword. He drew his and followed.

"Hello, boys!" Alys called as her helmet echoed of the words in the guttural language of the Fomorians. "I'm sorry, you're not going to be kidnapping anyone's kids today." Lifting her sword, she charged with that ringing Mad Alys cackle.

Davon ran after her, leaping at the nearest Fomorian. And the battle was joined, the two Magekind falling into their old familiar pattern: Alys firing blasts after blast at the lead Fomorian, spaced so tightly they overwhelmed his shield. The instant it fell, Davon leapt forward and swung his sword. Fomorian armor wasn't quite as good as theirs -- the Fomos depended more on their magic to shield them -- and he'd learned precisely the right stroke to cleave through armor, bone, and flesh.

The Fomorian's head tumbled away, trailing a violet spray of blood.

Another warrior lunged at him, and he spun aside, avoiding the Fomo's hurled blast. But even as they fought, Davon worked his way toward the edge of the woods, watching Alys from the corner of one eye. She was having a great time, hurling blazing magical blasts like fastballs. Ferociously alive, as she always was in combat.

Two Fomorians charged her, and there it was: she dropped her shield to swing her blade in that that fucking figure-eight sword swing from the vision. Davon snapped his eyes off to the left. Sure enough, a white-hot point appeared in midair, swelling outward into a gate. The one the eight Fomorian would step through.

His gut clenched, and he shot an agonized look at her. And longed to tell her this wasn't a betrayal. Ached to stay and fight for her, to save her from the horror that awaited her…

*I have one chance -- humanity has one fucking chance. And that's for you to believe me and follow the plan.*

Cursing himself -- cursing her -- Davon wheeled and ran, sprinting for the woods that lay at the edge of the yard. *They won't kill her. She swore they won't kill her.* He heard Alys's startled shout. "'Von? Where the hell are you…" Her voice sounded high with disbelief and a hint of panic.

But she had no time for more as the Fomorians closed in. *She'll think I betrayed her.* The thought rasped over his heart like sandpaper. But he didn't stop, didn't slow as he raced into the woods.

*I have one chance -- humanity has one fucking chance. And that's for you to believe me and follow the plan.*

Just ahead, a white-hot spot appeared in midair, the dimensional gate generator they'd planted the night before activating at his approach. Davon threw himself into the gate without breaking step. His feet hit the ground on the other side, and he slammed to a halt to keep from running into the hotel room wall. Tripping over his own feet, he hit the floor so hard his armor rattled. Behind him, he heard a distant *whomp* as the gate generator destroyed itself, leaving no clue where he'd gone.

\* \* \*

Alys watched in disbelief as Davon fled, a streak of glittering armor in the moonlight. "'Von? Where the hell are you…"

The instant's distraction was lethal. She saw something fly toward her from the corner of one eye. She whirled… right into a magical blast. She didn't have a shield up -- she'd been in the middle of an attack -- so there was nothing to protect her except her helmet.

Her helmet wasn't enough. Light and pain exploded in her face.

She saw nothing else.

\* \* \*

Davon crouched where he'd fallen, staring at the carpet beneath his braced hands. The great sword lay on the floor where he'd dropped it.

*They have her now.* Mechanically, he picked up the sword and stood. Walking over to the second of the two beds where he and Alys had left his gear piled, he put the sword down on the mattress.

The Do Not Disturb spell Alys had laid on the door had kept housekeeping from discovering it. If anyone touched it, they'd believed they'd already serviced the room. Then they'd remember something else that urgently needed doing.

Moving slowly -- his body ached as if he'd been beaten -- he reached up and took hold of his helmet. At his touch, it released its grip on his armored neck, allowing him to pull it off. His hands continued the business of removing his armor on autopilot, touching his breastplate, his gauntlets, his boots, his scale mail vanishing into each piece as he removed it.

Naked but for his briefs, Davon put it all away in the waiting metal case, then closed the case and locked it.

With a sigh, he picked up his sword and sat down in the desk chair beside the window. In the street beyond, brilliant electronic billboards lit up the towering buildings, advertising *Hamilton, Kinky Boots,* and *Les Mis.*

They'd booked the room the night before, finding it as miraculously available as Alys's vision had predicted. Which was how he'd ended up with a room overlooking Times Square in one of the most expensive hotels in the city. Damn, he wished he were sharing it with her instead of waiting for all hell to break loose.

Watching the lights flash, he absently spun the hilt of his sword between his palms. One thought pounded in his brain. Over and over, like the tolling of a bell. *She'll think I abandoned her. She'll think I betrayed her.*

The lights of the signs blurred, and something cold lay across his throat. It was only then that Davon realized he held the sword's edge pressed to his own carotid artery. He didn't even remember lifting it. With a curse, he tossed the weapon on the bed, getting it as far away from himself as he could.

Bending over, he pressed the heels of his hands against his eyes as the first sob tore his throat. His gaze fell on the minibar under the television, and he had a strong impulse to get very, very drunk. But the last thing he needed to do was fuck up his self-control with the sword lying across the bed.

He couldn't save her if he were dead.

A muffled voice sounded from his armor case. Morbidly curious, he stood, walked to the bed and flipped the case open. Arthur Pendragon's voice rang from his helm. "Fredericks? Fredericks, where the fuck are you?"

He slapped the case shut again. According to the vision Alys had re-created for him, by now the Magekind would have arrived at Carilla's house to find everyone gone. Arthur and Morgana would assume they'd both been captured by the Fomorians.

Thankfully, the spells Alys had placed on the armor would keep even Morgana from being able to track him. The Magekind wouldn't know where he was until sometime tomorrow night, when all hell broke loose.

After that, it was even odds whether Arthur would kill him personally.

* * *

The dragon was about the size of a Labrador retriever, if you discounted its long neck and tail. Considering how fast the species grew, it was either a newborn or damn close to it. In the dim light cast by the containment spell, its tiny scales gleamed gold, making it look like a pile of coins. Huge liquid eyes glowed spring green under a pair of tiny horns, and its pointed muzzle was much shorter than Kel's.

It almost radiated terror.

"I won't hurt you."

The little creature jerked and wound tighter around itself, as if it didn't understand her. Alys wished she could speak to it telepathically. Once again, she tried to reach out to its mind, but once again she failed.

She wasn't particularly surprised. She and the little dragon were imprisoned in a cavernous stone room lit by globes of blue light that bobbed against the ceiling high overhead, reminding her of trapped helium balloons. The floor for ten feet around them was deeply inscribed with shapes she recognized as draconic glyphs, along with other symbols she didn't recognize at all. She was willing to bet this was the Fomorian equivalent of a spell circle, though it was less ring than some kind of intricate alien shape.

Whatever it was, the spell it generated was an effective one. She couldn't seem to draw on the Mageverse at all. She'd never been so completely cut off from her magic, and it made her feel as if she'd gone blind.

Then again, if she'd abducted a newly-hatched dragon, she'd have erected the most powerful spell she could manage, too.

Sir Kel had told her once that dragon young had psychic links to their mothers that were almost impossible to break. Somewhere there was a terrified scaly mama searching frantically for her missing hatchling. Damn, Alys wished she could get out a distress call to her, whoever she was. The female would rip apart Bres's palace -- assuming that's where they were. She'd damn sure kill the Fomorian king and everyone else involved in the kidnapping.

The mental image of that searching dragon made Alys think of Davon. Where was *he*? Was he looking for her? Why had he run? She knew it wasn't cowardice. He'd demonstrated his rock-steady courage too many times.

Besides, cowards didn't become Magekind in the first place. Either the Majae's Council rejected them, or they went mad when Merlin's Gift transformed them. *So why the fuck did he run*?

But that thought only intensified her agitation, so she shoved it away. Better to concentrate on soothing the baby. Its fear was the only thing she could do anything about. Not that she could protect the little creature, but making the attempt was better than stewing in her own terror.

The dragonet gave a pitiful moaning cry that wrung her heart. She wanted to give it a hug, despite the inch-long talons and all the teeth concealed in that scaly little muzzle.

What the hell. It wasn't as if she had anything to live for. Bres was going to try to use her against the Magekind, probably through the same contagion he'd used to infect the werewolves and Prince Dearg's bodyguard. But though her head ached fiercely, she didn't feel sick. It was possible they'd infected her while she was unconscious, but she had the feeling they hadn't gotten around to that yet.

They'd stripped her of her armor and sword, of course, leaving her in the thin one-piece suit she'd worn beneath her kit. Which would offer very little protection if the hatchling decided to take a bite out of her.

The dragonet moaned again, and she began to inch toward it, crawling on the icy stone in a bid to appear less frightening. The little gold head raised and it gave a warning hiss, its open mouth revealing an impressive number of a very sharp teeth.

"I'm not going to hurt you," Alys said softly. "I'm a prisoner too."

The hatchling only curled in on itself tighter, quivering. She stopped a short distance away, crooning softly. Big green eyes met hers, blinking slowly, the nictitating membranes sliding back and forth across its liquid eyes. It uncoiled a little.

Alys reached out a hand to touch one thin foreleg. Unlike Kel's adult scales, the hatchling's felt thin and smooth, reminding her of the delicate skin of a human infant. When she inhaled, the dragonet's scent was sweeter and lighter than an adult dragon's heavy, dark musk. The baby gazed at her, eyes widening as the vertical slits of its pupils expanded slowly, eating up more and more of the green.

It moved in a blur. Before Alys could even cry out, she had a lap full of dragonet, its tail encircling her waist, wings curled around her back. It ducked its little head between her breasts and quivered.

Alyssa wrapped her arms around it and cuddled it close as a fierce determination rolled through her. "I don't know why they're holding you, but it can't be anything good. I'm going to get you out of this."

"No, you won't." The voice rumbled, edged in a hiss, so menacing it made her blood chill. It spoke the Draconic language. Bres must have bespelled her to understand.

Alys jerked up her head to see that a doorway had opened in the cavern wall, revealing the hunched emerald form of a dragon, eyes glowing orange, plumes of smoke wreathing its huge, frilled head. She thought it might be a little smaller than Kel, though thirty feet of dragon was still thirty feet of dragon.

In her lap, the dragonet made a high, terrified squeak and ducked lower in her lap, its heartbeat rabbiting against her chest. The green dragon slid endlessly into the room. Instinctively, Alys scrambled to her feet, lifting the hatchling's seventy or so pounds with easy Maja strength.

The dragon laughed at her, each breath a puff of smoke. "You clutch that creature as if you could protect it. You can't even protect yourself. Once Bres has cracked your mind and Avalon falls, we will slay the Sidhe and Magekind alike."

"And what would the God of dragons say to that?" She was proud her voice didn't shake. "I doubt Cachamwri would approve."

"He is no god," the dragon snarled. "He's turned us into the slaves of those bipeds. I will free my people from that false idol."

Staring up at the huge head gloating at her, Alys got a sudden, wild idea. "You're mad, lizard. Cachamwri will feast on your heart -- if Kel doesn't eat it first."

Hissing, the dragon reared, his huge head shooting up on his long reptilian neck. Alys readied herself for its attack. She'd toss the dragonet to safety and throw herself at the dragon. A flying kick into one of those big orange eyes might kill the thing. It was worth a try. It would definitely distract the green fucker long enough for the hatchling to…

"Farek, wait!" a deep voice barked in Fomorian. "If you break the spell barrier to get at the witch, the child will call its mother. You don't want that, do you?"

The dragon's head snapped around, eyes blazing orange as a great cloud of smoke rolled from his mouth. "You don't tell me what I do and do not want, Bres!"

"Of course not," the king said, strolling into the cavern. "But do you really want to allow a *human* to so manipulate you? She only wants you to kill her now so she can avoid her just fate."

The dragon snarled, but the smoke thinned around his muzzle as he closed his mouth.

*Goddamn it.*

Bres turned toward her. He was a towering figure, standing on his toes like a werewolf in robes of some iridescent, glittering fabric. Gemstones draped around his blue, hairless head, dangling from the crest of stubby horns that ran down the center of his skull to his spine. Each stone shimmered with magic, probably designed to amplify his power. "Now," Bres said, his voice low and rich with anticipation as his gaze locked on hers. "Let us begin."

Farek murmured a liquid snatch of spell, and the dragon glyphs suddenly shrank, wrapping tight around the hatchling. It cried out in distress as the spell pinned it to the floor. Simultaneously, Bres gestured and the Fomorian glyphs dimmed. Alys felt a trickle of returning magic.

Instantly, she exploded into motion, leaping into a spinning kick. But before her foot could slam into his skull, Bres's magic froze her in midair. She flung her magic against his, trying to break his hold, but it was like being trapped in industrial vise. The pressure clamped her so viciously her bones seemed to howl. The hatchling wailed in terror as she clenched her teeth against a scream.

Bres stalked toward her. Cold red eyes met hers as she hung helpless in the air. "You are arrogant, human. You need to learn your place. I'm going to crush your mind and leave you an empty shell."

*Go fuck yourself,* she thought, and hurled her will against his.

His magic began to tighten around her mind, seeking some vulnerability he could exploit, but she concentrated on making her consciousness as smooth and reflective as a mirrored dome, offering no purchase to his scrabbling mental claws.

He tightened his hold even more. *You will give in,* his mind told hers. *You have no hope. Even if you manage to fight me off for the moment, I will simply infect you with the virus and you will become my puppet. But that will take hours of suffering. Give in now, and none of that will be necessary.*

*I'm in no hurry*, she snarled back. *I have all the time in the world.* She'd spent centuries using magic on Mortal Earth, dragging what she needed from the Mageverse. She'd survived her transformation to Magekind without going mad.

She'd endured innumerable horrific visions, the crushing stress of being distrusted even by other Magekind agents. She'd withstood the weight of fear, the constant battle against dark futures -- the Nazis getting the atomic bomb; Nikita Khrushchev refusing to turn the Russian ships around and triggering World War III; the nuclear conflagration following the 9/11 that never happened. Davon's inexplicable act of betrayal, which had thrust her into the hands of this vicious son of a bitch.

She'd survived all that. She'd survive this.

Alys heard Farek's laughter as if from a great distance. "You'll never break her. She is too strong for you."

"Then you do it. Or do you fear you are no match for her either?"

A hiss of rage. "I would crack her like an egg. But then I'd have to touch her thoughts, and I'd rather bathe in sewage. Infect her and be done with it."

Bres snarled in frustrated rage. And just like that, the crushing pressure was gone. Alys sucked in a breath. The Fomorian lifted a three-fingered hand, and a long, thin dagger materialized in his grip. She tried to jerk away, but his magic still held her paralyzed.

She could only watch in flinching horror as the king plunged the blade into her stomach. The pain boiled up from her gut in a white-hot explosion that scoured her consciousness. Alys gritted her teeth against the screams that fought to claw up her throat.

Bres smiled at her slowly. "Oh, don't worry. I'll heal you in a moment. But I dipped the blade in the contagion. Within the hour, three at the most, you will belong to me."

"It won't do you any good," she gasped. "They know I've been taken. They'll have locked Avalon's shields against me."

"Oh, I know. But *you* know how the shield is constructed. I'll slay the dragonet and use the magic liberated with its life force to shatter the spell. We'll sweep in and wipe every last Human off the face of this planet." He smiled, smug and sure.

As the pain intensified, she realized he had reason to be.

The contagion raged through her body much faster than it had the werewolves'. But then, she didn't have a werewolf's resistance.

Alys shook and burned, vaguely aware of the dragonet moaning softly in the darkness. Did the hatchling know they were going to kill it? She longed to comfort it, but she was too sick to move. Her every bone and muscle ached as she shook with fever, and her mouth was so dry, her swollen tongue tasted like a dirty sock.

As she grew sicker, Bres wormed his way into her helpless mind. And there was nothing she could do about it, because the contagion had opened a huge hole in her psychic shield. She fought him anyway, trying to drive him out, but nothing worked. It seemed he filled her every cell.

Then the vision hit.

It came pouring from the depths of her mind, images that seemed... odd at first, lacking the usual razor clarity...

Then that thought vanished, drowned in horror.

Farek flew over Times Square, blasting gouts of fire into the towering buildings, which instantly roared up as if they were built of balsa wood instead of steel and glass. Alys rode astride his back -- she was distantly surprised he allowed it -- flinging magical blasts at the mortals fleeing below like panicked sheep. Magekind battled Fomorians in the street, swords ringing on swords amid crackling blasts of magic.

She glimpsed a familiar armored figure, felt the powerful blaze of Excalibur's magic. Arthur Pendragon, his wife hurling blasts of magic by his side. Heard her own laugh, sounding too deep.

No, not her laugh. Bres's. He bellowed over the sound of the wind, the screaming, the crackling fire. "There's Arthur, Farek. Kill him."

The dragon folded his wings and plummeted, talons reaching. Arthur spun, his head cranking back he stared at the sky in terror. Farek snatched him off the ground in both taloned hands and ripped his body in two. Blood and gore sprayed as Guinevere screamed in mortal anguish. And fell dead, slain by their Truebond link.

Trapped within her own skull, Alys screamed.

\* \* \*

Davon had never had such nightmares. All day long, he dreamed of Alys, terrified and confused, not understanding why he had abandoned her. He dreamed of a dragon's vicious mockery, a blue face twisted in fury and hate. Crushing pressure on her mind, magic probing, seeking a way in

Then the flash of a knife. Heat and unbearable pain.

And then Bres. Filling her consciousness…

When the sun set, Davon didn't so much wake as claw his way from sleep. He found himself on his feet, crouching naked, his lips peeled back from his teeth in an enraged snarl. Fear and guilt hammered him. He hoped to hell nothing he'd seen had been a vision.

Turning, Davon eyed the bathroom, craving a shower with a need almost as intense as his aching desire for blood. But he didn't know when the fight would start, and he was afraid to risk it.

He couldn't afford to miss his cue.

So instead he donned his armor, letting it enclose him in magical mail and the sweat stink of his own guilt. God, he burned to see Alys again. Even if she stared at him in betrayed fury, he needed to know she lived. She'd predicted she would, but that was no guarantee.

Once the rest of the suit was in place, he opened the shoebox-sized case and took out Maeve's gauntlets. At his touch, the opals began to glow, spilling alien magic that made his nervous system reverberate and set his teeth on edge.

Carefully, he drew them on over the scale mail that covered his arms. Alys had altered his suit to accommodate them. With another bone-rattling hum, the gloves snapped tight around his forearms. His skin stung as they sank magical teeth right through the scale into flesh.

Shuddering a little at the sensation, Davon withdrew a long, narrow case from among his luggage and put it down on the bed. Flipping back the lid, he gazed down at the two very different blades stored inside: Reaver, in its magical scabbard, and the

Unicorn Dagger. Hopefully, the gloves' opal power reservoirs would hold a charge long enough to get him through the coming fight.

Lifting the sword from its case, he buckled it diagonally across his back. Davon drew the weapon, then sheathed it again, making sure it slid in and out of the scabbard smoothly.

Next, he pulled out the dagger, with its spiral blade like a unicorn's horn and the delicate crystal globe that formed its pommel. He'd have to be damned careful not to break it. Davon buckled the weapon around the biceps of his left arm, then checked that he could draw it, too, without it getting caught on anything.

Davon frowned. Alys had said the enchanted weapon should work. Yet she'd also admitted her vision was a little hazy on that point, confused in a way that meant there were many possible futures. He and Alys had explored some of those alternative fates last night, during that interminable training session.

In some of those futures, he died. In others, she did. All Davon could do was trust Alys, trust the plan, and hope they were both alive at the end of it. And pray Arthur Pendragon didn't kill one or both of them for treason, because that, too, was a possibility.

Restlessly, Davon turned from the bed and walked to the window. The spell Alys had laid on the glass had blocked the light that would have otherwise burned him during the day.

He scanned the street below, looking for any indication it was beginning. Nothing so far.

Christ, he hated this. It was a hell of a lot easier to follow her visions when she was there with him. After all, Alys had four hundred years of experience, while he was barely forty. Which had sounded old to him until he'd begun hanging around with people who knew Merlin.

*She thinks I betrayed her.* The thought stabbed him in the heart.

*You'd better damn well hope that's what she believes. Because if she doesn't, that fucker Bres will know you're trying to trick him.*

Alys feared the Fomorian King would penetrate the spell on her mind and see what she'd attempted to hide beneath it. If Bres saw her memory of the original vision, he'd call off the attack, wait for daybreak on the city of Avalon, and wipe out every witch and vampire in the city. He…

Something flashed past far below, moonlight rippling along a huge, scaly body. Davon jolted out of his preoccupation and plastered himself against the window, looking in the direction whatever it was had gone.

Twenty floors below, a huge green dragon banked and strafed the sidewalk with gouts of flame. A small armored figure rode the creature's back, firing magical blasts in concert with the beast's attacks.

Alys, leading the attack as Bres's puppet. Just as she'd predicted.

## Chapter Seven

What he really needed was a good war, Adam Parker thought as he walked into the video editing booth to put together that piece on the newest cell phone.

Cell phones, for Christ's sake. It was enough to make you miss Syria. *I'm a combat shooter, for Christ's sake. I've got to get back overseas. I am so Goddamn bored.*

Adam winced, realizing what he'd just thought. Every reporter, cop, EMT, and nurse would tell you the last thing you ever wanted to think were those two deadly words: "I'm bored." It was an engraved invitation for the news gods to fuck you up the ass.

So he stifled his discontent and threw himself into a chair in front of the bank of video equipment. He was just reaching for the computer keyboard when his cell phone rang. He touched his wireless earpiece, activating it. "Parker."

"All Goddamn hell is breaking loose in Times Square," Donovan Cable News night director Carol Jamison snapped. "Grab a camera and haul ass. Don't even bother with a car, you wouldn't be able to get close anyway."

"You got it." As his heart instantly began to pound, Adam bolted out of his chair, slammed the door open, and broke into a run, heading for the equipment room. "What have we got?"

"You wouldn't believe me if I told you. Shit's on fire and people are dying. Get your ass out there and try to stay alive. Get me some fucking video."

*Jesus Christ!* As he dodged a panicked production assistant, he wondered if the news gods were about to give him that ass reaming…

\* \* \*

Even through the thick glass, Davon could hear the screams as terrified mortals ran for their lives. Meanwhile, a thousand Fomorian warriors and their allies charged from dimensional gates all around the square to fall on the evening crowd. An armored centaur ran down a woman in a Statue of Liberty costume, crushing her beneath his great hooves.

Davon stared down, feeling sick. It was all coming true. *Why the fuck couldn't she have been wrong just this once?* Though if she had been, it would mean the Fomorians were butchering people in Avalon. And the body count would end up far higher.

Davon spun away and strode toward the gate generator he'd set up at the foot of the bed. He pressed one foot on the device, activating it. The gate spiraled open, and he stepped through.

He and Alys had erected the destination generator on the hotel's flat roof. Davon stepped out into cool air ringing with the sound of screams and heavy with the smell of smoke and the stench of burning flesh. Grimly, he hurried to look over the parapet. Far below, the dragon strafed the sidewalk with flames. A hysterical chorus of agonized screams rose as people burned and died.

Davon drew Reaver as he watched the dragon intently, trying to ignore what the creature was doing as he watched for the moment Alys had predicted. They'd practiced over and over last night, working on the timing as he fought illusionary dragons in scenarios based on Alys's visions.

Four times Davon had plummeted to what would have been his death. Future Alys/Bres had decapitated him twice. He had to time this exactly right or this entire thing would be for nothing. Then the death toll would be even greater -- and it was going to be horrific as it was.

The dragon flew in spirals far below, incinerating humans. According to Alys's visions, a few insane souls were even now shooting cell phone video, and network news crews were on the way. *Arthur's going to be seriously pissed.* The Magekind had kept humanity in the dark about their existence for fifteen hundred years, but he and Alys were about to blow that right out of the water.

As the dragon banked, Alys shot a fireball through the window of a Starbucks down below.

*And there's my cue.* As Alys had taught him, Davon willed his gauntlets to extrude claws. He flung himself off the roof, aiming not for where the dragon was, but where it would be after the updraft of the explosion caught its wings and pitched it skyward.

Falling like a stone, Davon felt his face draw into a rictus of terror behind his faceplate. *Fast, fast, so fast, I'm going to hit the pavement and splat, the vision was wrong, we're all gonna...*

Suddenly the dragon's back appeared beneath him, shooting up toward his feet. He landed hard, bending his knees and thrusting the claws into the thick armored plates on the dragon's spine. He hung on for dear life as the dragon twisted through the air, riding out the turbulence.

This time Davon *didn't* fall off and get incinerated.

Just ahead of him, Alys perched in a harness astride the dragon's neck. As she started to turn, he snatched the Unicorn Dagger from its upper arm sheath. If she got all the way around, she'd see him and shield, and he'd be screwed.

He pounced, slapping one hand down on the back plate of her armor. It recognized his magical touch as she'd spelled it to do last night, the scales rolling up into the chest plate, leaving her back bare. Davon raked the knife in a hard, shallow cut across the small of her back, drawing blood, and sheathed the corkscrew blade again in the same smooth motion.

She twisted with an infuriated shriek in Fomorian. Her gaze met his -- impossibly cold and alien. And definitely *not* Alys Hawkwood. Lips twisting, she sneered in English, "Oh, look, it's the coward. Did you finally grow balls?"

*Shield!* he thought at the gloves.

The barrier sprang up around him a heartbeat before her fireball blew him right off the dragon's back. He plummeted thirty feet toward the pavement. Luckily, the shield absorbed most of the impact, though the landing still jarred every tooth in his head. Davon bled off more momentum with a combat roll and surged to his feet.

Alys and the dragon swooped toward him. His stomach clenched.

Now came the hard part. Nobody else could take the dragon out but him. If he didn't kill it now, the creature was going to bring down the Marriott. The resulting magical blaze would wipe out Times Square before the Magekind could extinguish it. Davon leaped into a ten-foot bounce, barely dodging the gout of flame as the dragon flashed past.

"Stand and fight, coward!" Bres shouted as his mount banked to wing toward him again.

"Easy to say when you're flying around over my head, asshole!" Davon roared back in a battleground bellow he'd learned from Arthur. He drew Reaver, and the sword exploded into crackling magical light.

"Come get some!" From the corner of one eye, he glimpsed the glint of a camera lens. That would be the news videographer. *And not my problem right now.*

"That puny thing?" Bres sneered as the dragon started toward him. "I'll show you flames!"

*Here we go...* If her vision was wrong, he was fucked. But Alys had told him she'd seen this event five different times in five different timelines, and it was always the same. He'd memorized it like a stunt man practicing a choreographed fight scene in an adventure flick.

The dragon barreled toward him, jaws gaping wide. It blew out a thundering plume of flame. Davon leaped aside, feeling the blast furnace heat of it even through his armor. "Missed!"

The dragon whipped its head around, great jaws opening. For a heartbeat, Davon stared at teeth longer than his forearms. He somersaulted backward, avoiding the snap, feeling the brush of teeth across the sole of one boot. He hit the pavement and rolled to his feet, spinning to swing Reaver in a crackling arc. His skin tingled, burning despite his armor's protective spells. He'd have second-degree burns -- and would be lucky if he didn't end up with third.

The slice barely missed the dragon. It twisted aside, just as he'd known it would, roaring something his helmet translated as, "You'll pay for that, human!" As it snapped, its long green neck whipping, Davon spun and leaped, throwing himself one way and then the other. The dragon chased him like a cat after a yarn ball. If it got him, it would fry him into an oily streak on the pavement.

\* \* \*

Adam had spent twelve years covering some of the nastiest shit in the Mideast for Donovan Cable

News. But he'd never seen any Goddamn thing like this. It was like being trapped in the middle of a Marvel movie, complete with giant flying monsters destroying Times Square.

He wondered if he was about to shoot his own death, live on national TV. Sweating, he panned his camera over the chaos -- the armored figures chasing terrorized tourists and cutting them apart with swords, for God's sake.

He'd be lucky if he didn't end up sushi.

New York's finest were out in force, periodically blazing away with pistols or shotguns. Trouble was, every time they fired, blue hemispheres would appear around the targets, and the bullets would ricochet.

*God, I wish I had my bulletproof vest.* But this was fucking Manhattan, not Falluja.

A thought skidded through his mind. *If they thought Sandy Hook was fake, what the fuck are they going to say about this?*

One thing was for sure, the death toll was going to be a hell of a lot higher. Bodies lay up and down the street, most either smoking lumps of charcoal or surrounded by pools of blood from horrific sword wounds. He had a horrible feeling there wouldn't be many survivors.

"Give me another pan," Jamison said in his earpiece. "You're still live."

Adam swung the camera the other way slowly, hoping no one would shoot him or run him through while he was doing it. Which was when his camera's viewfinder filled with a shot of some asshole in armor playing St. George and the Dragon with a lizard the size of a school bus.

Sucking in a breath, Adam focused on the tiny armored figure who leaped around, dodging the dragon's snapping lunges. His heart plunged into his throat. It was going to fucking eat the guy...

"That!" Jamison yelled. "Hold that shot!"

* * *

As the dragon darted at Davon again, he gripped his sword and leaped ten feet straight up, avoiding the charge, hearing the vicious snap of jaws. He badly wanted to use Reaver, but Alys's visions said he'd miss.

Bres's magical blast caught him in midair, batting him across the pavement. He crashed to a halt and immediately dove left, avoiding another thunderous snap as he shot to his feet. *Now now now...*

Davon swung Reaver before he even turned all the way around, knowing where the dragon would be. He put his full weight, strength, and momentum behind the stroke...

And rammed Reaver into the center of the dragon's great head. Snarling, he poured all the gauntlets' remaining power into it.

Flames ignited in the dragon's skull, and it screeched in frenzied agony, rearing skyward even as the fire spread. No non-magical blaze could have damaged the creature's fire-resistant hide, but this was Elementalverse magic.

And it burned the dragon just the way it had the troll when they'd rescued Dearg.

Davon didn't hang around to watch. He whirled and ran, throwing himself into long, furious bounds.

Alys landed just where the vision predicted she'd be after throwing herself off the dragon. She hit the ground in a crouch, knees bending as she absorbed the impact. Davon slammed into her in a tackle he'd once used playing high school football, knocking her right off her feet.

God, he hated this part of the plan.

They hit the ground with Davon riding Alys like a sled as she skidded over the pavement on her armored back. As they came to a stop, he drove his fist viciously into her helmet. It didn't crack -- the witches had done too good a job reinforcing it -- but the impact bounced her head against the helm's shell.

"God, Alys, I'm sorry!" He slammed his fist down again, and again with all his strength, until her eyes rolled back. Out cold. And now there was a tiny hairline crack in the visor. The dragon's fire, combined with his punches, had weakened her faceplate just enough.

Davon flexed his fingers, and three-inch claws slid from the gauntlet again. Carefully, he thrust the claws into the crack, then curled his fingers against the faceplate and jerked. Fragments of magical plastic went flying as the visor shattered. Davon snatched the Unicorn Dagger from the sheath strapped to his upper arm. To his relief, its tear-shaped glass pommel now glowed a brilliant crimson. The spell was done. *Now, if only it fucking works.*

Flipping the dagger over in his hand, he drove it downward. The glass pommel smashed against Alys's mouth, bloodying her lip. A wisp of red smoke drifted up her face from the shattered globe. Alys jolted and came to, staring up at him with wide eyes as she sucked in an involuntary breath, inhaling the smoke. Drinking in the cure the dagger's magic had created.

Her eyes narrowed, taking on the vicious expression he'd learned to recognize as Bres. "Well, it seems you don't love her as much as she thought," the king sneered. And yes, it was obviously Bres. The contempt and arrogance dripping from her voice had nothing to do with the woman he loved.

Bres's fireball took him right in the face, flinging him off her. He hit the ground rolling, his helmet smoking. The dagger went bouncing, but its job was done anyway. Davon somersaulted to his feet as he drew Reaver, only to see that the great blade looked blackened and dark. It had been completely drained.

*Oh, shit.* The gauntlets were dead.

"I'm going to cut you to pieces, boy," Bres snarled. "And I won't even need magic to do it."

He might be right. Davon was no match for Alys, despite his greater strength. Four centuries of combat experience were so thoroughly ingrained in her muscle memory, Bres could probably beat Davon even without her cooperation.

But that didn't matter. All that mattered now was buying enough time.

Bres stalked him, his expression vicious in the frame of the visor. He lunged forward, and Davon barely managed the parry. Alys's sword rang on Reaver's powerless blade. He disengaged and danced back.

From the corner of one eye, he saw a figure run past in the distinctive armor of a Knight of the Round Table. Whoever it was charged a centaur, howling the Magekind battle cry. "Avaaalonnnnn!"

He knew that voice. *Arthur. Thank God. Though we're all out of the closet now.*

The mortals were getting brave now that the dragon lay crispy in the middle of the square. Beyond Bres's shoulder, Davon spotted a ballsy cameraman shooting as Arthur swung Excalibur at his opponent. The centaur reared, dodging the stroke, hooves fanning the great warrior's head. *Yeah, that's going to be on loop for the next week.*

Then Davon had no more time to think about it. Alys/Bres was raining blow after blow on him, and it was all he could do to keep his head on his shoulders. He kept dancing, ducking and spinning around her, furiously blocking sword thrusts powerful enough to click his teeth together.

Davon had been an athlete as a mortal, and he'd gotten stronger and faster since becoming a vampire. Alys had spent the past decade building his strength even more. But as he fought her now, he realized it still might not be enough.

* * *

Alys stared out of the cage of her own skull in terror and helpless fury. She had no idea what the fuck was going on. It was like being trapped in a movie where you had no control over the movement of the camera or the action. All she could do was look where the camera was pointed, unable to do anything about what was happening.

And overlaying it all was the greasy evil of Bres's mind. She could feel his need to reduce everyone around him to piles of rotting meat or sycophants crawling for his approval. Begging for his mercy. And she knew exactly how little mercy he had.

Now Bres was stalking Davon. Her partner's face looked cold with expressionless concentration.

He'd abandoned her. She couldn't understand why she hadn't foreseen any of this -- not Davon's betrayal or her own capture. Why the hell hadn't her visions warned her? Though it could've been worse -- what she'd seen following her capture could have come to pass. In that vision, Bres had turned Times Square and its surrounding buildings into a blazing magical inferno the Magekind had been helpless to extinguish. Without Arthur's leadership, they'd had been easily overwhelmed and slaughtered.

Bres, of course, had promptly set out to bring that vision about. She'd fought him with every ounce of strength, but he'd blown through her defenses like wet tissue paper. When she'd sworn to kill him, he'd only laughed. Then he'd thrust her down to the depths of her own mind until she was barely aware.

At first that had almost seemed a mercy as the horrific images from the vision battered her.

Then came a spinning nightmare of sensations: Bres's vicious anticipation, the jolting impacts on her arms and legs she'd recognized as combat. The first thing she'd truly been aware of was the impact of something hitting her in the mouth. Gasping in pain, she'd tasted blood. And found herself stared up into Davon's face, into the fury and despair in his dark eyes.

Shocked, she breathed in a lungful of red smoke that smelled of ozone. Had to be a spell. She'd immediately buried the thought, knowing Bres would read it out of her mind. Fortunately, he was thoroughly distracted by trying to pilot a strange body located in an entirely different universe.

Davon wasn't making it easy on him, either. He'd whirled and leaped around her, the black blade of his sword ringing against Bres's. It wasn't his usual weapon. She spotted a curving cross guard that looked familiar and wondered if it was Reaver. That couldn't be. Davon didn't have the magic to generate the sword's flaming blade.

But he had more than enough skill to use it as a non-magical weapon. Swinging the sword with effortless strength, he pushed Bres hard, driving the puppet master backward. Davon was six inches taller than Alys, and his vampire strength was that much greater.

What was more, Bres hadn't anticipated the challenges of intricate sword work in the body of a puppet. As the Fomorian focused all his attention on Davon, Alys's awareness grew. From the corner of one eye, she glimpsed a huge, charred husk that appeared to be a dragon. She hoped it was Farek and not Sir Kel. It was a good sign that she was on her feet rather than riding the green dragon, as she had in that horrific vision.

With every moment that went by, her awareness sharpened, until she no longer perceived everything through a fog. Things were finally beginning to make sense, her consciousness no longer seeming to float.

And she could feel her body, feel the effort of straining muscles as Bres drove her ruthlessly. He didn't care if she died as long as he killed Davon.

The last time she'd seen Davon, he'd been running away -- leaving her to be captured by the Fomorians. Abandoning her to the infection, to the psychic rape that was Bres's possession. What the hell was he up to?

Desperately, she tried to think. Her body was slowing, weighed down by exhaustion, by the burns and bruises she could feel forming beneath her armor. Something must've been fucking hot to burn her through the enchanted mail. Had she been aboard Farek when the dragon caught fire?

That would explain a lot.

She could hear Bres's mental voice hissing through her brain. *The Fredericks boy is good, but he lacks experience. I've got to finish him off before the witch drops.* Beneath that was a boiling frustration. *Should've invaded Avalon. I could have killed them all by now. But no,*

*I wanted to humble Arthur, terrorize the mortals with my power, and enslave the lot of them.*

Yeah, that was pretty much what Alys had figured. And she'd seen all too clearly his plan for the Earth and what he saw as its infesting Human monkeys.

Bres flew into an uncharacteristically clumsy lunge, aimed at Davon's chest. It was a feint, designed to lure Davon close enough that Bres could blast him. And it would work. In a flash, Alys saw it all -- the fireball exploding in Davon's face, burning right through his armor and setting them ablaze.

Bres dropped his weapon a fraction, leaving a tiny opening as he pretended to miss the parry. Even as he did so, he drew on her magic, preparing a lethal blast. As the power burned down the length of her arm, Alys threw her will at the muscles of her biceps and forearm. Her hand jolted aside just as the blast boiled out. The fireball slammed into a neon sign, which instantly burst into flame.

*You little bitch*! Bres roared, incredulous. *You dare? You'll pay for that...*

His power slashed at her, trying to sear into her brain and knock her back into the dark, leaving him free to do whatever the hell he wanted to Davon.

*Fuck! You!* she snarled back, and grabbed for the Mageverse, for the power he had blocked away from her mind.

And there it was, in all its blazing glory. Alys drank it in like a drowning woman sucking oxygen. Then she poured it back out again, blasting it into Bres like a fire hose, shoving his stinking presence out of her head. Freeing herself.

Distantly, she heard his roar of outrage. *You little whore, you will not...*

*Yes, you asshole, I will*! Snarling, she poured so much power into her psychic shields that they blocked him out of her mind like a titanium wall.

In the next breath, she seemed to catapult into her own body, expanding into her legs and arms and pumping chest. Everything was hers to command again. Triumphant joy filled her...

Just as the ground came up and slapped her right in the face. She lay there, dazed, distantly aware of terrified screams, the crackle of flame, Fomorian howls, a deep voice bellowing curses. *Sounds like Arthur.*

But she couldn't spare attention for any of that. Bres still remained in her body despite her shields. She could feel the lingering slime of him beneath her skin, a corruption that filled her with revulsion. He seemed... distributed throughout her body somehow, even in her very brain. Revolted, she reached for him.

Small. He was impossibly small even as he seems to be *everywhere* inside her.

*Well of course. It's the fucking contagion.*

And it was dying. She could feel it weakening, almost as if someone had hit it with penicillin or something.

But it wasn't *just* a disease, or it wouldn't reek so of Bres. She remembered Davon talking about scientists using viruses to cure genetic diseases by inserting bits of DNA into them. They'd then inject the viruses into the patient so the virus could insert the new DNA into their cells.

Bres must've done something similar, inserting his own DNA into the contagion, then using that to infect his victims. His DNA had acted as a conduit for his magic, bypassing his victims' normal magical protections.

*But a conduit works both ways. That's why he couldn't let us get our hands on his puppets. We'd have followed that magical connection right back to him.*

Alys could use the virus's magical link to his brain and body. But she had to strike now, before he realized his vulnerability and protected himself. Unfortunately, she didn't have the strength to take him on alone. Not after the abuse she'd taken. Her magic was all but burned out, her body drained, her will worn down to a nub. How the hell could she...

"Alys?"

She opened her eyes to see a pair of booted toes inches from her face. One of those boots was planted firmly on her sword. Davon stepped back and kicked it away, then lifted his own weapon. "Are you back with us?"

Painfully, she rolled over on her side and looked up at his face. And realized instantly what she needed to do. *But he betrayed me...* Left her to be captured by the Fomorians.

*But he's here now. He risked his life for me again and again.* And as she stared up, into his dark, concerned gaze, she realized Davon Fredericks was no more capable of betrayal than Arthur Pendragon. He was honor all the way to the bone. Whatever he'd done, he'd had a damned good reason. She groped for the visor of her helm, only to find the faceplate missing, evidently shattered. "Davon?" she rasped. "Davon, help me up!"

He stared at her a long moment before dropping to one knee beside her, though he still held the sword ready. "Looks like the cure worked."

So he'd been responsible for freeing her from Bres. Alys wasn't at all surprised, but she didn't have time to ask how he'd pulled that off. "Davon, we need to Truebond. Now."

# Chapter Eight

Brown eyes widened behind Davon's visor. "Truebond? But…"

"We need to go after Bres. He used his own genetic material in the virus, which gives me a potential magical backdoor into his mind. But I need you to reinforce my magic because I don't have the strength." Basically, she'd be using him both as a battery and psychic reinforcement. Something in her rebelled at the thought of forcing such intimacy on him, but they had no choice. "We've got to do this now, while Bres is still shocked. Before he realizes the…"

A chorus of screams rose, answered by the guttural roar of a troll. Instinctively, Alys and Davon simultaneously ducked and spun, just as a group of New Yorkers raced past in full panicked flight. Behind them, a team of Magekind were exchanging magical blasts with two trolls, a pair of centaurs, and a dozen Fomorians.

Davon grabbed her arm and hauled her into the shelter of the nearest alley. "Alys, we're in the middle of a battle, for God's sake! Arthur and the Magekind need us. We can't just…"

"If we can take Bres out, the Magekind won't have to worry about the fucking war. And we've got to do this *now*, before he realizes how vulnerable he is."

He stopped, staring at her, then gave her a crooked smile. "Good point."

"I'll cast an invisibility spell on us. That'll protect us while we get this done." Alys grabbed for her magic and wove a quick enchantment. The sounds of battle instantly faded, blocked by the spell. Looking up at him, she hesitated, remembering the visions -- what happened to Truebonded couples when something went wrong. "But you need to keep in mind, if we Bond, and I get killed…"

Davon pulled off his helmet, his gaze dark, intense. "My life wouldn't be worth living anyway. What do I need to do?"

There was no hesitation in his eyes. No doubt. Alys reached for his face, only to realize she was still wearing gloves. This needed skin-to-skin contact. Instead of taking the gauntlets off, she rose to her toes and took his mouth in the kiss she'd craved for a decade.

His lips felt impossibly soft as they parted in surprise against hers. She groaned softly, started to slip her tongue…

Memory barreled into her brain like a tank going full speed as the amnesia spell broke as it was designed to -- with the kiss she'd foreseen three days before.

Alys saw it all -- the visions of Avalon's destruction, the frantic search for a solution. The delicious hour she'd stolen to make love to Davon. The preparations and the planning, and the way he'd had to execute all of it alone. She gasped against his mouth, realizing the cost the plan must have exacted.

All leading up to this inevitable moment.

But there was no time to consider the implications, not if they were going to do what had to be done. Alys grabbed for the Mageverse, pulling the energy in even as she dropped every psychic barrier she normally maintained. Then she took that power and began to weave a net of magic around their minds, drawing them closer together, spinning more and more threads. Pulling those bonds tight. Making them one.

He threw himself open to her. Let her see it all -- all the pain, all the guilt he'd felt when he let her be taken. How it had tormented him to imagine what she must be going through. What she must think of him.

But she also saw his beautiful, crystalline memory of the moment their bodies joined, when she'd kissed and touched him for the first time. When he'd felt her touch. But most of all, Alys felt *him*.

It was the first time she'd had more than brushing contact with Davon's mind. She'd known how intelligent and driven he was, of course. Idiots didn't become trauma surgeons. But he'd also demonstrated his character with his determination to learn every technique she'd tried to teach him. With his unceasing efforts to build his strength and speed. Despite the effort it had cost him, the pain of pulled muscles, the strain of lifting hundreds of pounds. And that was aside from his relentless efforts to learn swordplay.

But over and above all that, Alys felt Davon's love for her. Love he'd carefully hidden and tried to deny for the past decade. The love he'd thought she couldn't possibly return.

It was a good thing she'd never tried to touch his mind. If she had, there would have been no way she could have resisted the need to Truebond with him. And if she had, he would not have been able to save her. The contagion would have given Bres the means to seize control of Davon's mind, as well. But God, the price they'd paid. The years they'd wasted…

*All that's over now,* Davon told her, joy ringing in the thought. *We're together now, and he's not going to be able to stop us.* With that, he flooded her exhausted, battered consciousness with his warm strength.

She took what he offered with such generosity, using his power to heal her injuries, reinforce the cracks in her battered psyche, the wounds Bres had inflicted. Seeing the memory of what she'd suffered, Davon recoiled in new horror.

*No. It had to be this way,* Alys told him. *As painful as it was, it was better than the alternative.* She showed him the image of the troll carrying his severed head. *We must make sure the bastards don't get a second chance. Bres is going to try again, and we can't afford to let him succeed.*

Sensing what she needed without her even having to speak the words, Davon wrapped himself around her, through her, reinforcing her mind with his, despite his own exhaustion. Giving her the last full measure of himself without question. Because she needed it. And because that was just who he was.

Alys took that power and reached into herself, seizing the magical link Bres had created between them with the virus -- with his own DNA. Then she flung them both up that dying link, hunting the king on the other end. Together, they drove like a spear into Bres's mind -- right into the core of his brain where that magical link had been born.

Alys and Davon found themselves looking through Bres's eyes as he crouched in the center of the spell circle, one hand gripping the dragonet, the other holding a dagger poised to drive into the hatchling's heart. The baby writhed and whipped under his hand, screeching in terror as Bres prepared to drink its magic.

*I don't fucking think so!* Alys snarled.

Bres recoiled in astonishment, sensing their sudden presence. *What? Where did you... Get out!*

*No!* Alys eyed the spell inscribed on the floor around them. The draconic symbols that had strengthened it were gone. Farek's death must have broken his part of the spell. Which was why it was taking everything Bres had to block the hatchling's psychic link to his mother.

Drawing hard on Davon's strength, Alys grabbed Bres's magical connection to the spell that bound the baby.

And snapped it.

The dragonet wailed, a psychic screech of such power, Davon, Alys, and Bres shrank under its thundering blast. *Every dragon for miles will hear that,* Alys thought in satisfaction. *Particularly its mother.*

*No!* Bres screamed, clawing for his magic in a frantic effort to reconstruct the spell. But Alys clamped down over his mind, blocking his brain's access to the energies of the Mageverse.

Simultaneously, Davon wound his consciousness around the fucker, freezing his every muscle, holding him still so he couldn't hurt the hatchling. *The problem with kidnapping people's children,* Davon snarled, *is that it tends to piss them off.*

Panicked, Bres fought, his mind battering theirs with all his impressive magical power, flailing, howling in rage and terror.

Alys realized there was no way she could have held the king by herself, even with her restored magic. She'd taken too much of a beating. But Davon bound Bres like chains to a battleship's anchor. He might not have a witch's power, but what he did have was will -- the will to keep Bres from using his magic and the will to help Alys use hers.

A thought winged through her consciousness. *I never realized just how strong Davon is.* She'd been blinded by his doctor's compassion, by his loyalty and willingness to follow her. But he'd never obeyed out of weakness. Partnering Mad Alys had taken incredible strength. Never more so than today.

The white-hot point burst above Bres's broken spell circle, widening into a dimensional gate. A seven-foot-long head thrust through the opening, frantic red eyes sweeping the room.

The hatchling made a desperate little cry.

The mother dragon's eyes widened in unmistakable joy. Her magic flashed out to scoop up her baby like a cradling hand. She lifted the child and wafted it through the dimensional gate. All the while, the great beast stared at Bres, her eyes burning crimson in her great white head.

*Let me go, damn you!* the Fomorian king shrieked at Davon and Alys, writhing in animal panic as he fought to break their hold.

*How do* you *like being helpless, motherfucker?* They clung to him grimly as his mind battered theirs in a frenzy.

*I'll give you anything, just…*

*The only thing we want from you is your death.* They held him right up until the moment the mother dragon opened her jaws and screamed in flame. Howling in agony, the king began to burn.

\* \* \*

Alys damn near died with Bres, but at the last moment Davon's mind clamped around hers and dragged her away. They fell into their bodies with Bres's screams ringing in their minds.

For a moment, Alys thought she herself was on fire -- that the magic of the dragon's breath somehow spread her body.

"It's all right," Davon murmured. "It's all right, we're alive, we're safe…"

Alys sucked in a breath, realizing that her mouth still pressed against his in that kiss they'd begun when they Truebonded. With a moan of relief, she kissed him hard, letting him feel her humble gratitude.

"And look at that. You were right, Gwen. That spell was hiding our missing lovebirds." Something cold and bright touched Alys's jaw. "Would you like to tell me what the fuck is going on?" Arthur Pendragon asked coldly.

Alys and Davon jerked apart to find Excalibur's point pressing against her throat as the once and future king glared at them.

He was in full King Arthur mode, black brows lowered over furious eyes, the corner of his mouth twisted in the frame of his beard.

The memory of a vision flashed through Alys's consciousness: *Excalibur's swing taking her head...*

A gauntleted hand reached up and closed around the great sword's point, pushing it away. "You may want to hold off on the execution," Davon said coolly. "She just killed Bres."

Alys shot him a look. "*We* just killed Bres." Then she shrugged. "Actually, we held him still so a mother dragon could fry him for kidnapping her hatchling. But the end effect is the same. The son of a bitch is dead."

Arthur's eyes narrowed as he studied them for a long, cold moment. Alys's heart thundered like a bass drum by the time he finally spoke. "Where is Bres?"

*Oh, thank God. He believes us.* "At his palace," Alys said, and described how he'd used the virus to turn her into his puppet -- and how they had turned his spell against him.

"That was cleverly done," Morgana Le Fay observed. She'd evidently walked up in time to hear the conversation. Then she frowned. "Though it doesn't explain how he was able to use that kind of spell on those werewolves, given their immunity to magic."

"No, think about it," Alys explained. "If Direwolves were truly immune to magic, they wouldn't be able to shift forms. What they're immune to is magic coming from *outside* their bodies. Once Bres got the virus *inside* them, he bypassed that protection."

Morgana nodded slowly. "I suppose that makes sense, but I still don't understand how he overcame the werewolf immune system."

"He overwhelmed it," Alys said. "At least, according to what I saw when he was occupying my head."

"That must be why the infected carriers had to bite their victim so many times," Davon suggested thoughtfully. "It had to be a massive infection to overpower the werewolves's natural immunity long enough for his magic to get a foothold. That's why it took so much less to infect Alys."

Arthur studied them, some of the suspicion gone from his dark eyes. "How did you manage to break his control?"

"Once Davon administered the cure --" Alys began.

Morgana's eyes widened. "Wait, you have a cure? How the hell did you do that? And why didn't you mention it before now?"

"Unicorn Dagger," Davon explained. "I cut her with it, and while I fought her, it created the cure in a magical reservoir. Then I broke it under her nose to administer it."

Morgana stared at Alys. "You altered the unicorn spell and put it on a dagger? That enchantment normally takes an hour. How the hell did you get it to work fast enough?"

"Naked desperation. I knew what was coming."

Arthur's head rocked back, his eyes narrowing. "And you didn't fucking warn us?"

"I couldn't," she snapped, out of patience. "If I could have, I would have. Every other alternative future I saw resulted in Bres invading Avalon during the day and killing absolutely everyone."

"What about Maeve's spell?" Morgana demanded.

"It didn't work -- because you were the one he gained control of so he could invade."

"Shit." Arthur rubbed his forehead as if it ached. "And Bres? The mother fried him?"

"Like a bucket of chicken," Davon said with satisfaction.

"I predict the palace won't be standing in an hour," Alys said with a certain grim satisfaction. "Not once mama dragon gets through with it."

"Chances are good that entire city won't be standing in an hour," Morgana said. "The Dragonkind do not like death magic, especially not when one of their young is the intended sacrifice."

Arthur squared his broad shoulders. "But meanwhile we've got to finish dealing with all these fucking Fomorians."

"The Fomorians are not going to be a problem," Lancelot announced, striding up, Galahad at his side, along with their wives, Grace and Caroline. "They've all gated away. Every last one of them is gone, including the trolls, centaurs, and giants they brought with them."

"They didn't retreat in good order either," Galahad added. "More like stark panic."

"No wonder, if a dragon just fried their king." Arthur scanned the square. "Unfortunately, that still leaves us with one hell of a mess to clean up down here."

Alys looked around, and her heart sank. Buildings burned on either side of the street. Teams of Majae worked frantically to extinguish the magical blazes as their vampire partners carried mortals to safety. Other witches were busy healing the injured and comforting the grieving.

"This is a mass casualty event," Arthur said. "We have just been catapulted out of the closet, boys and girls. There's no way in hell we can stuff it all back in."

"I don't know about that," Morgana argued. "We could restore the buildings, then clean up the memories of any bystanders. We've done it before."

"Yeah, right." Arthur jerked a thumb over his shoulder. "Morg, look over there."

A cluster of videographers, photographers, and reporters stood looking at them, their expressions a blend of avid curiosity and anxiety, as if they were trying to figure out whether they dared approach and try to get an interview.

Beyond them, a mob of bloody, filthy, soot-covered cops stared at the Magekind with grim expressions and more than a little hostility. Probably trying to decide whether to arrest them or just open fire and pray.

"Oh, shit," Davon muttered.

"We're surrounded by a dozen live news trucks," Arthur said, "not to mention New Yorkers with cell phones making live Facebook posts. And that doesn't even count the cop body cam footage and the helicopters I can hear circling overhead. There is no way we're going to be able to cover this up." He sighed and scratched his beard. "I'm not even sure it's worth the effort. Merlin warned me one day humanity would find out about us -- that we wouldn't be able to remain a secret forever. And it looks like that day has come."

They all exchanged dark looks.

"Oh, here we go," Guinevere muttered, nodding toward the journalists.

A tall, dark-haired woman in a wrinkled, sooty blouse and dirty slacks started toward them, a microphone in her hand. The mic bore a Donovan Cable News logo. A brawny blond man with a camera balanced on one shoulder followed her. He had a kind of battered good looks, along with the haunted, wary eyes of a man who had seen the edge of hell a few too many times.

Alys, looking at him, felt that too-familiar sense of *knowing*. "Oh hell," she muttered. "That blond photog's a Latent."

Arthur stared at her, appalled. "You've got to be shitting me."

"I can believe it," Galahad said. "I saw that suicidal fucker escape death half a dozen times tonight. He's got big brass balls and the luck of Satan."

"Terrific." Arthur sighed. "And we're going to need this lunatic?"

"Yep," Alys said, and shook her head. "Not exactly sure how or why, but we will."

"Fuck me," Arthur muttered, then squared his broad, armored shoulders and gave Morgana and his wife a look. "We'll deal with him later. Right now, we've got our first press conference to give, God help us. The rest of you lot, help our people put out those fires and heal the mortals."

As the three started toward the reporter and the Latent, the rest of the press surged toward them, mics extended, already beginning to shout questions, eyes gleaming in crazed excitement.

* * *

The rest of the night was an exhausting blur, between the press conference, healing injured innocent bystanders, answering uncomfortable questions from mortal authorities, and making magical repairs to half-demolished buildings.

And someone still had to figure out what to do about Adam Parker, DCN cameraman, Latent, and potential vampire recruit they were going to need for some unspecified reason.

Fortunately, that was a problem for a Court Seducer, not Alys.

The only bright spot in the entire mess was Kel's report from the Dragonlands. The dragon knight had gated there to learn that sure enough, his fellow giant lizards were justifiably pissed at the Fomorians.

The mother dragon and her hatchling were home and safe. She had indeed torched Bres's palace, and her outraged relatives had gated in after her to make sure the lesson stuck. By the time they were through, they'd made it abundantly clear that kidnapping dragonets was *not* acceptable behavior. And would be *punished*.

After gating back from the Dragonlands, Kel informed Arthur and Morgana that the mother dragon had confirmed Alys's account. She'd sensed the presence of the two Magekind as they'd worked to keep Bres from killing her daughter or escaping her vengeance. As far as she was concerned, she owed them her child's life.

"So our alliance with the Dragonkind is now doubly secure," Kel reported.

Arthur turned to Alys and Davon, who were taking a break from rescuing mortals. "Good work," he said, giving them a genuine smile. "We'll talk more after you've had enough time to recover." Pausing, he gave Alys a significant look. "Or to put it another way, get lost. You look like shit."

Dismissed, Alys attempted to open a gate home -- only to wince as agony stabbed her in the temples. "Oww."

Davon glanced around. "Could someone open a gate? Alys is pretty well drained."

"Of course," said Morgana, much to Alys's surprise. Generally, the liege of the Majae did not coddle her agents. But she gestured and a gate bloomed.

With a sigh of relief, Alys stepped through it, Davon at her heels.

She expected to end up back in Avalon's central square, so she was surprised to find they'd returned to her bedroom. "Thank God. I was not up to that walk." With a groan, she collapsed on the bed and leaned forward, bracing her elbows on her knees.

"I'd have carried you." Davon knelt at her feet, taking one of her boots in his hands. His fingers brushed the magical contact, and the scale mail retracted down her leg into the boot. He eased it off and went to work on its mate.

Alys watched him, thinking she really should help, but it seemed like too much effort. At least returning to the Mageverse was already beginning to refill her magical tank. When she reached for her power, the thunderous banging in her temples quieted. She sighed in relief.

Still on his knees, Davon removed her gloves, then pulled off the chest plate. Alys let him do it, admiring the strong lines of his handsome face, the swoop of his broad nose, and the sensual, intent line of his mouth. Remembering of the feel of those lips on hers, she felt a slow smile grow.

"We survived." She blinked at the note of wonder in her own voice. "And it's all because of you." She remembered the sight of him battling Bres and the dragon in Times Square. The fluid power and speed, the elegance in every attack and parry.

Her eyes widened as she remembered the vision that had landed them in this situation. "Did you... did you really jump off the roof of the hotel?" An image spun through her mind with sickening clarity -- Davon missing the dragon by a fraction of an inch to splatter on the pavement...

Davon shrugged. "Well, yeah."

"What if you'd missed?" *And why the hell did I push him to do it?* Actually, she knew the answer to that. She'd been driven half insane by the future she'd foreseen. Willing to do absolutely anything to avoid it.

"But I didn't." Davon stood, taking off his right gauntlet -- which, like the left, was thoroughly drained. "Because we drilled that move over and over again until I knew it like one of those Elizabethan dances you're so fond of."

"I know, I remember, but..."

His dark gaze met hers. "I still wouldn't have been able to keep my balance on that dragon's back if you hadn't spent the last decade trying to turn me into a combination Olympic gymnast, fencer, and track star." Davon smiled slightly. "Damn good thing you did, or I never would have made it through today alive."

He looked into her face, and for a dizzy moment she saw herself through his eyes. *Why, I'm beautiful.* She'd never thought of herself in those terms. In a world filled with the likes of Morgana Le Fay, Guinevere, and assorted other fair-skinned beauties, she'd never really considered that a possibility.

"Bullshit," he told her. "You more than hold your own." Reaching down, he hooked a hand behind her neck, bending low for a kiss. His hand felt warm as it cupped her head, his lips astonishingly soft and pliant as they molded to hers.

With a low moan, Alys opened her mouth for his tongue. The slick stroke of it sent a shiver of arousal through her.

A joyous thought flashed through her mind. *We are alive! We survived*! Her aching exhaustion vanished, drowned in an abrupt wave of crazed survivors' lust.

Alys grabbed his chest plate, which released under her magical touch. She tossed it aside and let herself admire the stark sculpted beauty of him. He looked like carved obsidian, hard and dark and beautiful.

Davon snorted at the comparison. "Carved obsidian that probably smells like a horse."

"I don't give a damn. Come here." She made a quick, inpatient gesture, and the rest of armor swirled away to his room in a flurry of sparks, leaving Davon looking tall and delicious and very naked. Wrapping both hands around his brawny shoulders, she pulled.

With a huff of laughter, Davon slid a knee onto the mattress and followed her down. When he started to stretch out over her, she gave him a little push onto his back. He rolled over, seeing what she wanted in the Truebond.

Alys pounced, licking and kissing her way from his knife-blade jaw, tasting the salt and smoke of his skin mixed with that exotic musk of vampire.

Davon groaned as she stretched full length along his body. He dropped a hand to the curve of her ass as the other tangled in her thick corkscrew curls, drawing her head down for another hungry kiss. She felt the length of his fangs against her lips as his cock pressed hot and fully erect against her belly.

Alys moaned, remembering the many times she'd imagined this, *craved* it, knowing she didn't dare take what she wanted so badly.

All of that was done now. They were Truebonded. There would be no more lonely nightmares for her.

"Or if there are," he murmured against her mouth, "I'll kiss you awake."

"God, yes," she breathed, her eyes sliding closed as she imagined all the peace he'd bring her. Imagined how her life would be a little less lonely.

He cupped her breast, one thumb playing back and forth over her nipple. She threw her head back with a gasp at the hot rise of pleasure, and he echoed the sound with a groan. As pleasure fed lust, they stroked and squeezed and caressed each other, reveling in the shared sensation, pleasure piling on pleasure.

Davon tumbled her onto her back, reared over her, and began kissing his way down the length of her body. Alys reached down and found his impressive width, all velvet skin and rigid heat, weeping a sweet bead of arousal from the tip. She groaned as their joined lust burned fiercer. *Make me forget. Forget the pain, forget the terror and confusion and despair. Leave no room for anything but you.*

"Yes!" He surged to his feet, wrapping strong hands around her hips and lifting her lower body into the air, leaving her head and shoulders braced on the mattress.

Alys gave a startled yip as he pulled her legs up and draped both them over his shoulders. Cupping her ass cheeks, he lifted her until he could feast between her thighs while she hung upside down, only her head supported. She flung out both arms to steady herself as he subjected her to a long, slick lick.

"Jesus, Davon!" she gasped, as he started eating her like a peach, his tongue playing up and down between her pussy lips, stabbing deep into her, then retreating again before swirling upward to catch her clit. Each lick, each flaming stroke poured honeyed delight the length of her body right into her brain.

Hunger boiled through his consciousness, with his enjoyment of holding her so helpless in his arms. Because he knew just how much it aroused her.

"Let me..." she gasped, only to feel his instant refusal to free her. "But I want to make love to you too!"

*Darling, you don't have to do anything but feel,* he told her in the Truebond. *Feel my mouth. Feel my cock. Feel my hands.* His long fingers tightened on her hips right to the edge of bruising as his tongue circled her clit again, then lapping down to slide deep into her. He hummed with pleasure. *Delicious. Like candy.* Then he sealed his lips around her clit and pulled in hard, ruthless sucks that made her eyes fly wide and her helpless hands grope for his muscled thighs.

She cried out in a strangled squeal, but he went right on licking, dragging more and more pleasure from her quivering nervous system until it seemed her brain lit up inside her skull. As the pleasure whipped through her, Alys writhed, arching into his mouth.

An image flashed through her mind -- Davon's view of her breasts, topped with stiff, eager nipples. She could smell her own arousal through his keen vampire senses, taste it on his tongue, intoxicating and erotic. He savored the sight, the sound of her moans, the flavor and the scent of her as she went mad for him. Until he sucked the first bright, scarlet ribbon of orgasm right out of her body. It lashed through her, more whip than ribbon, until she shrieked.

Something stung her thighs, a sharp pain.

No, not her thighs. His. Her nails were digging into his skin hard enough to draw blood. She started to relax her hold…

*Don't you dare.* His order shot through her head.

She cried out, impossibly aroused. Which was when he saw what she wanted. What she absolutely had to have.

Davon lowered her ass off his shoulders, parted her legs, and drove the entire length of his cock hard into her body in a single driving lunge. Her voice spiraled into a cry of delight and lust.

He wrapped one hand around her ankle and lowered the other leg, draping it over a hip. His gaze hot and predatory on her face, he began to stroke. Hard, driving deep. Pumping in and out as his free hand delved between her thighs for the hard pearl of her clit. As he fucked her, he strummed her with his thumb, seeking exactly the right rhythm, zeroing in on the motion that created the strongest sensation. And banged her in pounding strokes that massaged her juicing flesh into a searing ecstasy on the edge of pain. Knowing exactly what she found most arousing, plucking it right out of her mind and using it to give her the most intense orgasm she'd ever had.

Alys came, howling, bucking against his big body as he watched her with possessive eyes, until the frenzy of her pleasure combined with the tight grip of her cunt to drag him to his own climax. Pleasure fed pleasure, a twisting, twitching, mad cataclysm of rapture that left them both sprawled in a sweaty, delighted heap.

* * *

Davon gathered Alys in tight as she wrapped her arms around him and they both quivered in every muscle from the aftermath. "God," he groaned against her hair. "Sweet Jesus, I love you."

She smiled, feeling just how completely he meant those words. Every bit as much as she did. "And I love you. Just as I'll love you until the day I die."

She felt his cheeks move against hers as he grinned in happy delight. "God, yes." He hesitated a moment, then asked the question even though he was well aware of the answer. "Marry me."

"I think I already have."

"Yes." The words sounded a little smug. "But let's make it official."

"God, yes."

For a long, delicious moment, they curled into one another, floating in dazed, sated pleasure. Finally she spoke. "It's going to get damned messy now that the mortals know we exist."

"Yeah," he admitted, a smile curling his lips anyway. "But we can handle it. After today, we can handle anything."

She opened one eye to give him a sly look. "Even a wedding?"

"You bet your pretty ass." He laughed, his deep voice ringing. "We fucking earned it."

# Dedication

This is my first interracial romance, mostly because I was afraid of getting it wrong. I was encouraged to make the attempt by two wonderful IR romance writers, Stephanie "Flashy Cat" Burke and LaVerne Thompson. Flash and LaVerne helped me with all kinds of details that would never have occurred to me, like the question of braids versus dreadlocks.

They also gave me great suggestions on how to handle the more painful and delicate aspects of the story. I hope I'm as good a critique partner to them, because they gave me the confidence to try something I've wanted to do for a long time.

I also want to thank Joey W. Hill, the best erotic romance novelist I know. As always, she helped me find plot holes and the spots where I had trouble giving the romance the proper emotional weight. Again, I hope my feedback on her books is as useful to her.

One of the secrets of my success as a romance novelist is my friends. These wonderful women have always been willing to read early drafts of my books and give me honest critiques of my work. I can't tell you how many times they've saved me from some embarrassing mistake or error in logic.

Last, but definitely not least, I want to thank my copy and line editors, Karen "Moon Tygr" and Emilie, who save me from those "Oh, shit!" moments down the line, and my editor and publisher, Shelby Morgen of Changeling Press, whose support and friendship mean more than I can say.

But most of all, I would like to thank you, my reader. I can't tell you how much it means to me that you're still following the adventures of the Magekind after all these years.

Sincerely,
Angela Knight

## Angela Knight

*New York Times* best-selling author Angela Knight's first book was written in pencil and illustrated in crayon; she was nine years old at the time. A few years later, she read *The Wolf and the Dove* and fell in love with romance. In addition to her fiction work, Angela's publishing career includes a stint as a comic book writer and ten years as a newspaper reporter. Several of her stories have won South Carolina Press Association awards. Angela lives in South Carolina with her husband, Michael, a detective with the Spartanburg PD.

Angela at Changeling: changelingpress.com/angela-knight-a-26

## Changeling Press E-Books

More Sci-Fi, Fantasy, Paranormal, and BDSM adventures available in E-Book format for immediate download at ChangelingPress.com -- Werewolves, Vampires, Dragons, Shapeshifters and more -- Erotic Tales from the edge of your imagination.

### What are E-Books?

E-Books, or Electronic Books, are books designed to be read in digital format -- on your desktop or laptop computer, notebook, tablet, Smart Phone, or any electronic ebook reader.

### Where can I get Changeling Press e-Books?

Changeling Press ebooks are available at ChangelingPress.com, Amazon, Barnes and Nobel, Kobo, and iTunes.

ChangelingPress.com

Made in the USA
Coppell, TX
15 September 2020

37521546R00252